PRAISE FOR CELTIC KNOTS

CELTIC KNOTS – A Mysterious Journey on the Irish Coast

In this, intricately plotted, heartfelt, easy to read novel, we experience the world through the eyes of Lily and Eve, childhood friends for 30 years, living in Southern California. Both have Irish family roots, but in the humdrum of keeping their lives afloat, given work, romance, family and financial challenges, both struggle to define who they are and what they want out of life. A series of events and coincidences lead them to take a trip to Ireland, bringing them closer to their ancestral past, pulling them into romantic relationships, and providing new professional opportunities. However, while Lily has the time of her life, Eve falls prey to her own worst attributes, taking risks that lead her to trouble, a divergence that ultimately pushes their long relationship to the breaking point. Against a backdrop of ancient ruins, mythical and historical characters, and mouthwatering fare, what sets this book apart is the wonderful knitting together of romance, adventure, mysticism, and thriller elements as well as brilliant plot twist at the very end, making this a story well told, as well as fun to read.

    -Deborah Glik, Professor, UCLA

The novel *Celtic Knots* is part pleasure-filled frolic through the gorgeous Irish countryside, mythical stories and all, and part serious exploration into the turning points in the lives of friends, Lily and Eve. Ms. O'Donovan brings us a very satisfying novel about the perils of a close, loving friendship of opposite souls, who change in ways they never expected. The story is riddled with love and friendship as well as distrust, violence and loss.

Ms. O'Donovan writes with great descriptive prose. Most fascinating are the studies of the land, the skies, the moors and the unique mood of Ireland. The setting becomes a character in the book. Add to this, her descriptions of the Irish lore, the ancient queens, pookas, demons and faeries. It is a book that will especially attract travelers to Ireland as well as those interested in women's literature and the topic of psychology and friendship.

-Elizabeth Atherton, retired Art History Professor

This tale skillfully weaves together two women's compelling stories of self discovery with mythology, Celtic culture, modern-day spirituality, and more than a little fantasy. Ms. O'Donovan writes with a strong sense of place. I found myself googling the Cliffs of Moher, the Burren and other Irish locales because of her vivid descriptions that made me want to get on a plane to Dublin. In fact, as I was reading this, I thought it would make a great movie. (Netflix, are you listening?) If you are looking for a good, transporting read, you will find it here.

-Pamela Westcott, owner of Westcott Communications

Celtic Knots – A Mysterious Journey on the Irish Coast is an intriguing novel [about] the bond of two childhood friends, Eve and Lily as they venture to Ireland. This captivating story [provides] twists and turns as they encounter alluring men while exploring the Irish/Celtic countryside. Jealousy and a change in their relationship will challenge these two friends, making you root for them to overcome their differences. This is a must-read for anyone who has had a toxic relationship [where] sometimes letting go is the best option to move forward. I loved this book, and even though it is fiction, I found it very helpful, having experienced a situation like this myself. I also highly recommend this book to anyone who is fascinated with Celtic mythology!

-Rebecca Stahl, Pediatrician and Screenwriter

Celtic Knots is an engaging new read, by the author of *The Chosen Shell*, which weaves together romance, folk tale, history and suspense in the charming, magical and potentially deadly setting of Ireland. The heroines are truly moving, as they struggle to keep their friendship alive amidst the increasing chaos caused by the knots they create.

-Denise Westcott, Author of "Hearts," a short story winner.

I had no idea about the rich Irish folklore Ms.O'Donovan wove so gracefully into this story. I really enjoyed learning about it. The character of Maeve became more and more mysterious as I was easily swept along into her magic.What a delightful character, firmly rooted in the real world (her trials with her son Seamus!) as well as a wonderful catalyst.(Wish I could try some of her mysterious Irish tea!)

I really liked Lily....her inner thoughts were totally plausible and well developed. At first I thought she was a bit naive for a widow with two daughters, but then realized how young she had been when she married and how she had spent the last 18 years tending to a husband and children, not to herself. She was still a young woman! She was multi-dimensional and real.

Eve is, of course, much harder to like....She certainly remains consistently self-absorbed and so very NEEDY throughout. Her confinement in prison and in a halfway house was an appropriate way to force her to face her issues.

Every single sex scene was tasteful and pleasurable. The author also tastefully described Eve's trysts and ended them at the correct point before they became disturbing. The men themselves and their general behavior toward her - Brad and Ian and Seamus - were disturbing enough. I found the jealous lover/hotel shooting to be quite creative.

O'Donovan's descriptions of the Irish countryside, the gardens, and Eve's visions were so well written and rich in imagery...the flow was so smooth. I believe the author experienced all of the places Lily and Eve traveled.

I want to add that it's very obvious that Kathleen O'Donovan has been honing her craft in the years since writing her first novel, *The Chosen Shell*.

-Diane Libertella, retired Special Education Instructor

Lily and Eve are lifelong friends whose life choices are extremely opposite. Lily became a wife and mother while Eve became a successful traveling wine salesperson. Eve is self centered and promiscuous while Lily is giving and devoted to her husband and daughters. These two diverse personalities...collide, weakening their strong bond. The reader will travel with them to Ireland and meet people who. . .[are] instrumental in offering Lily and Eve the opportunity to take the risks to change, risks that will be life changing for them both.

I really enjoyed this novel. The author provides tragedy, loss, love, mystery, forgiveness, surprises, and of course, sex. Kept me up reading, even in the wee hours.

-Lucy Perricone Klumok, Partner at Perricone Farms

Lily and Eve are best friends who grew up together in southern California. After they both experience deep, painful hardships, they make the decision to go to Ireland. You will love the experiences these two 40-year-old friends encounter. There are also many surprise visits from a diminutive, elderly and mysterious Maeve, who pops in and out of the story. Also, Lily and Eve will discover their Irish ancestry among many other important findings in their life. You won't want to put this book down!

-Mary Slavik, School Administrator

CELTIC KNOTS

A MYSTERIOUS JOURNEY ON THE IRISH COAST

KATHLEEN O' DONOVAN

DREAM TRAVELER PRESS, LOS ANGELES

Celtic Knots - A Mysterious Journey on the Irish Coast is a novel by Kathleen O'Donovan
www.kathleenodonovan.com

Published by Dream Traveler Press
First Edition, January 2022

Copyright January 2022 by Katherine Burns Sartori

ISBN 978-0-9883746-2-1

ISBN 978-0-9883746-3-8

Printed in the United States of America

Book design by Ruth L. Snyder https://ruthlsnyder.com

Cover and Map design by Author William Withrow

DEDICATION

After visiting Ireland, I was inspired to write this book
in honor of my Great Grandmother, Annie O'Donovan,
who, at the age of 14,
left County Cork, Ireland in 1871,
and traveled by ship to the United States.
Later, she met and married my Great Grandfather, Patrick O'Keefe,
a baker by trade, and settled in Pennsylvania with their six children.
In 1925 when Annie was 68, she led the entire family out west, by train,
to settle in southern California.

I have taken the liberty
to name my endearing character, Gram O'Keefe,
after my own Great Grandmother (O'Donovan) O'Keefe.

ACKNOWLEDGMENTS

Many individuals have continually supported me while I drafted this story and then revised it, not once, but several times. If they had not praised my work and encouraged me, this book would never have been published.

Though my mother and husband have passed on to a better life, I want to thank them both. When I was only nine years old, my mother told me I had a very special talent as a writer, and I am forever grateful to her. Also, when I began writing this novel, my husband's avid interest in my progress spurred me on to stretch my talent and follow my dream.

In addition, I want to thank all of my family as well as my long-time friends, Jeannie Russell, Judy Young, Kathie Ollivier, Lucy Perricone Klumok, Peggy Scheurich-Slavik and Denise Westcott for all of their gentle nudgings and positive inquiries about my writing over the years. More recently, my cover designer, William Withrow's, enthusiasm about this book has helped me to spread my wings and reach the finish line.

My critique groups have offered invaluable suggestions too, coupled with much praise for this story. Many, many thanks to Elizabeth Atherton, Deborah Glick, Rebecca Stahl and Joanne Park. They, along with my publishing mentor, Adam Houge, have kept my desire to publish this novel very much alive!

CONTENTS

The British Isles

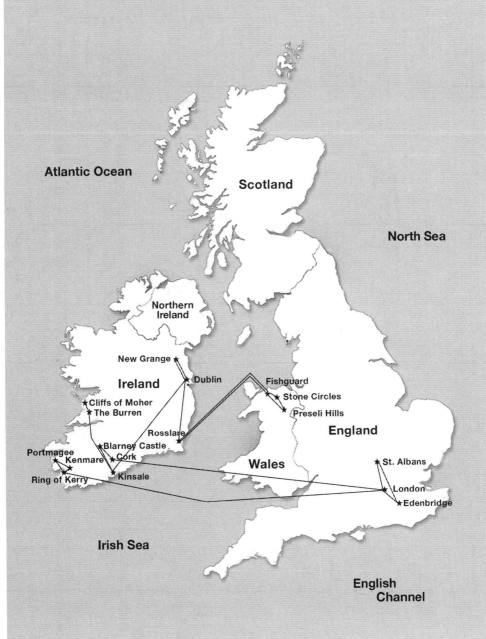

Atlantic Ocean

Scotland

North Sea

Northern
Ireland

New Grange

Ireland

Dublin

Fishguard

Stone Circles

Cliffs of Moher
The Burren

Preseli Hills

Rosslare

England

Portmagee
Kenmare
Ring of Kerry

Blarney Castle
Cork
Kinsale

Wales

St. Albans

London
Edenbridge

Irish Sea

English
Channel

PART I

The Celtic Knot represents family and unity of spirit
enclosed in a circle, with no beginning and no end.
The circle protects the symbol, so the spirit cannot be broken.

CHAPTER 1

*E*ve Olson dabbed her favorite scent, Gucci's *Guilty*, on her wrists. She slipped the vial of perfume—Brad's gift—into her makeup bag, squeezed it into her suitcase and pressed down on the stack of clothes containing bright summer tops, shorts, pants and lace bras with matching thongs in a rainbow of colors. A teal bikini, too, skimpier than she'd ever owned. Would he like it? Eve stroked the ebony satin negligee she placed on top of the crimson one. He'd like these too. *Our love-making is sensational now. Brad's made a lot of changes.*

She'd tried to convince Lily to like Brad, but no luck. Her long-time friend still didn't believe he had any good qualities. She'd never given Brad a chance. Was it envy?...*but she doesn't have a jealous cell in her body. She's gotta be depressed. Angry, too. Ever since Frank's diagnosis. Who wouldn't be?*

Eve laid her white lace wedding gown on top of the other clothes in her suitcase, carefully folding it so it wouldn't wrinkle. The dress reminded her of her mother's curtains wafting in the breeze and her Irish lace tablecloth covering their Christmas table when she was very young. But that was long ago. After Mom died and she'd turned eighteen, Eve had always celebrated Christmas with Lily's family and, of course, Lily's Grandma O'Keefe, too.

Checking to make sure her white satin heels were tucked underneath her clothes, Eve pressed the suitcase shut. She glanced at her bare left hand for a moment, then slammed the suitcase onto the floor. There it was again—her resentment. She couldn't dismiss it. Her co-workers at the winery were right, though she'd silently fumed when they offered their opinions. Lily hadn't minced words either after ten days went by and Brad was still making excuses about taking her shopping for a ring.

She twisted her mom's ring now, part of her inheritance. She wore it on the middle finger of her right hand. She'd always loved its vintage style and told her dad often when he was still alive. When she'd turned twenty-one, she'd paid for a new setting that combined her mother's diamond and the blue sapphire her dad had given her mother before they were married. He'd showered her mom with so many presents.

Eve stroked her neck and shoulder, trying to ignore the subtle discontent she'd felt lately. She wouldn't let everyone's comments about Brad spoil her excitement. To calm herself, she began wrapping a blue ribbon around a miniature safety pin. Attaching a tiny picture of her parents to the ribbon, she lifted her blouse and pinned it to her bra. "'Something old...something blue,'" she whispered. "It'll be next to my heart this weekend. Mom, I know you and Dad will be watching over me."

She had it all planned. She and Brad would leave the San Gabriel Valley early and arrive in Tahoe by late afternoon. She would contact a florist and order her favorite roses, the ones he always gave her. Long stems in a red so deep it was almost black, surrounded by baby's breath, to carry in her bouquet and wear in her hair. No veil this time.

She was locking her suitcase when the phone rang. Brad's voice sounded strange. She could hardly make out his words. "Meet me at Langley Park in a few minutes."

She agreed, but questions crowded her mind. *Why now? Why at a park?* Only last night he'd told her to pack her car so they could leave by nine o'clock, since it would take six or seven hours to reach Tahoe.

She glanced at the clock. Eight fifty-five. She ran a brush through her long blonde hair and picked up her suitcase.

❧

The California sun blazed so brightly on the sparkling fountain it almost blinded her. The August temperature had already climbed into the 90s. As she walked up the slope toward the pond that surrounded the fountain, moist spray wet her arms and the air was heavy with the scent of eucalyptus. Where was Brad? She spotted him sitting under the trees near the duck pond. She blinked. For a moment, his blonde hair, lit by the sun, and the curve of his broad shoulders made her think of her dad. Absently she put one hand to her breast, memories pulling at her heart.

She moved forward. "How are you?" She planted a kiss on Brad's warm cheek.

He picked up a large eucalyptus branch and stared at it instead of kissing her. "Not good."

"Why? What's going on?" She settled next to him on the stone bench and watched him tear leaves off the branch. The rustling of the trees and the birds' squabbling were the only sounds. Three lone ducks paddled across the pond. The park's green slopes were empty, except for large black crows devouring bread chunks.

Brad began ripping the bark off the branch in his hand, not looking at it, but squinting at the cascading fountain. Eve couldn't see his eyes behind his designer sunglasses, his prized possession. Once she'd misplaced them after spending the whole afternoon cleaning his apartment. He'd turned on her, saying she'd thrown them away. His accusation shocked her.

Eve's thumbs began picking at the ragged cuticles of her fingers. She could still hear her mom. "Evie, stop! Your nails are bleeding. You're ruining your dress."

Finally she managed, "Brad, are you okay?"

He stood up, tall and bronzed, his chiseled arms exposed by his sleeveless shirt. His legs were a deep tan, too, from weekends playing in beach volleyball tournaments. At the sight of him, a feral hunger grew inside her.

As she watched, he strode toward the pond and flung the naked branch past the ducks. It hit the glittering water and sank. A duckling waddled on the path near his feet. He kicked it into the water.

"Don't!" Eve watched the duckling right itself and swim toward the others. She walked up to him, but his back was a massive wall. "Please," she whispered, "can we—?"

He turned and suddenly hugged her, but he squeezed her too hard, crushing her. She gasped, half from anger, half from longing. "Don't. Not now."

"*Don't?* You don't ever get it, do you?"

She tried to push him away, but he was too strong. His massive strength and his perspiration mingled with his familiar musky scent tamed her resistance. His arms were around her then, crushing her. His lips found hers with a sudden urgency, as if he wanted to drink from somewhere deep inside her. All her resistance melted away then, and she clung to him, unable to push him away, until his mouth began to wound hers, his tongue pushing too hard.

"No! Stop!" She pushed his chest, trying to gain some space. But he kept on kissing her, his grip overpowering her. How dare he resurrect this old game! His mouth moved down, sucking hard at her neck. Suddenly, he lifted her in his arms.

"No!"

Cradling her, he gripped her legs so tight they began to throb.

Though she felt pain as he headed toward his Porsche 911, she was afraid of falling; she had to hold on.

"For god's sake," she yelled, "put me down!" She pushed at his shoulders and kicked, forcing him release her. Finally able to stand, she tried to squirm out of his grip, but he dragged her by the arm down the slope as the squawking crows rose up and flew off.

He opened the door of his Porsche and shoved her in. He slammed the door and she cringed, fingering red welts on her arms. Suddenly he was in the driver's seat, jabbing his key into the ignition.

"Brad, stop this! Where're we going? My suitcase is in my—"

"Nowhere. Put your seatbelt on." He revved the engine, threw the car into gear.

"This is one of your sick fantasies, isn't it?"

"Shut up, bitch. I said put your seat belt on!"

She shook her head and gripped the dashboard. The Porsche careened forward and just missed her parked BMW. She glanced at his foot pressing down on the accelerator. She held on, her throat closing. They streaked past a school crossing guard, who glared at them as he raised his stop sign in the air. The speedometer was rising fast. "Stop!"

"Stop? You're reneging on *me*? Backing out?" His tone was dark, sullen.

She tried to fasten the seat belt, but it was stuck. Nothing for her to do but grab the handle above the door.

"Where's your staying power, Evie? You used to like it unexpected. Wild and rough too. *Damn* Tahoe. That was *your* master plan, not mine. You've been hassling me about it forever." His laugh was ugly. "It was all 'sposed to be for 'better...*and worse.*' Right? Even without a ring." He laughed. "You had it all planned, and...and a family too."

She glared at him as the Porsche roared down the quiet street. She'd seen his moods turn crazy like this before. His sex games, too.

7

But not for a long time. How could she have been so naïve? So goddamned stupid, thinking he was finally over it? That he was going to be normal. She pulled at the seat belt again. It wouldn't budge.

He was racing toward Main Street. The signal turned yellow, then red.

CHAPTER 2

"Mom, I can't find the pajamas you bought me! Where'd you put them?" Tanya's high-pitched wail pierced the blare of her sister's music. "I'll never hear your answer if Lisa doesn't shut off that noise!"

Downstairs, Lily held her tongue as she scraped leftovers into her Rhodesian Ridgeback's bowl. *Lisa never showers without her rap music, and Tanya never fails to complain about it.*

"Mom," Tanya yelled again, "did you hear me?"

Her daughter's bellow shot up Lily's spine. She wouldn't miss this racket. So why did she feel so depressed? All year, with Tanya finally pulling better grades at the nearby community college and Lisa winning a scholarship right before her high school graduation, Lily had counted the days till her daughters would go off together to college, but now that their departure was near, she felt numb. All week, a strange heaviness had weighed on her, oppressing her when she woke up each morning. The pains in her stomach still blazed off and on. Finally she'd become alarmed enough to dial Dr. Blanchard. But when she'd finally gotten through to his office, the girls had interrupted her and she'd never made an appointment.

Frank tried to talk her into calling again. "Lily, doctors don't bite. God knows, I ought to know. Lately I've seen enough of them. Why won't you get to the bottom of this so you can stop holding your stomach?"

Had she been complaining that much? Frank's criticism seemed unusually sharp these days, ever since the oncologists had told him his cancer was in remission due to the last round of a new chemo treatment, but they recommended radiation next. Lily decided Frank must be fed up with cancer treatments or he didn't trust the doctors—his faith in them had never been strong. *He used to be so patient.* She crammed the last plate into the dishwasher. *He's short-tempered with everyone now, but how can I blame him?*

"I like doctors about as much as you like baths," she whispered to Kinza, who was licking her leg. "But I better make an appointment." She patted his cinnamon coat as he nuzzled her.

"Mom!" Tanya screamed.

That child will never change. Demanding as ever. Ever since she was a baby.

How had she managed when the children were smaller, with a colicky infant who never slept and another toddler with interminable earaches? *But raising kids is like that. Besides, there've been plenty of high points. I just can't remember them today.*

"Coming," she called with an enthusiasm she didn't feel. She wiped her hands on a towel and climbed the stairs to the girls' bedrooms. "Calm down, Tanya, I put your new PJ's in your closet with your other new clothes. I'll find them for you."

Two large open suitcases covered Tanya's bed and clothes were piled in stacks all over the floor. She was sitting in the middle of them, polishing her nails. She looked up as Lily strode into the room and opened the closet.

"As usual," Lily said, "you aren't even looking. They're right where I left them."

"How would *I* know that? Geez, why are you so cranky?" Tanya put two opened bottles of nail polish aside. She didn't look up as she painted her thumbnail then her index finger. She waved her hands in front of Lily, who placed the pajamas in her daughter's open suitcase. "Look, Mom. One finger's blue and the other is a metallic...it's called Passion Plum. Like it?"

"Tanya, how many times have I asked you not to do that? You'll end up spilling nail polish all over the new carpet!"

Tanya jumped up. "Mom, don't put my PJ's there." She snatched the pajamas and dropped them on a pile near her feet. "Let me pack. If you do it, I'll never find anything."

Lily swallowed her irritation. A confrontation with her daughter now would only delay their departure. She forced a cheerful tone. "Okay, but you'd better start. *Now*. We have to leave at three if you two are going to catch the plane on time." Vague pains jabbed at her stomach. Why was she not surprised?

Tanya blocked her from leaving the room.

"What is it now?"

"Did you talk to Lisa yet?"

"Yes, sort of."

Tanya towered over her mom's chunky frame. "What does 'sort of' mean?"

"I hinted that you were going to select a new roommate when you both arrived on campus."

"Mom, 'hinted' isn't enough. You've got to *tell* Lisa. I've lived with her all my life. I can't live with her this year. Please, if I broach the subject, she won't speak to me for months. You know how stubborn she is about forgiving anybody. Just like Dad."

Lily took a deep breath. "Okay. I'll talk to her before we leave. Better that she's mad at me than you. I'm expecting you both to look out for each other at college, but that doesn't mean you have to live together. In fact, I think it'll do you both good to have your own space."

Tanya grinned. "Right on, Mom."

CHAPTER 3

*T*he Doyles' Ford van was piled high in back with matching satchels and suitcases, plus tennis and pickle ball rackets and golf clubs. Frank was maneuvering the car through a traffic jam about twelve miles from Los Angeles International Airport. "Why do they have to work on the freeway this weekend?" he grumbled. "Only three lanes."

Lily kept quiet. They'd been told to get to the airport at least two hours before flight-time. Time was slipping away. Luckily her stomach pains were milder today. She'd swallowed several Pepto Bismol tablets earlier. She looked at her watch.

"I know. We're already fifteen minutes late," Frank snarled. Though he'd insisted on driving today, his voice grated with aggravation. Beads of perspiration had formed on his bald head, because the van's air conditioning was broken. Frank always repaired the car himself, but lately fixing anything exhausted him. Lily pressed her lips together and stifled a reply.

"Dad," came a voice from the back seat, "you don't have to go this way. Try getting off at the next exit. It's a shortcut Danny and I used when we dropped off his friends here."

"Lisa, I know what I'm doing."

Can't that child see how her father is struggling? Lily fumed. *He needs so badly to be in charge of this family again.*

"Leave Dad alone," Tanya said. "He'll get us there. He always does."

Lily stared at the stagnant traffic stretching out for miles on the freeway in front of her. She'd looked forward to this day. It had seemed perfect for her daughters to go off to college together. So why did she feel so down now?

Just then Frank hit the gas and swung the steering wheel wide, cutting in front of a truck in the car-pool lane. A horn blared and Lily bit into her bottom lip.

"Whew, it's sweltering in here!" Tanya turned her back on her sister with an exaggerated flounce and opened her window.

"What's with you?" Lisa sniped.

"None of your business!"

"Enough." Lily growled. "You two sound like you're eight years old. Keep quiet so your father can concentrate on the traffic."

"I won't have any trouble keeping quiet, Mom," Lisa said. Lily turned around to see her

daughter staring straight at her. Tanya had called it right. Lisa was furious, at Tanya and at her, maybe at the whole world too. When Lily had broached the topic of Lisa finding another roommate besides her sister, she'd exploded and then dissolved into tears. She was still oozing anger.

Lily faced front again. *Remind me, God, why I became a mother. Right now I'd like to disown them both. I hope they never live together again, at least not in my house.*

The next half hour was a web of nervous anxiety to get the girls to their gate on time to board the plane to Oakland and on to University of California at Berkeley. Their hugs and "I love you's" seemed rushed, though heartfelt, and Lily was glad to see them both pause longer to say good-bye to their dad. For all their teenage

14

angst, they seemed sensitive to him after all. Frank and Lily finally waved good-bye as the girls joined the line for security checks.

They'd just started the drive home when a deflated feeling took hold of her, as if her heart were a punctured balloon. She wouldn't share her feelings with Frank. She rarely did, and he had enough to worry about. She'd already noticed his wet forehead, and even though the car windows were open, the hot Santa Ana winds brought little relief. Besides, he was never one to say much, even when she summoned up the nerve to tell him how she felt.

This drive had been a supreme effort for him. Two weeks ago he'd finished his final round of chemo, and she was eager to fatten him up while he was undergoing radiation.

Minutes later, a Pasadena hospital called her. "Hello, can I speak to Lily O'Malley Doyle?"

"That's me."

"You're named as an HOPA on the medical I.D. we discovered in Eve Olson's purse. Do you know her?"

"Of course. She's been my best friend for over thirty years. What's a HOPA?"

"It means she's given you Power of Attorney over all her health decisions. We've managed to access her legal health directive from one of her doctors. She's in the ER. Can you come to the hospital as soon as possible? Unfortunately, she's been injured in a serious auto accident."

Lily was stunned, but after a few minutes she managed to share the shocking news with Frank. After a quiet hour's drive, they finally exited the freeway and headed to the hospital. "It's too hot out here. Why don't you come with me," she said. "You can wait in the lobby. They have comfy chairs there and AC. I don't know how long I'll be with Eve."

Frank didn't reply, and Lily was suddenly aware that the quiet between them had become unbearable. Was this what she had to look forward to with the girls gone? Well what else could she do?

Once in a while she'd thought of divorce, but it was out of the question. She'd just be more alone.

Frank turned the van into hospital's parking lot and pulled into the first empty space. "I'll be back as soon as I can," Lily said. "Then we'll go right home and I'll fix your favorite dinner. Meat loaf and baked potatoes, okay?"

He shook his head. "You don't have to. I'm really not hungry. Take as long as you need." Lily gazed at him. His eyebrows were almost gone, only a few dark hairs left. They reminded her of the shock of thick black hair she'd always liked. Gone now too, thanks to the all his treatments. New lines appeared around his mouth and eyes too. He'd lost nearly forty pounds.

Frank Doyle. A man of few words and a hard worker. Though he'd been an almost silent companion all these years, he'd always been someone she could count on. Her mother had introduced them at church when Lily was barely nineteen. No one had ever looked at her twice before that. Chubby girls rarely went out on dates. She was no exception; she was shocked when Frank asked her out. When months of going to movies and watching baseball games together had turned into a year, Frank had fumbled for the right words to ask her to marry him, and saying yes had seemed the only thing to do. When her parents and her brother Colin also nodded their approval, she knew she'd done the right thing.

No, Frank hadn't changed much in all the years she'd known him. A quiet partnership, mostly—that was her married life—but at least it had been a companionable silence. Unless, of course, you counted the clatter of her pots and pans in the kitchen, the TV's constant blare of football, baseball and hockey games, and after only a year, Tanya's baby cries and then eighteen months later Lisa's, followed by their endless chatter. Oh, once in a while, Frank would discuss the bills with Lily and how she needed to cut her spending. Every year he'd talk about the Christmas presents he'd bought and where he'd hidden them from the girls. Once in a while he'd mention his work at Boeing, but not often. Yes, Frank's words were few. But, as her mother had told her years ago, "He's dependable." *Mom was right.*

Lily hesitated, then gave her husband a quick kiss on the cheek. "Please, Frank. I'll find a nice cool spot for you to wait in the lobby."

He scowled but followed her through the parking lot. After she got him settled, she gave him one last look before she stepped into the elevator. They would keep following the directives of the best oncologists in southern California. She would pray hard too, that his horrible cancer would stay in remission.

The elevator opened and she turned and plodded down the hall, noticing how much her whole body ached. *This,* she told herself, *is what stress can do.* She blinked back tears and moved her shoulders back and forth as if that small gesture might lighten the burdens ready to crush her.

CHAPTER 4

*R*ounding the hospital corridor, Lily approached Eve's room and saw several doctors gathered around her friend's bed. A middle-aged nurse ventured toward her. "You can't go in now, dear. A special consultation is going on."

"Why is Dr. Blackman there?" Lily asked. "He's my obstetrician...and Eve's."

The woman's eyes told Lily the terrible truth. "No." Lily backed away from the doorway and leaned against the wall.

"I'm glad you came quickly. She'll have a lot to deal with when she wakes up. That's why the doctors felt we should phone you immediately."

Lily could hardly talk. "Will she. . .will she be able to get pregnant again?"

"I...I can't say, dear. Maybe, since you're named in her AHCD, you can talk to the doctor later."

"So many acronyms, what is AHCD?"

"Her Advanced Health Care Directive."

Lily stared across the hall at the waiting room for several minutes then looked back at the nurse's kind face.

"Eve always wanted to have kids," Lily blurted out, "but the time's just never seemed right between her career and all her stormy relationships. In the last few months, she finally started talking about being a mom, but she never said anything about being pregnant. Maybe she didn't know it herself." Suddenly Lily wished she hadn't divulged so much to a stranger.

"I can't say, because she's been unconscious since she was admitted," the nurse said as she put her arm around Lily's shoulders. "Why don't you wait here while the doctors finish. Then you can be with your friend." She walked Lily down the hall to another waiting room. "I know the shock of her injuries will be difficult, but your friend looks like a healthy woman and that's in her favor."

"Was anyone else in the car? What happened to him? She was with Brad, wasn't she?"

"All I can say is that luckily we were able to airlift her companion to a special neurological facility in northern California. He'll get the best care in the state."

They'd reached the waiting room and she took Lily's hand. "I'm so glad you're here to help Eve. Apparently, she has no family—"

Lily nodded. "We've been friends a long time, since middle school. Her dad died when she was nine, and her mother passed away when she was eighteen. My family is all she has. Besides her friends at work, probably her only other visitor would be my brother Colin. But he's serving in Afghanistan."

"You look awfully pale." The nurse steered Lily toward a comfy, stuffed chair. "Why don't you sit down here. Can I get you something? A glass of water? Tea?"

"Thank you. I have some vague stomach pains, but I'm sure it's stress. Yes, I'd love some warm tea." She noticed the TV. "Please, can you turn the news off?"

As the nurse left the room, Lily slumped into the chair, fished a tissue out of her purse and wiped perspiration from her forehead. She had to be strong for her friend. She chewed on an antacid and stifled tears by shutting her eyes. *Maybe meditation will help.* She would ask her Mysterious Maker, as she'd called God for years, to infuse her with strength. She'd need it to help Eve.

🍃

Lily leaned against the white antiseptic walls of Eve's hospital room. The doctors had suddenly left and she was alone with her friend. She sighed as she peered out the window. Why did the world look so normal? Across the street, palm trees swayed in the hot Santa Ana winds, and the setting sun bathed the stucco shops and red hibiscus bushes in a luminous amber light. Three young women were sauntering toward the grocery store. Coming out, a blonde child trailed behind her mother's overflowing cart. Next door, a man in a business suit pumped gas at the Arco station.

Everyone's doing what they always do...except Eve and me. Strange...to feel no part in it.

Lily shut the blinds and sat next to Eve's bed, pressing her forehead with both hands. The pungent hospital smell mixed with bodily fluids swirled around her, making her slightly nauseous. How bizarre, to be back in this same hospital so soon after Frank's surgery. She struggled to breathe as she dismissed those days. Had it been only two months?

Though Eve still wasn't conscious, Lily shifted her body in the narrow chair next to Eve's bed and forced herself to talk to her friend, comforting her, as the nurse had suggested. A tube protruded from Eve's mouth, allowing her to breathe, and her right cheek was bandaged. Her flaxen hair was hidden completely by bandages too and a forbidding steel medical halo. She didn't stir.

Like a child, so helpless...

Music might help her. Lily chose some calming tunes Eve liked, calibrating a low volume on her phone.

Trying to calm herself, Lily rooted through her purse for her

21

checkbook, sifted through its pages, scrutinizing entries, balancing the amounts. Frank was an accountant; he expected her to be precise. That task completed, she looked at Eve again. No movement, but she was still breathing.

CHAPTER 5

*W*hile the music played on, Lily sat next to Eve's bed looking through a photo album on her cell phone. She'd created it for Eve on her last birthday, even scanning several old photos too, one taken years ago when she and Eve were teenagers traipsing around the mall. She found a newer one of her and Frank sitting across the table from Eve and Brad at a pub last St. Patrick's Day. She'd never liked Brad, always wondered what Eve saw in him...except all the expensive gifts he gave her. She had to admit she'd disliked most of Eve's boyfriends over the years.

Studying the photo, she heard her grandmother's words again, ones she'd heard often while growing up, "Lily, you're my dark-haired beauty. Don't forget that. And don't compare. You and your friend, Eve, are like lilies and roses. Each gorgeous in your own way, and as different as the two primal women you were named after."

Lily still didn't know what Gram O'Keefe meant about "primal women," but she'd always talked about ancient characters from old books, especially Celtic ones. Lily had always secretly decided Gram was only half right. She didn't consider herself a beauty and she never would. Eve was the one who turned heads.

Lily found another photo. Eve in her cap and gown on the college steps, her ivory complexion and sky blue eyes accentuating her tall, svelte body. Lily was standing next to her, a round mound in a black robe.

She towers over me. In more ways than one.

Though Eve was a year younger than Lily, her friend had always seemed older. Eve was bright too; she'd even skipped a grade in school. And her opinions were always so right-on. Eve never hesitated. She could always persuade others. Even the most stubborn, like Lily, would eventually shake their heads in submission. Many times over the years, Lily had held up her hand and said to her friend, "Enough already. I hear you. Give me some peace so I can decide for myself!" More often than not, though, she ended up following her friend's lead.

The truth was, and she'd be the first to admit it, Eve was her only real friend. All her life, Lily had suffered ceaseless insults and snide whispers about her body and her weight. But not from Eve. Not ever. In all the years they'd know each other, Eve had never criticized Lily's appearance. Her short, chunky frame, her double chin, her dark, impossibly curly hair.

Eve was popular, too. She'd always had friends; her beauty and smarts attracted people from every clique. Lily sometimes envied her, but she told herself envy was silly because she'd always be grateful that Eve had found some engaging qualities in her, enough to be her closest friend— though Lily still didn't quite know what those qualities were. Maybe it was her mean fastball when they'd played softball in school. One thing she was good at, even now, was sports.

Lily shuffled through the photos and found one of their championship team. She was the pitcher, with Eve at first base. They'd shared the MVP award in their senior year, and that had definitely cemented their friendship.

Or maybe, Lily thought, Eve had stuck around because of Gram

O'Keefe, who eventually became Eve's surrogate grandma. Her warmth and mysterious wisdom and all those annual outings when she'd taken Lily, and Eve as well, to stay at her mountain cabin.

*Mom couldn't wait to get rid of me, and Dad was always away on some military mission...*but riding horses among the pine trees, swimming in the lake and listening to Gram's stories by the fire had been more than enough for Lily, especially with Eve by her side.

Lily found an old Fourth of July photo she'd scanned. Her brother, Colin, clowning at the beach, dragging Eve, a long-legged teenager, into the waves. He'd loved Eve as well, and his wit had cheered her when tragedy struck. After Eve's dad died, it was Colin who persuaded Eve to attend all their holidays at Gram's house, and bring her mother along too.

Mom never showed an ounce of enthusiasm when it came to Eve, Lily mused, *but when Colin wanted something, he got it. Mom never said no to her perfect boy...*

Years later, when Eve's mother died, Lily remembered how Eve's heart had filled with more sadness than she could bear, so much so that Lily wouldn't let her friend be alone.

After a couple of years, Lily married Frank and he'd actually welcomed Eve into their family too. That was a surprise.

Lily smiled at a photo of Lisa's baptismal day. Godmother Eve beaming as she grasped Tanya's chubby hand, her other arm holding baby Lisa. Yes, Eve was still an integral part of Lily's family. Whatever the glue was that had held the two friends together during these last thirty-something years, Lily thanked God for it.

She clicked her copy of Eve's photo album to off, selected more calming tunes for her friend, then laid her cell phone on her lap. Reluctantly, she focused her attention on the hospital bed, watching the gentle rise and fall of Eve's chest. Yes, she was still breathing, but her skin looked ashen and her long slender body was shrouded in white.

Helpless. Of all people, Eve, the one who stands up to everyone. And they always admire her for it. Except Brad...

Lily knelt down on the hard tile floor beside her friend's bed and lifted her hands to her cheeks, finally letting a few tears come. She folded her hands and imagined herself as a child in the pew of a Catholic church. "Dear God, please heal Eve. After everything with Frank, well... Just this once, please grant my wish. And soon!"

CHAPTER 6

*I*n the late night hush, Eve lay motionless—intravenous tubes puncturing her flesh, her head immovable. Eyes closed, she licked her upper lip, breathing quick and shallow, then she gulped for air. She tried to press her lips together, but something was in the way. She inhaled more deeply. It hurt. She tried to form a word. Impossible. She managed only a faint murmur. What was that metallic odor? Sleep began to pull at her like the undertow of a grim riptide, a blackness reaching for her like oily liquid, enveloping her.

Far away, a tiny light pierced the gloom. She tried to reach it, but she couldn't move. Ever so slowly, the light widened, becoming a white glare that blinded her. She heard a loud crunch of steel, shattered fragments of glass flying into the air. She felt the stabbing of innumerable knives and touched her arms. A thick wetness. All over. She forced her eyes to open. Everything was red. Everywhere. Blotches on her, covering Brad, too. His head, his chest.

She screamed. Darkness descended again, but now a shadowy figure was standing beside her bed. Silent. She shut her eyes.

Minutes ticked by. Or hours? An intolerable quiet. Her room was empty now. She closed her eyes again, and the images bombarded her.

Strange...he's bent over the wheel. That familiar stare, but...but I don't think he's... Can he see me?

Brad!

He always glares like that. I hate it!

Brad, say something! Please.

I detest it when he won't talk! He likes to punish me. It makes me feel so alone.

Tears leaked out, laying wet paths on her cheeks. She couldn't wipe them away. *I'm sorry*, she heard herself say. *Forgive me. I know I talked you into it. But you'll like it once we're married. I know you will. We can buy a house, and have the baby. I want to be like everybody else. Brad, don't be mad anymore. Please, say something. Just one word.*

She felt her eyelids quivering. The hospital room was a jumble of shadows now, but above her she saw the filmy outline again. Gossamer faces. The faint scent of lavender. Her mom's dark blue-marble eyes. Her dad's face behind Mom's, harder to see. Soft words in her ear. *Eve, you must go on. Don't hold on to him. You always did that. Clinging to your dad, telling me those ridiculous stories about him. You can't get the past back. I told you over and over, but you never listened. ...Stubborn child. Stop that whining. You have to let go.*

Her mom's graying blonde hair faded away, but Eve could still make out her straight nose, her thin lips. The rest was a murky curtain surrounded by haze. Her dad's bright blonde hair was still shining. Vague remnants began to fade, but she could still make out his kind eyes.

Daddy, don't leave me alone again! His face began to disappear. Until only his whisper remained. *Go on, Evie. Hear me? Look to your future. Be my brave girl—*

She began to whimper. *Be my brave girl—that's what he always said.*

28

The unearthly outline vanished completely. Only deep shadows and the scent of lavender hovered.

Eve moaned, soft sobs choking her. She gave up her energy to the dark, yearning for a sleep that would not end.

CHAPTER 7

A bouquet of sunflowers caught the early morning light streaming through the hospital window. The golden flowers were the first thing Eve saw when she woke up. She admired

their flamboyant display, wondering who had brought them.

Oh, Lily, of course. But which day?

Eve couldn't remember. In fact, she didn't know how long she'd been here. *Must be a week at least. More?* She paused. *Yes, now I remember.* Her friend had arrived yesterday loaded down with a box of See's Candies, two paperbacks and this large vase of flowers. "Ten days is enough," Lily had announced. "I brought these gifts to celebrate your move out of ICU."

Eve smiled at the memory. *That's who Lily is. Today it'll probably be dancing girls and balloons. I'm lucky to have her as my best friend.*

Sure enough, when Lily arrived later, she was carrying more goodies, this time several magazines. "I bought just a few." She showed Eve the front cover of *People* magazine. "Thought you might want to read the latest about Hollywood's best and brightest stars or," she held up another magazine, "if that doesn't float your boat, you can flip through this one for decorating ideas." She put the magazines on Eve's bed. "I can help you spruce up your new condo when you go home."

"Thanks." Eve's voice was faint. She didn't feel energetic enough to get out of bed, let alone think about decorating. She couldn't help noticing the sympathy in Lily's eyes.

Lily chose a chair next to Eve's bed and pulled a large book from her briefcase. "That's not everything. I want to share this book about Ireland with you. It's full of travel ideas and lots of Irish lore and Celtic faerie legends. I consider it a treasure, but I'm willing to leave it with you for a few days. I found it on sale in the college bookstore and couldn't resist."

Lily held up the front cover. Against a bright blue sky, grassy velvety squares covered rolling hills, with gray stonewalls curving around them. A rectangular strip of golden Celtic designs framed the cover. "Does Ireland really look like this?"

"Looks like the real deal," Eve said, "but my memory isn't working very well these days." She tried to scrunch herself up in the bed as Lily pressed a button to lift the top half of her mattress and then put another pillow behind her head. For a moment the pain in her leg was so sharp Eve couldn't breathe. Very slowly she sucked in a few breaths, trying not to aggravate her fractured ribs. Usually, deep, easy breathing helped her to relax. She sank back on the pillows and pulled the blanket closer.

"Can you...can you show me some more pictures in your book? It'll take my mind off this pain. But before you do that, do you...do you think the nurse will come soon with my meds?"

Lily got up and made for the door. "I'll go find out."

She's trying so hard to cheer me up, Eve thought. *I want to please her, but it's difficult.* The pain felt like it was scalding the side of her leg with fiery fingers. She closed her eyes and tried to endure it, but images of Brad and the accident—images she didn't ever want to think about—invaded her mind. She opened her eyes. *No! I won't go there! Not if I can help it.* She yearned for some special pills that would bury her memories as well as her pain.

The nurse arrived with Lily behind her. She bustled around the room, taking Eve's temperature and blood pressure and checking the levels in her IV bags. Finally, she gave Eve her pain meds with a tiny paper cup of water and left.

Eve quickly swallowed the pills. After a few moments, her question pierced the quiet. "Where's Brad?" She hadn't dared to ask until now, but the past days were so jumbled up in her mind she didn't know if she'd asked anyone before or not.

"He's not well at all, Evie." Lily's voice was as cold as stone. "I couldn't find out much. All I know is that he was airlifted to a special hospital up north."

"Will he...? Will he live?" She felt like a gaping hole was growing inside of her.

Lily shook her head. "I don't know, and after what he did to you, I don't care." She turned away from Eve and looked out the window. "Eve, you need to forget him."

The stillness in the room closed in on them. Only the sounds of patients shuffling by, dragging their IV poles, reached their ears. A minute later the lunch cart clanked as it passed, followed by the sound of the attendant delivering trays to neighboring rooms.

"Do you know..." Lily broke the silence. "Do you have any idea why he ended up almost killing you in that crash?"

Eve heard a new hardness in her friend's voice. She tried to answer as calmly as she could. "He...he was really mad. Turned out he didn't want to...he didn't want to be a fath—" She took another deep breath and found other words. "He didn't want to marry me after all."

Eve closed her eyes, but felt Lily take her hand and whisper, "I'm so sorry."

She was relieved when Lily picked up the book on Ireland again and slowly flipped through it, showing her the pictures of sights she'd never visited and places she'd already seen.

Suddenly Lily changed the subject. "Talking about Ireland... Remember my Gram O'Keefe when she told us all those Irish tales? Because of her I loved anything to do with faeries. I didn't believe in them, but Gram sure hooked me with those stories."

"Yes, I remember, but I liked her Celtic stories about the after-life," Eve said. The pain throughout her body had diminished, but she still ached all over despite the meds. Though she was beginning to feel drowsy, she knew her friend was determined to turn her thoughts to happier times, so she tried to keep the conversation going. "How could I forget her always telling us about Ireland's ancient rivers, sacred wells and the mystical journeys the Celts took 'beyond the veil'? As if their after-life lay behind a flimsy curtain and they had only to slip over to 'the other side,' where happiness imbued everything."

"Yes," Lily said, "I still love those ideas. That reminds me, I found a short story I wrote for one of my college classes; it's about us when we were young. Remember when we went to that first Celtic Faire near Gram's mountain cabin?" She held up several type-written pages. "This story was stuffed into one of my old diaries. Maybe...what if I read it to you now? You can just lie back, close your eyes and listen."

Reaching up to hold her forehead for a moment, Eve nodded yes. "I'd like that. Such a long time ago, but I still remember some of it," her voice fading away.

"Well, it'll allow us both to escape to a simpler world," Lily said and she began to read aloud:

Blue-gray shadows shrouded the cabin. I squeezed my eyes shut, hoping for another hour of sleep. Soft steps scuffed across the floor. My eyes flew open. Who was that dim figure standing by my bed? Head and shoulders hidden in the shadows. It moved closer and I recognized a long robe, and white hair curled around pink sausage rollers.

Not a ghost. Just Gram.

"Wake up, you two," she said.

I sat up and stretched, then glanced over at my friend Evie, who was sleeping in the other bed.

"Up with you both, sleepyheads," Gram said. "I only go to an Irish Faire very early in the morning or late at night."

"Why so early, Gram?"

Evie's sleepy voice chimed in. "Yes, why?"

"Because it's the dawn mists that make everything grand and magical. The same clouds play tricks with the moon and stars at night as well." Gram winked.

For as long as I could remember, Gram had loved secrets.

Patting my head, she opened the window over our beds and let icy air flow through the room. Gram loved fresh air.

"Ah," she said as she gazed outside, "the mists are still thick, even among these redwoods. The same fog as in me old country, where it hovers over the emerald hills and cliffs. Quick, me little ones, we must get down to the meadow soon."

She left the room, and soon I heard her rummaging through the kitchen cupboards. Would she make raisin bread French toast, slathered with warm butter and syrup, like she always did on vacation? I could hardly wait to find out.

Hungry, I hopped out of bed and slipped off the gold chain and small Celtic Knot emblem I usually wore, then found my clean clothes. I had to be first in the shower or I'd have to wait forever to eat. I was eleven and Evie had just turned ten. I knew she would spend way too much time in the bathroom, primping in front of the mirror, admiring her golden hair and slender figure. Gram said Evie looked like a long-legged colt. I was rounder, like the bears that roamed the mountains, plus my dark curls did nothing but frizz, especially in the shower.

But I told myself I didn't care today. I felt luckier than my best friend in other ways. Besides, it was the beginning of spring break with a promise of bright days all week. As usual, I would be sharing them with

Evie at Gram O'Keefe's cabin, and we'd have nothing but fun until school started again.

"Evie, get up. Today's gonna be something special! Gram told me today is the first Irish/Celtic Faire to be held here in our California mountains at Rocky Point."

Evie suddenly sprang out of bed. Slam! She banged the window shut. "It's frigid in here!" She jumped back into bed and pulled the quilt over her head.

Ignoring her, I turned on the shower. Evie always used important words like "frigid." And she always said them loud to make sure everybody heard. She couldn't help being smart, though. Cripes, she'd even skipped a grade. Plus, Miss Gates, the principal, said, "She's the brightest star in fifth grade."

"You better not go back to sleep or you'll miss everything," I shouted from the bathroom as I pulled off my nightgown. "I've never been to an Irish Faire. Have you?"

Evie pulled the quilt down a smidgen. "No, and I'm only closing my eyes for an instant. I can't do anything till you're done, anyway. So get going. I'll invade your shower if you don't."

There she goes again with those special words. Instant and invade. "You wouldn't!" I said.

"Oh yes I would!"

Breakfast over, the two of us walked side by side, the top of my curly head reaching just above Eve's shoulder as we followed Gram on a path through the tall trees. The shushing sound my pudgy legs made as I walked annoyed me, but the swollen creek on our right distracted me. I loved the sound of water tumbling over rocks! Hearing it was enough to banish my bad feelings about being chubby.

The fog, hanging mid-air in magnificent puffs, enclosed both of us in a gossamer world. I reached out to catch the drifts wafting around my waist and shoulders and stomped at the wisps lying at my feet. I grabbed Evie's fingers to get her attention, but she pulled away and went skipping off in a new direction. I sighed, lifting my eyes to the mammoth redwoods and pines, watching the chalky vapor touch their crowns, the lowest clouds I'd ever seen.

Silence enveloped the woods. Evie was gone, but I still walked with Gram. The magic might come if I don't talk, I thought. The elves and faeries I'd read so much about filled my head. I wondered if they really lived in the tree trunks and under the boulders scattered beneath these trees. Maybe I was being silly. Evie said none of those faerie stories were really true.

Soon the woods gave way to a meadow filled with bright green tents with yellow, white and purple flags waving above them, all still wrapped in the soupy fog. I saw no sign of people.

Evie suddenly reappeared, her eyes sky-blue pools. "Look!" She nudged me. "In that cluster of trees." I looked, but all I could see was more mist.

"What?"

"Don't you see him?"

"Who?"

Evie's yellow rosebud dress billowed out as she turned and ran ahead, strands of her golden hair flying about. She veered right, off Gram's path again, and pointed at something, but then the mists closed in again, covering her like a curtain. I could barely see her.

"Come back!" Should I follow her?

I looked up ahead. Gram was waiting near the first green tent. She smiled at me. "Evie will come back. Don't worry about her."

I was just opening my mouth to ask how Gram could be so certain when a petite lady in white came out of the tent. With pale hands, she reached out and took Gram's in hers, then they hugged each other. Her robe reminded me of Gram's bathrobe, though it was white satin. Why, I wondered, did it have flowing sleeves and such a large hood? Silver threads on the robe caught the light as the sun peeked through the trees at the meadow's edge. She looked...magical. I turned toward the woods, looking for Evie again.

The little lady in the hooded white robe spoke, "Come over here, dearie. I know you'll eventually be fallin' in love with flowers and plants, and this is the perfect season for it. Did you know the ancient Irish welcomed the spring sun with nothin' but glad hearts? Its dancing rays always wake up the sleeping earth to new growth after a long winter's nap."

I watched the little lady's hands move as she talked.

"Your grandmother tells me you've read many faerie tales, but I have Irish faerie artifacts to show you and ancient Celtic tales to tell that truly happened."

I looked around for Gram, but she was nowhere near me now. So I followed the lady into a white-flagged tent, and though the light was faint, I could see sparkling rocks set up in a labyrinth on a table draped with green fringed cloth. The lady named them as she pointed. "Fine crystals. Purple amethysts. Agates. Amber, too. This one is obsidian." She put the black stone into my hand, and my fingers curled around its cool sharp edges.

Evie will love this, I thought. I better go find her.

The lady pointed at the other treasures visible in the dim light. "More of the faeries' favorites."

I saw tiny mushroom stools, semi-precious stones, jars of hazelnuts, lichen stones and lots of flowers in tiny pots—fuchsias, forget-me-nots, pansies and cowslips.

"And I have Irish storybooks here, too," the lady said. "You can take one home." She took a book off a shelf and handed it to me. "Ancient Celtic rules were written down centuries after the Celts were gone. They're contained in here." She opened the book. "For instance, 'Don't rile the pookas, faeries and elves that dwell in every wood.'" The little lady's whispery voice was mysterious, but I found her twinkling eyes and smile fascinating.

I fingered the pages of the book and looked at the drawings of beautiful, winged creatures hiding in giant leaves. One was sitting in a daisy that formed a tiny boat floating near lily pads. I handed the book back to the lady and bent to smell the tiny cowslips. "I've read about faeries since I was four, but I've never really believed in the little people. What does riling the pookas and elves mean?"

The woman pulled her hood down, and I couldn't help noticing her curly dark hair. It was like the wavy mane of a horse I'd ridden last summer in these mountains.

"Well," the lady said, "we Irish really do believe in them. You see, a lot of the magic is caused by the Others or the Little People, as they're called, and they've been livin' in our ancient Isle and under its hills and mounds for many long centuries. I believe they're here in California too."

"Really?" I said, but I think she knew I doubted her.

"They're everywhere in nature," she insisted. "You mustn't ever disbelieve, Lily. It might insult them, diminish their benevolence, and then they'll be sure to play tricks on you. They're powerful, they are."

"Benevolence?" I knew Evie would know what that word meant, but I didn't.

"Their natural kindness."

"What kind of tricks do they play?"

"Oh, they've been known to play in gardens, steal secrets or food, and even babies. Sometimes they take treasures."

How could faeries be so mean?

I wasn't going to tell the lady I didn't believe her. After all, I figured Gram was her friend. Sure, it was fun to imagine faeries. But really believing in them? That was kid's stuff, like Santa or the Tooth Fairy. After all, I was eleven now. Almost a teenager.

The tent flap opened, and I saw Evie's face, unusually pale, scared, as if she'd just watched a horror movie. "They said you'd be here." Her voice was softer than usual, even squeaky. "Please come here. Just you, Lily."

I spied Gram over in the corner of the tent, got the nod I wanted and rushed out to hug Evie. "I was so worried. Why'd you leave me?"

"I didn't." She pointed toward the trees. Her eyes looked funny, like she'd just woken up. *"I saw him over there. I swear it."*

"Who? Who'd you see? Evie, what's going on?"

"My dad," she whispered. *"He spoke to me. He was there. A minute ago."*

Lily suddenly realized she'd better stop reading her story. The ending would make Eve too sad. She looked up from the pages and noted Eve's deep and measured breathing, and guessed her friend had fallen asleep. "Are you still listening, Eve?" No answer, so Lily settled into her seat again; she might as well read the rest, but silently now.

I put my hand on my hip. "Don't fool with me, Evie. I know you've been dreaming about him, since... Well, if this is one of your jokes, I—"

Evie's face was paler than I ever remembered. "Honest! It's true!" she said. "I've never seen him since.... You have to believe me. But don't tell anyone. Promise me. Not even your grandma."

I'd never seen Evie this upset. Except last month...I felt her fingers grasping my shoulder, shaking it as her words tumbled out. "He told me that he didn't really die, Lily. He said he just took another shape. He can do that now."

"What?"

"I might even see him again. He went to the...Well, he called it the Other World. I asked him to describe it, but he only shook his head. His face was sort of...it was all lit up and shining when he talked."

"Really?" I knew I'd better not show any doubt. Evie looked very serious. She was lost in another world. But I couldn't really believe what she was saying. I looked more closely. Did my best friend, who'd skipped fourth grade, actually believe that she'd just talked to her dead father? Had the smartest girl in the fifth grade lost all sense of what was real?

I'd never forget the funeral, the first one I'd ever attended. Was it only a month ago? I saw Evie's dad in his coffin and joined Evie and her mother in the first pew of the church. They got up and knelt beside that big, long box. After them, I ventured toward it, examining his large muscular body dressed in a navy suit and tie. His face was still tanned, his eyes closed, and he was surrounded by cool white satin. Evie almost never cried, but she began to sob so hard she had trouble catching her breath. I'd never heard crying like that before.

No!--I clenched my fists and gritted my teeth. Evie's dad, the man who'd always laughed and rough-housed with us...he didn't belong in this box!

Evie's words cut into my memories of the funeral. "Then, just now, he hugged me good-bye. I felt his hug, Lily! I did. And you know what? He smelled just the same."

Hearing her say this, all I could do was choke down my own sadness and put my arms around her.

"Then when the sun broke through the mists," Evie whispered, "he disappeared." She took a step back. "You believe me now, don't you?"

I looked into Evie's eyes and felt tears stinging my own. I reached out and gently brushed a golden lock of her hair off her forehead. "What do you think? We're friends forever. Of course I believe you."

But I didn't believe Evie's dead father had appeared out here in the woods. Instead I was wondering how my friend, who rarely believed what anyone told her without proof, could believe in a ghost. It was probably only her imagination mixed with the morning fog.

"Hey—where's your Celtic Knot necklace?" Evie's question felt like a shot. She was staring at my bare neck.

Oh, no! Gram's sacred baptismal gift was gone! I always took it off when I showered, but I always put it back on. Did the chain break? I tried to stifle a choking feeling.

With a sudden turn, I raced back into the tent and began searching. Except for the sparkling rocks, I saw nothing. No Celtic Knot pendant. I noticed the tent was empty now. Gram must've gone off with the strange hooded lady. I got down on my knees and searched the dirt floor again. Nothing. I retraced my steps, running all the way back to Gram's cabin, tearing through the bedroom, tossing pillows aside, scouring the bathroom and shower stall. The kitchen too. My pendant was nowhere to be found.

Were the faeries playing tricks to test me, like the lady had said? Why?

I was afraid to tell Gram I'd lost my gold Celtic Knot pendant, so I wrapped her green scarf around my neck and left the cabin. I shuffled my feet as I walked, swiping the pebbles and dirt on the path as I returned to the meadow. I looked around. Where was Evie? I wanted to ask her if she remembered anything about my pendant. Poor Evie, I thought—I wonder if she's back to normal?

The sun was pouring through the trees now; the fog had drifted off. People were gathering in the meadow, some carrying napkins with slices of soda bread, frosted with warm butter and honey. It smelled like Gram's cabin. I had to find her. Evie too.

Suddenly I looked up. The little dark-haired lady in the white robe was looking right at me. She put her hand to her lips, "Shh, don't tell anyone, but I know you'll find it. Please believe me, child."

"How do you know...?" I whispered.

Before the lady could reply, Gram came up, smiling. "Lily, I told you magic happens in the mists. You found my Celtic scarf, did you? I brought it from the old country years ago."

What did all this mean? Did the lady know about my missing pendant? But Gram didn't know it was lost. Or did she? Would she be smiling like that if she did?

I was surprised again when Evie popped out behind Gram. She looked normal now, and that was more important to me than anything.

I felt the lady touch my shoulder. "I told you to believe in the Others, remember? Don't worry. Their trick won't last—not this time."

Clenching my teeth, I closed my eyes to focus on the deepest wish I could muster. I summoned up every bit of faith to believe in the magic beings that dwelt here under the rocks, in the flowers, behind the mist. Maybe that would help.

Gram interrupted my prayer. "We need to be goin' home, my girls.

The sun's moving up." She led Evie and me back on the path. "We'll come back tonight to see the moon," she said. "Now it's time for swimmin' and sweepin' out the cabin. Maybe some blueberry pie too." She waved a thank you to the white robed lady and ambled ahead.

This time I took Evie's hand so she wouldn't run off. As we walked, I looked up at the gigantic trees and the granite boulders.

Evie was unusually quiet. Finally she asked, "You won't reveal my secret, will you?"

"No. Not if you don't tell Gram about my lost Celtic Knot."

Hopping out from behind a redwood tree, a rabbit and her babies suddenly appeared. I jumped away, unlocking my hand from Evie's. I knew, from Gram's stories, that rabbits were a Celtic omen of good luck. The bunnies came nearer, then suddenly vanished into a bush near a tree so wide it looked like a house.

Seconds later, I saw something sparkle on the ground near that same huge tree. Evie saw it, too. Glimmering next to a small puddle of water was my gold Celtic Knot pendant on a chain! It lay on a green oak leaf, with hazelnuts arranged in a perfect circle all around it.

Finding it hard to return to the harsh reality of Eve's hospital room, Lily breathed a sigh and stared at the last paragraph of the story. *What really happened on that day long ago?* Finally she looked up. Her friend was still breathing deeply. Eve finally appeared peaceful and out of pain, and Lily was glad. Then her thoughts flitted back to the mysterious story in her lap.

CHAPTER 8

*G*arden Getaway. *The name couldn't be more perfect*, Lily thought. She opened the door of the cozy shop, nodding hello to an elderly, petite lady who was watering mounds of pink and purple petunias that surrounded a bubbling fountain.

Lily pulled a piece of graph paper out of her jeans pocket, found a pencil in her purse and put some finishing touches on her sketch: a rectangular garden with a meandering path leading to a wishing well and a bird bath.

"What might you have there, lassie?" the white-haired woman asked as she put down her watering can. Not even five feet in height, she was dressed in a green and white plaid blouse and a white skirt. On her head was a jaunty green tam, and as she looked up at Lily with twinkling blue eyes, a strange feeling came over Lily.

"I'm...I'm taking a horticulture class." *To keep my sanity*, Lily thought, but she didn't dare say it out loud, even to a friendly stranger. "This is a rough sketch of what I want to do in my back-yard. I need a bird bath or maybe a wishing well." She handed it to the store owner.

With the girls gone and Frank still weak due to cancer treatments, Lily had decided she'd go mad if she didn't find something to keep her mind off her troubles. So when she'd received a brochure from the nearby community college, she'd combed through the list of courses and decided it was time. Time to keep busy, time to redirect her thoughts, or at least have somewhere to go during the long, quiet autumn evenings when she knew Frank and Eve would fall asleep early.

Yes, now she had two patients who dozed off after dinner every night. After much pleading, Eve had agreed to come home with Lily when the hospital released her. Still nursing multiple leg and rib fractures and with a periodic loss of memory, Eve was mending slowly. The hardest part for Lily was her friend's chaotic mood swings.

The little lady was still speaking. "I'll be showin' you plenty of bird baths in the back, my dear, but the only wishing wells I have in me shop are wee ones over here."

"Wee ones?" Lily smiled, charmed by the lady's brogue.

The little woman pointed at a shelf full of miniatures. "It's a special hobby of mine, it is. These Irish things for making lovely faerie gardens. I learned it at my mother's knee in the old country." Her eyes fixed on Lily. "I never forgot it, you see."

"What a great idea," Lily laughed. "I've heard of faerie gardens, but I've never made one. Sounds like a wonderful idea." She began looking at the miniatures. "I listened to plenty of Irish and old Celtic faerie tales from my Irish grandmother. Gram bought several books for me when I was a little girl. Too bad she's gone, or she'd probably help me with this project."

The woman picked up a tiny twig house complete with brown leafy shutters around the windows and a hinged door she began to open and close. "I'm wonderin', child, what would you think of this? No homeless dwarfs or faeries would be turnin' down this tiny mansion, now would they?"

Lily was transfixed. She took the house and began examining every detail.

Next the lady held up a plastic bag of pebbles. "Take a look inside. There'll be a miniature cylinder made of bark in here, too. See? You'll need a bit of glue for makin' your own wee wishing well, and then you can set it out for the faeries." She pointed to the well in the bag with some other items. "And," she paused," if you're lucky, someday you'll discover real gold coins in the well, a sign from the faeries that good fortune is comin' your way!"

Lily delighted in the lady's Irish fantasy.

The owner went on, waving her hand at the other shelves. "All of this came all the way from Ireland, my dear. I ordered these tiny items from my dear friend Rose O'Sullivan. She actually works at Blarney Castle and grew up near the cliffs of the Western Isles..." she paused and looked into Lily's eyes again "...where the winds blow and the mornin' fog hides the faeries and the pookas. They really do still dwell there, they say."

Lily's imagination took off, and her heart began to sing, as if she were ten years old again.

She laid the little house and the bag of pebbles and bark in her basket and turned to pick out some flowers to plant later. "I love your idea," she said, "and I'm so glad I met you!"

"I'm thinkin' the same, lassie, and I don't mind tellin' you that I knew somehow it would happen. . . ." She held out her hand to take Lily's and nodded her head. "Call me Maeve, child."

"My name's Lily. Because of you I'm going to make some changes to my garden plan. Where did you say your large bird baths are?"

The little woman led her to the back of her shop. Lily's homework wasn't due for two weeks, but she couldn't wait to get started. This new project had stoked an old passion of hers, a slice of her life she never wanted to forget.

CHAPTER 9

*L*ily was standing in a wrecked landscape. *This backyard looks like a wasteland! Except for my new faerie garden.* Four uneven stumps were all that was left of the lush ficus trees that used to shade Lily's entire patio. Now the raised planter that traversed her backyard wall contained only a few puny bushes. She'd cut away mountains of diseased branches while trying to salvage the hibiscus and gardenias she'd planted so carefully fifteen years before, when she and Frank started renting this house. As if all the dead brush wasn't enough, only random clumps of green grass remained. The rest of the lawn was now the color of burnt ochre.

She sat down to rest in a wrought iron chair surrounded by trays of plants she'd bought while visiting the Garden Getaway again last week. Her dog looked up at her. "Kinza, this yard is a mess." She took off her gloves and scratched the Rhodesian Ridgeback's ears. "Between the city cutting down my trees, that horrible white-fly disease, plus too many summer heat waves and you watering my lawn..."

She shook her head, got up and walked toward the lone corner in the garden that still held promise: a newly planted oak tree sprouting next to a magenta bougainvillea whose gangly branches were spewing wildly in all directions, a welcome riot of color. Sitting down next to the large stone birdbath she'd bought, she noticed a bird dipping its beak into the water. Lots of birds took baths in it every day at twilight, but this one was unique, with white, gray and black feathers and a flash of red on its head. It pecked as if it were trying to get her attention. Tap, tap, tap. Again, tap, tap, tap. Then it flew away.

Mid-October had finally brought cooler weather, a perfect time for planting. "This bougainvillea bush survived the summer, and thank you, God, the flowers I planted in my faerie garden last month are thriving too." Kinza began licking her ankle. Lily smiled, then picked up the little twig house resting among the flowers and found another place to put it. She suddenly realized her stomach pains had disappeared since she'd begun working in her garden. *Doc Blanchard said I was heading for an ulcer.* Yet it was Gram's words that lingered long in her thoughts, "It's the ancient magic of the faeries and sprites that might heal us."

Lily loved gardening. Her backyard, though small compared to her neighbors, had become a special retreat. Over the years, digging in the dirt, nourishing it with compost, yanking out weeds, and then sitting back under the trees, the serenity here had renewed her soul. She needed this precious oasis! The flowers, the birds and the butterflies nourished her when the world and its people couldn't. Trouble was, during the last year, with the overtime she'd put in at Graylock, her girls going off to college, and now Eve's and Frank's daily needs, the backyard had taken a beating.

She bent down and created pathways of small river stones at the foot of the fledgling oak tree. An array of purple foxgloves and yellow pansies already circled it, with saffron crocuses sprouting in front, their petals revealing pistils with scarlet stigmas. She'd read in a faerie book that crocuses held "the famous golden seeds of ancient days."

"I wonder what the golden seeds will buy? Or should I wait till I find those mysterious golden coins in the wee wishing well that Maeve mentioned?" she joked as she patted Kinza's head, his nose now buried in the flowers. *He's in heaven. These smells are like birthday cake to a hound.*

She moved the nursery trays closer. Today she would plant Irish moss, creeping thyme and white baby's tears around the small flat stones she'd placed in front of the faerie house. Since talking with Maeve a couple of times at the garden shop, Lily had dug her old books out of the closet and begun reading a faerie story each night. "They're better than sleeping pills," she said to Kinza as she turned the soil over and began digging holes for her plants.

A strange tinkling sound distracted her. She sat still, noticing Kinza's ears perk up. The sound was like a xylophone plinking out the notes of a rainbow. But different too...foreign, like a breeze blowing tones up and down the scale of a wind chime. Once, then twice, now three times! For a second it went silent, then it sang out again.

How strange! Though the warm Santa Ana winds had raged last month, now her new tree's leaves were completely motionless. No breezes today! So where was the music coming from? A thrill went through her and she suddenly grinned. Maybe the faeries were trying to tell her something! Did they like their new garden? Laughing to herself, she checked the faerie wishing well. "Well, no gold coins yet."

The dog nosed the flowers some more, his tail swinging back and forth, as if they had company, but no one but Lily sat beside him. Just then an unusual blue butterfly emerged out of nowhere, alighting on the faerie flowers. It sat very still. Lily held her breath. Blue? She'd never seen a bright blue butterfly like this! With Kinza so close, the butterfly's trust amazed her. Now it landed on Kinza's nose! Really? She heard the tinkling bells again as she watched the dog's tail switch back and forth. He turned to chase the butterfly.

Lily's heart filled with a girlish joy she hadn't felt in decades. Maybe life's magic still existed somewhere.

"Lily!" Eve's call came from the upstairs window.

"Be there in a minute!" Lily yelled back. She wiped her hands on her shorts and stroked Kinza's back. "C'mon, buddy, let's leave this garden to the faeries and go see our patients."

On her way to the stairs, Lily crossed her dining room and spied the silver trays in her china hutch, Eve's wedding gift to her, trays so lustrous and gleaming years ago, but now darkly tarnished. They reminded her of Eve's former sparkle. Would the happiness she used to see in Eve's eyes ever return?

Reaching the top of the stairs, she tiptoed past the master bedroom so as not to wake Frank. Now that his radiation treatments were over, he was still perennially tired and slept late, not arriving at work until the afternoon.

She entered Tanya's bedroom, where Eve was staying. "So how are we feeling today, my friend?"

Eve was sitting up, trying to bolster a trio of purple pillows behind her back with one arm. "Tolerable," she replied crossly. "Better than yesterday, though." Her complexion was still pallid, her tall frame thinner, her eyes lifeless.

Lily smiled. "Don't expect so much. It's only seven weeks since the accident."

"*Only?*"

Lily wondered if Eve would ever recover from the shock of losing her unborn baby and the awful news that she probably couldn't bear children in the future. What worried Lily most was whether Eve would keep her distance from Brad when he was finally released from the neurological rehab center. Though she'd heard Eve asking Frank to mail letters for her, nothing had arrived for Eve except cards from co-workers. Lily knew this because she was the one who commandeered the mail every day. Plus, their family computer hadn't been up and running for weeks. *So the bastard can't email Eve*, Lily thought, *nor can she contact him*—at least not as far as Lily knew because she'd confiscated her friend's laptop, iPad and cell phone. And so far, strangely enough, Eve hadn't asked for any of them. She'd seemed content to watch TV, read, exercise a bit and sleep much more than usual. The accident had taken its toll.

Lily watched Eve pull herself out of bed, her face contorted with pain. She hobbled, stiff-legged, to the bathroom. "Back in an hour," she called over her shoulder.

"Eve, let me help you."

"No. I travel on my own. Always have. I can't be a burden to you forever."

"You're not a burden." Lily watched her painful progress. *Please, God, find someone special for her in the days ahead, someone who truly cares about her.*

Eve closed the bathroom door and Lily was alone. As the minutes ticked by she looked at Tanya's soccer trophies and picked up one of her blue and white pom-poms from high school. Pursing her lips, Lily let the room's memories tug at her heart. Images of both of her girls filled her thoughts and a familiar ache took hold. How could she make this awful malaise go away?

She hadn't heard from them much in the last weeks. Her anger had flared when two whole days had marched by after their departure with only one text from Tanya saying they had arrived safely. She'd finally phoned the dorm and managed to connect with one of Tanya's new college friends.

Tanya took her time calling back. "I got a fantastic new roommate, Mom. Yeah, her family's rich. They're from Vail. She's got awesome clothes, too, and guess what? We're the same size, so we can share. Yeah, Lisa's fine." Her voice suddenly sounded bored. "Her roommate? I don't know. Gees, Mom, I'm not her shadow! I haven't seen her lately. This campus is huge, and we only have one class together. Why don't you call her?" Tanya hadn't said much more before she'd started saying good-bye.

All the flurry of their departure, a brief callback from one daughter and a mere five-minute, very sullen phone call from the other echoed through Lily's mind yet again—Lisa was probably still furious at her for suggesting she live with someone other than her sister.

After that, except for a few random text messages, weeks of silence ensued, though she'd tried calling them and left messages.

"Hey, Lily, where'd you go?" Eve was inching her way back to bed.

Lily put the pom-pom back and wiped the dust off the bureau with her hand. "Nowhere," she said. "Just thinking about the girls. You know, daydreaming, worrying. Like always."

Eve reached the bed, wincing as she sat down on the high mattress, and twisted her body to lift her legs. "So what else is new? You're always worrying...about everyone. You have such a wonderful way of taking over, so no one else has to lift a finger. Me, Frank, the girls. We all rely on you way too much."

Lily kept dusting the shelves with her hand. "Well, I can't change. You know I've tried." She picked up a framed photo of the girls, turned away from Eve and blew away the dust on it.

Eve doesn't know what it's like to lose two daughters at once. Somehow her friend's remarks sounded like criticism. Well, she *had* tried. Promised herself she'd stop listening to the voices in her head that worried about her daughters and Frank—Eve too. Tried over and over. But her damned imagination had a way of constantly conjuring up bad news. How could she turn away when her loved ones needed her? Besides, taking care of people was the only thing she was good at.

Eve was still talking. "...you're not angry at me, are you? I didn't mean to stomp on your feelings." Her question made Lily banish her thoughts. "Lily, honey, you've been a great support to me during the last few weeks."

Lily faked a smile. "I'm tired. That's all."

"*Bone* tired, I bet." Eve ran her fingers through her tangled blonde hair. "My goal is to be out of here. Soon. You know that, don't you?"

"Eve, please stop. I'm not tired because of you. I was just wishing the girls—"

"Would call you more often? Honestly, they're in an incredibly self-centered phase right now. It's not about you, it's about them. I know. My grandparents sent me away to college after high school, right after Mother's passing. Remember? But it was a good thing." Eve's voice cracked a little. "And this is just the beginning. You're going to have to accept that Lisa and Tanya aren't your little girls anymore. They need space. If you don't hear from them, that's normal. They're working out their own lives."

"I know all that. I've been trying to let go, but it still doesn't feel right, not in here." Lily pressed her fingers to her breast. She knew she sounded cross and depressed, but she couldn't help it.

Eve opened her arms. "Aw, come on. Let's not argue."

Lily bent down to press her cheek to her friend's.

Eve's arms wrapped around her. "You're too good."

Lily tried to back off, but Eve held her close. "Forgive my harsh words," Eve whispered. "Without you, I'd be totally alone. You've taken such good care of me. You always have." Her voice broke and for a moment they were quiet, holding on, as if by clinging to one another each could dispel the loneliness within.

CHAPTER 10

*N*o one was home except Eve. Lily had taken Frank for his monthly blood test.

Eve hated the silence. Making her way to Lily's bedroom, she opened a drawer and lifted her laptop out for the first time in several weeks. A smile crossed her lips. *Lily thinks I don't know where she stashed it.*

Back in Tanya's bedroom, she clicked on a favorite iTune, "The Time of My Life," and leaned back against her pillows to read her business emails. There weren't many; her manager at the winery must've told her co-workers not to bother her. Next she perused her territory's sales reports. The sales woman hired as her substitute seemed to be satisfying her clients, though Eve didn't notice any large orders. For a moment, she worried about maintaining her status as "top salesperson of the year," but a part of her didn't want to think about her job. Besides, the doctor kept ordering her to leave social media and email alone for a while, to avoid stress. But Eve had to admit it. Today, for the first time, she was just plain bored. Did that mean she was getting well?

Suddenly she clicked off her email, knowing if she didn't, she might violate her vow to cut Brad out of her life. Though she'd sent him a few get-well cards without Lily's knowledge, he had never replied. So far, she hadn't tried to contact him any other way. But her thoughts often still turned to the special times they'd shared, even though she kept reminding herself what he'd done to her. He was dangerous. Finally she could admit it, but never to anyone else. And yet, she was still obsessed with him. As for the other things he'd made her do? She couldn't think about that. She was too ashamed.

To distract herself, Eve began searching the Internet, clicking on half a dozen websites devoted to decorating. Maybe she'd shop for some new items for her condo, to go with the London purchases she'd made on her last business trip. Better yet, why not come up with a new plan for her bedroom? Brad was gone now, and hopefully, she'd return home soon. Wouldn't it be wonderful *not* to be reminded of him there at all?

Wait till I tell Lily. Her eyes will absolutely glow. She totally hates Brad!

What about a gray and white color scheme for the walls? With that deep, almost black red I love—in a bedspread! She looked at some ads, then ordered sparkly, beaded red pillows and black and white ones too. To make things pop. She scrolled through the products offered on a European website and ordered an expensive crystal chandelier.

Shopping done, she got out of bed and wobbled to Lily's bedroom. Earlier in the week, overtaken by nostalgia, she'd asked Lily to bring several storage boxes from her condo. She found what she was looking for in Lily's closet: *Eve's Memory Box,* inscribed in gold letters, a gift from Lily years ago. She hadn't searched through it in years, but today something was urging her to open it.

Sure enough, inside were several old books her father had read to her when she was a child. She stopped to gaze at *National Velvet,* its worn cover a dark red. *It'll go perfectly with my new bedroom palette,* she told herself. *And remind me of Daddy, too.* She set it out on her dresser, tracing the black horse's outline on the book's cover. How she'd loved the sound of her father's voice as he read her this story over and over. Even better were the days they'd ridden together in the mountains. Dad had given her Star, her very own pony, when she was only seven years old. Though infrequent, those special days were enthroned in her heart. *Always so much fun to be with Daddy! When Mom wasn't around to spoil everything. No man ever treated me like he did.*

ﭸ

Evie watched Daddy as he reached into his pocket for his handkerchief, wiping perspiration off his face. He winced when he touched a large bruise on his forehead. She wondered about it. Then she noticed his initials sewn into the handkerchief, a gift from her last Christmas! Lily's grandma had helped her empty her piggy bank, and taken her to J. C. Penney's to order the softest ones they could find. Evie picked out the color of the embroidery too. Blue. Daddy's favorite.

"Dry your tears, my sweet girl," he said now, patting her cheeks with the other side of the smooth linen cloth.

She gritted her teeth, trying to hold her tears back. Daddy didn't like it when she cried. She couldn't hold back the pain in her heart. It was like nothing she'd ever felt before—sort of like scissors cutting into her finger or the kitchen knife that sliced her hand when she'd tried to cut a roll in half. The throbbing in her heart felt like that now, sliced open. Yet being with Daddy was the best comfort of all whenever she felt sad.

Evie wiped her cheeks with his handkerchief; then he lifted her up to put her on her pony. "Here you are, my brave girl. See? Star is waiting to take you for a ride." He tucked her boots into the stirrups and gave her Star's reins. "You have two good friends. Right here! You know that, don't you?"

KATHLEEN O'DONOVAN

"But why did I have to give up Amber?"

"Honey, sometimes we have to let go of a friend," he said in a soft voice. "Amber is a great pup. He'll miss you, but he'll be happy in the home he has now. Maybe we can even visit him." He patted her head as he always did, and she tried to smile for him because she knew that's what he wanted. But Evie also knew she would never see Amber's red-brown tail wagging at her again, no matter what Daddy said.

She had come home from school yesterday to find the house empty. It wasn't unusual to find her mother gone in the afternoons, though she would never let Daddy know how often, because Mommy would punish her good. At first she'd wondered why Amber wasn't waiting for her. Every day after school, as soon as she opened the back door, he'd jump up on her and lick her entire face. Then she'd drop her book bag on the couch and they'd race outside to play their favorite game: she, throwing his Frisbee as high as she could and he, running for it, as it swirled up into sky, then sloped down to earth, where he waited to catch it in his mouth. He caught it every time. She'd taught him how, with Daddy's help, of course. Then his tail would wag like crazy, and he'd scamper over to sit at her feet, holding the Frisbee and gazing up at her, begging her to throw it again.

That wouldn't happen anymore, not ever, because Evie had suddenly remembered why the house was empty. Mommy had decided the puppy was too much trouble. "Two pets are way too much for a seven-year-old child," she'd announced the night before at dinner.

Recalling her Mommy's words, Evie's heart felt like it would break. She'd seen her daddy's shoulders flinch too that night, and the muscles in his cheek quiver like they always did before their row began. At first, he'd sat silently, like she had, but when Mommy's voice turned hard and shrill and loud, he'd pulled his chair out and yelled at her, again and again. To Evie, their arguing sounded like a blast of car horns in a horrible traffic jam.

She knew how it would end. Helpless, she let her tears drip down her cheeks as she rushed away to hide in her room, hands over her ears, trying to block out their burning rage. Afterwards, Daddy started up his convertible, its wheels screeching as he streaked out of the driveway and down the street.

Star's whinny and the tossing of her head interrupted Evie's thoughts. The pony was telling her she wanted to trot. Evie shifted her weight in the saddle and nudged Star with her legs to go faster, or Daddy might disappear ahead of them on the mountain trail. She patted Star's mane and held on, as a cool breeze whisked her hair and the sweet chill of the morning nipped at her cheeks. Nothing was better than this!

Even though she'd barely slept last night, today was a new day and in spite of all the ruckus lately, Daddy had kept his promise. She felt elated about that. She'd fallen asleep last night, doubting she'd see him today, but, as he'd promised, he'd walked into in her bedroom before sunrise, whispering, "Rise and shine, my sweet girl. We're going to spend the day riding in the mountains. Remember?"

A thrill had streaked through her, because their riding trips together were just about the best times in her whole life. Today would be full of fun, so she decided she wouldn't let herself think about Mommy today. Though her mother would ignore them both when they returned home tonight. She always refused to speak to them after they'd gone riding together. But as Star picked up speed and the breeze whipped her hair and cooled her cheeks, suddenly Evie didn't care. Not one bit! Mommy and all her drama and her harsh, mean ways were far away! She and Daddy were riding on this gorgeous mountain trail where the sun's pink rays were just beginning to paint the sky.

CHAPTER 11

Graylock Inc.'s cafeteria was filling up fast as Lily made her way through the food line. She lingered by the pizza and sandwich counter before choosing a low-calorie lunch. When she headed toward an empty table, Holly, a slim, red-headed co-worker, fell into step with her.

"You're being so good," she said, eyeing Lily's tray. "Only cottage cheese and a fruit salad. Is that *all* you're going to eat?"

Lily sat down across from her co-worker and nodded toward her plate. "I'm not like you. Fried chicken and mashed potatoes will show up on my hips tomorrow if I eat any today."

"Well, your diet must be working. I've noticed you've lost weight." Holly picked up a drumstick and carefully bit into it.

"Thanks." Lily started on her fruit salad. "As of today, I've only lost eight pounds on this new food plan. But at least I weigh less than I did three weeks ago."

"How much do you want to lose?"

Lily hesitated. "A lot," she said, careful not to reveal too much. "I'm sure dieting is the last thing *you* need to worry about." She wondered how Holly could eat so much and still be so slim. But Lily knew how fast Holly moved and worked. As editor among twelve technical writers in Graylock's publications department, Lily marked up the drafts that writers gave to her. She also kept track of all the airline maintenance manuals written and revised in the department. Holly had earned the reputation of top technical writer in the department by completing several manuals in record time each quarter. She was an impressive talker, too, and everyone liked her.

Yet, strangely, Lily had never edited Holly's work. Their boss, Ken, had told Lily that Holly didn't need an editor. She was that good. So last week, Lily was taken aback when he'd suddenly asked Lily to edit Holly's latest project. From the beginning, every other writer always submitted their work to Lily for not just one, but several edits before the manuals were corrected then sent off to different commercial airlines like Boeing and Airbus, who bought Graylock's airplane parts.

Lily's confidence had grown in the three years since working at Graylock. In the beginning it wasn't easy. She had worked part-time in another large corporation, writing and editing brochures and newsletters, and had taught a business writing classes at a local university but she'd never tried technical writing. When the bills from Frank's surgeries and cancer treatments became intolerable, Lily spread the word that she needed to work full time. A friend recommended her to the manager of Human Resources at Graylock, and shortly thereafter, Lily sent in her resume, was interviewed twice and was offered the job. For the first few months, she'd constantly bitten her nails for fear she wouldn't measure up, but finally her anxiety faded away and, thank god, her nails had grown out, too.

"How are your classes going?" Holly asked between sips of her Diet Coke and big bites of mashed potatoes and gravy.

"I'm taking only a horticulture class at the college this semester, strictly for fun," Lily said. "I won't teach any classes for a while. I have too much to do."

"Seems like you've been either taking classes or teaching them forever."

"You said it. I guess you know I finally completed my master's degree last May. So that's the end of homework and exam pressure. What a relief."

Holly smiled. "Wow! A master's degree? No, I didn't know. Impressive. Why did you put so much effort into getting degrees? The rest of us just worked our way up here. It took a while, but that's really the way things are done. I got my job repairing Graylock's products after high school. Put ten years in, doing different manufacturing jobs, then I submitted writing samples. That was all I needed to finally become a tech writer. We all did it that way."

"I knew you started here when you were barely twenty," Lily said, "but I didn't realize everyone else did. Well, my dad is the one who urged me to go to college. Maybe because he never did. He always said it would give me financial independence if anything serious happened to my husband. Now, with Frank sick, I want to keep my work options open. Earning my master's degree might help."

"Hmm...your work options? Oh, I get it. You won't be stuck here forever, that's what you're saying, right? By the way, how *is* your husband?"

Lily tried to smile as she returned Holly's gaze. "He's holding his own."

She didn't want to share any more of her personal life—in fact, she'd probably shared too much—and since her plate was now empty, she stood up and smiled as she excused herself. Holly was one of only two coworkers Lily felt comfortable with since she'd taken this job, but even spending time with her stressed Lily out. And Holly's pointed remarks today made Lily realize she wasn't like the others--Lily would never consider herself a lifer at Graylock.

Also, early on, Lily realized the whole tech writing department spent way too much time gossiping, Holly too. She hated it, but that was the culture here: constant rumors and comments and nitpicking. She refused to get involved in any of it, so limiting her conversations with co-workers had become her best choice.

&.

Steve Friedman's return call was a godsend. After mulling it over, Lily had called him to help her straighten out several errors on some hydraulic blueprints, a very touchy subject. Engineers didn't like it when a technical editor discovered mistakes on *their* documents. In fact, Steve was one of only two or three engineers Lily could approach in situations like this. Most of them found excuses *not* to help the Tech Pubs department. Some were even hostile when asked a technical question. Since most writers lacked the confidence to question an engineer, it was Lily who braved unpleasant confrontations to assure a manual's accuracy, though her boss, Ken, kept saying he didn't want her to "bother engineering."

Today an unusual deadline loomed, and Lily had to get the data right on an Airbus manual Holly had recently revised. While editing it, Lily had discovered glaring inconsistencies in the manual compared to Graylock's engineering documents—so many errors! That's why Lily had called Steve. Sure enough, he'd not only called back, but he'd left his answer in an email. Lily's next challenge was to sit down with Holly. She dreaded it because Holly's manual was riddled with even *more* technical errors. Lily could tell she had not checked it against the blueprints, and this stunned Lily. Sighing, she braced herself for the worst. Holly supposedly didn't need an editor's corrections. *Yeah, right!*

Minus her usual smile, Holly showed up for her appointment at two o'clock. Lily tried to put her at ease at first. But as Lily showed her the numerous technical mistakes she'd missed, Holly listened in stony silence, folding her arms and sitting stiffly, her mouth scrunched up like a fussy baby. Trying to keep her voice neutral, Lily continued explaining the inconsistencies between the manual and the blueprint data. Holly's face became a blank mask. When Lily finished, she shook her head and spoke so low Lily could barely hear her. "I thought you were my friend."

"I am," Lily said, "but I can't ignore these errors. Our manuals are used to repair parts on airplanes. If they're not accurate, it could affect a plane's flight. That could be dangerous. You must've forgotten to review the blueprints. I can accept it this one time, but, Holly, this isn't like you. However, you'll be relieved to know that not every error here is your fault. The blueprints were inconsistent, too, so I took it upon myself to call Steve Friedman to clarify which data to use. Here's the email he sent me. You can use it when you correct these mistakes."

Holly glared at Lily. "Oh, so you took it upon yourself to go to Steve? I thought that was a no-no; that's what Ken always tells *everyone* in this department." Her face pink with irritation, the redhead picked up the manual. "Oh, and thanks for not even bothering to ask me before you contacted Steve. He knew this was *my* project..." her voice cracked, "but then I've heard you often end up doing everyone else's job around here. It'll probably look good on your resume when you start looking for...what did you call it? 'Other work options'?" She got up from her chair, flounced over to her desk and immediately picked up her phone. Lily could hear her sugary tone. "Hello, Ken? Oh yes, everything's perfectly fine, but something *has* come up. It's important. I'd appreciate it if you could see me as soon as possible."

Lily already knew the Ken couldn't resist a request from Holly, since she was the star writer in his department. She watched Holly swagger past her desk and go into Ken's office, almost, but not quite, slamming the door.

Though Lily knew things would never be the same now, she

tried to focus on a new project Ken had given her. But right after Holly left Ken's office, he asked to see Lily. In his usual, weasely way he hinted that Lily had been too hard on Holly. But, he also made it clear that from now on he wanted her to edit *all* of Holly's manuals. "Only correct her technical and spelling errors, though," he said. "Ease up on her style mistakes for now. I'm sure you won't find many."

After that, he launched into a lengthy tirade about how Lily shouldn't bother Steve Friedman so much. "If errors surface on the engineering documents, you should *never take over* a writer's project by contacting an engineer. Instead, come to me. I can straighten out any discrepancies with the engineers. Then *I'll* settle everything with the writer, in this case, Holly. Do you understand, Lily?"

She understood...but her whole body ached, like she'd just finished *last* in a marathon.

By the time she emerged from Ken's office it was the end of the work day and most of the writers had already left. Not Holly. She was over by the copier, engrossed in a conversation with Belinda, the only other writer in the department who had befriended Lily. Both women stared at her, and then went on talking. Lily shrugged, picked up her jacket and briefcase, and made for the door. As she walked down the stairs to the lobby, she tried to dismiss today's ordeal, but she couldn't help feeling like a student who'd been sent to the principal's office for punishment. *Engineering made some errors and Holly made plenty more and I just saved them from lots of trouble. So why do I feel so shitty?*

She moved her shoulders up and down, trying to release the ache that often settled there. As she walked to her car, all she could think of was food. She spied a McDonald's on the way home and decided to pick up dinner. *Frank likes fast food and Eve won't mind just this once.* At the drive-in window, she ordered two Quarter Pounders for Frank and, on a whim, two for herself, as well as a Filet-O-Fish for Eve. She set the bag of food in the middle of the passenger seat. "Diet be damned!"

After dinner, Lily went out to sit in the cool autumn air in her backyard. Exhausted, she was aware she was clenching her teeth and a frenzy of adrenaline was racing through her body. She tried to focus on her faerie garden; the twilight cast shadows on it, making her smile. Were the wee ones getting ready for their nightly dance? She looked up to see a full moon already glowing in the sky. The whole scene began to calm her. Just what she needed.

Her cell phone rang. She was surprised to hear Belinda's voice. "Is this a good time?"

"Sure. Are you okay?" Lily said.

"Oh, yes, *I'm* fine. It's you I'm calling about."

"Me? Well, I guess you heard an earful this afternoon from Holly—"

"Yes, I did. But...well, Lily, I think I'd better... I hate to do this, but I need to clue you in. Holly's not the only one complaining about you. The others have been too. For a while. Since Holly had the best reputation in the department, that is until now, she always stuck up for you along with me, and they listened—"

"Stuck up for me?"

"I...I never wanted to tell you about how they sniped at you behind your back. It really wasn't *that* often or that bad, but now... well, without Holly putting in a good word for you, they're all gunning for you. Holly is *really* mad, especially because everyone knows about all her errors on that Airbus manual."

"How would they know?"

"Apparently, Sean snooped around and saw all the markups you made on her manual and told everyone in the cafeteria this afternoon. And he's the absolute worst enemy you have. You knew that, right?" She paused. "Oh, Lily, I kept wondering if I should tell you... but then...well, I know you'd do the same for me."

Lily's stomach churned. "Of course I'm glad you told me,

Belinda. No, I didn't know about Sean, or that the other writers were so upset with me. No one said a word! From the beginning I've tried to be tactful and professional when I hand back their manuals for corrections. Yet, they're all so standoffish, I should've figured out how they felt. But I've had so much to do and so much on my mind, I didn't—"

"Well, I wanted to warn you," Belinda said. "I know you're in an awkward position because we never had a professional editor in our department before. We just looked over each other's work. And Ken keeps saying we have to get used to it."

All Lily wanted to do now was get off the phone. "Yes. Well, thanks for letting me know. You're right, Belinda, I'd do the same for you. I won't let on that you told me, okay?"

"Okay, good. I hope this won't totally ruin your evening. Let's get together sometime after work. Maybe take in a movie? I hope you sleep okay tonight."

"Sure. Yeah. Thanks, Belinda. Good-bye." Lily put the phone down.

Slumping in her chair, Lily hugged her aching stomach. Finally she looked up at the moon again, shining bright and magical above the trees. This time its light only enhanced the darkness closing in on her. "Please, God," she whispered, "if you're near at all, give me strength. I feel so alone."

Three weeks had passed and Lily was still trying to endure her isolation at work. The tech writers were shunning her. Only Belinda spoke to her now and, of course, Ken.

This morning it taken all of Lily's energy to get out of bed. As she set both feet on the cold floor, she was keenly aware of a sick loathing that gnawed at her whole body. She glanced at the clock; her annual review with Ken was at ten o'clock. The last thing she wanted to do was set foot in that company today! She was beginning to hate her job. *But I have bills to pay, and they're stacking up. Frank needs me to support us.*

The truth was that Frank hadn't opened a bill, let alone paid one in weeks. He wasn't himself at all. Still exhausted from his past cancer treatments, he found it difficult to resume his activities or go to work, even part time. Lily had taken over their finances temporarily, even though he'd protested. Despite his growling, the bills needed to be paid, and she was determined to overcome his lack of confidence in her when it came to money.

In spite of the revulsion plaguing her, Lily dressed quickly, laid out breakfast for Frank and Eve, and dished out Kinza's food, petted him good-bye and tiptoed out the back door. She popped antacid pills as a precaution, while driving faster than usual to Graylock. She would arrive early. *It's been a long time since I've had a real breakfast. It might cheer me up.*

Sure enough, her steaming cup of Starbucks coffee and the aroma of blueberry pancakes plus eggs with bacon on her tray were already lifting her spirits as she paid the cafeteria cashier.

"Splurging today?" the cashier asked. "I don't see you in here much."

"Well, now that you mention it, I've been dieting," Lily said, "but I decided to treat myself this morning."

"That's a delicious idea. Go for it." The girl smiled and Lily felt better.

The regular cafeteria tables were cordoned off, perhaps for cleaning, so Lily made her way toward an adjacent conference room also used for breaks and meals. As she neared the open door she heard her name.

"Lily? Yeah, she gets her review today." It was Holly's voice.

Lily stopped, trying to hear the conversation; she couldn't see who Holly was talking to.

"She was in Ken's office for over an hour yesterday," Holly

continued, "with all our marked-up manuals. When she came out, she had on that Cheshire-cat look. That pseudo-control of hers, always so cheerful. Well, I've told Ken plenty about her lately, and he's finally been listening. I know she'll go crazy for sure when he's done with her today. I can't wait."

Sean voice chimed in, "She's always so god-damned superior with those high-fa-lootin' degrees of hers. Rest of us paid our dues, came up the hard way and worked on the shop floor for years. But she can't take the real world. And she can't take criticism."

"I knew that about her from the start," Holly said.

"You got that right. Ken never should've hired her."

"'Course nobody ever asks *us*. She's gonna lose it today. And I'm glad."

"Oh, c'mon guys, lay off her. Look at the time. We better get upstairs."

Was that Belinda's voice?

Lily couldn't move. She stood transfixed outside the room for a full minute. Then she turned around so fast that the tray in her hands tipped and the Starbucks mug went crashing to the floor, coffee splashing everywhere. But she couldn't clean it up. Not now. Instead, she set the tray down and rushed through the cafeteria doors, making it to the elevator. As she stepped inside, and the elevator doors began closing, she saw Belinda coming, with Holly and Sean behind her. Belinda's eyes were wide as saucers. Lily held her gaze until the elevator closed.

Sitting at her desk, Lily glanced at the clock, seven-thirty p.m. Everyone else had gone home. Today had been her worst day ever. No matter how she tried, she couldn't push the details of this morning's meeting with Ken out of her mind. *What a disaster.*

She moved a six-inch-thick aerospace manual to the side. This was the huge Boeing 757 revision project that no one else in her department had wanted to touch, let alone finish. But this year, to everyone's surprise, she'd taken it on as a challenge. This assignment would guarantee her more money to pay Frank's endless medical bills, or so she'd thought. It had taken lots of overtime, but she'd checked every detail in the manual for accuracy and updated every page, when necessary. After that the manual was formally reviewed and signed off by the engineers. She'd finally completed it, as well as all her other responsibilities, even though it cut into her daily care of Frank and Eve at home. After ten long months, it was finally done!

She leaned forward, laid one arm on the Steelcase desk and rested her head on it, the fingers of her other hand grasping the desk's cold frame. Though she'd lost weight, she still hated how her buttocks overlapped the edges of her seat. Absently, her fingers found her thighs. *I detest these bulges!*

Waves of pain pierced her stomach again, too. *Too much stress, not just today but...* She'd have to get another refill of the meds the doctor had prescribed. He'd finally told her she was struggling with an ulcer. *Big surprise.* She raked her fingers through her curly hair.

Lately, she'd been staying late, as often as she could talk her neighbor into giving Frank and Eve their dinners. She used the overtime to finish other projects. But the truth was that all her extra hours hadn't counted at all. Ken made that clear today.

Her dogged dedication. For what? A mediocre review and a *one percent* raise? She knew her co-workers' peer evaluations had swayed Ken a lot. Her mediocre raise wouldn't even begin to pay off Frank's bills.

What a fool I was! She hadn't felt rage like this, ever. In fact, she rarely allowed herself the freedom to...to even *feel angry*. She sat up and slapped both hands on the desk, then again and again. Soon she began to pound, the sounds echoing through the long room of desks lit by cold, white fluorescents.

She blinked and tears began running down her cheeks. She wiped her face.

I'd like to throw all these friggin' manuals off my desk for good!

She leaned to her right and shoved two loose-leaf binders off her desk, and watched with a feeling completely new to her—was it wicked glee?—as the binders broke open and papers fanned around her chair, covering the space between her desk and Sean's. She couldn't believe she was doing this...but suddenly...

She. Didn't. Care.

Better yet, I'll scatter these pages all over everybody's desks! That'll cause a stir. Give them something else to talk about. No one will know I did it.

She grabbed bundle after bundle of the loose-leaf manuals and tossed them on adjacent desks. As radical as she felt, she took satisfaction picturing Sean and Holly gossiping about this mess tomorrow. It wouldn't be the first time.

Her mind reeling, Lily picked up another pile of manuals and marched over to Holly's desk. "This has gone on too long! But I *will* find a way out!" she yelled. Was that really her voice? Oh, it felt *good* to let go. She couldn't remember ever allowing herself to be this angry. Frustrated, irritable, yes. But not like this. She raised her arms and let the stack of manuals crash to the floor. Holly's framed photos and pencil holder keeled over and everything else scattered.

From the beginning she'd tried so hard to be courteous when she handed back their work, full of her meticulous markups. Even tried to make friends. She'd considered Holly a friend. Now she didn't dare count on even Belinda's friendship anymore.

Well, I guess there'll be another feeding frenzy tomorrow. They'll be gossiping about their victory, my paltry raise. Lily knew they'd instigated what Ken had said to her today during her annual review. He was such a wuss.

They've been chewing me up all week in that cafeteria, waiting for me to see their peer-evaluations, all the condemnations they wrote out so carefully. Well, I hope they choke!

She found her chair, leaned back and howled like the coyotes she heard in the hills at night, her voice high and piercing. She wailed again, long and low. A hollow quiet closed in on her and she stood up. All she wanted now was to go home to Eve and Frank.

CHAPTER 12

The November sun illuminated the yellow and gold leaves of the maple trees, contrasting with the dark evergreens. The vivid colors, amidst the dappled afternoon light, lifted Lily's mood as she turned a corner, driving faster than she should have, to pick up Eve. When she reached the crowded parking lot, she swung her SUV around the last aisle, speeding toward a vacant spot as a Lexus convertible zoomed into it.

"Damn!" She hit the brake, beeping the horn.

A lanky athlete in a navy polo shirt stepped out of his sports car and saluted Lily with a jaunty grin. He walked near her open window. "Sorry. I didn't see your car." He winked, "Chill out, mate. Life's too short."

Lily stuffed away her irritation and managed a smile. She loved his Aussie accent. As he gave her another carefree salute and swaggered away, she couldn't help admiring him. Maybe he was right. Lately she was over reacting to everything.

Just then an older man in a blue shirt and yellow tie came up, waved at her and pointed to his parked black Jeep.

"Guess there's some courtesy still left in the world," she muttered.

He backed his car out of his space and gave her the high sign. She nodded, and then maneuvered her KIA between the white lines.

As she waited in her SUV, Lily gently rotated her neck, hoping to release pent-up stiffness. She closed her eyes and tried to conjure up a relaxing scene. Eve kept nagging her to try this. As the minutes ticked away, she visualized cascades of foaming waves moving toward a foggy shoreline as the sun dipped into the ocean. . .*only an hour away. When was the last time I took the time to walk on that beach?* She breathed in through her nose, then exhaled slowly, eyes still closed, almost smelling the salty air. Why couldn't life be as simple as that?

Eve hobbled up. "Napping? Can't imagine why *you'd* be tired."

Lily jumped out to open the passenger door for Eve. "No, I was trying that visualization technique you keep telling me about."

"You mean. . .badgering you about? Did it work?" Eve got in, sat still for a moment, then pivoted to face the windshield, clenching her teeth as she lifted her long legs into the SUV.

"I hate to admit it," Lily said, "but I actually think it did." Making sure Eve buckled up, she started up the car, looked over her shoulder and backed out. She lowered her voice. "I was trying to forget about my buddies at work."

"Yeah, they're your *buddies*, all right. I've heard enough stories about them. Not lately, though. And we haven't talked about your job since you got your review. Has Ken finally realized how lucky he is to have you in the Tech Pubs department? "

Lily couldn't tell Eve everything. She'd mentioned her co-workers' interminable gossip several times, but nothing about her paltry raise or...or how she'd almost lost it the other night. How could she share her work problems with Eve, who'd always been so successful in her career?

But Ken knew how fed up she was. He'd tried to make things

good by calling her into his office yesterday and promising her some business travel.

Lost in thought now, she braked for a stoplight and gazed into the rearview mirror to put on her sun visor. Her face looked glum-- she pulled at the extra skin under her chin as she always did. Her usually cheerful lips slanted downward, her dark, frizzy hair curling around her face.

"Hey," Eve said. "Where'd you go?"

Lily looked away, focusing on the traffic. "Sorry, there's nothing much to tell you. How'd your physical therapy session go?"

"Fine. The therapist said I need to do plenty of leg exercises for the next few months. Supposedly, it'll help me get back to normal. She showed me how to do them. The neurology guy says my brain is better. How he knows that, I'll never know. I certainly don't remember not remembering things."

Lily forced a grin.

"Good! I got a smile out of you," Eve said. "The bad news is I can't work full time for a couple of months. I hope he'll allow me to drive pretty soon. I want to move back to my condo before Christmas. But, wait a minute, you keep changing the subject. Tell me what happened at work."

Lily hesitated, then dove in. "It's not all bad. Really. Ken asked me to take on a new project today, that's all."

"What now? And what about your review? And your raise?"

"Oh, it was all pretty routine...the raise, I mean. But I'll now be heading up the outsourcing of all the new Boeing aircraft manuals. Managing not one but two outside vendors. It'll enhance my experience *and* my reputation in the company."

"Sounds like you're parroting your boss." Eve tapped her index finger on the console between them. "So what else did old, reliable Ken offer you?"

"Don't be so negative." Lily was well aware that her career was far from glamorous, unlike Eve's, but she didn't have much choice right now, did she? Besides, Ken had said he'd try to pull some strings to give her some perks. She knew he was trying to make up for her meager raise. Anyway, revealing the truth to Eve would only make her feel worse.

Eve straightened up, facing forward. Her fingers played with the silver chain around her neck. "Okay," she said. "Tell me the rest. I promise I won't criticize."

Lily summarized quickly. "This new project will take at least eight months, and I'll have to put in more overtime, but I'll get to travel to other divisions of the company. I'm kind of excited about that. I just hope it won't interfere with caring for Frank. If so, I'll hire a home health aide to stay with him."

"Will they *pay* you for your overtime?"

"No extra money this time. But Ken said I'll have an expense account when I travel. I know you take it for granted, but I've never had one. And he said if I complete the projects on time, he might have something 'down the road' for me."

"What?"

Lily squirmed in her seat and tucked a strand of hair behind her ear. "He didn't say."

"C'mon Lily, do you remember the promises he made to you last year? If you checked and revised every detail in that huge Boeing manual? You know the one I mean, the manual from hell that no one else would tackle. What did you get for that?"

"You said you weren't going to criticize."

Lily lapsed into a long silence. Eve's career with a major California winery had skyrocketed in the last two years, and she'd often traveled to several countries in Europe. By contrast, Lily's raise was worse than measly, and her co-workers' scathing peer reviews still stung. How could she not feel wounded by her boss's spineless capitulation to them?

Why? Why do they all despise me so much? It's my job to point out their errors! Maybe I am proud of my degree and maybe they feel it. But they could go to college too. The company would pay for it. She wasn't exaggerating. She *did* work hard. She didn't stand around talking. Didn't take a dozen breaks a day. This past year she'd completed more projects than anyone else in the Tech Pubs department, and Ken knew it. He'd praised her many times, though only in the privacy of his office. But when her peer evaluations reeked with negatives, he wouldn't dare face down her co-workers.

So, she'd ventured into Ken's office again yesterday to ask if she could write a rebuttal to the peer criticisms she'd received and turn it in to Human Resources. Documenting all her accomplishments would balance her co-workers' negative comments. Why was she surprised when Ken advised her to ignore her peers' comments? He'd minimized her request, hinting her coworkers were only envious of her because they didn't have college degrees. "Look at it from their point of view," he said.

Of course! How easy. She should try really hard to understand them and simply forget their vicious comments. *Yeah, right.*

No, she *had* to fight back by listing all her achievements and forcing HR to put it in her file or she'd never be able to respect herself. She'd hammered away with her persuasive pitch and Ken had finally acquiesced. *Big surprise. Truth was, he couldn't say no to anyone.* She'd handed him the rebuttal she'd written, and he promised to forward it to HR. Then he'd asked her to take on this new responsibility, making it sound really important.

They were near Lacey Park now, and Eve was staring out at the pond with its sparkling center fountain. The sun's rays flashing through the trees scattered light and shadows on the lawn where several mallard ducks were resting. Off to the side, several crows were pecking at the grass. Lily knew she was remembering the day of her accident.

Eve suddenly faced forward. "I'd better keep quiet. You're awfully touchy about Ken and your job. I'm sorry, I just want everyone to value you the way I do."

Lily laid her hand on her friend's. "I know. You're my best fan. Always looking out for me."

Eve sighed. "You know what?" her voice rising. "We haven't gone out to dinner in months. Let's not go home yet. You said Frank seems a little better in the last few days. Why don't you call him and tell him we deserve a girls' night out?"

Lily smiled, feeling her whole body relax. "If you're up to it, I'm game." She pulled her cell phone out and dialed her home number.

CHAPTER 13

A tall waiter lingered at their table. His bronze tan looked like a surfer's, and his gleaming dark hair was slicked back in a ponytail. Lily noticed a tiny silver hoop decorating his left ear. She couldn't help noticing how his eyes scoured Eve, from her long blonde hair down to her shapely legs and slim ankles.

He never glanced her way. *Why would he?*

"Appetizers with your bottle of Pinot Grigio, ladies?" he asked.

Eve was studying the menu. "Let's indulge ourselves," she said, meeting the waiter's eyes. "Two orders of escargot--and a filet mignon—medium, please, with a Caesar salad for me."

Lily locked eyes with her friend and began to protest.

"C'mon, try the escargot. Trust me," Eve said.

The waiter stood beside Eve until she looked up again, his russet eyes lingering on hers. "Of course," he said smoothly. "Two escargots." His tongue wet his lower lip, and he smirked just enough to hold her gaze. "Can I offer you anything else?"

She smiled. "Not right now."

Lily tried to get his attention. "Really, I don't think I can manage escargot. Shrimp cocktail for me. And a small Cobb salad."

"Whatever you say," he said to her, but his eyes were still on Eve.

As he walked away, Eve leaned in toward Lily. "C'mon, be a little daring for once. Promise me you'll at least taste mine."

Lily wrinkled her nose. "Okay. One bite." She paused. "What do you think of that guy? He sure was coming on to you."

"Think so? He looks familiar. We had a winery meeting here last year. He probably remembered me." She straightened her slim black skirt and fingered the sparkling topaz that hung from a silver chain. "Seems like forever since I thought about the opposite sex." She started to add something, but stopped.

The pause lengthened as Lily gazed at her, hoping her friend would open up. *Please, at least say something about Brad and the accident.* Eve always avoided talking about her feelings, but Lily knew she desperately needed to share the events of last summer. She'd been silent for too long.

Eve suddenly spoke. "I...I still have dreams about Brad. No surprise to you, I guess," She held up her glass, stared at the tawny, golden wine and sipped quietly.

"You haven't mentioned him since you left the hospital," Lily replied, "and I didn't want to pry."

The smile Eve offered looked fake. "It's okay. I'm all right. The counseling sessions the doctor suggested have helped. Thanks for taking me every week." She fidgeted with her necklace again. "I guess I miss him. A lot. Don't look so shocked. You must think I'm crazy."

Lily decided not to say anything.

"...And I don't know why," Eve continued. "Our relationship was pretty rotten sometimes, and now when I look back, I can see how unhappy I was." Her words tumbled out. "On one level, well...I thought I loved him. But on another..." She folded her hands on the table. "I've finally begun to admit it to myself..." She took another sip of wine. "We both know it," she said so softly only Lily heard her. "He wasn't good for me."

Lily chose her words carefully. "In the beginning you two seemed to hit it off. Remember our high school reunion dance with Frank and Brad? We all laughed ourselves silly. But during this past year, Brad's anger got worse and worse. It scared me. It scared Frank, too. We've both been worried. Brad became sarcastic and abusive toward you, even in public. He *knew* he was hurting you. I worried about what he might do in private."

Eve let Lily's last sentence die without a response. Lily hoped her friend would continue.

Instead, Eve took a bite of the escargot the waiter placed in front of her, not looking up as he poured her a second glass of wine. She began drinking it so fast that Lily got agitated, twisting the napkin in her lap. She knew from long experience that if she dared to say anything, Eve would snap shut and not utter another word.

Eve replied, again in a low voice. "Now I can admit it. He cut me down a lot this past year. But I *allowed* it. For a long time. Now I'm trying to figure out why.

"I thought...I thought I was in love with him. I loved watching him play sports and win all those trophies. He took me to so many exotic restaurants and clubs--and remember when he took me to Tahiti? He gave me these very expensive presents too." She held up her right hand where a large aquamarine ring and another, with an Australian opal, graced her fingers. "But in the end," she muttered, "it was this strange rage he had...It made him...." She drained her glass and ordered another.

Lily kept her voice soft. "What made him so mad at you on that particular day?" She hoped Eve would release the grief Lily had seen every day painted on her face.

"I haven't allowed myself to think about it."

There was something guarded about Eve's eyes and her tone of voice, something foreign; Lily wondered what she was holding back.

Eve plunged on, "He called me early that day. At first I didn't get it. Why would he want to meet me at the park? We'd agreed to meet at my house, then head for Tahoe right after breakfast. I'd packed a wedding dress.... " Her voice broke and she poured herself more wine.

Lily could hardly control the anger erupting inside her. *How could Brad--*

Eve went on, "and...and then when I saw him standing by the pond, I could tell he was in one of those black moods. He got that way sometimes. I thought after the counseling he.... But I was fooling myself. He kept accusing me of things, saying I was manipulating him, that all I wanted was a...a child." Tears glistened in her eyes. "I saw him act crazy like that before, but I couldn't break up with him. He was so hot...especially in bed. I couldn't resist him.

"But on that day he acted like I'd talked him into everything, said he never wanted to get married, all I ever did was rag on him." Tears trailed down her face. "Maybe I did. You know how much I always wanted..." she almost swallowed the next words, "a family." She wiped her eyes and paused for what seemed like a long time. "Do *you* think I manipulated him?"

Hearing Eve share these private thoughts and blame herself was so rare, Lily felt breathless. She reached across the table and took her hand. "I've known you since we were kids. You didn't manipulate him into marrying you. I'm sure you didn't. You don't need a man that much. I've always looked up to you. You're so independent. You started fighting to be self-reliant at eighteen, back when your mom died. I've always admired you for it...how you made peace with your aloneness."

Eve still looked inconsolable. After a minute, Lily went on. "Sure, Brad was gorgeous. But he had issues. Big ones. I could see it. Frank saw it, too, after a while. He had a strange rage inside. You said it yourself. It was getting more and more out of control." She had Eve's attention now so Lily went on, "I even caught him taking it out on Kinza once. He kicked him so hard I yelled at him to stop. You know what *really* scared me? He didn't think he'd done anything wrong. Anyone who abuses animals...well, ask your counselor. It's definitely a sign of much deeper problems. Believe me, it wasn't you. Brad was at war with his own demons. Sometimes I thought the demons were winning." She took a deep breath. "I tried to let you know."

Eve looked down at the granite table, her finger making circle after circle on its flecked gold surface. Her hair had fallen forward, hiding her eyes. She lifted her head and tried to smile. "Don't feel guilty about what happened. I remember not listening to you, Lily.

"He couldn't control his anger. That's what did him in. He was speeding on purpose that day. No matter how much I screamed at him, he wouldn't slow down. No surprise that we crashed. I heard he was transferred to a neuro rehab hospital. He may never be the same again, mentally." She wiped her cheeks with the napkin, and tucked strands of her blonde hair behind her ear. She finally met Lily's eyes. "Some people seem hell-bent for self-destruction. Brad was...*is* one of those people."

In spite of the pain on her friend's face, Lily was sure this sharing had helped her. But during all the weeks and months since the accident and even now, Eve still hadn't mentioned losing the baby. *She has to talk about it sometime. If she doesn't, she'll never heal.*

Lily's cell phone sang out and she picked it up.

"Please come home." Lily could barely hear Frank's voice. "I just called 911."

CHAPTER 14

*C*hristmas lights twinkled in the tops of the tall palms lining the boulevard, spilling their glitter down each trunk. Dusk was drawing a curtain on another hard day as Lily dashed out of Graylock's back door, late as usual. She'd snatched cheese and crackers from the vending machine and munched on them as she wove her SUV through rush hour traffic. Frank had been at St. Vincent's Hospital for almost a month and a half. His cancer had returned with a vengeance. First his throat had closed down and he'd struggled to breathe or eat. The doctors solved that problem, but as the weeks wore on, one complication after another besieged his body.

Spotting the freeway exit sign, Lily abruptly changed lanes, maneuvering onto the exit ramp in the left lane. Someone honked and she jumped as an oversized Chevy truck sailed past on her right, the driver gesturing at her. At the stop sign, she pulled up next to him and braked. Even though she sank down in her seat, she saw him pointing at her. She also noticed the backwards Angels cap hugging his head. Why was he shouting? Lily reluctantly lowered her window.

"F'r god's sake, lady, put your lights on! You want to get killed?"

She clicked on her lights and yelled, "Thank you."

He saluted and smiled. "Merry Christmas! You want to enjoy the New Year, right?"

As the traffic moved forward, Lily accelerated and waved to him as he sped away. "Yeah, I'd like that! Merry Christmas to you, too!"

Cars sped around her as Lily looked at her watch, her thoughts suddenly flitting to Frank's cuckoo clock, a special gift from his grandfather many years before. Last night she'd noticed it was broken. The music no longer played on the hour, and the little figures wouldn't come out to dance. The tiny door was shut tight.

Her heart felt locked up, too. An overwhelming numbness took its place. Her husband didn't even look like himself anymore. When the girls had come home on Christmas break, their dad's condition upset them deeply. She couldn't blame them. They were shocked to see him so changed: dark circles under his eyes, his skin a sickly yellow, his hair and eyebrows completely gone and sharp bones replacing muscle. She and the girls had to face it. Frank was dying.

A wish darted through her mind—*maybe it'll all be over before Christmas*—guilt overtook her then. Her mind rushed back to the girls, who were having a very difficult time. They'd come to the hospital with her several days ago. But their visit with Frank had lasted only five minutes before they'd rushed out on the pretext they needed to pee.

On the way home from the hospital and for the rest of that night, nothing she'd said or did could console them. They hid in Tanya's room, refusing to come out. The special Mexican enchiladas, chorizo and beans she'd made sat cold on the stove. She'd skipped a meal again too. She knocked on their door so many times, heard them talking and crying together, but they wouldn't let her in, and she didn't have any strength left to demand entrance. She wanted so much to hug them, comfort them. In her bedroom later, she crumpled to the floor by her bed, her grief erupting in sobs, until the house closed in on her with empty silence.

After that she knew they wouldn't return to his bedside on their own, so two days ago she'd begged them to go back to the hospital one more time with her and tell their dad good-bye. Like most of her motherly pleas these days, this one fell on deaf ears.

Later Eve had phoned to see how she and girls were, asking Lily if she should call them, and Lily said yes. When Lily asked, "What can I do?" Eve warned her to have a serious talk with them.

So Lily gave it a try. Even though she felt sapped of energy afterwards, she'd spoken to them firmly about everything their dad had given them. She reminded them of their happy childhood, talked about events and memories they seemed to have forgotten. As her talking wore on, Lily finally saw the girls' fears melt away. At last they allowed her to hug them like the old days. And even though she knew her own faith was terribly weak, she'd spoken to them about Christ's resurrection and the peace and happiness that lay in store for their dad. "We must all be at his bedside now," she said. "We have to stand together...now that he's going away. But I truly believe it's just for a while. I know we'll see him again someday."

Sure enough, the girls had appeared together at their dad's hospital room yesterday, flanking Eve on both sides, holding on to her. Lily had felt a twinge of anger that no one had even thought to call and tell her they were coming, but she'd hugged both of them and they'd squeezed her so hard she thought she couldn't breathe. She'd yearned to say something more to them than a weak thank you, but she decided to hold her peace. Each of them slowly said good-bye to their father while gripping Lily's arms as if she were their lifeline. After Eve took them home, and Frank closed his eyes to sleep, Lily had never felt so alone.

As she drove near the hospital now, searching for a parking place, she wondered how Frank would be tonight. Would he even open his eyes? Would he squeeze her hand wordlessly, like he'd done last night?

The hospital elevator opened onto the bustling oncology ward, and the nurses nodded to her as Lily heard Eve calling her name. Eve came toward her, still walking with a limp, reminding Lily of the shock of those first days after Eve's accident. She knew her friend hated hospitals as much as she did, and another surge of gratitude swept over her as Eve reached out and folded her into her arms.

"I got here early. I'm afraid Frank's...he's slipping away. The doctor came in a minute ago to check on him. He gave him more morphine so he won't feel any pain. I...I don't think it will be long now. Maybe you should talk to the doctor. Do you want me to call the girls for you? Or send an email to your brother?"

Lily tightened her arms around her friend, clinging to Eve's strength. "Yes, please try to reach Colin, but don't bother the girls. They said their good-byes yesterday."

She turned toward Frank's room. "The nurses told me last night that even if he doesn't seem to know me, I should talk to him. He might still hear me."

They walked down the hall in silence.

A Christmas wreath hung in the window of Frank's room, multi-colored lights blinking off and on. Lily absently fingered some of the little green elves and glittering faeries she'd fastened to the wreath. She'd told Frank some old Irish stories the day she decorated his room. He always liked hearing her stories and he loved the traditional lights, so she'd strung them around the window too. Now she moved toward the wooden manger scene, which sat on the windowsill. They'd bought it their first Christmas together. She stared at the faded figures and the bits of straw still clinging to the animals.

As Eve limped out of the room to give her privacy, Lily stepped closer to her husband's bed. His breathing was worse. Each time he gulped for air, his chest and shoulders rose as if he were trying to suck in a few more minutes of life. The horrible, lurching gasps he'd begun the night before ripped at her heart now.

Lily clasped his hand, thankful for the tiny pressure she felt in his frigid fingers. She bent down and kissed him on the cheek she knew so well, now hollow and gray. Picking up a Kleenex, she wiped his forehead, her own tears wetting his sallow skin and dropping on his pillow. "Frank, I'm here with you," she whispered. "It's...it's okay. We're here together." She kissed him again, not even seeing him because her eyes were drowning in tears. "We'll be fine now," she whispered, "the girls and I will be okay. Don't worry about us anymore. It's okay—you can give up your fight now. I love you, I love—"

His throat rattled, he lurched forward and his eyes opened. He stared past her, as if he saw something in the distance. Lily grasped his hand tighter and gazed straight into his eyes. "You can go to God when you're ready," she whispered. "Thank you for being...for being a great father and..." she smiled at him, "for always being a loyal partner. I love you, my Frank."

She broke down, leaning into him, laying her cheek against his, gripping his hand. She felt no response, only his limp, icy fingers. His tortured breathing finally ceased. When she looked up, his eyes were still open so she reached out to close his lids.

CHAPTER 15

*D*awn was rising over the San Gabriel Mountains, the entire sky a rosy glow, as the two friends climbed up the bleachers. Neither had ventured to the Pasadena Rose Parade in years, but here they were in the middle of a mob of spectators, braving the chilly weather.

The seats were filling up fast on either side of the parade route. Lucky to have a superior view, Eve and Lily tucked a plaid blanket around their legs and began to sip their steaming café mochas to stave off the cold. They watched street vendors blowing raucous New Year's horns while others hawked balloons, feathered dolls and Rose Bowl football pennants to the boisterous crowd.

"I know you're feeling sad," Eve had told Lily only ten days after Frank's funeral, "but please promise you'll celebrate New Year's Day with me. I can't bear to be alone, and with Colin so far away in Afghanistan, you shouldn't be alone, either. We'll do something different together."

Even though Lily had never quite agreed to go, Eve had called a co-worker and conned her into selling her Rose Parade tickets, though at an exorbitant price. Then she persuaded Lily to come with her, at least for a little while.

Restless already, Eve stood up now and shaded her eyes against the brightening sun, trying to make out what was happening down the street where the parade started. Silently she wondered if she'd made the right decision to drag Lily here so soon. *But it's a waste to sit at home,* she thought. *What's life for, anyway? Every minute is precious.*

Spotting the first float moving down the street, Eve turned to Lily. "Look! The Grand Trophy Award winner. See the banner? The float from Taiwan always wins a prize. Look at those gorgeous cherry blossom trees. Amazing!" Decked out with hundreds of roses and exotic bird of paradise blooms, the float featured a giant dragon that spewed pearl smoke. Young Asian women with long, gleaming hair waved to spectators.

Eve pulled Lily to her feet, and they waved back. Squinting over the heads of the people in front, Eve spied the marching band she'd been waiting for, behind the float. As *Stars and Stripes Forever* floated up to them, Eve laughed. "I've heard that tune before."

"Me, too," Lily said in a weak voice. "I wish my father had talked to me once in a while instead of constantly playing all those patriotic songs. He was hardly ever home, but when he was—"

Trumpets and tubas drowned out her words as the people around them stood up and began clapping in rhythm. Excitement permeated the air.

Eve nudged Lily. "Whoever decided to come here today—it was a spectacular idea!"

"You decided for both of us," Lily said. "You manage one good idea per year. So you've already made your quota."

Eve knew Lily's heart ached, but she also knew her friend would try hard to keep their banter going. Though she must've lost at least 20 pounds in the last few months, Lily's cheeks were pink from the cold wind. Only a few days ago her skin had looked gray, her eyes puffy from crying. Now, thank god, her face shone with a faint gleam of anticipation.

Eve and Lily joined in the clapping as the military band marched by in their dress-blue uniforms playing, "To the halls of Montezuma, to the shores of Tripoli..." the famous *Marine Corps Hymn*. Eve had heard these military melodies many times when she'd visited Lily over the years. Lily's dad, a retired Marine, had never missed a chance to sit them both down, share his music and tell them stories about the war, even though, like Frank, he was generally a man of few words. She would never forget his ardent patriotism. Her eyes stung as she remembered him...and her own dad. Eve turned away to slip her sunglasses on. *They're all in the Great Somewhere together now...Mom, Dad, Lily's father and mother, Lily's Gram. . .and now Frank.*

A crowd of teens caught Eve's eye across the street. She tapped Lily's shoulder and pointed. "Look! Your girls made it after all."

Lily waved both arms. "Wow, I'm surprised. I told them where our seats were, but I never expected them to find us." She raised her arms again, trying to attract her daughters' attention.

Surrounded by their friends, the girls were dressed in jeans and black or dark purple jackets. Even from a distance, Eve could see the new fluorescent pink streaks in Tanya's hair. But it was Lisa's new look that had shocked her, and Lily too. Her long blonde hair was no more. Chopped short, it was now stark ebony, matching her clothes.

Eve waved with less gusto than Lily, but the girls didn't respond, and Eve began to wonder if they would wave back even if they did recognize them. Would they try to come over and say hello when the parade ended? They'd been so stoic and distant during the funeral service—*they were probably in shock.* Secretly, she hoped the girls would return to college right away. *The last thing Lily needs now is to cater to their whims.*

Meanwhile, Lily's gestures were becoming frantic.

"Cool it, hon. Let's find them after the parade," Eve said, as she pointed to the next float. "Whoa, isn't that totally gorgeous?"

Two hours seemed to fly by as each flowered marvel rode down the street along with cavalry groups from all over the world, their horses decked out with silver harnesses and draped with flowers. Waving señoritas in lacy Mexican dresses rode by on prancing steeds; baton twirlers hurled their batons high into the sky, turning cartwheels before catching them. The crowd roared. Young women in sparkling costumes twirled flags as the bands marched along. Eve watched Lily's face with satisfaction. Caught up in the sparkling glitz of the parade, she seemed distracted from her sorrow.

Suddenly, even though the parade was more than half over, a small, white-haired little woman started climbing over people in the bleachers. Carrying a basket, she was heading toward Eve and Lily, and reached the one empty seat next to Lily. She squeezed in and sat down. "Hello there, lassie. Do ye remember me? 'Course you do." She reached into her basket.

Lily nodded, "Why yes, what a surprise! Eve, this is Maeve. She and I met a few weeks ago at the Garden Getaway shop. What a coincidence that you have a seat right next to us today."

"Can I offer you some of me homemade goodies?" Maeve asked. "It's gettin' close to lunchtime and I baked them meself, I did. Early this mornin'. They'll be fresh, all right."

Lily shook her head. So did Eve.

"Aw, please. You'll be hurtin' me feelin's, if you refuse." Her red striped, knitted cap hugged her head at a jaunty angle. "What're the holidays for if we can't share? These are my recipes from the old country, mind you." Her wrinkled face looked like Irish linen.

"Okay," Lily said, noticing the parade had stopped due to a float's engine trouble. "You talked me into it. I'll have a cookie."

"When did you come here from Ireland?" Eve asked.

"Well, aren't you the smart one now," Maeve said, as she

handed a cookie tin to Lily. "I'm straight from County Meath, I am, and how'd you guess?"

Lily selected two cookies and passed the tin to Eve.

Eve smiled at Maeve and winked, faking a brogue. "Well, now, I'll not be knowin' how I figured that one out. But just maybe...maybe it's the influence of me friend's Grandmother O'Keefe, who told me so many tall stories, she did."

Maeve's eye twinkled mysteriously, and she smiled as if she knew a secret. "I like the way you talk, missy. It's makin' me homesick." She nudged Lily. "So your ancestors come from my wee island, too? You never mentioned it when you were pickin' out all those faerie houses and plants and things." She took the tin back and offered them napkins decorated with green shamrocks.

"I've always wanted to visit your homeland," Lily said, "and spend time finding my relatives in County Cork or anywhere else. If I have any left."

"Well now, me child, you should promise yourself you'll do just that. You'll never be quite the same afterward. I'm meanin' that in a good way, you know."

"Oh good, they fixed the problem. The parade's started again," Eve said and bit into one of the Irish shortbread cookies. "Mmm, these are good!" She grinned as she added, "Almost as delicious as a pint of Irish ale."

Maeve smiled back at her. "Why would you be thinkin' any different? 'Course they are." She reached deeper into her basket. "Here are some more goodies. Irish soda bread and scones. Try them, too. Please?"

Eve laughed. "I'm trying to watch my weight, but, sure, I'll split a slice with Lily." When Lily nodded, Eve added, "I went to Ireland once. On business. Mostly I ate pub grub. One thing I'll never forget, though, is Irish soda bread!"

The old lady reached into her basket and slathered strawberry jam over a generous piece of bread. Then she drew out a china plate, also decorated with shamrocks, and she placed it under a small scone. She cut the scone in half and presented a piece to Lily and Eve. "Here you are now. This should convince you about me Irish bakin'. *And* it'll be makin' you homesick for my island, Eve. You should go back, you know, and take your Irish friend along with ya. I'm going meself pretty soon."

While savoring the sweet bread, Eve marveled at the next float coming down the street. It was covered with yellow-gold mums and featured tall evergreen trees. As they watched, a small bear made of flowers zoomed along a zipline stretching from tree to tree as the music grew louder. When Lily's face broke into a smile, Eve knew for sure that she'd made the right decision to come today.

She turned to Maeve and tried to mimic the old woman's brogue again. "You and these delicious goodies are surely talkin' me into to travelin' again, you are. I'm supposed to go to Ireland again on business. Maybe I'll be makin' that trip sooner rather than later. I have some Irish roots, too. On me mother's side. Thank you for these Irish treats. I'd repay you, but I'm not much of a cook."

Maeve beamed. "I like yer brogue, my lady. No need to repay me. I'm happy to be sharin' with you on this first day of the year. I wasn't going to come out today, but then I said to meself, 'Maeve, just because your son couldn't make it to your party today is no reason to stay home and be gloomy. What about those you're goin' to meet? They'd be likin' some Irish treats now, wouldn't they?' And sure enough, I made it here to this great parade, late as I am, and found you two, as I knew I would, didn't I?" Her eyes sparkled as she looked at Lily. "Must be a dash of little people's magic," she added, "me meetin' up with you again, eh?"

Lily wondered what she meant.

More floats had passed while they talked, and now only two were making their way down the street, with spectators following behind them. The people in the grandstand began gathering up their blankets and sacks of food and started down the bleachers.

Maeve began to fold up her blanket too and put the treats into her basket. Eve turned to her. "May I help you?"

"No, no," the old woman said as she carefully tucked away the plates, "I'm plenty strong, I am. I can carry all this meself. I'm not as old as I look, you know." Her expression had turned quite serious and Eve wondered why--*this little lady is a bit of a mystery.*

CHAPTER 16

The three women climbed down the grandstand, reaching the confetti-strewn street. Multicolored streamers were tangled around street lamps and trees, and debris littered the street.

"Can we walk you home?" Lily asked.

"Thank you, child, but I only live a block away." She gestured in the direction they were going. "You needn't be botherin' yourselves about me."

"We're walking that way anyway to find our car," Eve countered, trying to keep up with the wiry little woman who insisted on quickly threading her way through the crowd.

Lily was falling behind. "I'm scanning the crowds for the girls," she called to Eve.

"Any luck?" Eve asked, as she picked up Maeve's hat where it had dropped.

Lily caught up. "I lost sight of them. Oh well, they'll probably get home soon. I'll see them then, I hope. Tomorrow they leave for college; they both have part-time jobs to get back to before the new semester starts."

As Maeve scooted farther ahead, Eve gave Lily a questioning glance.

Lily rushed toward Maeve. "Are you all right?"

Maeve shook her head. No smile now. "You don't have to be walkin' me home, child. I told you I live right near... " She shut her eyes for a moment, then her eyelids flickered and she opened them again. "I guess I'll be needin' some of my special tea," she said. With that she turned away and started off, nearly running, and Lily and Eve couldn't determine why. Almost running after her, they arrived at the end of a long, narrow driveway where Maeve had turned in, but now she was nowhere to be seen. They stopped in front of a makeshift, clapboard shed in back of a large old house. Weeds and brambles had choked away most of the grass in the yard. The hut must have originally been a garage behind the 1930s main house. What used to be the garage door was now a gray, wooden wall. The roof sagged, and the peeling paint sorely needed a fresh coat.

Eve looked in a window and saw white ruffled curtains. She also noticed a neat, rectangular garden of flowers below the window. Surprised, the two friends admired the tidy oasis. No weeds here. Instead, camellias bloomed in bright pink next to red poinsettias and a thriving holly bush. Over to the right was a bed of Irish moss surrounding a small stone faerie house where a miniature pebble path led to a tiny bird bath.

As Lily leaned down to inspect it, they heard Maeve's voice crackle. "I was tellin' you girls all along I could get here by meself, I did, but you wouldn't listen. I'm here now, and I'll not be needin' your help any longer."

She'd opened her front door just enough for them to see her wrinkled face. Her round blue eyes held no merriment now.

They both nodded to her, managing weak smiles.

Eve held out Maeve's striped knit cap. "Here. I think you dropped this."

"That I did." Maeve kept her arms folded.

Eve made sure her voice was calm. "We just wanted to thank you again for your Irish treats—and return your hat."

Maeve began to close the door, then paused, which irritated Eve. This whole incident was becoming a bit ridiculous. Why didn't the woman just take her cap and be done with it? Should she lighten the lady's mood with a joke? No, better to exit now, but it wasn't going to be easy to pry Lily away.

Unexpectedly, Maeve produced a half smile. "I guess you two might be thinkin' I'm a poor refugee," she let out a sigh, "livin' in this old shack here all by meself." She opened her door a bit wider, stood up straight and braced her shoulders. "Well," she said, dignity dripping from her words, "if you want to know, this is only temporary. My son's gone off to Dublin and he'll be sendin' for me soon, he will."

Lily spoke softly. "Why no, Maeve, we weren't thinking anything about your place, except we're grateful to you for sharing this special day with us. It was such a surprise to see you again." Lily took the cap from Eve and offered it again to the little woman. "We just wanted to make sure you're okay, that's all, so you can travel safely. You looked a bit tired just now, and you said you were leaving soon for Ireland, right?"

Maeve finally seemed to relax. "Well, we all get tired once in a while, now don't we, child? I'm sure you've felt that lately with all you've been through, now haven't you?" Her eyes were fixed on Lily as she let herself slump a little against the door and finally accepted the cap Lily held out. "Yes, and I don't mind telling you two that I'll be feelin' mighty glad when I get to the Emerald Isle." She opened the door wide this time and waved her hand at them. "Well, won't you come on inside, please? We'll be havin' some special tea if ye like."

Eve tried to hide her aversion to Maeve's invitation, but a nagging question began to bother her. How did this little woman know what Lily had been through? Her curiosity overcame her antipathy, and when Lily stepped into the shadowy dwelling, Eve followed.

The tiny place was barely more than two rooms, except for a small bathroom Eve glimpsed on the right. A tall screen almost hid an antique stove and an old-fashioned tiled sink. An electric hot plate, like one Eve had seen in antique shops, sat on the counter. The one window was covered with curtains, making the place so dim the visitors could barely see. Eve began to feel uncomfortable and reached up to massage her temples, hoping the new throbbing in her head would go away. Impatient, she waited for an opportunity to excuse herself and leave, even as another question began to gnaw at her. How could Maeve have baked all her delicious treats in that ancient oven? Impossible, because the stove was covered with piles of newspapers and looked like it had been used only as a counter, for years.

Before her visitors knew it, Maeve put on a crisp white apron and started humming a tune. She switched on the lone lamp in the room. Now she was setting china cups and saucers, rimmed with pink rosebuds, on a sparkling silver tray she pulled out of nowhere.

She's certainly a woman of contrasts, Eve thought.

"You both will enjoy my tea, now, won't you?" She gestured for them to sit down at her modest table, which, they suddenly noticed, was spread with an immaculate, sky-blue tablecloth embroidered with purple violets. She produced matching napkins and handed one to each of her guests. "There now," she said. "You'll be havin' some more of my tasty treats too. And we'll relax and have a pleasant talk now, won't we?" A shiny silver kettle on the hot plate began to whistle.

Eve noted the old woman seemed both mysterious and desperate to serve them tea. Maybe to save face? She decided they dared not refuse. The pain in her forehead was spreading, but she reluctantly sank down in the nearest chair beside Lily.

Maeve began pouring the amber liquid that was somehow

already in the rosebud teapot. She no sooner asked if they wanted milk and sugar, than she sprinkled what looked like sugar into their cups, not waiting for a reply. After that she set a delicate sugar bowl on the table along with a matching pitcher of cream. "I brought these Belleek Irish pieces all the way from my homeland. Very pretty, aren't they?" She arranged more cookies and some scones on a plate and placed it in the center of the table. "There now. You'll be havin' these too, won't you now? I baked them all this morning."

Eve sipped her tea, surprised it wasn't sweetened after all. She added sugar and took one cookie. Her eyes drifted to the knick-knacks arranged on a nearby shelf as she listened to Maeve chattering in her rhythmic brogue with Lily about this recipe and that one. She decided to sit quietly and assess Maeve's little—*what would you call it? A hovel? Well, no, it's not that bad. Maybe it's just the tiniest old cottage I've ever seen here.* As she finished the cup of tea, the headache that had threatened to overcome her minutes ago began to fade a bit, and an unusual feeling of elation took its place.

The others were still talking as Eve noticed a silver-framed photo of a brawny man with attractive, dark hair, graying at his temples. He wore an ivory, ribbed fisherman's sweater, a wide blue-green sea visible behind him. His blazing blue eyes and his dimpled cheek resembled Maeve's. *Hmmm, not bad. I'd say he's in his mid-forties.* Eve felt strangely warm all over now.

"I see you're noticin' me son there, are you now?"

"Why, yes." Eve felt Maeve staring at her.

"Well, I have to admit my Seamus is a looker, he is, and all of a sudden he got it into his head to start studyin' at Trinity College in Dublin."

As Maeve talked while pouring her a new cup of tea, Eve noticed a faint glow over the whole table. Had the midday sun's light moved? She looked at the window curtains, which still blocked the sun. *No, of course not.*

"Anthropology is his subject," Maeve was saying, "but I'll be daft if I know what that is. Do you? Finally now, my scholar son has sent for me." Her face brightened, and Eve had the perplexing feeling that a rosy spotlight was now illuminating the entire room. Everything gleamed bright and new. Lily's face was flushed in a radiant smile, and Eve's spirits had lifted too as she drained her second cup of Maeve's unusual tea.

Eve pointed to the photo. "I thought he must be your son. He looks like you."

"That's a compliment, for sure. My Seamus is a handsome one, he is, and he likes the ladies, but, mind you, he'll never sit still. Always dreamin' of a new adventure." She sat down again and offered them both another scone. A dimple formed in her cheek as she smiled. "This time it's studying for his doctorate, mind you. Whatever made him think of that, I'm not sure. When he got the notice that they'd take him, he just up and left me and sold the front house as quick as a wink," her face clouded up, "but, of course, he arranged for me to rent back here. All this is temporary, mind you. He'll be settled soon." She stared at her guests again. When neither commented, she reached over and took an envelope from the drawer of the lamp table. "If you don't believe me, here it is, now, as fine as can be. My ticket's inside." She held it up and smiled as she raised her teacup to her lips.

But Eve could see light shining through the envelope. It looked totally empty.

"You'll certainly want to be in good shape for your trip," Lily said. "Are you feeling okay now? I certainly am."

"Of course I am, my lass. My tea solves all kinds of problems. It's a brew I got from an ancient Celtic source. A secret recipe." Her lips formed the widest smile Eve had seen yet, and her wrinkled face was suffused with a mysterious glow.

Now it was Lily who was checking her watch and seemed to want to leave. She stood up and pulled on her coat. "I think we'd better go," she whispered to Eve. "The girls should be home now."

Eve wanted to ask for a third cup of Maeve's wonderful magical brew, but Lily kept talking fast and thanking the old woman, telling her they had to go.

As they waved good-bye, Eve realized her headache was completely gone and she hadn't felt this energetic and upbeat in a very long time. Looking at Lily, she guessed her friend felt the same. Attending the Rose Parade today had turned out better than she thought! She looked back at Maeve waving good-bye, pixie merriment shining on her face.

CHAPTER 17

*E*ven with her arms full of grocery bags, Lily managed to pick up a stack of mail as she pushed the kitchen door open with her foot. She set the mail on the counter with the bags, and flipped the lights on. She'd texted Eve two hours ago, and then called her. Still no reply. Now she tried again. *Where is she when I need her?*

While Lily let Eve's phone ring, she unpacked her groceries: dog food, canine treats, Weight Watchers frozen dinners, berries, low fat yogurt, pita bread, tuna and lunch meat. Gone were the days when she'd delighted in trying new recipes. Only lackluster meals awaited Lily now, but she had little appetite.

Tanya and Lisa had boarded the plane to northern California two days ago. Lily had gritted her teeth to stifle her tears when she kissed them good-bye. She hadn't seen them much after Frank's funeral and only briefly on New Year's Day after the parade. Eve kept reminding her that "girls are into their peers and boyfriends and partying at this stage. You might as well be invisible for the next few years. Get used to it." Eve was right. But that didn't make it any easier.

She looked around for Kinza and his wagging tail. He loved to greet her by licking her hands and even her cheeks when she came home. Tonight he was asleep on his plaid cushioned bed in the corner, snoring, but softly whistling too. Lily smiled. *He must be chasing cats, or better yet, lizards.*

She was ready to hang up her phone when Eve finally offered a sleepy "Hello?"

"Hi."

"I must've dozed off," Eve said.

"Sorry I woke you. I can't believe you're in bed so early. It's only eight-thirty."

Hearing voices, Kinza woke up and started jumping on her, so Lily dished out food for him while she talked. "Are you feeling okay?"

"Don't know what's the matter with me," Eve said. "I only had a short meeting at work today, but I'm exhausted."

"*I* know. This is your first week back after a month in the hospital and almost two here at my house. How did it go?" She stowed her purchases away as she talked.

Eve sighed. "Just okay. I'm only putting in half days, and everyone seems genuinely glad to see me. My customers are demanding, though. They want someone to service them constantly. Not a big surprise. You remember that woman the company hired as my replacement right after the accident?"

"I think so." Lily set the Weight Watchers chicken dinner on a plastic plate.

"Well, even though she mucked a few things up, I know she's waiting in the wings in case I can't take on my whole sales territory right away."

Lily unsealed and popped her dinner into the microwave oven. "She's not plugging for your job, is she? You don't need stress like that."

"She's competitive," Eve said. "That's clear. But I can handle it.

Luckily, she's not part of a stab-you-in-the-back gang like you have at work." They both chuckled. "Actually, I think she's willing to help me. She's aware of my reputation and knows if she performs well, they'll offer her some plum accounts later, but not mine. But hey, you didn't call to talk about my—"

"No, and I'll make this quick so you can turn in for the night. I got a message from Mr. Turle today. Our family lawyer. He wants me in his office tomorrow morning at nine. Could you...possibly come with me for moral support? I...I just can't go alone—it's too soon."

"Sure. No problem. I'll meet you in the morning and show up at work after lunch. Shall we meet at his office?"

"Yes. Thanks." A wave of relief calmed her. She rarely asked for help, but when she did, she knew she could count on Eve. She opened a can of Diet Coke and sat at the kitchen table.

"Why didn't your lawyer contact you sooner?" Eve asked. "Tanya and Lisa kept talking about their father's will when they were home."

"My fault, I guess," said Lily, absently patting her thighs. They seemed to lack some of the pudginess she'd always hated. Yes, she'd shed some pounds, but she didn't know how many. The scale was her enemy, always had been. Kinza was licking her free hand, and when she ruffled his ears, he laid his head in her lap. "I kept procrastinating because I didn't want to face the...the *finality* of it all." She stroked the dog's coat. "I'll have to handle it myself now, but your support will soften the ordeal. *Then* I'll call the girls.

"Oh, and one more thing, Eve. I bumped into Maeve this evening after work. I picked out more plants for my faerie garden project at the Garden Getaway shop. She was getting ready to close the store.

" That woman is *strange*. Didn't she show us her plane ticket to Ireland on New Year's Day? Or am I going nuts?"

Eve cleared her throat. "Why? Does it matter? Why are you getting involved with her?"

"I'm not. I just wondered. Tonight she told me something different, that her son is *sending* her the plane ticket. By Federal Express."

"Maybe she's mixed up. She's definitely erratic."

"Either that or...."

"Or what? How was she?"

"Seemed cheerful this time. Wanted me to come back to her place, so I did, and she sat me down for tea again. She was as chipper and friendly as she was in the grandstand. I felt wonderful when I came home. Can't imagine what she puts in that special tea of hers." Lily paused and scratched the dog's ears for a few seconds. "I don't know, though. I worry about her for some reason. Did you get the feeling she's trying to hide things?"

"I can't answer that," Eve said, "but my reading on her is she didn't want us to walk her home because she was embarrassed."

"About what?"

"Didn't want us to see that she lives in that cramped little shack. She was hell-bent on rushing away when the parade was over. That's why she ran ahead."

"Oh."

"You didn't figure that out? Anyway we'll never know for sure, will we? C'mon, Lily, don't immerse yourself in Maeve's problems. So what if she doesn't make sense? For god's sake, you're always taking care of people. She's a stranger. We hardly know her."

Eve's words stung even though Lily knew her friend was only trying to pry her out of a bad habit. She *was* always losing herself in others' problems. She fumbled through her mail, dropping one on the floor. Picking it up, she separated out Frank's hospital bills while she talked. "It's just that she's all alone."

"Stop it, will you?" Eve changed the subject. "What's the plan tomorrow with your attorney?"

Lily twisted a tendril of her dark curly hair. "We're going to open Frank's private safety deposit box. He never shared its contents with me, and I never asked. Mr. Turle says that's where he kept his will. He never shared that with me either." She drained her Diet Coke.

"You can't be serious! Really? Frank handled *all* the finances? He—"

"He never trusted me with money—I was such a spendthrift when we got married. You knew that, Eve."

"But that was *years ago*. You were married how long?"

"I know, but Frank couldn't forget *any* mistake I made with money. He cut up my credit cards, too." She forced a lighter tone as she peeked into the microwave to see if her dinner was ready. "I've never been good at budgeting," she confessed, "so maybe I had it coming." She picked up a potholder, pulled the dinner out, scowling at it, and set it on a plate. "Meeting the attorney tomorrow probably won't take long," she said. "Maybe it's silly of me to ask you to come."

"It's not silly," Eve assured her. "Of course I'll be there. I don't go back to work full-time until next week." She paused. "Hey, I'll get all my travel assignments soon. Can't wait!"

Lily felt a smidgen of dread when she heard the anticipation in Eve's voice. She knew her friend was looking forward to plunging back into her career and traveling again. After all, she'd won a shelf-full of awards as top salesperson at Moncino's, a well-known winery upstate in Napa County. They'd lavished her with prizes over the years too, sometimes cash awards. Eve never boasted outright, but she'd shown Lily the black leather luggage she'd won, and the French perfume and high-class restaurant gift cards too.

Like clockwork, Eve would always call Lily right after her business trips were assigned, happily enumerating the countries she'd be visiting. As Eve went on and on now about how much she loved traveling, Lily managed upbeat replies to hide the feelings that always washed over her—hopelessness and yes, envy. It was all so predictable. So why didn't she change her life if Eve's travels depressed her so much?

Lily's discomfort was as palpable as her hunger for the two chocolate donuts she spotted on the counter. Leftovers from yesterday's work meeting. As she took a bite of her Weight Watchers chicken casserole she gazed at them. Her stomach growled. *No, I won't eat them.*

Lately she'd been waking up every morning full of trepidation about going to work. She wanted to pull the covers over her head and hide forever. Her new tech writing projects were more complicated than she'd expected and required tons of unpaid overtime. Plus, so far, Ken hadn't mentioned one prospective business trip. *Not one. Good old Ken, the BS artist.* Oh well, her job paid her expenses. Or most of them.

Still listening to Eve, Lily took another bite of her dinner, got up and stacked the hospital bills on Frank's desk with all the others.

"See you at nine a.m. tomorrow then?" Eve asked suddenly.

"Yes, and thanks, Eve. I feel better now, knowing you'll be with me. I've never even met the lawyer. I don't expect any earth-shattering news, though. God knows, Frank managed our savings account down to the last penny so we could fund the girls' college expenses. He did share those details with me."

After Lily hung up, she shoved her half-eaten dinner into the garbage, poured herself a small glass of Bailey's Irish Cream and grabbed the two chocolate donuts before heading up to her bedroom.

CHAPTER 18

*E*ve took inventory of the stocky attorney's office while Mr. Turle searched through his file cabinet, his back to the two women who sat in front of his massive walnut desk. Thick manila files were stacked everywhere, some spilling over onto the floor. The once-white mini-blinds on all the windows were gray with dust. The faint smell of cat urine pervaded the room. *Thank god for the ceiling fan!*

Mr. Turle finally turned around, a fat file in his hands. Following Eve's stare, the little attorney laid it on his desk and pulled his white shirt over his bulging belly, re-fastening the middle button. He straightened his yellow tie and sat down.

"We got an update on Frank's assets a few minutes ago by email," he said to Lily, who was clasping and unclasping her hands beside Eve, "but I'll cover that in a few minutes." He cleared his throat. "Well, let's begin." He took a stapled document out of the file and started reading. "I, Frank Doyle, of sound mind..."

Eve's thoughts strayed as the lawyer's monotone dragged on. She'd heard it all before, first when her father died when she was nine—she'd sat on her mother's lap in a dark room while two lawyers peered down at her as her mom cried softly. She didn't remember much about that day. Nine years later after her mother passed away, she'd sat straight as a rod, unable to cry or hardly breathe, as the lawyer read the will. After that nightmare was over, Lily came to see her, hugging her as Eve told her friend about the generous financial dowry she would inherit—her dad's dying gift.

Eve was aware that the reading of the important part of the Trust, her friend's inheritance, wouldn't happen for a several minutes. As they listened, she felt Lily's cool fingers reaching for hers. She clasped Lily's hand, knowing how difficult this was. An ache in her shoulders and back had already begun to rebel as her own memories crowded in on her. Her normal habit of stuffing all unpleasantness away was no use today. But she wasn't going to let past ghosts win. Besides, she was a different person now...more mature, independent and self-reliant. The reading of her mother's will had occurred twenty-one years ago. *That was then,* she reminded herself. *This is now.*

As Mr. Turle's voice hummed on, Eve studied the beads of perspiration popping out on his forehead and under his bulbous nose. Why was he so nervous? She noticed the copy of an email he'd set aside on his desk directly opposite her. Reading it upside down wasn't hard. Something about "property" somewhere "in Pennsylvania." She saw Frank's name, too.

Noticing her gaze, Mr. Turle suddenly picked up the printed email and tucked it under the sheaf of papers he was holding and continued reading the will.

Minutes later, Lily spoke up, "What does that mean exactly? I can't understand this legal gibberish. Please explain in regular language."

"I'll try to be candid, Mrs. Doyle. Uh, or are you using your maiden name now?-- O'Malley?"

"Most of the time," Lily said.

"I. . .I'm sorry to say this, but the parts I just read mean that

Frank's assets, except for one item, are quite modest. Despite my advice, he insisted on managing his financial portfolio himself. As a result, many of his stocks lost a lot of their value in the last couple of years. Of course, you can keep the shares and hope their value will rise in the years ahead—"

"And the value was?" Eve asked.

"Just over $80,000, when he inherited it several years ago at his father's death."

"And now?"

"I'm afraid his stocks have dwindled to about $11,000. No one was managing his portfolio."

When Lily's shoulders crumpled, Eve put an arm around her.

Mr. Turle kept his eyes fastened on his paperwork and wiped his forehead with a handkerchief. He picked up another document. "However, you'll be happy to hear that his life insurance policy paid for all the funeral and burial costs."

"Well, that's a big relief," Eve said. "Anything left for my friend at all?"

The lawyer shook his head. "No, I'm afraid not. Frank didn't believe in buying a sizeable insurance policy. And, as you know, he always preferred renting, not buying your house. He was depending on the stock portfolio he inherited to be your retirement savings, Ms. O'Malley, since he'd set aside his company's savings plan to pay for your daughters' college education." When Lily nodded, he seemed relieved. "Did you know about the stocks he inherited?" he asked.

"No, I only knew about a small bank account Frank opened for our girls," Lily managed. "I contributed a little to it, too. Frank was a very private man, and what he inherited was his. That's all I knew."

Now Mr. Turle produced the email Eve had spied earlier. "Oh, yes, I forgot about that account. It is very small. Only $2,500. Well, he had one other asset of interest. I'm looking into it."

Fat chance Lily will be able to retire on that, Eve thought. She'd never trusted Frank's financial know-how.

"It's his only other asset." The attorney scratched his nose, and Eve turned her gaze elsewhere—she couldn't stand to look at him —though Lily's eyes were riveted to the flimsy sheet of paper Mr. Turle was waving in front of her. "It's a small restaurant, a pizzeria actually, that his great-uncle owned in Pennsylvania and Frank inherited. The original manager Frank's uncle hired is still running it. Did he ever tell you about that?"

Lily inhaled deeply and shook her head. "No, Mr. Turle. I need to go outside for a moment. It's stifling in here. Please, I need air."

Before the lawyer could react, Eve whisked her friend out to a forlorn patio outside. An old, tinkling fountain in a shady corner provided their only comfort. She pulled two wooden chairs together and Lily collapsed into one of them. Eve sat across from her. Lily was so silent it made her nervous. She began talking nonstop to try to comfort her friend.

Lily put her hand on Eve's arm. "Stop," she said. "It's okay. It really is. Frank was my ever-silent partner. He took care of every-thing himself. That was his way. He took pride as the provider of our little family. In his mind, no one else needed to know the details. That's why he hired Mr. Turle. To shield me from worry."

Eve had no idea how to react to this. Finally she said, "But, Lily, what about this restaurant he never bothered to mention?"

Lily's face sagged with exhaustion. "Uncle Matt died five years ago back east. Neither of us even went to his funeral; Frank hadn't seen him since he was a boy." She moved her lips, trying to smile. "It's ironic that Frank would inherit Uncle Matt's pizzeria. He prob-ably wanted nothing to do with it. So that's exactly what he did —nothing."

"Nothing but turn it over to Mr. Turd...er...Turle. Sorry, Lily, but why couldn't Frank have hired someone a little more savvy, or...at least more professional?" Eve didn't dare say any more.

"It worries me, too," Lily admitted. "He never even brought me to meet Mr. Turle. Oh, you know how Frank pinched pennies. 'What does it cost?' was always his first question."

Eve couldn't say a word. She hated the disappointment written all over her friend's face. A tidal wave of depression had transformed Lily, like a full-color photo suddenly turned gray. All Eve could do was nod toward the lawyer's office. "Well, if you've gotten the air you needed, let's go back and get this over as quickly as we can. Then we'll figure it out, together." She steered her friend back inside.

Lily sat down in the same chair, and Mr. Turle resumed. "Mrs., um, Ms. O'Malley, I have a bit of good news. Pennsylvania real estate has appreciated recently." He gave her his first smile. "That's something you'll be happy about. I wasn't aware of it until I received the comps on the property this morning."

"Comps? I told you I'm not familiar with legal jargon, let alone real estate terms."

He wiped his forehead again with a handkerchief. "Oh. Sorry. It just means comparable. From a list of recent *comparable* sales in the area, it looks like the land is worth $170,000, if you're lucky. When you arrived, I was pulling together the restaurant's business assets, the annual profits, the IRS statements and the manager's accounting books. If you'll excuse me a minute, I have to make a couple of phone calls, then I'll tell you the approximate worth of the restaurant and the business also."

"So Frank was trying to sell the whole thing? The land, the building and the business?" Eve asked before he could pick up his phone.

"Well, yes, but not until he took a turn for the worse right before Thanksgiving. He called me from the hospital shortly after he was admitted."

"Any offers?" Eve persisted.

"Yes, surprisingly."

"Surprisingly? I thought you said land has gone up and this was a positive for my friend."

"Ms. Olson, I have to admit that my expertise is not in real estate. Or the sale of restaurants. And prices in Pennsylvania are a lot lower than California. Frank asked me to find some reputable property agents in Pennsylvania, so I did. Then, well, everything happened so fast, plus I was traveling all during the holidays in the Caribbean, so..."

"Oh, I see," said Eve. She tapped her fingers on his desk and leaned forward, choosing her words. "Let's get to the bottom line, Mr. Turle. Mrs. Doyle, uh, sorry, Ms. O'Malley needs to know exactly where she stands. How long does she have to wait?"

Mr. Turle's eyes bulged as he picked up his cell phone again. "Only a few minutes."

Eve suddenly stood up. "Your office is intolerably hot. I can't believe your AC is broken. We'll wait in the lobby while you make this call. The air is fresh *there*." Eve fumed inside as she steered Lily through the door and sat her down near a water cooler. She poured water into two large paper cups. Obviously, she thought, as she looked around, Frank had found the cheapest lawyer in town. Not to mention the most incompetent! She opened the outer door to let in the morning breeze, and then came back to Lily. "You don't look well, hon. You're white and clammy."

Lily looked up. "You know me. I'm not good at any of this. Finances aren't my strong point. And the thought of working as a technical editor at Graylock for the rest of my life is pretty depressing too."

"As far as Graylock, I get it. But when it comes to your finances, stop putting yourself down! If I can learn it, so can you."

"Yeah," Lily retorted, "you who skipped a grade. I love the way you assume everyone has your IQ."

"C'mon, you can do anything you set your mind to. For god's sake, you earned your college degree, you even got your master's.

Tanya and Lisa were in junior high when you started back to college. So why *can't* you tackle your finances? Stop talking yourself out of it!"

"You're always so sure...sure about everything." Lily's voice was as tremulous as a frightened child's. Lately Eve had witnessed first-hand how chaotic Lily's emotions were, especially since Frank died. She would seem completely normal, but minutes later she'd start to cry, and always at the oddest moments. Often she didn't seem to think things through either—what bothered Eve most was her helplessness to do anything about it.

"I wish I could be half as confident as you," Lily said. "I've never lived alone, that and the unknown scares me. Always has."

Eve put both hands on Lily's shoulders and looked straight into her eyes, parsing her words. "You. Can. Do. It. And I'm here to help you. Now drink your water."

Lily gulped down the liquid. When she heard Mr. Turle's voice behind her, she jumped.

They both noticed a marked change in him. His face was beaming. "I think I have some *very* good news," he said as he stepped into the lobby.

"You *think?*"

"I'm happy to say that if you'll sign the escrow papers today, Mrs. Doyle, uh, I meant Ms. O'Malley, we have the beginning of a definite sale! The agents in Pennsylvania say this buyer wants this small pizzeria and land *badly*. He happens to be the manager of the restaurant. He'll pay the *full* asking price of $300,000 for the restaurant, $210,000 for the land and $60,000 for the business "

Lily couldn't believe her ears. "Didn't you say the land was worth $170,000?"

"Well, I guess...yes, but that was my error. Uh, well, it really wasn't a mistake..."

"What's the buyer's total offer?" Eve demanded.

Mr. Turle took a step forward. "Uh, apparently, the restaurant is small but successful. Tasty Italian food as well as pizzas, with a local following that's growing. The manager of the restaurant doesn't want a landlord to raise his rent and possibly damage his business, so the Realtor bumped up the land price because commercial plots there are rising weekly. Now with two other buyers vying for the land, the manager offered more, $570,000 total!"

Lily could hardly breathe. Her back was still partly turned, so Mr. Turle couldn't see her face, but Eve could. Lily reached up to feel her warm cheeks. She mouthed her words, "Should I?"

"Do you have to ask? Imagine what you can do with that kind of money!" Eve said.

Lily squeezed Eve's hand. "Okay," she said, nodding to the lawyer, "It's a deal."

CHAPTER 19

February drizzle coated the windshield. Eve shivered and buttoned up her blazer, regretting that she'd hadn't brought a coat or a rain slicker to work this morning. As she steered her SUV into her condo's parking space, she felt the hairs on the back of her neck tingle. Had she left that light on in the living room? No. The kitchen lights were blazing, too. Her body froze.

Switching off the ignition, she forced herself out of the car, clutching the small can of Mace attached to her key ring. She tiptoed through the gate. Even from here she could see the automatic security light burning outside her kitchen window. Who set it off? Her breath became short gasps and her heart beat louder.

Wait a minute, isn't Lily coming over tonight? She has my key.

Patches of bright light from the windows glistened on the wet porch. She ventured closer, but could see no one inside.

Where's Lily's car? She looked back down the driveway and spied a white Toyota parked across the street. *Oh, yeah—Lily's van is in the shop. That's probably her rental.* She inserted her house key into the lock and turned it, pushing the door open an inch. "Lily?" She heard low jazz, Lou Rawls' voice, *"It's a rainy night in Georgia..."*

She knew. A half-forgotten thrill enveloped her body, like a soft leather glove.

Brad came forward, humming, forcing her briefcase out of her hand, laying it down on the chair by the door, offering her his familiar, crooked grin. She stared at him. Then he leaned toward her and kissed her on the neck.

She pushed him away. "How dare you!"

Those familiar cobalt eyes...specks of gray making them shine. *Still irresistible.* She felt herself melting, but... she couldn't... "It's been almost six months," rage saturated her words, "and not one fucking word from you! And...you almost killed me."

He handed her a giant margarita, but she waved it away and turned to leave. Where could she go?

"Aw, c'mon, Evie." That voice, so smooth and coaxing, "I was flat on my back for months, and they kept laying those psyche tests on me. Like solitary confinement. I just got out. Please, you know how I like to surprise you. C'mon!" He held out the drink. "Raspberry, just the way you like it."

A taste from her past...he'd remembered. She'd gathered raspberries as a child at her grandpa's farm upstate, and she'd loved that flavor ever since.

Though her anger burned inside, the longing that pervaded her body was automatic and intoxicating. They'd played out this kind of scene together so many times. And, *well...I did have a difficult day at work.* But she glared at him, even as she kicked off her shoes and licked the rim of the glass, feeling the thick, icy liquid ooze down her throat. So sweet. Brad smiled...and all the images of the crazy fun they used to have came flooding back...their tipsy hilarity in bed many times, long ago.

As he turned toward the kitchen, she recognized the aroma. He was frying veal slices with mushrooms and white wine. His famous Italian sauce and pasta were bubbling on the stove. His specialty.

Rawls' throaty singing in the background accompanied Brad's

casual remarks as he disappeared into the kitchen, brandishing a spatula. "Relax, pigeon. I'll be done in a minute." He stuck his head back out. "I hope you're hungry."

She hadn't heard that low, breathy voice in eons.

She could see candles shining in the dining room. Her Tiffany vase on the glass coffee table was overflowing with Black Beauty roses, the deep red she loved. Two expensive champagne bottles glistened with beads of moisture in her silver ice bucket. All her favorite things. Oh, she knew this scene *so* well.

He must go. Right now. Before I let my guard down.

She let out a sigh and her shoulders sagged. If she weren't so exhausted she would show him the door... but...but she was hungry. She'd skipped lunch, her back ached and her bad leg was terribly sore from working all week. She pulled her phone out of her purse and read the latest text. Lily wouldn't be able to make it tonight after all.

That did it. Eve shed her business jacket and sank down into the couch, stretching out while balancing her margarita, then sipping it again. *Just a couple minutes. Please. It's been soooooo long. I need this...pampering.*

❧

They hadn't even finished their meal before he lifted her into his arms and laid her on the bed, darkness covering them and the sound of soft pelting rain from the open window weakening her faint resolve. He undressed, then peeled her clothes off, oh so slowly. She felt her nipples harden and her body stirring, a wetness down below. When was the last time they'd made love? Too long ago. Then Brad slipped off her thong.

His breathing lingered near her ear, his lips rubbing her neck. His passion inflamed them both, and she felt his warm breath heaving. She knew she fed his lust like no one else. She'd dreamed about him so often during these last, interminable months. But he was real now—and the thrills vibrating through her body were real, too.

His fingers became silk sentinels triggering frenzy through her body. His tongue explored her mouth, her breasts, the inside of her thighs. She arched her back and opened herself to him, quenching a longing she'd suppressed for months.

They wound their legs around each other then, licking and caressing until their sweat mixed together and she climbed on top of him, her hips plunging down again and again, riding him, and wanting more.

Then he rose out of bed and, with a force she'd forgotten, pulled her down off the mattress, ordered her to kneel beside it, him behind her, his hands fondling her waist, massaging her hips. Then he bent down behind her and ran his tongue over her torso. He began biting her, softly at first, as his fingers moved to find her wet center, stroking her, and the moist pungent scent of her permeated her space. Suddenly he penetrated her and the force of him hurt. She cried out. Once, then again. But he didn't stop and the pain got worse. She cried out over and over as the familiar ritual of pain and pleasure intensified. "God damn you," she gasped. "Stop it! Please." She tried to move away.

He stood up. "Yeah, I'll finish you. You're dripping for me." He pulled her up out of her crouch and pushed her forward again. His rough plunge inside burned again, but she didn't make a sound this time. She knew if she did, he'd hurt her more.

Then he threw her down on the bed and thrust his thickness into her, hard and deep. She screamed.

"You like it! You know you do. You're such a lying bitch!" His voice was husky with pleasure. She knew what he wanted next, and she cringed. He slapped her thighs hard; she felt his tongue and teeth again, and she remembered the pain, the bruises and, sometimes, the blood. It was the way he finished her.

No! Not this time!

It took all her strength, but she untangled her body and pulled herself up onto her bed.

"What's wrong?" He was out of breath.

She lifted her eyes enough to see his flushed cheeks and lips. Then she saw his eyes and remembered his awful rages. Before he could speak again, she raced for the bathroom and locked the door. "Not this time!" she yelled. "I'm not gonna take it. Don't you know how sick you are? Out of control. I don't need this anymore. Hear me?"

"You don't need this?" She heard something slam. "You're just a cheap pussy. I'll find someone else, then. I'm outta here!" Another slamming sound. "Got that?"

She trembled at his threats, but she knew a feral, dark part of her still wanted him. She couldn't bear it if he went away again. But not like this...it disgusted her. If only she could quell his roughness and his anger. She'd done it before. She wanted his lovemaking, but tame and gentle and passionate. Like it was in the beginning, when they first met.

He was pounding on the door. "If you don't come outta there, I'm leavin', you little bitch. Hear me? And you'll pay!"

Her teeth clenched, she leaned against the door. "Please, Brad, I want it nice. You know, like it was in the beginning."

"So you *do* want me, huh?" His voice suddenly became softer. "Oh, baby, I can behave. I promise it'll be good." He kept it up. "Please baby, it's been so long. You don't know how many times I thought about you in that prison...your wet pussy yearning for me."

Her heavy breathing began coming in waves. She licked her top lip but still held onto the doorknob.

"Aw, Evie, it'll be like the old days. C'mon, open the door. Please. C'mon, baby."

She couldn't will away the wetness between her legs. Oh, the incredible hunger, everything inside her craved him. Her fingers twisted the lock open.

"Aw, there she is." She could hear his smile—and the triumph—in his voice. "I knew you wouldn't cut me off. You missed me, didn't you? I know you, baby. C'mon. Let me see that cute ass."

She tiptoed over to him, held her breast up to his lips and let him suck on her, while his fingers played between her thighs. Yes, he was making it last, doing it for her. He stroked and kissed her, long and deep. But when she cried out with pleasure, he yanked her to him. Her knees taut, her nipples pebbled, she let him caress her till she was crazy with the strange, unquenched need she always felt with him. She climbed up on his body, grasping his smooth shoulders, then spread her legs and rode him. On and on it went, oh the pleasure of it! When she'd had enough, and thought she'd die from the exploding pleasure, he tossed her over on the bed, pulling her. "Get down, bitch. Kneel like a doggy for me, you cunt!" He lifted her, even though he knew she didn't want it. But he plunged into her anyway, and it hurt so bad it seemed to rip her apart...

Rain was rattling at her windows, the first thing she heard. She opened her eyes to a gray morning. Puddles of water were saturating her new, pricey bamboo floor. *No!* Up she scrambled, slamming the window, using thick towels to soak up the storm's mess.

Her bed was empty. Brad was gone. *Why am I not surprised? Did I expect anything different?* Her whole body hurt. In her heart, it was as if someone had knifed her.

It's your own fault. He uses you...you always let him. You must like it. She pounded the pillow. *You're a sick bitch!*

The rain drummed on the roof. Wind shook the windows. She lay down again, staring at the Austrian chandelier she'd purchased. She'd finally come home from Lily's house, energized with the idea of redoing her bedroom. Tears burned her eyes as she remembered how fired up she'd been. Ablaze with starting over, making a new life, she'd convinced herself she'd be so strong, repeating over and over, *I'll never see him again. Never. No more abuse.*

Yeah, I made a new life, all right.

The searing ache from the accident lingered in her leg like the cold draft in the room. Out of bed, twisting in front of the mirror, she inspected the welts on her body. She'd hide them from everyone, like always. Actually, she wished it would hurt more, to remind her *all* day, *all* week, how utterly stupid she was.

She lay down again and turned over, inflicting more pain down her leg on purpose. Maybe the next time it would hurt this bad she'd remember, enough to run away when she saw him.

Damn him. Damn me! Pulling her teal satin robe around her, she heaved herself off the king-sized bed, slid her feet into satin slippers and headed toward the shower. *Enough.* She must get ready for her business trip—she was flying to Rome tomorrow.

CHAPTER 20

"Sure," Lily said, hanging up the phone. She rose, leaving her desk cluttered with airline manuals behind her. She checked the time. Five minutes before five o'clock. *Strange, Ken never works late. Why does he want to see me now?*

Normally, her boss rushed out at five sharp to pick up his two little girls at school and drive them to the local swimming pool, where they practiced daily for state competitions. His daughters were all he ever talked about.

Ken looked up as Lily entered his glassed-in office. She remained standing in the hope that whatever he wanted wouldn't take long. Refusing to look at her, he swiveled sideways to snap his briefcase shut. *Click.* "Sit down for a minute, Lily."

She held her breath. *Something's up.* She sank into the office chair across from him.

Unexpectedly, Ken got up and took his trench coat off the hook. He stayed standing, looking down at her. Was he going to leave? *That's weird.* Suddenly, he handed her a memo with two timecards attached. "I'm sorry about this," he said, "but you know...uh, you knew...how important the company regards our team commitment.

I had no choice. Graylock's new attendance policy demands that I strictly enforce company rules regarding time off, even for funerals."

Lily skimmed the memo. Addressed to her with a cc: to the Human Resources manager, Ken's note stated that she had knowingly deviated from company policy. He ended with a standard warning that if she transgressed the company's personal time off policy again, she would face grave consequences. Lily stifled a shout. *Bastard!* She wanted to rip up the memo. Instead, she dropped her hands into her lap to steady them and watched Ken scuttle around his office. He turned his back, switched his trench coat to his other arm and then shuffled through a stack of files. Finally he turned around to face her again. He was a rat trying to find an escape hole.

"If you want to discuss this with HR," he said, avoiding her eyes, "they're ready to listen." His face was pink. "Again, I'm sorry, but all our team members," he gestured toward her co-workers' desks, "felt that any deviations from policy must be documented in your file."

Lily couldn't look at him, though she heard his voice trembling loud and clear. "You knew," he said, "how lax on attendance our department's been in the last three years. You knew my boss tightened up the rules this year." His voice took on a pleading tone, "Everyone has to abide by the same standards, Lily. I hope you can understand the position you placed me in by your excessive use of time off."

"The position *I* put you in?" Lily could hardly form the question. She sat up straighter; her body felt immovable, rigid. Inwardly steaming, yearning to shred the memo, she slowly folded it in half in front of him. Her words were solid blocks. "Ken, I Only Took One Extra Day." She breathed deeply. "Frank died on Christmas. I used the last sick day I had the day after Christmas and all my funeral leave after that. I just couldn't go anywhere after his burial. I could barely move, let alone come to work. I'm sorry, but I was too weak to pick up the phone to call you. You never said a word when I returned to work after New Year's or since." She kept her voice steady. "Now, almost two months later, you write me up?"

His face turned crimson. The whole department always joked about it. *"Uh-oh, Ken's got a sunburn!"* They all knew when he confronted someone—which was rare—his fair complexion turned bright red.

Lily watched him fiddle with his briefcase, then turn to go. *He's going to walk out and leave me here.* She heard someone laugh outside and turned around. Two co-workers, Sean and Holly, sat at their desks staring at her through the glass enclosing Ken's office. They were grinning.

She stood up. Crumpling the memo and timecards in her hand, she finally erupted. "I don't believe this! After all the overtime I've put in without pay! You, of all people, know how hard I've worked. For that I got a *one percent* raise. And now you write me up? Of all your employees, I've completed double the amount of publications than any other tech writer in this department. Not once, *but every friggin' year!*" She wadded the thick timecards into a fist-sized ball and aimed it at Ken. He had to duck. The paper ball flew across the room, hit the glass and dropped to the floor. He stood for a minute, dazed, then started to bolt.

Lily blocked his path.

Her rage at this big, cowardly oaf of a man had smoldered for months. He looked like a football halfback: six-foot-four, broad chest and shoulders, healthy shock of hair for his fifty-plus years. Yes, he was an upstanding, cover-your-ass company man all dressed up in his pin-striped suit. Truth was, he was a namby-pamby weakling with no backbone. She'd lost respect—no, she'd *despised him* for a very long time.

She wasn't the only one. *Everybody* knew about Ken. Even the department's slackers agreed. He'd bend in *any* direction, wherever the power in a group swayed him or wherever his boss dictated.

"He has no balls," were Frank's exact words, spoken months ago. Yes, even her quiet, nonjudgmental husband had disliked Ken and said so after she'd recounted several ludicrous episodes at work. Ironic that her quiet, peace-at-any-price husband had uttered a negative opinion and now, by taking one extra day to settle Frank's affairs, she'd lost any chance for a promotion. Yes, Ken had finally taken a stand against her, at her co-workers' urging. He'd written her up, and that stupid, crumpled-up memo would remain in her personnel file for all to see.

She turned her back and marched out of his office. No wonder Sean, Holly and the rest of them hadn't gone home yet. They were all sitting in their cubicles, heads bent, pretending to work. *Of course.* They usually skipped out the minute the clock struck five. Not today. They were waiting to assess damage control and jeer at her behind her back. "There goes the college graduate," they'd titter. She'd heard it all before.

She strode toward her desk, her thoughts churning. *No, I didn't work "in the shop." All I did was raise two daughters and work my ass off at night to get my degree. They've had it in for me ever since I was hired! For god sake, they probably drafted the memo for Ken. He's such a pansy!*

Her cell phone rang. She dug it out of her purse. "Hello?" She began packing up her things.

"Hey, I'm back from my business trip. Two weeks away was just what I needed," Eve's voice, chirping on the other end, irritated Lily. "It was fabulous. I want to tell you all about it! I'm sitting on the 210 freeway in a limo, backed up for miles, just came from LAX airport. I see Tia Maria's up ahead. How 'bout my driver drops me off, and you come and meet me for drinks and dinner? You can drive me home later. How 'bout it?"

"Sounds perfect!"

"You mean it?" Eve said. "I was ready to spend the next five minutes trying to talk you into it. Are you okay?"

"Just fine. See you in a few." Lily put her cell phone away, picked up her briefcase and her black cardigan sweater, and walked as calmly as she could toward the elevator. Ken was ahead of her, waiting in front of the elevator doors that began to open. When Lily approached, he rushed down the employee staircase.

Coward. Fuck him! Fuck them all!

CHAPTER 21

*P*iñatas hung from the dark ceiling beams at Tia Maria's, an after-work hangout for business types not far from Eve's condo in Sierra Madre. Sitting at the bar, she raised a margarita to her lips, this time savoring its salty, lime taste. A muscular guy wearing a golf shirt caught her eye. She assessed his scruffy black hair and the sunburn on his cheeks. Locking eyes, she licked her lips to tease him, then had second thoughts. *I'd better watch it. He'll be over here in no time if I don't stop.* Quickly she averted her gaze, focusing on the Mexican blankets and silver-trimmed sombreros hanging on the wall.

She hadn't slept much on the plane, and though she was exhausted from her nine-hour flight, her adrenalin was still racing. She sipped the tart drink, her spirits basking in her memories of the Umbrian countryside, plus Rome and Florence. "A jewel of a trip," she'd said to Lily before she left, and she'd been right.

Strange how she'd been afraid to leave the comforts of home and her best friend to go off to Europe this time. *Silly fears.* Probably due to her painful weeks in physical therapy trying to walk again—made her feel so vulnerable—plus endless sessions with her therapist to free herself from Brad. His last visit invaded her thoughts. *All that therapy didn't do much good, did it?* She remembered every sordid detail of that night. *He made me feel like trash. But I let it happen....*

Thank god she'd left on a business trip the next day. Even in Italy, though, she couldn't put him completely out of her mind. She'd resisted for several days, then she'd given in and texted him at least twice. No answers. Nothing. *The whole thing was a sick obsession. I'm sick!*

Exasperated, she'd called her psychiatrist from Italy. She could hardly believe it when he abandoned his professional reserve and offered her blunt advice, "I've tried to warn you, Eve. Brad's dangerous. First, you can't allow your thoughts to dwell on him. Focus on other things. Use mind control. It takes effort but you can do it. You've got to move on! Rebuild yourself. Only then will you be ready for relationships with other men."

So, she thought ruefully, *Dr. Stein's fed up with me, too.*

Move on? How? Going back to work helped, and flying away to Europe transported her to another world. But she had to come home sometime. How could she lock Brad out of her thoughts and her life? She'd loved him....he'd even gone to counseling when she asked. For two years she'd filled her dreams with him and planned to marry him. Despite his flaws. The whole relationship had been crazy-making. *How on earth can I finally close that door and throw away the key?*

But I have to. She drained her glass and raked her fingers through her golden hair. The waiter set her second margarita on the table. He smiled at her before turning away to serve the swarm of professionals pressing for refills. Stuffing her credit card and wallet back into her Gucci bag, she pulled out copies of her sales reports to distract herself, scanning the pages. This trip had been a godsend, culminating in several sizeable orders. She couldn't wait to see her boss' face tomorrow. He'd probably take her someplace expensive for lunch.

Such glorious shopping in Italy too. She'd shipped home a stone fountain—the second authentic antique she'd ever owned—to decorate the atrium she'd transformed a year ago. Trailing orchids and Australian ferns adorned her glassed-in terrace now, matching the condo's modern décor: gray walls, ebony and silver furniture. She loved her framed Picasso and Dali prints. She'd allowed only a splash of color: vermillion tulips in slim glass vases and a crimson fringed blanket thrown over her black leather coach.

The red Italian tapestry she'd bargained for in Florence would look stunning hanging in her bedroom above her headboard, and lit by her new chandelier. *And Brad will never, ever set foot in there again!*

Eve gulped her drink down, checked her watch and scanned the throng milling around the room. She stood on tiptoe to wave at Lily, who was coming through the mammoth, wooden front door. As her friend jostled through the Friday night revelers Eve noticed Lily's new look. *Whoa, she actually looks slim!* Lily's curly dark hair glistened with new auburn highlights and framed her face in a longer style, but her eyes were brooding and her mouth was set—Eve knew she was clenching her teeth. *She hates crowds. But she looks fantastic!*

Lily finally reached Eve and hugged her. "Hi, stranger. I'm glad you're home safe."

"Of course I am," Eve said, leaning closer, "you worry too much. What's up? You look slimmer and I love your hair, but you don't look happy at all."

The noise in the lounge was rising as men in the latest Ralph Lauren shirts leaned on the bar next to women dressed in tunic-length sweaters, leggings and boots. Their hilarity was beginning to sound harsh.

Lily cupped her mouth with her hand and muttered in Eve's ear. "Today was the worst day ever at work!"

"What happened?" Eve almost shouted, pointing at her margarita and gesturing a question to Lily.

"Yes, order two for me!" Lily put up two fingers.

Eve's eyebrows went up. "Wow, you *did* have a bad day! Don't tell me... Ken offered you another golden opportunity? With lots of unpaid overtime, of course."

Lily's eyes told another story as she shook her head. "I've taken way too much shit, from him *and* my co-workers. You never let me forget that, but today was—"

"That's the trouble, you keep *taking* their shit!" Eve jumped in. "You're been a slave to that company! What happened now?" Eve turned her back on a guy in a navy golf shirt who was heading in her direction. She leaned closer to Lily to hear what she was saying.

"Thanks for bolstering my confidence, friend. Just what I need. Tonight of all nights."

Eve couldn't miss the tears in Lily's eyes. She put her arm around her waist and grabbed her jacket and drink, moving her forward. "I'm sorry. Let's find a quieter table so we don't have to blast our personal stuff to the whole world."

They pushed away from the rowdy group at the bar, heading toward an adjacent room with a cozy fireplace and candles flickering in wrought-iron lanterns.

Two hours had passed and the happy-hour crowd had finally moved on, but Lily and Eve were still huddled together in the corner, nursing their drinks and munching on chips with guacamole and salsa.

"So," Lily asked, "you're not going back to Italy soon, are you?" Her eyes were puffy from crying. She'd shared every detail of the day's heinous confrontation with Ken.

"I go to Ireland next," Eve told her. "I'll have to go back to Italy in a couple of months. I sold a monthly contract for wines to several hotels in Umbria, but I know I can double that if I call on them more often." Eve's smile lit her sky-blue eyes. "Plus, I have more places to go. Visits to Milan, Verona and Venice in the late summer wouldn't be hard to take."

"Yeah, right," Lily said, playing with the chips on her napkin. Wrinkles were forming between her thin, dark eyebrows again. She took another gulp of her margarita.

Eve tried to cheer her up. "C'mon, why so down? I don't think you realize it, but you have options now. Ken's done nothing but mistreat you for a long time, and Graylock has taken you for granted since you got hired. Admit it. What he pulled today borders on outright cruelty after all your hard work. He's just covering his ass and cow-towing to his employees for fear they'll report him to the higher-ups.

"Did you," Eve continued, "finalize that offer on Frank's restaurant while I was away? By the way, I guess Mr. Turle isn't as incompetent as he looks. Before my plane took off for Rome, I checked out the real estate deal he mentioned. I phoned the restaurant manager in Pennsylvania. It was all on the up and up.

"So, if you accept his offer, you'll have plenty of money now. Why stick around at Graylock so everybody can whip you some more?"

Lily flinched. "That's how you see it? How you see me?" She covered her cheeks with her hands.

Eve reached for her friend's hand. "I didn't mean to be so harsh, but they've treated you harshly. I keep waiting for you to realize it."

"Well, I called Mr. Turle while you were away, so the restaurant is in escrow now. But, Eve, I've worked for Graylock for almost three years. What about tenure? And my pension? If I put in a few more—"

"Good, I'm glad you're going to sell the restaurant." Eve nodded her head. "Now pitch the job! Corporate pensions are slim pickings these days. Please, Lily, promise me you'll quit. Give them what they deserve. Ken will never expect it. If anybody deserves a shock, it's him. How can he survive without you? You handle all his pet projects." When Lily offered no reply, Eve gently covered her friend's hand. "Did you hear what I said? When escrow closes you can bank the restaurant money, even invest it. C'mon, this is your golden opportunity! Get even for once in your life."

One hand wiping her cheek, Lily looked down at her drink.

Eve snapped her fingers. "Hey! I've got a great idea! I told you I'm going to Ireland. The winery is giving me a month or more over there to improve our wine sales. Lily, come with me! You've always wanted to go there. A vacation in the British Isles will make a new woman out of you."

Lily could only stare at Eve, who was already planning their trip. "I can take some vacation days in the middle of my business trip," she said. "That'll extend our time. Maybe we could even stretch the trip out to two months. C'mon! We'll have a fabulous time in Dublin. Seeing the sights. Shopping. I'll show you Trinity College, too. We might squeeze in some of the smaller villages where the wine pubs are. Maybe we could drive around the Ring of Kerry and see the western coast too. I've heard it's gorgeous."

"Eve, I'd love it, but...but you know how I hate to fly. I haven't been on an airplane in twenty years. It's easy for you, you're used to traveling, but I—"

Eve lifted her margarita. "Do what I do. Take this for your stress. C'mon, don't focus on your fears. Think of the fun we'll have! You've wanted to go to Ireland as long as I've known you." She put her fingers under her friend's chin and raised her head. "Lily, just think, we could visit the wee folks you read about all during your childhood."

Lily's eyes began to sparkle. "Did I tell you about the new class I'm taking for fun? It's called Celtic Culture. All these years I've been reading faerie tales. The Celts had an amazing story-telling tradition. Their faerie tales are different from the so-called American fairy tales in the books I used to devour. That's partly why I wanted to start a faerie garden last summer—"

"See? You already know about the Celtic Isles. If anyone deserves a trip, *you do*." Eve smiled as she lapsed into a brogue. "It's in your blood, it is. And how can you turn away now from your ancestors when they're just waitin' to be discovered?" Lily's eyes were glowing now, so Eve pressed on. "Hey, I have another idea! We could look Maeve up in Dublin." Her smile turned devilish. "Meet her brawny son, Seamus, too."

Now Lily's smile widened. "Oh, you. You're always on the prowl!"

"Why not? Flirting's harmless. Besides, I'm free, single...and well over twenty-one. Why shouldn't I flirt with gorgeous men?"

"Maybe you should think about finding a good man, you know...settle on a nice, predictable guy who will—"

"Take care of me? I don't think so. The guys I choose either slap me around, drink with me or use my money. You know that better than I, Lily, but you're too nice to say it. No, I don't want a steady guy." She paused. "Brad was the last one, and it's still taken me a ton of strength not to talk to him in the last two weeks."

Lily looked alarmed. "Brad? Two weeks? What do you mean? You never mentioned—"

"No, I didn't. And for good reason. I didn't want you to know how weak and demented I am."

"What do you mean?"

"Okay, here it is."

Their high spirits while planning their trip to Ireland disappeared as Lily listened to Eve tell only a few of the details of her shocking rendezvous with Brad.

Leaving the most painful parts out, Eve ended the story, "He pulled out all the stops, and, dammit, I fell for it. Again! Oh how I love to hate myself." She'd never divulge how low she'd fallen that night. Lily would be horrified.

As it was, Lily was frowning deeply. "He didn't even contact you beforehand? After all these months, he barged right in?"

Eve waved her hand as if swatting a fly. "That's Brad. Years could go by. He'd never think of calling me and *asking* me before he showed up."

The sunburned guy in the golf shirt walked by, eying Lily this time. Eve noticed how Lily's eyes met his for a second. Then she squirmed in her seat, straightened her black skirt and reached for her drink.

Hmmm, she's interested. That's new.

Lily wasn't finished quizzing Eve. "Have you seen or heard from Brad since that night? Tell me the truth."

"Not a word. Typical, though." *Trouble is,* she mused to herself, *I sit here now and rag on him, but last night I took a sleeping pill to keep myself from phoning him from Italy."* Eve lifted her glass and drained it, savoring the sweet and sour taste. "I'm a mess," she said and signaled to the waiter.

Lily signaled to the waiter, too—to stay away. "Please don't, Eve. You've had plenty."

"Okay, *Mom.* I wasn't going to order another, anyway." She nodded to the smiling waiter. "Check, please."

CHAPTER 22

*L*ily drummed her fingers on her desk. She'd arrived at work early, her stomach quivering, but she hadn't summoned up the courage to venture into Ken's office. Not yet.

Fired up at dawn, Eve's words still swirling in her head, she hadn't been able to sleep. Finally, at five a.m., she'd started planning what to say to Ken. But now that she was actually sitting at her desk, all the old fears that had beaten her into submission all her life gripped her body.

"I'd better get to it," she muttered. "I've got to have it out with him. Otherwise I'll be skulking around here like always, taking whatever shit he shovels my way. Enough is enough!"

She stood up and slipped into the ladies room to reapply her lip gloss. She knew she was procrastinating. She fidgeted in front of the mirror, adjusting the silver dangle earrings Frank had wrapped and put under the Christmas tree a couple of days after Thanksgiving. Just looking at them made her sad. Would Frank approve of her quitting? Of course not. *But he's not here and he won't ever be again.*

Besides, he left me plenty of money. She tucked her magenta blouse into her basic black skirt and pulled in her stomach. Her new size-ten clothes had even begun to sag a little so that her blouse ballooned around her midriff. When she'd bought this outfit before Christmas it had fit snugly, but since Frank's funeral, she'd lost more weight. No one to cook for now, and when she ate, nothing tasted good.

She checked her hair. She was letting it grow longer. She liked what she saw. Her stylist had applied masque oil; it had not only tamed the frizz but made her hair shine. Plus, her auburn highlights warmed her complexion.

Well, it's time to escape this shitty chicken coop! She marched out of the ladies room. Noting Ken was off the phone, she made a beeline for his office. All the desks were empty. Her co-workers always met for breakfast in the company cafeteria at eight thirty.

Full speed ahead!

She hovered in the doorway. "Ken, can I speak to you for a minute?"

His face looked sheepish when he met her eyes. He gestured for her to sit down, even as he focused again on his laptop.

He's such a god-damned coward!

"I...uh, I hope you didn't go home too upset last night, Lily. Nothing personal about that whole thing yesterday, you know." His gaze flicked between the paperwork on his desk and his computer screen.

"Upset? Why no, Ken. That doesn't begin to describe how I felt. Fact is, after meeting with you I went out on the town with a friend. To Tia Maria's. Fabulous margaritas there! We were having so much fun we didn't even stop to eat."

He stared at her, his mouth gaping open, then he diverted his gaze again, focusing on his laptop.

Lily almost lost it then. *Don't you dare ignore me. You'll listen now, you big oaf, and you'll listen good!*

She clasped her hands together and took a deep breath. "Ken, I know you're terribly busy, and the last thing I want to do is take up your precious time. So I'll be brief." She handed him a letter. "This is my resignation. I'm sure you can find someone else to take over all your special projects. As soon as I clean out my desk and gather up my things, I'm out of here. My time is valuable--I have tons of packing to do. I'm leaving for Ireland soon."

Ken's face went pink. His eyes stabbed at hers. Finally he was giving her the attention she'd craved for years. She reveled in the glory of this moment.

"Ireland?" he stuttered. "Uh, how long do you need? For a vacation, I mean. I can..." he stacked some papers on his desk, again avoiding her eyes. "I can probably make that happen if...if you need it. No problem. Anything else?"

"You didn't hear me, Ken. I don't need your permission anymore. And, by the way, I'm no different than I was yesterday or the day before. So why are you offering me perks now? I told you, *I'm done*. In a few minutes I'll be out of here. For good."

Ken face grew redder by the minute. "Uh...Lily, you don't mean it. You've worked here for...isn't it three years this summer? You'll earn tenure after only two more. Don't do something rash. Frank wouldn't want—"

"You don't have a clue what Frank would want!" She stood up and only turned to look at him when she reached the office door. Her co-workers were filing toward their desks now, checking out what was going on in Ken's office. She opened the door and raised her voice. "There's nothing rash about my decision, Ken. Far from it. In fact, it's the smartest, most rational decision I've ever made. Have a nice life! All of you!"

Ignoring their stares and whispers, she quickly cleaned out her desk and stuffed her personal belongings into her briefcase. When the slam of her desk drawers subsided, the ticking of the clock above took on the eerie quality of an echoing gong, marking a huge milestone in her life.

Ten pairs of eyes watched her clamp her briefcase shut. She marched past all of them, down the stairs, away from Graylock Inc. and out into a new world of possibilities.

PART II

*The Celtic Knot represents family and unity of spirit
enclosed in a circle, with no beginning and no end.
The circle protects the symbol, so the spirit cannot be broken.*

CHAPTER 23

"*I*t'll be clear blue skies and about 17 degrees Celsius out there this afternoon, folks," the Aer Lingus pilot announced. "And for those of you travelin' from the States, that's sixty-two degrees Fahrenheit. Take a look out yer window now, will ya? See that beautiful green patchwork below? That's our Emerald Isle down there, i'tis. Oh, and those spots of white you see? That'll be herds of sheep rovin' on all sides. You'll be seein' lots of lambs as you roam around our island... "

Looking out the window, Lily sighed with pleasure. The waning afternoon light cast streams of glowing amber on the rolling slopes below. Gathering mists on the horizon were blending with the clouds that surrounded the shimmering sun. She squirmed in her seat. "My stomach's doing flip-flops, I'm so keyed up." She pressed the tip of her nose to the cold window. "Aren't you?"

"'Course I am," Eve said. "But not as much as you. I visited Dublin once before. I'm not surprised your stomach's upset, though. To be honest, I thought you'd have more trouble."

"I kept up my prayers," Lily answered, fingering Gram's gold

Celtic Knot around her neck. "That keeps my fear in check, and the melatonin pills you talked me into helped me sleep."

"I'm glad they worked."

"It's amazing down there! I can't wait to walk those roads and talk to the people. Don't you love the pilot's brogue?"

As if he'd heard Lily, his voice came on again. "We'll be headin' over to Dublin airport now, folks, and we want to thank you today for flyin' with us. We'll be landin' in about 15 minutes. So, you'll need to gather your coats and sweaters and carry-ons up top when I tell you, but for now, fasten your seatbelts and don't be poppin' out of your seats, or you might find yourself in a Dublin hospital, and we wouldn't want that, now would we?"

"He's a character," Lily murmured as she studied the landscape below and snapped a couple shots with her new iPhone. Then she took her airline socks off and put on her sneakers.

"So you're not going to hold it against me for forcing you to come?" Eve asked with a smile.

"You're priceless," Lily said. "*I* talked *you* into it! Don't forget, when Brad phoned you the other day, you almost called off this whole trip."

"I know." Eve's voice turned low and serious. "In the end, though, I couldn't let you down. After all, you're my best friend. And we'd bought the plane tickets, and you'd already walked out on Ken. Besides, my counselor warned me this was *the* most dangerous time to see Brad, because I've never refused him like this..."

Lily nodded, digging her nails into her palms. She'd harbored fear that her friend would give in to Brad. "Well, you turned the tables on him. Finally. Now he knows you're determined to stay away, not for a few days, but for a long time. It fired up his rage because it's new to him. You've never taken a business trip *and* a vacation in Europe before. And never after he demanded to see you." She leaned over and squeezed Eve's hand. "I'm proud of you!"

Eve nodded. "Would you be shocked if I admitted I can only think of one other time when I said no to him? My counselor's been working on me for months, but he became insanely adamant after I...," her voice lowered, "after I saw Brad last month. Dr. Stein even urged me to prep the office workers at the winery, in case Brad calls, looking for me. So I warned them all and I was firm about it. I'm sure they won't tell anyone my itinerary."

Lily's mouth went dry. The deep anchor of dread she'd been feeling for her friend still weighed her down. "That's a relief." She swallowed the last of her bottled water, then gathered up her magazines and stowed them in her carry-on, which she stuffed back under her seat. A random thought calmed her. "Brad's scary *and* unpredictable. Don't forget, he's lazy, too. I doubt he'll pursue you if he finds many roadblocks in his way."

"Yeah, you're right. Thanks for your pep talk the other night, Lily. I'm glad I left my apartment and stayed overnight with you, in case he showed up again. When he called me I almost caved. I...I never wanted to admit it, but the reality is he's got plenty of other fillies in his stable." Eve crossed her index fingers as if she were protecting herself from a vampire. "Let's hope he gives up on *this* mare."

Lily noticed the wrinkles between Eve's brows and the tears shining in her sky-blue eyes. Just then the sun coming through the window backlit her golden hair. Lily couldn't help wondering why her gorgeous friend had become so obsessed with this good-for-nothing abuser. Maybe, she thought, it had something to do with losing her dad when she was so young. He'd been athletic and good-looking too, like Brad. *Her dad was always gone a lot. She adored him. And he spoiled her terribly by buying her that pony. Brad showered her with gifts too...in the beginning.*

As if Eve read Lily's thoughts, she whispered, "I have a hard time saying no when certain men want me. It's my downfall."

Lily fastened her seatbelt then patted her friend's hand. "I'm glad you're safe with me. After you're gone for a month, he'll forget you. For a while at least. That's his history, you know. And, we can concoct lots of foolproof ways for you to disappear after we come back to California."

Eve smiled but didn't look convinced.

CHAPTER 24

"*D*riving on the wrong side of the road is tricky, especially with the sun in my eyes," Eve said as she turned their rented Opal to the right, to leave the airport. They were headed for the heart of Dublin. "I've only done this once before," she added, "in London." As she drove through the city, she gestured out the window. "Look over there, in the distance. It's much more rural than I remember."

In the bright sunlight they spotted tiny sheep grazing in the fields. Miles away, a river glistened in the light. "I bet that's the Shannon," Lily exclaimed.

"Is it as magical as you thought it would be?" Eve asked.

"More!"

Eve smiled. "We're lucky it's not raining. March is always cool here. As we make our way through the city, notice the different colors of the front doors. It's a Dublin trademark."

"Yes, I've seen it in travel books but this...this is so exciting!" Lily was clasping and unclasping her hands.

After a while they discovered Grafton Street. "Look at those hanging flower baskets and the lanterns outside the shops. Everything looks so quaint," Lily said. "More affluent than I expected. All the houses and shops are freshly painted—love the pastel colors. I'm itching to go shopping here."

Eve nodded. "*You* shopping? I never thought I'd hear you say that."

One hand on the wheel, Eve fumbled through her purse and pulled out a larger map, which she handed to Lily. "My phone isn't working. Help me out, okay? We need to find the Shelbourne Hotel. I marked it." As Lily studied the map, Eve went on, "I'm supposed to meet the area's most important wine merchants there. I made reservations for us to stay two nights. You can join us at the Wine Geese Banquet tomorrow evening."

"Wine Geese?" Lily asked. "What a strange name. I vaguely recall you mentioning it. But, Eve, I won't feel comfortable at a banquet with your customers. Please don't expect me to attend."

"The name Wine Geese is sort of a poetic description of lonely geese traveling across the skies," Eve said, as they stopped at an intersection and watched shoppers meandering past the stores. "And the Celts had a thing about birds," Eve continued. "They claimed birds carried messages or were harbingers of the future."

Lily found the paragraph she'd just read in the guidebook, "But the name Wine Geese has nothing to do with the Celts. It says 'thousands of soldiers who fled Ireland in the 1600s. Many became vintners in France and Spain, and smuggled wine back into Irish ports later on.'"

"Hmm, that book should come in handy as we travel," Eve said. "And you're a master at changing the subject, too. C'mon, Lily, you have tonight and tomorrow to rest up for the banquet. It'll be fun! You can meet the locals and some merchants from the south of Ireland. You'll be a knockout in that dress you bought. It shows off your new, svelte body. *And* it matches your green eyes."

"Svelte?" Lily had to giggle at the word. "I've only lost forty pounds, at least according to the scale this morning. With more to go."

"That's six pounds more than a few weeks ago. Enjoy it, girl."

Lily looked up from the map. "There's the hotel. Wow, talk about old world charm. Compared to the new housing tracts we see all over California, this is so different...very historical." Eve maneuvered the car into a parking spot.

The Shelbourne's stately brick facade, colonnaded entrance and the doormen in top hats welcoming each guest were drawing plenty of attention from tourists on the street. Eve and Lily climbed the steps of the luxury hotel, nodded to the doormen and handed over their luggage. Both of them in awe, they entered the high-ceilinged foyer with its gleaming marble floors and Palladian columns. A sparkling chandelier overhead caught Lily's eye. She stopped to stare at two gigantic black candelabras trimmed in gold and the central staircase with its wrought iron and mahogany banisters. Finally she looked up at gold-leafed, coffered ceilings. Everything literally glowed.

"I never expected our hotel to be so lush," she whispered to Eve, "but believe me, I'm not complaining!"

As they checked in, she delighted in the lilting cadence of the young man's brogue who was checking them in. He kept smiling at her and welcomed them both. Lily couldn't help but notice the cinnamon freckles sprinkled across his nose and the dimple in his chin. His green eyes were only a shade lighter than his dark uniform.

"This is my first trip to Europe," she told him. "I wanted to start with Ireland because my ancestors are from here. I used to worry about traveling, but not now. I'm thrilled to be here." This wasn't like her—to blurt out personal details to a total stranger. But she was in new territory now. Maybe she was in for more changes on this magical isle. Who knew what might happen?

Up on the second floor, the two friends walked down a long,

thickly carpeted hall. They finally came to Eve's room, and as she shoved her key card into the lock, she looked at Lily. "I'm exhausted. How 'bout you?" The door opened and she stepped inside. "I'm going to order in for dinner. I'll call you tomorrow morning, and we'll have breakfast before I see my customers, okay?"

Lily peeked into Eve's room before she chimed in that she was tired too. "I'll order in, too. See you at breakfast."

A surprise in her room, which was right next-door, stunned Lily. "One, no, *two* vases of flowers," Lily murmured, as she moved toward the large arrangement of yellow roses on the dressing table. She leaned in to smell them, and caught a glimpse of her flushed face in the antique mirror. Then, flouncing onto the massive white bed, she sank down on the soft mattress. After enjoying its pure luxury, she sat up against the satin pillows, excitement riddling her body. Sleep or no sleep, she had to call Eve. She picked up her cell phone.

"Dahling, my room is simply *exquisite*."

"Ah, that means you like it."

"I feel like...like...a queen. Can I come see your room again? You chased me out way too fast. Can I have my dinner brought to your room instead?"

"Of course."

CHAPTER 25

*T*he hotel's conference room was crowded with men the next evening. Though they'd entered and were now standing at the back of the room, Eve and Lily could tell who the members of the Irish Wine Geese organization were. Dressed in dark suits, each man wore a lapel pin in the form of a silver-winged bird, the group's insignia. Now an older gentleman with silver hair stepped up to the podium as a few men left the room and the rest took seats around tables. Empty wineglasses sparkled at each setting. The crowd quieted.

"Welcome to you all, lads," the old gentleman said in a hearty voice, "and...yes," he nodded," we have two lasses here tonight, too." Some of the men turned around to gaze at Lily and Eve. A couple of them smiled and winked.

At this point, the speaker paused and nodded to Lily and Eve. "C'mon and join us, lasses, take a seat down in front here. We don't want you thinkin' we're lackin' in Irish hospitality."

As she put out her hand to commandeer Lily forward, Eve felt over fifty pairs of eyes following them as the crowd clapped. *They look like lottery winners the way they're smiling at us,* she mused.

O'Sullivan timed our entrance perfectly. Two men waved them to their table near the front of the room and, with gallant bows, gave them their seats.

The old gentleman then placed both hands on the podium, his eyes creased with laugh lines. "Most of you know me, but for those of you who don't, my name is Sean O'Sullivan. I know you locals well. You enjoy a smooth pint or two here on many a night. Or is it four or five?" The crowd tittered. "Tonight we've gathered from other counties too, for something special—our annual wine banquet. We're here to remember our Celtic heritage, which dates back more than two thousand years, and also to honor our brothers who left Ireland many long centuries ago."

Sean O'Sullivan beamed. "As we sip these new wines this evening, lads—and lasses," he winked at Eve and Lily then his face turned serious, "let us remember those brave lads who left our fair isle after that fateful tragedy, the Battle of the Boyne. During that infamous time," he continued, "the Brits banished 14,000 of our defeated Irish soldiers. They could only continue to serve in the Irish brigade far away. Sadly, they were all marched south to Cork's docks, where they boarded ships with their families. Some joined the French, Spanish or Austrian armies. It became known as the Flight of the Wild Geese. And," he held up his glass of wine, "it's the vintages of their descendents that we'll be enjoyin' tonight, since our Irish brothers have squeezed grapes in foreign lands for many a long year. And, as you might already know, they also traded and smuggled their wine at great peril. Now, thanks be to God, we trade with ease."

The audience applauded and he cleared his throat to continued, "And, my lads, we have a special visitor tonight who has come from another faraway place. Napa Valley, California, a place where many an Irishmen started their own wineries. Let us welcome Eve Walsh Olson, a wine representative for a well-known American vintner called Monceno's. Stand up and give us all a nod now, will you, Eve?"

Eve rose, her hair hanging loose in silky blonde curls, her black satin dress framing her shape perfectly. With pleasure she noticed how the eyes of the audience seemed glued to her. The men's gazes triggered a thrill in her that was all too familiar. She licked her lips just enough, and brought her hand up to touch the lone diamond necklace, sparkling just above her cleavage, teasing them some more.

"Let's all make her feel welcome, men!" O'Sullivan said. The room broke into raucous clapping. "And let's also welcome Eve's friend from California, Lily O'Malley Doyle, who has also joined us tonight."

"See?" Eve murmured to Lily. "They're incredibly friendly. Stand up and give them a nod."

Lily neither moved nor spoke.

Eve nudged her friend's shoulder and whispered, "For god's sake, Lily, stand up. They won't bite." *What's she afraid of now? She looks prettier tonight than I've ever seen her.*

"Don't," Lily whispered back, the men still clapping all around her. She waved her hand in the air for a couple of moments, only rising for a second, and then sat down, remaining rooted to her chair. "You know how I am in front of a crowd. Especially people I don't know."

"That was then and this is now," Eve murmured. Why did Lily always have to let the past plague her? "Don't let an ancient fainting incident curse you forever." Eve knew her impatience was spilling out, and when she saw Lily's eyebrows rise, she knew her friend wasn't happy with her. Obviously, Lily had never gotten over an episode long ago when she'd tried to give a speech and ended up in the high school infirmary. The other kids had taunted her for weeks after that.

O'Sullivan kept clapping and smiling as he looked straight at Lily, though, then he introduced the first wine tasting.

A brawny waiter stopped by their table and grinned at them as he filled their glasses almost halfway. Like the men in the room, Eve and Lily swirled the sunny liquid in their spotless glasses, sniffed its bouquet and sipped.

As Lily nursed her second tasting, a third began to mellow Eve, banishing her irritation and the minor tremors of nervousness she'd felt during their entrance. She had learned long ago to hide her edginess because, she had to admit it, she craved the spotlight. Even though entering a roomful of strangers never failed to give her stage fright, she'd always managed to appear confident. She would never let fear control her. Not like Lily.

Some of the men were up and about now, swarming around the room, slapping each other on the back, beckoning the waiters for refills. The activity exhilarated her, and the wine had relaxed her, triggering her desire to flirt, a phase of her sales career she delighted in. She knew the game well. After working the room, she'd narrow her choice, pick them off, eliminate the average guys and go for the gold: the one hot guy who seemed to want her the least.

The man sitting next to Lily was trying to break the ice. Would she at least respond? After all, he was one of the most attractive men in the room. *Good, I couldn't leave her in better hands.* "I'll be back in a minute." Eve maneuvered away from the table and into the horde of eligible men.

Two broad-shouldered buddies were raving about their latest wine sales, so she sidled up to them to talk shop.

"...I've examined all the numbers, and Hong Kong and Vietnam top all the sales figures," one was saying.

"I know," said the other one. "They're racking up the largest buys of California wines lately."

"Is that so?" Eve smiled into one pair of eyes, then the other.

They nodded to her with obvious pleasure and made room for her to sit between them as the next wine tasting began. The more muscular of the two gave her his full attention. His eyes, she immediately noticed, were so dark they looked as black as his hair, which had an unkempt look. The knot of his tie was crooked and loose. Eve liked the shadow of beard on his chin and cheeks. He was different from the rest. That's why he aroused her interest.

"Well," she said, "you and your friend seem to know a lot about wine sales. Is Ireland going for it more than ale these days? "

"I wish," said the shorter, stocky man. "Pleased to meet you, by the way. I'm Timothy. I'm glad the world's giving California wines the honor they deserve." He turned to the scruffy guy Eve preferred. "Let me introduce you to my friend—"

"I'm Ian," the swarthy guy said. He extended his hand to Eve's, holding it a few seconds longer than necessary. "You look like a lass I'd like to know better. I collect special vintages." *Maybe he collects something else, too*, Eve mused.

She caught Lily's eye and waved to her, hoping to cajole her into joining them. To her surprise, Lily stood up and crossed the room. Within seconds of introducing herself to Ian and Timothy she gave them a weak smile. "Excuse me. I'll be back in a minute."

Eve was speechless. *Why couldn't she stay and make a little small talk with these guys? What a drag she is!*

Eve stayed put, swirling the newest wine sample in her glass and sipping it, then trying another. She was thoroughly enjoying this roomful of Irish machismo. Still, she tried to keep an eye out for Lily, every once in a while searching among the suits for a glimpse of her friend's green velvet dress. She had to admit when Lily had come to her room this evening, she'd gasped at the sight of her. The emerald velvet didn't hang on her, like all the rest of her clothes; it revealed a shapely body Eve had never seen before. Why, Lily actually looked sexy tonight, and Eve had told her so. Lily claimed she didn't believe her, but Eve knew her friend's confidence had risen because her cheeks immediately flushed after her compliment. Then she'd tried to bolster Lily's self-assurance more, lavishing her with praise so they could make a dramatic entrance together. And her plan had worked!

Eve gave up looking for Lily. Instead, she began moving through the room, focusing one by one on the men around her. The testosterone surrounding her was staggering! It stirred her whole body; she hadn't wanted a man like this for months. She leaned into their smiles and innuendos, moving so close to them she sensed their arousal. By the time dinner was announced her body felt electric from the thrill of their lingering gazes. *Careful*, she cautioned silently. She had to maintain her professionalism at all costs. She neared the dark-haired fellow she'd flirted with earlier, taking his arm lightly, forcing away an urge to nestle closer. What was his name? She'd met so many...

"Would you mind escorting me to dinner, uh...Ian?"

"I'll oblige ye, m'lady," he said but didn't smile.

Hmmm, maybe Irish men aren't used to assertive American women.

They reached the grand dining room where Royal Tara china and Waterford crystal gleamed in the candlelight.

Eve glimpsed Lily across the room, the only other female, seated next to the same guy she'd met earlier at the bar. She certainly hadn't bothered to spread herself around. *She's landed a live one, all right.* Eve tried to catch her friend's attention as the first course was served, but the twosome were eating, sipping and talking nonstop. They seemed to have no time for anything or anybody.

Though Ian had finally told a good joke, Eve was finding his stories too serious, plus she had the distinct feeling he was hiding something. He seemed restless too. Some of the other men at their table were boasting to each other about their latest wine sales to establishments in Wales and Belgium when the hotel's banquet chairman approached and asked Ian for his name, while scrutinizing her invitation list. Then she left the room. A minute later, she returned and pressed him to produce his Wine Geese Association card. He began to make a lengthy show of searching through all his pockets, muttering excuses. Only now did Eve notice he wasn't wearing the Wine Geese lapel pin like everyone else. The banquet chairman became impatient and signaled to a security guard. Without a word, Ian suddenly strode out of the banquet hall.

Puzzled and feeling suddenly abandoned, she searched the room again for Lily. What could she and that man be talking about all evening? She had *never* seen Lily engaged in conversation like this with Frank, not in all the years she'd known them.

The lavish dinner, with choices of cheese soup, Irish potato skins, shepherd's pie or corn beef and cabbage finally ended with Donegal's Irish sundae. Her male companions had just launched into a boring chronicle of current Irish politics, so Eve made her escape.

"Hey, you two," she said, interrupting Lily and her companion. "You haven't budged all night! You must know each other from another life."

Lily looked up. "Hi, Eve. Patrick, here...he and I...we sort of...," a glow spread across her face. "Patrick and I come from the same part of Ireland. And he's an O'Malley from his stepmother's side of the family. Isn't that amazing?"

"Hmmm, sort of related then?"

Lily nodded. "He's been telling me about the ancient mounds in Ireland and the legends of faerie hamlets where the little people lived before the Celts arrived. There are still wells amongst the wild places in the west; some believe their water is still magical. Oh, I can't wait to sightsee."

"Calm down," Eve said with a smile. "We'll do it."

"And Patrick says there are some circular labyrinths and whorls carved into ancient stones not far from here! They're over 5,000 years old." Lily's eyes were lit with anticipation. "I've always wanted to design a labyrinth garden. To go with my faerie gardens."

Eve tried to engage Patrick with her famous wide-eyed gaze. "Sounds fascinating. And that's why we're here, Lily. So, do I deserve an introduction to this handsome fellow?"

Patrick merely gave her a glance before returning his gaze to Lily.

"Oh, I'm sorry," Lily said. "Patrick O'Sullivan, this is Eve Olson, my childhood friend from California. Patrick's the nephew of Mr. Sean O'Sullivan." She gestured toward the silver- haired gentleman who'd opened the event, now conversing with men across the room.

Eve sized up Patrick as he stood up to shake her hand, slowly raising her eyes to finally meet his as she took in his tall, muscular frame. "Happy to meet you," she said. Large hands, wide shoulders, slight graying at the temples, nearly black eyebrows that almost matched his wavy hair. Kind eyes too. The inventory completed, she decided he'd be a good catch for any woman.

She set about immersing him in such a lengthy amount of wine talk that they were soon standing face to face, nearly alone in the dining room. At least thirty minutes had passed and almost everyone had left, though Lily still sat nearby, gazing out the window. Finally noticing the time, Eve turned to Lily and raised her voice. "Oh, sorry, I almost forgot you were here. Enough shop talk now. Why don't we all indulge in an after-dinner drink together?"

Patrick walked around the table shaking his head, and took Lily's hand as she rose from her seat. "Not tonight, I'm afraid. I promised I'd take your friend out very early in the mornin' on a drive. All me life I've been fascinated with the ancient sights here in Ireland. It's a hobby of mine. Since neither of us is part of the wine convention you're goin' to tomorrow, I volunteered to be her tour guide for a time." He looked at Lily again. "So, we'd best get some sleep now, shan't we?" He included Eve in his gaze. "Especially you two, after your long flight yesterday. Jetlag always has a way of lingerin', you know, for a couple of days or more."

"Tired? Not me. I'm sure I can find someone else to buy me a nightcap." Eve abruptly turned to walk away. Where was that dark-haired guy she'd met at dinner? In the hotel bar?

"I didn't offend you now, did I?" Patrick called in a voice that sent a streak of anger through Eve.

She turned around. Both Lily and Patrick looked slightly shocked. She gave them a broad, fake smile. "Of course not. You two go on and get your rest." She forced another smile. "I'm not an early-to-bed kind of person like you two. Unless, of course, things get too tempting to pass up. If you know what I mean." She summoned up the alluring stare she used on other men and offered it to Patrick. Most guys couldn't resist it. But Patrick didn't crack a smile, not even a curve to his lips. *Damn him!*

She turned around again and dashed away toward the hotel's No. 27 Bar, which she'd heard was quite a "happening place." She made a careful entrance, trying the same come-on she'd used minutes before, but this time she got exactly the result she was after. Several men turned to admire her. Ian hadn't left, after all. He waved his drink in the air at her. He had a buzz on, that was clear, and he was finally smiling. She headed toward him to find out why he'd left the banquet table so suddenly. Mysterious guys fascinated her. He'd taken off his jacket, too. *Ooh and I never noticed those hefty Irish shoulders.*

"Ah, this is so much better," she muttered under her breath. "Patrick and his ancient sights be damned!"

CHAPTER 26

The air coming in through Lily's open window made her shiver. Her mood was as chilly as the night air streaming through her room...and her heart too. She burrowed under the smooth sheets and soft blankets and tried to fall asleep, but nothing could make her warm, inside or out. Instead she lay there, going over and over what had happened tonight.

She had actually felt joy, for the first time in years, and she'd even felt attractive, all day! Yesterday, too, despite her endless insecurities. Everything had seemed so perfect. The exciting plane ride, this perfect Irish city, her gorgeous hotel room and especially her brand-new look in her emerald velvet dress. Eve's compliments were so unexpected. They'd given her a confidence she'd never felt before. Then Eve had pushed her into that nerve-wracking entrance into the banquet. Well, she'd gotten through it somehow...only to magically land in a seat right next to a super-attractive man. And he hadn't excused himself and suddenly disappeared like so many others in the past. No, he'd actually sat beside her *all* evening, eager to share his stories and listen to hers. He'd given her...yes, a new kind of bliss, the kind she'd spent decades watching other women receive—with his rapt attention and admiration, listening to her every word.

Then Eve had joined them and everything changed.

Lily still couldn't believe it. She'd never seen her friend act like that before. Well, maybe around other women, but never around her. Why had Eve spent so much time flirting with the *one* man in the room who actually seemed content to talk with *her*? The only man in the whole world, besides Frank, who actually showed a genuine interest in her.

Had Eve really left her sitting there, ignored, for over a half hour while she used every flirtatious trick she knew to lure Patrick away? Why?

Lily got out of bed, reached for the window and slammed it shut. No more blasts of cold night air. Enough!

When she awoke, blue shadows shrouded her room. This time thoughts of Gram filled her head. Gram, who'd always insisted on healthy "fine, fresh air in the morning." Because of Gram, Lily had slept near an open window all her life. She reached up to unlatch it. *If Gram could only see me now. I'm actually here in her homeland.* Lily looked out at the pale pink streaks of clouds trailing across the sky. *Maybe she sees me...from the Great Somewhere.*

Glancing at the time, 5:30 a.m., she pulled the soft white bedspread and the lush blankets back up around her. It was way too early to get up. Obviously, she hadn't adjusted to the seven-hour time difference between Ireland and California. No wonder she wanted to go back to sleep.

Though she smelled the delicious aroma of coffee brewing, she closed her eyes and, pushing all thoughts of Eve's strange behavior out of her head, she let her plans for today spill through her thoughts. Patrick would pick her up right after breakfast. He'd promised that they would visit a primeval burial site and see inscriptions of the ancient shadowy people called Tuatha de Danaan who had lived here centuries before the Celts. She knew a little about them from her Celtic studies. When she'd told Patrick, he'd launched into some legends about the "dark little people," as the Irish called them....

Minutes later Lily drifted off again.

Hearing her alarm two hours later, she threw back the covers, eager to begin her day.

What to wear? She rummaged through her suitcase. Shopping for her trip had never been so much fun. Clothes two sizes smaller actually fit her now! And instead of trying on twenty-four outfits and finding only one that looked good, she'd had trouble limiting her purchases. In fact, she'd spent triple what her budget allowed on five different outfits.

Ah, here it is. The blouse that clung to her body just enough to hide the slight tummy bulge that hadn't yet disappeared. She moved toward the huge oval mirror and admired herself up close. The color of the aqua top made her eyes look more turquoise than green, contrasting with her hair and its new auburn highlights.

Heading for the bathroom, she showered, then selected her new leather boots, which Eve had talked her into ("C'mon, Lily, they're sexy. Go for 'em!"), and her black leggings. She zipped up the boots, her thighs looking thinner than she'd ever seen them.

Eager to show Eve her new look, she reached for the phone and punched in Eve's number. No answer. *Strange, maybe she's so tired she can't hear it.*

After dressing, fixing her hair and applying makeup, Lily made her way down the hall to knock on Eve's door. Still no answer. Suddenly she spotted her barefoot friend at the end of the long hall, swaying as she took each wobbly step forward, and carrying her heels in one hand. She was still in her black satin dress.

Should she worry? The jolt in Lily's stomach answered her question. Years ago she'd first witnessed Eve's drinking and learned about her one-night stands. The aftermath was always tears and fierce self-condemnation. Back then, she'd listened to Eve for hours, but finally she'd urged her friend to seek out a professional counselor.

But...she hasn't done this in a long time.

As Eve slowly staggered up the hall, Lily decided she wouldn't say a word to her. *It won't do any good.* She'd warned Eve about her escapades before, but her friend never listened. Years had gone by, years of promiscuity after her divorce. Then she'd taken up with Brad. *And what a prince he turned out to be.*

Lily could feel her own body sag as she watched her friend come forward in a drunken stupor. Dark thoughts bombarded her: Eve's rudeness, ignoring her while she used all her wiles to gain Patrick's attention, then her sarcastic jabs that felt like knives.

Raising one hand in a futile gesture, Lily took a few steps backward.

Eve waved back. "I know," she called. "Don't waste your breath, my chaste Irish maiden. Oh, and have a fabulous time with Patrick today. I'm kinda surprised you're going out with a complete stranger. But he's definitely hot."

Lily turned and nearly ran back down the hall toward her room. Something inside her felt crumpled up, squeezed out, like a sheet of worthless paper wadded into a ball and thrown away. She tried to focus on the day ahead. She'd been so excited a moment ago.

As soon as she entered her room, she heard the phone ringing. *Must be Patrick.* But no, it was a voice she never expected to hear.

CHAPTER 27

"*D*amn this hotel!" Standing outside her room, Eve fumbled with the key card, waiting for the green light to signal open. She tried again and again, cursing. Finally the light blinked and the locked clicked. She pushed the door open, nearly fell into the room and threw her purse on the bed. Barely remembering to close the door, she stripped down to her lacy black bra and thong, and then pulled the drapes shut. Rooting through her purse she found her cell phone, rescheduled her morning appointment for early afternoon, then burrowed under the blankets. "Well, I did something right," she murmured, glad the darkness could transform everything into nighttime. She promptly passed out.

When the alarm went off, Eve had no idea what time it was, but crawled out of bed to turn it off, happy she'd placed it far away, forcing her to get up. Pain battered her head, but she took a warm shower, hoping it would help. As soon as she was dressed, she checked her schedule. Her sales call loomed only minutes away. Thank god she'd suggested lunch in the hotel's restaurant downstairs.

Sean O'Sullivan, the head vintner from last night, took her hand as she joined him. "So how are you feelin' my pretty lass? If you don't mind me sayin' it, you're lookin' a little more tired now than you did last night."

She mustered a weak smile. "I'm okay, Mr. O'Sullivan. Just a little jet lag. You know how it is." She decided to let him do most of the talking. Men loved it when women listened. Besides, she was feeling too nauseous to carry on a decent conversation.

The waiter asked for their order. She decided on a Bloody Mary; it sometimes relieved her hangovers.

"You're a bit under the weather now, are you, lass?" O'Sullivan murmured.

She smiled again, wishing she'd postponed their meeting till tomorrow.

"If you're not up to a lunch today, we can always cut this short."

She nodded, noticing how the room seemed skewed, even slanted, and she couldn't quite focus on the vintner's face.

She tried to talk shop, with an opening about how California wine sales had risen in Ireland in the last few years, but kept an eye on the waiter, hoping her drink was on the way. Next, she asked O'Sullivan several leading questions and, sure enough, he lapsed into a lengthy description of Irish vineyards in County Cork, which produced most of Ireland's wines. When he started enumerating wine sales figures, however, she cut him off by clinking her Bloody Mary glass against his. She hoped he wouldn't ask her any questions, because she didn't remember a word he'd said.

"What wines are your best sellers? I'm interested in percentages."

Oh great. He did want figures. She reached down for her briefcase, hoping to locate her iPad, since she'd forgotten her laptop. But just looking down made her dizzy, and her stomach turned over as she sat back up. Suddenly she felt like she was either going to faint or.... She jumped up, grabbed her purse, excused herself and ran for the bathroom to heave. Sure enough, that's exactly what she did. A few minutes later, leaning on the counter in front of the mirror, she wiped her damp forehead and touched up the smeared makeup under her lashes. She tried rubbing lip gloss on her cheeks, but she was still pale, even a little green.

Way to go, Eve. You've now made a lasting impression on the head wine merchant in the Wine Geese organization.

When she arrived back at their table, she could see he was upset but was masking it with his charming Irish banter and broad smile. Nonetheless, she knew she'd ruined her glowing first impression from last night. She'd have to turn on all her glamour and charm at her second sales call, hopefully next week. All she could do now was try to mend things by promising to email him the wine data he'd asked for. Relief washed over her a minute later, before they'd even ordered, when he abruptly stood up to end their meeting, mentioning they "should get together sometime, but only after she'd had a good rest."

Back upstairs in her room, Eve knew better than to keep her next afternoon appointment. She called to postpone it, then closed the curtains and stripped down to her underwear again. By now she was sober enough to realize she'd seriously damaged her reputation with one of *the* most important wine clients in all of Ireland.

"Damn," she whispered under her breath, "I wouldn't have gone off to the bar and gotten in trouble if Lily hadn't decided to devote herself to that complete stranger last night, and me so worried she'd do something crazy with him—after all, the only man in her *whole entire life* was Frank—what does she think she's doing trusting the first man she meets in a foreign country? And she's out with him today too! I was trying to protect her, as always. But she never gets it."

She gave up then, closed her eyes and soon fell asleep.

...she was calling Lily, calling her to come over, though the place where Lily was sitting kept shifting and lace curtains blowing in the window suddenly erased her friend. Eve kept shouting but the curtains

wouldn't lift, and though she reached out a dozen times, her fingers couldn't touch the fabric. The fragile lace soon changed into thick material, concealing her friend completely. Eve moaned and kept calling Lily, but all her words turned into grunts. When the curtains suddenly blew up from a stronger wind, she glimpsed her friend, dwarfed now. She'd turned into a dark-haired Alice in Wonderland, with a silly, serene smile on her face, far away now, yet sitting at a bar, but deaf to Eve. Then a miniature Lily moved off into darkness as Eve tried to follow her, resorting to yelling. Finally her guttural sounds turned into words.

"Lily, where are you? Wait! Wait for me!"

Her own shrieking made her wake up, and she moved to the edge of her bed, shaken from the dream, only half awake. Looking up, she was captivated by a dark shadow standing near the door. "That you, Lily?" she said, her voice quivering. Silence. "I said, is that you?" Anger rose in her chest.

The shadow moved forward. It was a man, taller than Patrick or Ian or even Brad, the tallest man she'd ever known. "Dad?" She hadn't seen him in such a long time. His light blonde hair glowed, and he was wearing his old, familiar riding boots. His face was only vaguely visible, but it was tanned as always.

"Don't be afraid," he said. He put his hand out, palm up, as if reaching to hold hers. "I miss you, honey."

Or was he speaking at all? Maybe it was only her thoughts.

"Is it really you?" she whispered, feeling like she'd crossed into another time zone. "I miss you too." She fought back tears and moved out of bed toward him.

The dark specter shifted, becoming only shadowed patches, and in seconds, her father dissolved completely. She found herself staring at the hotel room door.

Eve began to sob. "No. Don't do this! It tears me up inside. You always disappear. Even when you were...alive."

A counselor had once told her to write down her thoughts after startling dreams like this. She picked up a sheet of hotel stationery, found a pen and began to write.

Why? Why does he always leave me? Or send me away? All my life...

Especially at parties...he'd tell me to go upstairs, go outside, watch TV, anything. He'd rather laugh with Lily's mom and the neighbors.

Sometimes he did want me, though. We'd go off, just the two of us, ride our horses, camp together, make a fire and sing songs. So...maybe he did love me.

But he drove away, so many times... Why? My fault...because before he left he'd look at me with those sad blue eyes.

It always turned ugly when Mom was there. Fiery words back and forth, and she'd pick up heavy things and go at Dad...his hands covering his head. Then he was silent. Afterward, he was sure to leave.

And I'd be alone. For days.

CHAPTER 28

"*H*ow's my faerie garden friend?" The old woman's voice on the phone was like a warm shower of Irish bliss.

Lily's spirits lifted. "Maeve! Where are you? You, of all people, to call me here in Ireland. Today's only the third day of our trip."

"Don't you know I already know that, my young lassie? It was me who lavished praise on that marvelous hotel where you're stayin'. Don't you remember? Or was it your lovely friend I told?"

Lily gazed out the window, admiring how the sun was finally peeking out from behind a mass of white clouds. *That's funny*, she thought, *Eve never mentioned she talked to Maeve. And it was Maeve's idea to stay here.*

"Well then," Lily said, "I guess you get all the credit. I never dreamed I'd find myself in a posh hotel like this. I'm told famous people like Julia Roberts and Bono come here."

Maeve chuckled. "Wait till you see the garden across the street. I'm glad you're startin' to realize who's got the 'scoop,' as they say in the States, about the best sights over here."

"So you're here in Ireland?" Lily asked.

"Of course I am, child. I told you a while ago that me Seamus was flyin' me back to the Emerald Isle. I'm callin' you now so I'll be the first to show you the best gardens around--faerie gardens and Celtic sights that'll fill your Irish soul with glee. My promise to you, lass."

"How exciting!"

"I want me Seamus to meet you, and Eve, too."

Lily knew she was running late for her date, so the next few minutes were a rush of words to set up a meeting with Maeve. When she left her hotel room and went downstairs, she found Patrick at the front desk directing the tall concierge she'd met the day before to ring her room. Smiling, he put the phone down.

As she met Patrick's gaze, Eve's warning drifted through her thoughts. Her stomach tightened at the prospect of going out with someone she barely knew. *Frank's only been gone a few months. But what did we have together anyway?* She suddenly felt shy, too, but the twinkle in his eyes banished some of her anxiety.

"When, may I ask, is such a fine-lookin' lady ever on time?" he said, as he put his hand on his hip.

She had to smile. "Thank you for the backhanded compliment. Which, by the way, is a bit of Irish blarney, but I can use it this morning." She was amazed her words spilled out so easily. *I'm positively brazen!* she thought. It was so unlike her to banter with someone she hardly knew, especially a man. *Forgive me, Frank.* Though his face had intruded on her thoughts a couple times this morning, she realized what she was feeling now wasn't really fear or guilt. It was more like frenzied nervousness, but coupled with delight too. Why shouldn't she have some fun, after years in a lackluster relationship?

When Patrick stepped forward, she took his arm, and he steered her outside where his silver Opal waited. She settled next to him, feeling unusually comfortable. Soon they'd left Dublin and were speeding along narrow roads surrounded by green slopes dotted with grazing sheep. Despite the fact that she didn't know Patrick well, she felt at ease to talk about anything. After a few pleasantries, she settled in to admire the scenery.

"So," she asked, after a while, "is our destination a secret? Or are you going to tell me where we're headed? I'm keeping a journal of my trip." She took a small spiral notebook out of her purse and showed it to him.

"Well," he said, "we're headin' to *the* most renowned ancient burial ground in all of Ireland. It should 'knock your socks off,' to use a crazy idiom from the States."

Lily was fascinated at how Patrick could sound American and then quickly take up the brogue. "You must've lived in my fair country once," she quipped. "Your speech sounds like mine, then all of sudden you're talking like an Irishman."

"A checkered past, I have," was all he said. Since he kept his eyes on the road, she wasn't sure if he was joking. He'd certainly not revealed much about his past last night.

"Ah," she said, hoping he'd disclose more, "but Irish tales of the past are my cup of tea. Didn't you know that?"

He ignored her hint. "That's what you were saying last evenin'. And that's why I'll be showin' you these sights today."

Now that they'd left the city, Lily admired a flat green valley under a never-ending azure ceiling of feathery clouds. As he drove, Patrick told her anecdotes about his growing-up years with his brothers, which Lily enjoyed.

"What's the name of that river in the distance?" she asked during a pause in his stories. "And that round, flat hill?"

"That, me lady, is the River Boyne, bendin' its way near Newgrange, one of the finest passage tombs in all of Europe. It's as ancient as they come, i'tis, built in the Neolithic Age. Goes back to 5,200 years ago. 'Long before the Celts came here and even before the Egyptian pyramids at Giza were built." He pulled into a parking area. "Want to give it a go?"

A thrill she didn't recognize raced through Lily. These were the burial places of the ancient people who lived here even before the Celts! She moved to the edge of her seat and grabbed the door handle.

"Whoa, me lady, don't jump out till I stop this mare."

Patrick parked the car, and they were soon circling around twelve upright boulders or *menhirs*, he called them, standing in the grass. "Historians believe these were placed here after this mound was completed, sometime between 2200 and 3000 B.C.E.," he said.

"What strange, beautiful stones. This reminds me of pictures I've seen of Stonehenge in England. These are smaller, though. Have you ever visited there?"

"Yes." But he offered nothing more about his travels as he led her to the stone circle around a modern building that protected the pit grave. "But, can you believe it? These boulders are a couple hundred years older than Stonehenge."

The awe in his tone stopped her. She looked up, marveling at how the standing stones pointed up to the sky. "How were these heavy stones placed here?" she wondered out loud. "How could those primitive people possibly move them? What were they trying to say?"

"They figured out how to move them, so I guess they weren't as primitive as we like to think. Scholars don't know why, but they think the ancients were preoccupied with how the light marked the changin' of seasons and the passage of time. Come on, I'll show you."

Their tickets purchased, they followed a few other sightseers to the tomb's entrance, and Patrick pointed to a window-like opening above it. "If you come here at dawn during the winter solstice— between December 19th and the 23rd," he said, "you'll see a narrow beam of sunlight shine right through this opening, and on through the long tunnel and into the shadowed chamber inside. Photos show it illuminated completely—it's phenomenal! Though today we'll be in darkness."

"How magical—that's the winter solstice, isn't it?"

"Yes, the darkest time of the year. Think of it, Lily. When the sunrise lit this chamber in mid December, the ancient people marked the beginning of their next year. But some scholars say the people were afraid the darkness would remain and the sun might not continue on its path, so they performed rituals to guide it toward the warmth of spring."

"Brilliant, weren't they?"

Patrick smiled down at her and nodded. She noticed his thickly lashed eyes and that same twinkle in his eyes again, and all of sudden she wanted to get to know him better. This was a brand new feeling too, and she sensed he felt the same.

She stopped to study the large, horizontal entrance stone in front of them, carved with ever-expanding spirals. They reminded her of the ones printed on her grandmother's green scarf, the one she'd worn as a child at the Celtic faire.

Her mind suddenly fixed on another memory: Gram O'Keefe's old quilt, made from leftover bits of blue and green fabric, mostly scraps from Lily's childhood dresses. Gram's patched artwork was lovely, but her stitches of repeating whorls all over the quilt were *just like* the ones on this famous stone. While tracing the circling stitches with her fingers, Lily would never forget what Gram told her. "Life is like a quilt," she'd said many times. "You'll walk all kinds of paths, my Lily, up and down and around to places you never thought you'd go. Right on through the patchwork of life. You won't think you're ever going to find your way out of the confusing circles life brings, but eventually, you do. And mind you, child, before you reach your end, *you must get lost*, not once but many times. Losing your way and getting hurt will happen, lass. But, above all, you must take the path yourself. Remember though, at

185

the end, when you finally discover your true way, you'll realize the search itself is the mystery of it all, and the fun of it, too."

Patrick interrupted her reverie. "Hello? Are you still here?" The kindness in his eyes convinced her even more that he wasn't a stranger at all.

"Sorry. I guess I was daydreaming." Lily reached out and traced the circular grooves in the large stone with her finger. "These spirals remind me of my Irish grandmother, that's all."

"So, she knew about them, did she?"

"Yes, she must have. I saw these whorls long ago, stitched into the quilts she made for me. I think she was a lot wiser about this wild land and its inhabitants than I ever realized."

"Irish grandmothers have deep and wonderful ways," he said. "Especially the O'Malleys. You were lucky to have her."

"Well actually, her name was O'Keefe. Why do you say that?" Lily asked.

"Oh, uh...yes, that's right, the O'Malleys are on your dad's side. And I unearthed some history about them. Their territory was small, so they took to the sea and were legendary for their maritime prowess. In fact, in the 1500s the famous Grace O'Malley was known as a renowned sea captain. She killed her lover's murderers, and led her men into battle. Quite a female heritage you have!"

"Really? I can hardly believe a woman could become so famous back then."

"You have lots to learn about Celtic women. They were very strong and held in high regard by their men." Lily heard pride in Patrick's voice.

He gestured for Lily to follow the tour guide and step ahead of him. "You'll see more art in this tomb," he went on to explain, "and it's full of spirals, as well as zigzagged chevrons, triangles and other arcs. No one is sure what it all means. Some say the art depicts maps of this area or star formations or even the afterworld. Many agree the symbols represent the changin' seasons. The ancients were preoccupied with how spring followed winter, and they believed new life followed death."

Patrick's last phrase triggered a chill up Lily's spine.

"You look like you've seen a ghost, you've turned so pale," he said.

"No, Eve's the one who's always believed in ghosts. Not me. It's just that, well, my husband Frank, he...he passed away only a few months ago...."

"Oh, I'm sorry. I didn't know. Maybe you shouldn't go in after all." The concern in Patrick's tone comforted her.

"It's okay. Really. I believe in the afterlife, but maybe not quite like these ancients did, but...in these last few months, it's given me some peace. I was brought up Catholic, and though I haven't practiced in years, I believe the risen Christ promised us life after death. I clung to that belief to get through Frank's illness and passing. Though he's gone now, I'm sure his spirit lives on. Don't worry. Let's go on."

She felt his strong hand on her shoulder for a moment, reminding her of her brother Colin's protective ways. She took her place in a single-file line behind the other tourists and bent her head to enter the dark tunnel.

"There are lots of theories about why this passage tomb was built and what it means," Patrick whispered behind her. She could feel his breath on her cheek, he was so close, and a faint scent of mint.

The same rush as before streaked through her—a dash of joy, but mixed with quickening heartbeats this time. She wondered what these feelings meant. Maybe it was hearing about her ancient ancestors. Or...maybe not. He seemed so glad to share all this with her. Irish tales had fascinated her all her life, but this excitement when Patrick came near was hard to fathom. It made her breath skip.

"You probably want to hear more about this mysterious place, eh?" he said.

"Oh, yes."

Was it curiosity that was sending tingles through her?

As she stepped into the dim stillness of the tunnel, with only the guide's flashlight leading them forward, she began to feel something else, an unmistakable aura, a kind of spiritual presence engulfing her. Thoughts of Eve also flooded her mind. She'd always talked about her strange dreams and her visions of her dad. Did the dead not "go to heaven," after all? Did they still reside here and roam about the earth? That's what Eve believed. Was that what she was sensing now? No, not Frank's...but ancient spirits?

Lily noticed Patrick's silence. Maybe he, too, felt these otherworldly sensations. She shivered, sniffing the suddenly cold, musty air as she moved forward in the shadowy passageway.

Finally, crowded among the other tourists, in complete darkness now, they reached the inner chamber and stood still for what seemed like an interminable few moments. Trembling a little, an unmistakable alarm took hold of her...yes, spirits *did* still dwell here. She felt them. The guide began speaking and Lily forced herself to concentrate. He told how archeologists had discovered ancient skeletons here. With his flashlight, he illuminated side recesses where two stone basins sat. "Those were made by Neolithic carvers," he said. "Once they held remains, some human, some animal bones. Ashes were found here also, next to bone beads and small stone balls—indicating ancient burial rituals took place here."

The cold enveloped Lily now and her throat constricted. She began to shiver. It was as if the dead still roamed here and might control her. She held herself rigid, trying to fight back the peculiar, chilling presence overwhelming her. She had to keep calm and maintain her own inner power.

Finally the guide turned around and led their group back down the sixty-foot tunnel toward the entrance, but he stopped suddenly to flash his light on another design of three conjoined spirals carved on the wall. The sight of it brought up images of Gram's quilts again, and Lily felt a gradual warmth spreading through her. Finally her shivering disappeared.

When they were safely outside and beyond the stone circle, Patrick smiled down at her, though worry filled his eyes. "You were awfully quiet in there," he said. "Do you think an Irish pub will bring some color back to those cheeks?"

CHAPTER 29

*A*s Patrick guided her through the crowded pub, Lily took everything in: worn oak panels on every wall, shining from the light of wrought-iron chandeliers, the gleaming brass rail around the bar and open shelves above, crammed with whiskey bottles and mugs.

After finding them a place to sit on a bench with comfy green cushions, Patrick headed to the bar and promptly returned with two mugs of Irish ale. At the same time, a fiddler began playing and everyone began to clap. Lily was surprised at how many families were gathered here with children of all ages sitting next to their parents. Several men were hovering near the bar too.

"This is the real Ireland, i'tis." Patrick clinked his mug against hers and winked. "And this lovely ale will soon be chasin' away all those ancient ghosts, for sure, lass." He took a drink, grinned and set his mug down. "That is, as long as we don't drink too many pints."

"I love it when you lapse into your brogue," she said.

"Did you feel it too?" She brought the mug up to her lips. "I mean, for a while there, I was wondering if the ancient spirits might carry me off to who knows where."

"Ireland's full of strange ghosts, banshees and otherworldly beings. Hooligans, too. Better get used to it, lass!" He laughed and took another swig of ale.

As the fiddling ended, Lily's cell phone rang. All she needed to hear was Eve's "Hi!" and her stomach began to stir.

"What're you up to?" Eve asked. "My sales appointments are done for the day. So I thought I'd find out where you are." The gaiety in her voice sounded forced.

Lily tried to summon up a cheerful tone of her own. "Patrick and I are at a pub not far from the hotel. Want to join us?"

After Lily had given directions and hung up, Patrick said, "Your friend is quite the flirt, I've noticed."

Lily nodded. "Yes, I guess she is."

"Why are you turnin' so glum now, my lassie?"

She appreciated his effort to cheer her with his lilting brogue. "I'm not glum," she said, placing her hand on the table. "Just a little tired, I guess."

"Tired of tourin' already? Or tired of your friend?" His hand brushed hers.

She didn't move, aware of the new sensations she felt.

This man was perceptive. He'd noticed Eve's obvious come-on last night, to him and every man in the room. Again, Lily thought of her brother Colin, a take-care-of-everyone guy whom she sorely missed. But there was something else about him...something that moved her.

Not quite ten minutes later, Eve breezed into the pub, though not before Lily had managed to squeeze a few more tidbits out of Patrick. She learned that he'd studied genealogy as a hobby for most of his life and had visited the United States as well as several other countries. Offhandedly, he mentioned he'd "just embarked on a third career, writin' articles about ancient sites like Newgrange."

She was trying to find out what his first two careers had been when Eve squeezed in beside her with a full pint in her hands. She'd headed straight to the bar and ordered it herself, in spite of Patrick's protests to get it for her.

"Hi, there!" she said in her brightest tone. As she began to question them about their day, the fiddler started up again.

Glad she couldn't carry on a conversation, Lily timed her glances to study her friend. Eve looked hung over and checked her cell phone at least three times before the fiddler finished playing. "Did you schedule a late sales meeting?" Lily's asked her.

"Not at this hour. I wouldn't want to tie up my evenings with business and leave *you* in the lurch."

Lily couldn't miss Eve's sarcastic tone. Or...was she imagining it?

"Oh, there's Ian!" Eve exclaimed, as she turned toward the door to see him enter and wave at Eve before heading for the bar.

Lily recognized him from the night before, his tousled hair and that distinct, unshaven look she didn't care for.

"I remember *him*, all right." Patrick's voice was as hard as his icy dark eyes. He slaked his thirst, emptying his mug, then jolted up to order another.

Aware that Patrick's sudden departure made her nervous, Lily watched him stride toward the bar, then suddenly redirect his course to join Ian. Looking over Eve's shoulder, Lily saw Ian spy Patrick then quickly veer over to the far corner of the bar, slipping behind two brawny men knitted together in a drunken slouch. Neither man would let Patrick by, but stood like a wall, protecting Ian and forcing Patrick back as if inviting a fight.

Eve, who was facing Lily, couldn't see any of this. "My, my," she said, "you sure seem mesmerized by men these days. Can't take your eyes off of them."

Yes, it was the cutting sarcasm she'd used on others. But now... *I'm her target.* "Why are you using that tone with me?" she said. Eve glared back, but Lily went on, "I thought we came on this trip to have fun together. I don't want to get into a tiff with you."

"What are you talking about? Why are you so super-sensitive?"

She recognized Eve's reaction. Lily had seen her do this with other women, and they usually backed down. But never to her. Lily knew the best way to get her point across was to do the one thing Eve hated. Ignore her. Patrick's return to their table gave her the opportunity.

"What was that all about?" she asked him. "When Ian saw you, he looked like he'd seen a ghost."

Patrick's eyes were still cold. "That he did."

"Ian?" Eve turned around, scouring the room. "He just got here. Where is he now?"

"He high-tailed it out the back door when he saw me."

"Why?"

"It's better he did." Patrick took a drink. "He used to be nothin' but a hoodlum. Now he's plenty dangerous, and that's understatin' it. Around here, people label him a sociopath and I'd believe them if I were you. There was a time I didn't, but I was dead wrong, and found out the hard way. He never thought he'd lay eyes on me again. That's why he disappeared just now."

"You've got to be kidding!" Eve's tone was full of skepticism. "I was with him last night and he was—well, let's just say I had a fantastic time."

Lily's mind reeled with memories of Eve staggering down the hall that very morning.

Patrick's face turned serious. "You don't know me well, I'm sure of that, but if you did, lass, you'd pay mind to my warnin'. Pardon my frankness, but that man brings nothin' but trouble, and you'll rue the day you met him if you keep seein' him."

Eve leveled a cool gaze at Patrick. "I just love your Irish faerie tales." With that, she picked up her mug and made for the corner of the bar, where the group of men were swaying and laughing together.

Patrick watched her go. "That lass is full of herself and stubborn," he said. "Lily, how well do you know her? Can you talk her out of pursuin' Ian, or does she always have her way?"

"We've been good friends—for over thirty years." Lily knew she was sipping her ale too fast. "She can be stubborn, but normally she has good judgment. Lately though, uh, . . .not so much. I'm not sure what's gotten into her. I'll talk to her again about Ian. Is he really *that* dangerous?"

"Treacherous enough to kill someone. Maybe more than one," Patrick said.

CHAPTER 30

*W*hen Lily stepped into the Dublin teashop they'd selected as their meeting place, Maeve greeted her with open arms and an impish smile. She looked like a pixy this morning, dressed in a green plaid tam and matching scarf. Her white dress matched her hair and hugged her petite figure. Leather boots completed her modern look. "It's so good to see you, my lass. Where is your friend Eve today? I thought you'd be bringin' her with you too. I wanted you both to meet me son. I've got lots of treats planned."

"Oh, I thought I told you," Lily said. "She had to work today. She plans to land plenty of wine orders for the California winery she represents while we're in Ireland. I'm going to meet her later, though."

As the minutes sped by, Lily was surprised at how easy it was to chatter on and on with this sprite of an Irish lady. She'd really only spent time with her two—no, three times. They spent the next hour sipping Irish tea and eating scones slathered with strawberry jam, while Maeve plied Lily with questions about the wine banquet and the hotels where she and Eve planned to stay.

"My hotel room is perfect, and I hear the hotel in Kinsale is wonderful too," Lily said. "Oh, I know, lass. I'm so glad your friend liked all me suggestions," Maeve chimed in, describing more sightseeing ideas as Lily wondered again what Maeve meant.

When the plump waitress asked if she could bring more tea, Maeve nodded, then glanced at her watch and gazed through the window to scan the street outside. "Me son is suppose to be pickin' me up here soon, he is. Why don't you come with us this mornin', my dear? I had it all planned. You just told me Eve will be busy, but Seamus is plannin' on takin' us over to the college to show us around. He's so proud to be goin' to Trinity for his studies and all. A famous book is displayed there...I've forgotten its name." She held up her finger, landing it on her left temple. "It's bound to come round in a minute."

"*The Book of Kells?*" asked Lily.

"That's it, my dear."

Just then the door swung open and a tall, brawny man swept in. His presence seemed to fill the entire room. His dark hair was almost collar-length and neat, except for a liberal graying at the temples. With intense blue eyes he scrutinized Lily and then brandished a flashing smile edged with laugh lines. She noticed the deep dimple in his cheek as she stood up, and then she was enveloped in his warm, strong arms, savoring a fresh scent of pine.

As they settled around the table again, he surveyed them both. "I'm surrounded by two gorgeous women here, even though ya say the third is workin' today, and it's a gorgeous morning." His smile was magnetic and he was looking straight at Lily. "We need to move along. I've arranged a special tour so we don't have to wait on those long tourist lines. Then we'll have lunch at me favorite pub. Now how does that sound to ya?"

Lily hesitated. She'd promised Eve she'd meet her for lunch at their hotel. She'd never make it if she went on this tour.

Seamus leaned closer. "Why, you're not going to let us down, are you, lass? *The Book of Kells* is famous among the Irish, and you *are* Irish. I can see it as plain as your green eyes lookin' back at me. So, it's settled, isn't it?"

Lily couldn't resist. "You're right, I can't pass it up." She excused herself and called Eve, leaving a message about turning their lunch into a dinner date instead. Eve hadn't returned her call last night anyway and had barely spoken to her this morning. Apparently she was still miffed about Patrick's warning last night.

She probably went out with Ian last night in spite of Patrick's words. Lily's stomach tightened at the thought, and she couldn't help wondering if her old ulcer pains were going to spoil her time today. She popped a pill as a tinge of relief came over her; she realized for the first time she was glad to put off seeing her friend.

Done, Eve said to herself. *Three sales calls in one morning. That's a record. But snagging three large orders in four hours?—Phenomenal!* "Woohoo!" she yelled out loud inside her car, not a regular occurrence but sometimes it *felt* good to shout. Especially on the day that marked the beginning of her sales expansion in Ireland. She switched on the radio to play hit tunes as she maneuvered her car out of the parking lot of The Stone House restaurant. An array of her California vintages would now be sold regularly here, as well as another restaurant in the southern region of Cork County the owner had urged her to call on, since his brother was the owner. She planned a visit soon. She sang along with the radio as she opened her purse to look for her phone.

Stopping at an intersection, she checked for messages then listened to Lily's voicemail. "Shit! She's going off to Trinity College without me." *Busy, busy, busy. First with Patrick—now Maeve and Seamus. Where do I come in? She wouldn't even be here if I hadn't talked her into it.*

Eve managed the wheel with one hand while she punched out a text message to Ian. She'd been with him this morning—*truly an amazing time!*—but she didn't want to eat lunch alone again, plus she'd decided to take the afternoon off. When she didn't get a reply, she checked Lily's tour book and drove from Blackrock to Dalkey, a lovely seacoast resort town a few miles from Dublin. She scanned the streets for another pub and finally spotted a famous one. *Finnigan's, just the place for me!*

Once seated at the bar between two locals, she ordered a meal and began to flirt. Using her regular opening, she asked the men one at a time how they liked the local wines. Pretty soon the bartender joined in, and thirty minutes later the owner did too. By the time lunch was over and they'd all finished another bottle of wine, Eve was saying good-bye with another sizeable wine order tucked in her purse. Ian had never answered her text, but she'd decided she wasn't going to leave this pub alone. The best looking guy out of the foursome was leading her out to his car. Of course, she'd made an excuse to the owner that they were going sightseeing, but that was the furthest notion from her mind. *So many wasted months pining over Brad,* she thought. There was something so freeing about sampling the Irish men here as well as the brew. *Lily can have what's his name...Patrick...or for that matter, Seamus too. I don't care! I can walk into a pub in Ireland and have any man I want!*

CHAPTER 31

The Trinity College campus wasn't as massive as Lily had expected. She and Maeve followed Seamus as he showed them the main quadrangle and proudly explained, as they walked around, that Trinity was the oldest and most respected university in Ireland and a sister university to Oxford in Britain.

Soon they found themselves inside, moving along with the tour, to view the glass cases displaying *The Book of Kells*. The 1,220-year-old manuscript had been salvaged quite by chance after marauders destroyed everything of value in most Catholic monasteries in Ireland. She and Maeve stood for several minutes in front of the first glass case, studying the lively decorations bordering each page of the book in brightly colored, and silver and gold braided patterns, intertwined with images of animals and humans. Lily gazed at a lion head at the bottom of the page; its body twisted upward among the Celtic twinings and became a hawk. A snake's head appeared at the top border, its body slithering down the page in twists and turns until it emerged as a bear. She remembered what she'd learned in her classes:

The Celts believed in shape-shifting all during their lives and after death too. In their minds it was normal for animals to transform into other animals or for humans to take the shape of a bird, a selkie (seal) or other animal, sometimes temporarily, sometimes forever.

"Look, here's their shape-shifting beliefs in living color," Lily mused out loud. "Even though this is a Catholic Bible, the Irish monks were still holding fast to ancient Celtic myths.Seamus leaned closer to her. "How do you know about this amazing book, lass?"

"I studied a little about the Celts back home, but only for a semester. These designs remind me of their shape-shifting beliefs, that's all. It's fascinating."

"Yes, that it is. Celtic study is my area too. I'm here tryin' to get my doctorate in anthropology, so I can go back to the U.S. and teach. I've just begun takin' two courses in Celtic studies here."

"Really? What a great opportunity!" As she moved to the next glass, case Lily wondered why a man of Seamus' age (he must be fortyish) would be excited about attending college.

Seamus joined her. "I've never heard anyone compare these designs to shape-shifting before, but now I see it, lass! I've learned about some of their symbols, but I'm going to look up what these animal designs meant."

"Well," Lily said, "I'm sure scholars have noticed this long before I did."

Just then Lily was distracted by a bird sitting on a ledge outside, pecking at the glass window in front of her. She'd seen it once before, but couldn't remember where. White with gray and black feathers and a splash of red on its head, it pecked again as if communicating with her. *Strange,* she thought, as she watched it fly away then return. Tap, tap, tap. Then it flew off for good. Suddenly she remembered...a bird just like it had visited her faerie garden at home. *Strange, indeed!*

She stole a glance at the dimple in Seamus' cheek as he smiled down at her. He obviously hadn't seen the bird. His gaze seemed to summon her to take a daring swim. *I could get lost in his blue ocean!* But she turned away and walked to the next case so he wouldn't notice the blush she felt warming her cheeks.

"Do you believe in shape-shifting then, as the Celts did?" she asked. "See, here it is again on this next page. That deer is turning into a hare. I've also read that the Celts believed rabbits were a sign of rebirth and good fortune. What did they believe about birds?"

"Aw, you're not just a beautiful lass, you're a smart one too!" He moved closer to Lily, and she felt his warmth as she breathed in his clean scent.

Suddenly a bit breathless, she lowered her eyes, trying to distract herself by scouring the room. Where had Maeve gone? She'd come in with them and stood right beside Lily at first, but now she'd disappeared. "Where's your mother?"

"Talk about shifting shapes, me mother is a master at it." He seemed to be joking, but Lily wasn't sure. "Don't worry, she'll reappear any minute.

"And you asked about birds?" Seamus said. "They had different meanings for the Celts. Sometimes faerie folk appeared to humans as birds. And sometimes birds carried potent messages warning someone to stay home, not continue their journey, even foretelling bloodshed."

A streak of fear stopped Lily and she shivered. *An omen?* She quickly moved behind Seamus into the crowd.

Finally, Seamus looked at his watch. "We'd better be moseying over to the pub soon. You must be hungry. The lunch crowd is probably leavin', and the luck of the Irish is with us—I don't have to go to me classes all afternoon."

He steered her through the throng of tourists marooned in the gift shop, making a path for Lily so she could buy a book that explained *The Book of Kells*. She felt like a princess as Seamus opened the door for her amidst the stifling movement of the crowd. Soon he was maneuvering her toward the campus gardens. As they walked along, he introduced her to students and professors alike. *He's only been here a few months,* she thought, *yet he seems to know everyone.* She couldn't help comparing him with Frank, whose friends she could count on one hand. Seamus' upbeat words to each person was vastly different than the quiet, somber husband with whom she'd spent twenty years.

When Seamus opened the car door for her, he leaned in close, the touch of his fingers on her arm sending shivers through her, a totally new feeling. Never with Frank. Not with anyone.

She felt his breath again on her neck too. But she didn't dare turn around to face him or say anything. Instead she quickly slid into his car, and he closed the door.

Where's Maeve? she wondered again, and finally asked aloud.

"She'll meet us at the pub. I'm sure of it, lass." Seamus began showing her a few sights in Dublin, driving down one street and another, and now he was heading across the famous O'Connell Bridge, lit with twinkling lights now that dusk was near. He turned into a busy thoroughfare, gestured toward an imposing pub called Madigan's and parked the car across the street.

He was right. As soon as Seamus found a booth for them, Maeve walked right up to their table, her eyes alight with merriment.

"So how was your tour, me girl?" she asked, as she sat down next to Lily.

"Fascinating," Lily retorted. "Where'd you go? I was worried about you, but Seamus assured me you were fine."

"Me mother has some strange ways sometimes, she does," Seamus said. "But you'll get used to it, lass."

Maeve only smiled—and a glorious beaming pixie smile it was.

They were finishing their pub grub when Lily heard a familiar signal on her cell phone, a new text message from Eve: "Can't make it for dinner. Got an offer I couldn't refuse. Meet me for breakfast tomorrow at eight instead. Let's check out early."

Lily began to worry. Was Eve hell bent on getting in trouble again? *First Brad, now Ian.*

She mustered a cheerful tone, "Guess I'll get to bed early. Eve cancelled our dinner date. That's good. I'm tired."

"Tired, bah! Who do you think you're foolin', lass? Young as you are, all you need is a wee nap." Seamus flashed an alluring grin at her, then at his mum. "Why don't you both come out with me tonight? You're in luck. I have tickets for a play here in Dublin and no one to go with. We're sure to have fun."

Lily stood up suddenly. "I'll think about it, but now I must find the Ladies room."

Seamus chuckled. "You mean the *loo*?"

A bit embarrassed at her ignorance, Lily wound her way to the back of the pub as scrambled thoughts bombarded her. This was all becoming a bit too much. She hardly knew these people and she was spending more time with strangers these days than her best friend.

By the time she'd combed her hair and put on fresh lip gloss, though, she'd changed her mind. "On second thought, why not?" An image of Seamus crowded out her worries—his broad shoulders, his merry blue eyes. She gazed at herself in the mirror. *Yes, why not? What's to fear? Maeve will come too. It's an opportunity to see a real Irish play right in the middle of Dublin. When will I ever get that chance again?*

CHAPTER 32

*A*s twilight cast shadows on the Dublin streets, Seamus walked with Lily through a maze of theater-goers outside the famous Abbey Theater. Many people looked their way as they entered. Was that envy in the women's eyes? *In a million years, I never thought I'd see that!*

Earlier she'd dressed with care, wishing Eve had been around to help her. Knowing her friend owed her a favor, Lily used the extra room key and borrowed Eve's silver sequined top, which sparkled just enough and matched her dangle earrings perfectly. Glimpsing her reflection now in the lobby's mirrored walls she was doubly thrilled tonight at her slim profile. She'd lost a few more pounds. *Imagine! I'm wearing one of Eve's outfits!*

Lily had actually never worn dangle earrings. Even though her daughters had nagged her for years, "Mom, you need more bling," her husband had made it clear he didn't like it. *Forgive me, Frank,* she said to herself, *I need to do some things my way now.*

She turned away from the mirrors and looked up at Seamus, marveling that she was actually on a real date with this amazing

Irish man. *Who would've thought that meeting his mother Maeve in a Pasadena garden shop would lead to this special night?*

"I can read your thoughts, lass," Seamus said, his eyes flashing.

"You can? Then you know how excited I am!"

"Aye, I'm happy too. Me date is the most beautiful woman in the room."

She didn't know how to respond. This was only the second date of her life. First Patrick, now Seamus. All the others were with Frank long ago, and he'd termed it "hanging out." No one else had ever asked her. No one ever called her *beautiful* either. Overcome, she turned away from his penetrating gaze. "This is gorgeous artwork lining the walls," she said, "an extra I didn't expect."

"Yes, these paintings are renowned here in Dublin. Local Irish artists. No one has made off with one yet, either," Seamus said. "Me mother loves them. I brought her here a few weeks ago. Too bad she couldn't join us tonight—her health isn't what it used to be, lass."

Lily was mystified that Maeve seemed so unreliable at times, but Seamus' comment seemed to clear up her questions for now. She remembered Maeve's strange change of mood on New Year's Day and wondered if her health might've been the cause.

They made their way to the Abbey Bar to indulge in a cocktail before the play. The low music and plush surroundings ramped up Lily's mood as she meandered with Seamus around the room. One painting looked like an French Impressionist piece, but she knew it wasn't.

Lily sipped a French Pinot Noir from a sparkling glass. "I'll tell Eve about this famous bar. I know she'd love to call on the manager and sell him some California wines."

"Oh, I didn't know she was in the wine business. The manager's son is an acquaintance of mine—he's a doctoral student too. That's why we didn't have to stand in line. I could introduce them, if I ever meet Eve. She's a busy lass, isn't she?"

"Yes, she's spending her days calling on restaurants, hotels and places like this in Dublin, as well as other places we visit. So far, she's booked several large orders."

They made their way to their theater seats and settled into them. "And you?" Seamus asked. "What about you, lass? I've heard that you've been studying landscape design, besides, of course, bein' steeped in Celtic lore, as I've noticed. Me Mum told me one of her friends was duly impressed when she heard about your state awards. I think she'd do well to hire you, perhaps as an intern. Did she already mention it to you?"

Lily was shocked. "Why no, Maeve never said anything. I'm totally flattered."

Before Lily could dwell anymore on this strange piece of news, the lights began to flicker, on-off, on-off. The play was about to begin. As the music began and the lights dimmed, Lily began to imagine herself working in a lush Irish garden. *But how did Maeve know about my awards?* She was certain she'd never mentioned them. She'd even forgotten about them herself, since both awards had arrived in the mail right after Frank was hospitalized. *Me?— working here in Ireland? How incredible.*

As Seamus touched Lily's hand, then clasped it in both of his, Lily muffled a gasp. She actually felt a curious electricity! So this is what other women talked about...

As the curtains opened on George Bernard Shaw's *Pygmalion*, she settled back in her seat to soak up the magic of these moments.

CHAPTER 33

The windshield wipers whined as Eve maneuvered their rental car through the winding country roads on their way out of Dublin. Back and forth, back and forth...its monotonous rhythm echoed the dullness of the day. The dark sky and driving rain seemed to fit her mood and Lily's too, apparently.

Eve glanced briefly at her friend, who sat beside her leafing through her tour book, and decided she wasn't going to break the silence between them. She'd said "Good morning" to Lily earlier, but all she'd gotten in return was a grunt, and silence ever since. That response didn't surprise her. Whenever Lily was miffed, she became sort of passive aggressive. Eve knew Lily would eventually capitulate, or at least she thought she knew.

After all, it wasn't *her* fault they hadn't shared many meals or gone sightseeing together. Plus, she'd made sure she'd left a message for her friend last night that breakfast today would be impossible since Ian had kept her out so late. Of course, she'd hadn't told Lily that last part. But overall, Eve reasoned, Lily was the one who'd been gone lately, gone all day and night yesterday and the day before too.

Plus, my priority has to be my sales calls. It had paid off too. She'd secured plenty of wine orders, and if she'd squeezed in some unexpected playtime with Ian and that other guy too, well that was her business. And, Lily certainly didn't seem to be lacking for things to do...for a change. Eve had always wondered how her friend had put up with such a quiet, uneventful life all those years with Frank and the girls. *She's certainly making up for it now.*

As rain pelted the windshield, Eve thought about last night. Just as she'd stepped into the soothing bath water at around four o'clock, her cell phone rang. Ian wanted to see her right away. How could she refuse? Besides she loved spontaneity—even though Lily seemed to detest it—plus, she wouldn't get to see Ian for a few days, now that she and Lily were on the road again. And well...Lily couldn't possibly grasp *what an awesome time* they'd had last night... Yeah, he could be a little rough, but just on the edge, and that's what made it unforgettable.

Overall, she'd realized she never knew what to expect from Ian. First, he was all over her with attention and the next time he would barely say a word. One thing was certain, though, his lovemaking was just as unpredictable. But it was fantastic! Better than Brad, and a lot better than that strapping guy she'd taken home for a quickie after lunch yesterday.

A dog suddenly appeared in the middle of the road. "Shees!" Eve slammed on the brakes.

Racing across, the dog disappeared.

Eve reached over to Lily, who was holding her head. "Are you okay?"

"I guess so." Lily raked her fingers through her hair. "Whew. Close call."

"I wonder if the Irish leash their dogs? Or let them run loose like they do in other countries?" Eve said. "That one was blessed with the luck of the Irish."

"It's a wonder you don't run over more animals, these roads are so winding and narrow. I bet these sheep cross the road too when you least expect it," Lily said.

"Yeah, and I don't need more trouble." Eve maneuvered the car past a herd of lambs at the side of the road. Finally her friend's mood had turned; she was talking. *Good. Now to pump her about the new men in her life.*

"You must be tired from all your touring," Eve said. "What's been going on with you and Patrick? He's definitely not *my* type. Didn't take me long to decide that. But what about Seamus? I'd like to meet him. I haven't even had time to have tea with you and Maeve either."

"You're the one who should be tired," Lily said. "I called you at midnight last night because I was worried about you. I know you can't sleep through a ringing phone, so you must've gone out again. With that...guy? The one Patrick warned you about?" Lily was staring at her with the same accusing eyes she used on her daughters.

Eve suddenly swung around a curve in the road. "What if I did? And who is Patrick anyway? Why should we trust what *he* said about Ian? We hardly know him at all. Maybe he's the one who's had some bad history with Ian or...who knows? Maybe he's jealous."

"Jealous of who?" Lily said.

"You mean 'whom,' right?"

"Well," Eve went on, "I've been known to attract plenty of men —you know that. Maybe he's hot for me but doesn't want to admit it. So he's bagging on Ian."

"Oh, Eve, come on. Patrick's the real deal, very genuine. I'll admit, he's sort of mysterious about his past, but he's smart and he's caring. My take is he doesn't have a jealous bone in his body."

"How would you know? I don't want to hurt your feelings, but you really don't have much experience with men."

Lily reverted to silence again, opening her guidebook, and Eve knew to let her be. They'd soon be at Kinsale, where they planned to stay for two nights. She could hardly wait. Better to focus on fun things to do today than bitch at each other.

❧

The Lee River's sparkling waters finally emerged in the distance. "Look, that's an Irish postcard, if I ever saw one," Eve said.

Lily could tell she was trying to make up.

Green hills surrounded them and a fishing village came into view, with plenty of moored sailboats on the widening river. The road meandered for a couple minutes before they ventured into Kinsale. The shops were a patchwork of bright pastels with hanging baskets of flowers everywhere. Lily tried to take a few photos with her new iPhone when they stopped at an intersection. "Each scene is lovelier than the next. I loved Dublin, but for years I've pictured Ireland just like this."

Eve almost turned into a street the wrong way. Lily quickly put her hand on the wheel to warn her. "I'll try not to talk too much so you can navigate," Lily said.

Eve smirked. "Thank god." Lily rolled her eyes, but was relieved to hear Eve's familiar banter. "I hope they don't give too many tickets or I'll end up in jail. I noticed arrows to help tourists cross the street the Irish way, but driving is a challenge."

Lily began reading from her guidebook: "'A charming medieval village where boats dot the harbor and bright cottages line the coast.' They sure got that right." She pointed ahead at Charles Fort overlooking the river's edge, its imposing stone ramparts in ruins. "And it says that gray stone building over there on that hill is Desmond Castle. Do you think we'll have time for sightseeing? It's almost twilight now, but maybe tomorrow?"

"We'll see. I have to check my schedule."

Eve nudged Lily to find a map. "Look for Pearse Street, will you?"

They were in the heart of town now. "There it is. See that yellow building with blue shutters like this picture? " Lily pointed to the guidebook, "That's it. The sign says Blue Haven Hotel."

For March, the weather was unusually warm, and the tables, covered in white linen with sparkling tableware, filled the large patio near the hotel entrance. Diners were seated near outdoor lanterns since the sun's light was waning. The two friends walked by families eating an evening meal and drinking dark ale from large mugs. A few nodded and smiled.

After checking in and wheeling their suitcases upstairs, Lily gasped as she entered her hotel room. Golden brocade wallpaper matched burgundy and gold-striped pillows, trimmed in satin, that leaned against a cherry wood headboard. It was a king-sized bed too, which she'd never tried! Lily's phone rang.

"Want to finally have dinner together?"

Lily heard the warm excitement in Eve's voice. Keyed up, she rushed to get ready. They were going to sit down for a leisurely meal together, like old times.

CHAPTER 34

*M*aeve minced her way through the grassy fields surrounding Blarney Castle, her lavender print dress swirling to her dancing gait amid rose blooms and tall, dark-green trees. For a woman Lily guessed must be close to eighty, Maeve meandered like a twenty-year old. Lily couldn't deny that this petite, limber lady seemed more like a Faerie Godmother than a wrinkled senior citizen.

This day is turning out to be a wonderful surprise, Lily mused as she followed her newfound friend. *Thank God!*

To describe this morning's breakfast with Eve as "uncomfortable" was an understatement. Even after a fun dinner together last night, Lily had suffered through a breakfast of stony silence. She figured the mistake she'd made was telling Eve she was spending the day with Maeve and didn't have a clue what they were going to do because Maeve had insisted on surprising her. Finally, tired of Eve's moods, Lily had stood up and ended their meal, but agreed to meet her friend that evening. She hoped tonight's dinner would match the high spirits they'd enjoyed together last night, but she wasn't at all certain anymore what to expect from Eve.

Maeve had arrived only minutes later to pick her up this morning, and Lily was more than grateful. The tiny lady's ready hug calmed Lily, and Maeve's eyes danced with charm when she announced they were heading for Blarney Castle, about an hour away.

"I'm thrilled!" Lily told Maeve. "I've yearned to go there since I was a child."

Of course, Maeve climbed the famous twisting stone staircase of the castle with Lily. When they reached the seven-storied buttress to reach the famous stone, they marveled at the lush view of the green glens below. Maeve wouldn't accept Lily's refusal to bend over backwards to land a kiss on the famous Blarney stone. Instead she tried persuading Lily by promising her "the gift of Irish gab," the reward for following this well-known Irish tradition. When that didn't work, she badgered Lily about conquering her fear of heights, threatening "angry visits from Irish goblins this very night!" if she didn't comply. Maeve even promised Lily "Irish bliss a hundred-fold." So Lily finally performed the tourist ritual atop the castle's turrets while Maeve held her tight and then applauded, and Lily ended up elated at overcoming her age-old terror of heights.

As Lily followed Maeve now through the afternoon's shadowy pathways amidst myriad green hues of trees and grass and bushes, she couldn't keep her childhood fantasies from crowding out her thoughts. She thought she heard tinkling bells more than once, but the air was completely still. No breezes. Was that a blue butterfly appearing in the distance? She remembered that day in her faerie garden back home, how Kinza had allowed the tiny butterfly to sit on his nose. Now she'd glimpsed one a second time!

She was already nearing the Witch's Tree she'd read about months ago. She could hardly wait! Wherever she looked she thought she saw dwarf dwellings at the foot of the tall trees or tiny crevice lodgings in the large rocks dotting the landscape. *I must find the doors leading to the faeries' dwellings inside,* she giggled to herself, delighting in childish imagining. Since that event long ago near Gram's cabin in the mountains, when her Celtic Knot pendant had vanished and then mysteriously reappeared among the oak leaves, she'd become more open to Irish faerie superstitions. After all, Gram had believed in them. So perhaps the "little folk" *did* exist, and if they played tricks in the California mountains, they'd surely be hiding in droves here in Ireland.

There it was! They'd reached the giant, ancient tree where, it was said, witches' magic played out in inexplicable ways. As the sun began moving behind the clouds, Lily shuddered as she inspected the thick sinuous branches, curling around each other. It reminded her of a snake pit, packed with poison. *I'm letting my imagination get out of hand.* Clasping the gold Celtic Knot hanging around her neck, she shivered again. The clouds had completely overcome the sun's rays now as Lily reached out, tentatively at first, to stroke the rough, wooden bark. There was something sinister about the feel of it. An ominous sensation took hold of her. Quickly she pulled her hand away.

Lily heard Maeve calling to her, "Hurry, my lass."

She'd been so preoccupied she hadn't noticed the little lady was no longer with her. She rushed off to find the garden path, following the direction of Maeve's voice, passing azaleas, oak trees and yews. She knew them by name now since taking her horticulture class. Maeve called again and Lily remembered she'd promised a surprise when they entered the Blarney tourist shops. She rushed forward, like a birthday child eager to open her gift.

"Here you are, my lingering lassie," Maeve scolded, "I was afraid for a minute we'd be too late." She was standing in front of Ye Olde Irish Lace Shop, one of many tourist shops. Next to her was a silver-haired lady, thick at the waist and a head taller than Maeve. Dressed in a black skirt and a pale pink blazer with a matching blouse, she'd draped a flowered, wispy scarf around her neck. She held out her hand as Lily approached.

"Hello, Lily O'Malley. I'm Rose O'Sullivan," she said, nodding her head toward Maeve. "And I hear from me old classmate here that your ancestors not only come from our faire Isle, but you enjoy designin' gardens as well. I've decided from what she says that you're a young woman sure to titillate my own enthusiasm, since I'm always searchin' for new ways to decorate me own gardens here at Blarney Castle."

Lily felt her cheeks turn warm. Was this what Seamus had hinted at? Sure, months ago when they'd met, Maeve had helped her purchase a few twigs and plenty of faerie paraphernalia to create more than one college project. That was all. But now Lily noticed a mischievous gleam in Maeve's eyes and returned a quizzical look herself before stammering, "Why...why thank you. It's so nice to meet you, Mrs. O'Sullivan."

"I hear you met my husband a few nights ago? At the wine shindig, did you?" Rose said, while Lily tried to hide her reactions to this dual surprise. She'd never mentioned the Wine Geese Banquet to Maeve either, but perhaps the event was well known in Kinsale. Rose went on, "My Sean's the head vintner in all of Ireland's southern and midland counties, and I'm sure he introduced you to the whole group." She pointed up to Blarney Castle. "Sure *he* doesn't need to kiss that stone up there, and never did. Did you notice his Irish gift of gab?

"Come inside, will you both?" The shop's cashiers and sales clerks waved to Rose as she walked Maeve and Lily through the busy lace shop to the back, where a room appeared behind the door Rose opened. "I've got tea ready and we can talk a little," Rose said. Vases of flowers decorated the private room, and a silver tea service gleamed on a sideboard in the corner. They settled around a cozy table where, surprisingly, large picture windows overlooked a spacious green glen outside.

If Maeve had wanted to surprise her, Lily thought, she'd certainly outdone herself. As she listened to the two ladies talk and sipped her mint amber tea, she tried hard to collect her thoughts. Better to wait before plunging into the conversation with this important Irish lady. Unexpectedly, the conversation turned toward her.

"So, Lily O'Malley, I've heard about your faerie garden designs and how you've won some garden contests back in the States," Rose said.

How? Lily involuntarily nodded her head but didn't utter a word.

"Don't be modest, my dear. I'll let you in on a secret about Maeve. She has contacts in California and I can tell by your confused face you didn't know, and that's just like my old classmate here not to tell you a thing, now isn't it?" She looked over at Maeve, who let out a soft chuckle.

The rest of the afternoon sped by with Lily eventually answering Rose's questions about the awards she'd garnered for her horticulture designs. Never talking about it to Eve or Frank or her girls, she'd nearly forgotten how her college professor had urged her to submit several class assignments to local, then state competitions. Though her teacher praised her achievements when she'd actually won two major contests, Lily had quickly banked the $1000 prize money and slipped the award certificates into her bureau drawer at the semester's end. With Frank suddenly hospitalized and later passing away, and her working overtime, plus planning Frank's funeral then preparing for this trip, she'd totally forgotten about her Celtic garden designs. Her layouts of hedges and trees and flowers as well as the several miniature faerie gardens she'd painstakingly created on paper were still stowed away at home.

However, Rose seemed to know about them already, and the gracious lady showed such animated interest that Lily became embarrassed. She hid her feelings, though, trying to present a calm, professional impression in front of this woman who'd obviously gained high stature in this community.

After saying their good-byes, and riding back to the hotel, Lily chattered continuously about Blarney Castle, wondering for a moment where all her words were coming from. She questioned Maeve too about how she'd known about the prizes she'd won, but she never got a straight answer. The little old lady had a very amiable way of diverting the conversation. Then Lily fell into a long silence, which began to feel surprisingly comfortable. Though Maeve was almost a stranger and had certainly surprised her several times, Lily sensed a kinship and a kindness in her she hadn't felt since Gram was alive. She sighed and leaned back on the seat and closed her eyes.

"There now, my Lilith, rest those pretty orbs, I'll be getting you back to Kinsale, but it may take some time this evening," Maeve said. "You'll need your rest. I have some more exciting plans for us ahead."

Lily heard nothing. She was already asleep. That is, until the car broke down.

CHAPTER 35

*E*ve drummed her fingers on the table then checked her watch again, waiting for Lily a few minutes more. This would be their last night in Kinsale. The dinner crowd was slowly thinning out. The waitress kept coming over to replenish her wine, but Eve drained the glass and stomped out of the hotel's restaurant. She wasn't hungry. Apparently, Lily wasn't either!

Tossing her shoes in a corner of her hotel room, Eve settled herself on the bed and in minutes she'd dozed off while watching TV.

Eve's cell phone woke her up. She looked at the clock. Over an hour had passed.

"I'm sorry," Lily said. "I hope you had dinner by now. We're still stuck outside of Blarney."

"What do you mean: stuck?"

"Our car broke down. A hose problem in Maeve's rental car. She didn't have a cell phone and mine ran out of juice, so we had to depend on the kindness of a trucker who stopped to help us. Lucky for us, he finally found a mechanic who would open his shop. I'm using his landline now. It'll take a while longer before we get on the road again. Sorry."

Eve didn't feel like talking. Ian had never answered her texts, and Lily was becoming someone she didn't recognize: independent, too busy to see her, unusually social and undependable. After a few words she hung up, deciding to take a bubble bath to soothe her nerves, then go to bed. She'd spent the whole day calling on hotels and restaurants, but it had paid off again with sizeable wine orders. But tomorrow marked the beginning of the two friends' five-day getaway. She'd rise early and drag Lily out of bed just after dawn. *Oh, she'll love that!*

First, they'd fly to England and stay two nights, then back to Ireland to spend some time exploring the western coast. Eve had planned pure sightseeing and no sales calls during the coming days. *I hope Lily appreciates all the work I've done, booking rooms and arranging special tours. She used to be grateful for everything, but now... who knows?*

CHAPTER 36

$\mathcal{T}$he two friends' plane, headed to the London Luton airport, though early, landed right on time. Their British tour guide introduced herself as Susan, then quickly motioned for Lily to settle into her van behind Eve. "The drive to St. Albans will take less than a half hour," she said, while driving amidst sloping English hillsides where streams interrupted spacious blankets of green pastures. *Actually,* Lily mused, *this part of England doesn't look too different than Ireland.* After a time, the three women got out of the van, taking in an idyllic scene of sheep munching rich grass and wild rabbits darting about in this seemingly endless landscape.

"Have you heard of Boudica?" Susan began. "She's one of *the* most famous Celtic women, and many historians believe this is one of her battlefields." Susan found an elaborate illustration on her iPad. "Here she is." She lifted up the screen so both Lily and Eve could view a woman of imposing stature with red wavy hair flowing across her shoulders and down her back. She was dressed in green and blue robes edged in gold, with the same braided Celtic design that Lily had seen in *The Book of Kells'* pages.

"She's gorgeous!" Lily said. "Did you say *her* battlefield?"

Susan nodded, "Yes, Celtic woman fought right alongside their men. They were considered equals." Susan started off across the hills, waving her hands from right to left. "In 60 A.D. the Celts gathered here from many lands faraway. That's why the battle was so momentous. That a woman could lead thousands of Celtic soldiers was unheard of. History is a bit foggy, but many believe one of her most famous onslaughts occurred right here in St. Albans and later in London." Susan's face gleamed with admiration, "What is *unforgettable* is that a Celtic *woman* actually *won* these battles. She was Queen of the Iceni tribe and pulled together a massive rebel uprising against the Roman forces because, among other reasons, she had a personal score to settle."

"What was that?" Lily asked, as she admired Susan's pictures of the ancient warrior woman.

"Storytellers say her daughter was raped, and she became so incensed that, unlike submissive women of other ancient tribes, she vowed to get even."

Lily followed Susan and Eve at a distance. How could a woman command so much homage so long ago? The story was thrilling.

Susan continued, "Boudica's defeat of hundreds of thousands of Romans had never happened before, nor did it ever happen again. Unfortunately, as the battles raged, the tide turned and the Celts were eventually defeated. Boudica and her daughter were dragged away and murdered. But no one here will ever forget this great lady." Susan flipped through other pictures on her iPad again and showed them another of the famous woman leader armed for battle.

"Makes me feel powerful walking on the same ground as she did. Your story is very moving. She had Celtic blood like we do since we're both Irish," Lily mused, nodding toward Eve.

"Yes, as many times as I've visited this site," Susan said, "I get choked up every time. I especially like to bring women who have Celtic ancestors, whether Irish, English or Scots. We should never forget her bravery and her maternal fire of anger to vindicate her daughter."

Lily fell in step with Susan. "And her message to us is relevant today. To protect our sisters, our daughters and our friends—to never, ever submit to a man's violence. Or anyone's, for that matter." A thrill permeated Lily as if her veins were infused with a tangible fluid of strength. She felt a new surge of confidence too. Yet she noticed how quiet Eve had become. *She looks upset.* Lily moved near Eve as they made their way to the van, touching her arm. "Are you okay?"

Eve stared straight ahead. "Just thinking. I know you don't consider me introspective, but once in a while I do go deep."

"Well, I hope you're okay. I worry about you sometimes."

Eve only nodded, taking the back seat in the van this time, so Lily could sit in the front with Susan.

CHAPTER 37

*L*ily and Eve said good-bye to Susan and took an Uber to Atherton Castle, its imposing gray stone turrets visible from a distance. Lily found it in her tour book, "It was originally built in the in 12th century," she read, "when religious and political leaders were vying for money to build huge castles. They wanted to bring prestige to an area and also prosperity.

"We're actually going to stay the night here? Reminds me of a fascinating historical novel I just read, *Pillars of the Earth*," she said. "You should read it too, Eve. It illuminates the era as if it were yesterday."

Eve only nodded.

Once inside the castle, the B&B matron checked them in and directed them forward. The two friends peered up at the dark circular staircase. The entire room was paneled in a deep brown mahogany, as were the stairs. The only light lifting the shadows came from a green shaded lamp on the hotel's desk and a huge stained glass window above the staircase landing, two stories up. Made of odd-sized glass rectangles of bright colors, the yellow panes, numbering more than the others, allowed light to shimmer down to the entryway, lifting the gloom.

Soon Eve and Lily were climbing the stairs. They couldn't wait to compare each other's bedrooms: the heavy brocaded tapestries, bedspreads and draperies with tasseled ties, the medieval wrought iron sconces, the aged portraits of ancestors. Lily beckoned Eve to take in the view through an archaic diamond-paned window in her room. The grounds were bright green and hilly, stretching for miles. The castle was actually quite isolated, as they'd driven for over an hour from St. Albans and then to the nearest town of Edenbridge, before attempting to chug up the hill that wound around the crumbling but intact castle walls.

After an early dinner of wine, mutton pie and custard for dessert, they decided to take a walk before bedtime. The evening mist was beginning to rise on the hills as they ventured along the moors, so after about twenty minutes, they started back toward the castle. "I've also read English novels like *Wuthering Heights,*" Lily said, "but I never thought I'd actually walk on the moors. It feels squishy under my feet."

"I read that book too and lots of other British novels in high school," said Eve. "Remember how they piled the reading on me? Because I skipped a grade. Now that we're here, though, I remember those stories differently. Not everything about them was fiction." She raised her hand to point to the castle's turrets and smiled back at Lily. "Everyone should travel, right?"

A breeze turned into a wind, blowing the branches of the few trees that surrounded the castle. On the horizon the sun's last rays were sinking into a shroud of darkness. They pulled their coat collars up and wrapped their scarves around their throats. "We'd better go inside," Eve said. "It feels like a storm."

The rattling of rain pelting the windows seemed to go on for hours. Finally, silence pervaded, except for a moaning bluster outside. Eve turned over again and again in her large four-poster bed, hoping to fall asleep. It didn't happen, and after another hour, she got up and went to the window. The wind seemed to have quieted. Maybe if she ventured outside and let a brisk walk invigorate her, she'd tire herself out enough to come back and fall asleep.

Bundled up, Eve began her walk, looking up to find a full moon. As several clouds moved away, it cast an ethereal glow on the moors. The air wasn't as cold now, and she welcomed the breezes that played with her hair as she quickened her pace. Soon she'd put quite a distance between her and the castle and found herself enjoying her hike as she mounted yet another hill. Once past an old graveyard, she climbed further for a while, and then ventured downhill into a large, flat valley. The mists covered the moors around her now, and she picked up speed and began a slow jog. Nowhere did she see a small house, or even a structure in ruins.

Off in the distance she thought she saw a person walking up ahead. A tall man. He was far off, but Eve decided, for fun, to try to catch up with him. The only trouble was, the mists had thickened into fog in that direction. Sometimes she'd catch a glimpse of him and sometimes he'd disappear. Strangely, when she checked her distance from the castle, its turrets seemed closer, even though she was sure she'd been heading away from it. Soon she was immersed in large drifts of fog, clouds hovering everywhere.

The filmy whiteness lifted for a full two minutes, and she glimpsed the figure again, not far away. She picked up speed while nothing but fog surrounded her again. She glanced at her watch and realized she'd been hiking for over thirty minutes. Winded, she made it to a large oblong stone, which reached up to the sky, and as the mists parted, she found herself surrounded by several others. *My god, it looks so ancient here.*

Leaning against the standing stone, she surveyed the area as best she could, in spite of the murky whiteness. Then, over next to the farthest one, she saw the stranger; he too, was leaning against a stone, lighting his pipe. Eve hadn't seen anyone light a pipe in years! She ventured closer, sure he hadn't noticed her.

"How do you like all this, Evie?" He waved his hand at the stones. His voice sounded familiar.

She slowly moved forward. "What did you say?"

"I asked if you liked these mysterious stones. These moors. I expected you would." He stoked his pipe, and Eve saw the red glow of his match light his face.

Oh, my god! It can't be...

Eve couldn't move. "Dad...Daddy, is that you? It's been so long—"

"How's my brave girl?" he said. "I thought you needed me—to look after you."

Eve moved closer, but as she did he seemed to fade. She stopped.

"That's enough," he said. "Don't come closer."

She chose another pillar to lean against, nearer to him.

"You're disappointing me, Evie."

"Why?" Eve's heart plunged. She wanted get closer and hug him, tell him she was okay, she was fine.

"You're getting reckless again. Like you used to do with Star."

"Reckless with my pony?"

"Yes. Remember? I warned you about him over and over. You wouldn't listen. When he threw you, you didn't learn either. Stubborn. You always liked a little danger...too much so."

She couldn't look at him. Instead she gazed up to watch the waning moon trying to hold out against a buttress of clouds moving across the sky. Minutes ticked by as she thought about what he'd said. Soon the moon was almost covered and the darkness deepened.

She stared over to where she'd seen him, trying to distinguish his shape in the mist. She could barely discern his outline now, but glimpsed a red glow again as he stoked his pipe. A sweet, musky scent brought back more childhood memories. She tried to make out his face. "I'm sorry, Dad, I'll try harder." Involuntarily, she moved closer, but when she did his form shifted and now she saw only the large stone obelisk. She still heard his voice, though faint in the deep gloom.

"Don't tempt danger, Evie. Please look for a good man. You deserve better..."

Then the moon succumbed completely to the mounting clouds. Everything was shrouded in darkness. "Dad?" She stood rigid as the fog descended like a thick wall, barring her from all reality. She couldn't see the other obelisks now. "Dad, don't leave!" She waited, but all that was left was the pipe's scent. She was completely alone.

As lonely and as devastated as she felt, all she wanted to do now was find the castle...and Lily too. She gazed up, turning to her left then to her right, trying to find the shadowed vista of the castle's ramparts. Finally, the mists shifted and she saw it!

As she ran uphill, out of the valley toward the ancient structure, she pushed her dad's words from her mind. Far, far away. Tears burned and she wiped her eyes with the back of her hand, trudging forward and up, mounting the crest of one hill then another.

He did it again, she raged. *My entire life he appears...and then, just as quickly, he's gone again. Damn him!*

CHAPTER 38

"*I*'m glad you're up," Eve said on the phone to Lily. "Can you meet me downstairs in fifteen minutes?"

"Sure. I've been awake for a couple of hours." Lily was so keyed up about sightseeing, she'd finally risen and made her way to the window, watching the gray light transform into pink rays extending across the sky. She'd dressed in a hurry, putting on jeans and a fleece-lined hoodie, and was out of the castle in no time. "I actually witnessed the most gorgeous sunrise ever. It's pretty deserted around here, but beautiful. I wish I had time for a decent hike."

"I did. Last night," Eve countered.

"You didn't."

"Yes, I did. Are you going to warn me about danger too?"

"What are you talking about?" Lily said, squeezing out of her jacket and folding it into her suitcase while she talked. Just before the telephone rang, she'd checked the weather report, which predicted sunshine and a warm late March day in England and in Ireland too.

"Never mind," Eve said. "Let's meet for a quick breakfast. I hope you're packed. We need to put everything in the car fast and leave by nine to catch our flight back to Ireland. After that we have a long drive to the famous Ring of Kerry."

❦

They spent the whole day traveling after their plane landed in Ireland. Crossing miles of rolling pasture land, they watched as the sun's caramel rays gradually melted into the horizon. As darkness closed in, they arrived at O'Donnabhains bar and guesthouse in Kenmare.

"I'm exhausted from driving. Let's order a pint and some pub grub before we check in for the evening," Eve suggested.

Entering, they heard music. Five men, with guitars, a harmonica, a fiddle, as well as a tin whistle, were playing a lively tune. The two friends spied a man dancing in the midst of the people gathered around the pub. He wore a wool checked vest over a white shirt, and he tapped his heels to the spirited melody, jigging for all to see. The whoops and whistles and clapping of the crowd accompanied his dance, and the faces of the people shone with merry smiles. Lily noticed Eve's face brighten too.

As soon as their mugs were full of ale and a meat pie placed in front of them, Eve's words began to tumble out like a faucet long dry. "I guess I shouldn't have gone out last night. It was a risky thing to do, all alone. It was eerie out there and I saw someone. So I followed him."

"You did?" Lily shook her head, but vowed to limit her comments. Her friend rarely confided. If she did bare her soul, it would be brief, so Lily sat still, ready to not only listen, but to try to decipher the meaning beneath Eve's words.

"I was lucky to get a word out of you today. Now you look…" she hesitated, then let her words spill out, "well, you look like you've seen a ghost," Lily said.

"How'd you know?"

Lily stared at her friend's downcast face. "What?"

Eve was gazing over Lily's shoulder as if still in a trance. "It was my dad...I saw him when I hiked over the moors last night."

Lily turned to see where Eve was staring, but no one was there, yet her eyes seemed to see something.

Eve continued, still gazing off in space, "Dad warned me too. To steer clear of danger."

Lily put her hand over Eve's. "He did? I'm glad. I've been wanting to warn you myself."

Eve's vacant gaze turned hard and her eyes snapped. "Warn *me*? What about all the men *you've* been meeting? You better watch yourself. Let's face it, you don't have any experience when it comes to dating. You barely know Seamus, and Patrick isn't the most transparent guy I've ever met. If you want to know the truth, I think he's hiding something."

Lily felt her breath quicken with anger, plus she realized her friend had completely flipped the topic away from her own life and was now scolding her. She bit her lip, and decided she'd bide her time. Later she'd link her warnings with more talk about the ghost of Eve's father. Her advice might have more punch that way.

"Oh, Patrick's a good guy," Lily said. "He reminds me of my brother...smart, thoughtful. He's traveled a lot too, but now that you mention it, he does seem reluctant to tell me where."

"See?" Eve countered. "A mystery man—with secrets. So you think Patrick's smart? Book smart?"

"Yes, he knows a lot, but he's not stuffy and he's not a nerd. He's into genealogy too; it's his part-time job. When it comes to Celtic information and ancient tourist sites, he's an expert; he writes articles about it. Actually, he and Seamus have that in common—the Celts. They've never met, though, as far as I know."

Eve sat up, eyes alight. "Hmm, genealogy? I've always wanted to search out my family's ancestors. Ever since Mom died and I became an orphan. I wonder if I have any close relatives over here. I'm a Walsh, you know, on my mother's side. Remember?"

"Now that you mention it, I do. But with your blonde hair and blue eyes, you've always resembled your dad's Swedish side of the family, and you've never talked much about your Irish roots," Lily said.

The pub's music started up again, but Eve still seemed in the mood to share confidences, "Didn't I ever tell you? I hired a professional genealogist a while ago. I actually loved reading the research she unearthed about my ancestors, but I got stalled on the project after my accident." Eve tilted her head, as if mulling something over. "Maybe I'll ask Patrick about it sometime. But he doesn't like me much, does he?"

"Ask him about what? Oh, c'mon Eve, Patrick likes you. What he doesn't like are your flirty come-ons. He's more like Frank that way and my brother."

"Humph! 'Flirty come-ons.' Thanks."

Eve's eyes told Lily she was treading on enemy territory, but she decided it was time to press forward anyway. She knew Eve was still seeing Ian, and she felt sure Patrick was telling the truth about how dangerous he was. Eve *needed* a talking to, no matter how much she would fight back like a blazing spit-fire.

Lily faced her friend. She took a large swig of ale and dove in. "You're not going to like what I have to say, but I have to say it— because I care about you. A lot. But I don't want to hurt you in any way or make you mad." Lily noticed how Eve avoided her eyes and she was tearing her pub receipt into tiny pieces, but Lily went on anyway. "I think you're tempting fate by not protecting yourself. You left Brad behind, hopefully for good, and that was a great start on a new life, but now...you've started drinking and going to bed with strangers since we got here, like you did when we were young. You don't need that, Eve. You're smart. You're gorgeous. Be wise about this. Acting like this can affect your business contacts over here. But that's not the worst of it. What I'm most worried about is your heart." She reached out to put her hand over Eve's, but her friend promptly pulled it away, got up and strode to the bar.

Lily decided Eve needed time to cool off, but minutes passed and as usual, Eve was surrounded by men again. The guy who had entertained the crowd before was the most attentive. Funny...he actually reminded Lily of Brad, with his sandy hair, eyes the color of the sky. And...*Look at those arms. Must hang out at the gym every day.*

Soon the fiddle player began an Irish tune and the rest of the band joined in as "The Jigger" took Eve's hand and led her to the dance floor. He tapped his feet together, arms at his sides, perfectly straight and danced all around Eve, his eyes riveted on her. Others noticed too. "Aye, Sean, she's improvin' your jig tonight, she is!" Soon everyone in the pub was watching the couple dance, clapping to Sean's rhythm with Eve. They began applauding the gorgeous blonde couple, who seemed mesmerized by each other, as the tin whistle and guitars wailed to the timely drumming all around.

When the music ended, Lily stood up, ready to leave, but at that moment Eve caught her eye. She nodded to the crowd, and, bowing slightly to Sean and the others with her famous smile, she whispered something in his ear. The crowd groaned as Eve grabbed her purse and followed Lily on her way to the door. Surprised, Lily pushed through the crowd toward the pub's exit. The crowd clapped and hailed good-bye to Eve, but not before Lily noticed several good-looking men were checking her out too. Some smiled at her and one even winked. Startled at first, Lily smiled back.

The front door swung open as a new crowd entered, jostling Lily. She heard Eve's faint call behind her, "Lily, wait up."

By the time Lily reached the adjoining hallway of the B&B, Eve had caught up to her. "I'm going to turn in too. We've got a full day tomorrow driving to Ireland's west coast. Then two days more. Let's have breakfast here and then visit a few of Kenmare's quaint shops early tomorrow. You probably want to bring some gifts back to the girls, won't you?"

She must've actually listened to me after all or maybe it was her dad's warnings, Lily mused.

CHAPTER 39

*A*fter shopping in the morning, the two friends decided to head to Portmagee to meet Molly, the Irish tour guide Susan had recommended to them.

With a surge of new confidence, Lily asked, "I feel like taking on a challenge today. Can I drive?" A bit shocked, Eve nodded.

But before Lily started the car, her cell phone rang. She was surprised to hear Patrick's voice. "Aye, lassie, where have you been? I was plannin' to take you on some more jaunts, but you flew the coop."

"Eve and I took a side trip to England. But we're back in Ireland today, planning to explore the Ring of Kerry."

"Is that right? I'll not be far from Kerry meself. I'm doin' a project with a family nearby. You couldn't squeeze in a lunch or dinner, could you, lass?"

Lily knew Patrick would liven up their day and share lots of information about their sightseeing. She arranged a meeting time at a pub he recommended, then placed her phone back in her purse. She glanced at Eve, who didn't look happy. "You don't mind if Patrick joins us for lunch, do you?"

"Thanks for planning our day," Eve said.

"C'mon, he's got incredible knowledge about Ireland," Lily said. "When he took me to Newgrange I was blown away by everything he knew. He ought to be a tour guide."

"Well, I already arranged for Molly to meet us. I get the feeling you don't appreciate the fact that I've spent hours planning everything, Lily."

"Oh, yes I do...but aren't we meeting Molly this afternoon? Couldn't we have an early lunch with Patrick? Just for an hour or so? He's near here, working. What could I say?"

❧

As the day played out, Patrick's presence on their getaway was a godsend after all, because the tour company called Eve a few minutes later to say that Molly was down with a case of food poisoning and couldn't start their tour till tomorrow.

When Patrick arrived, he took charge immediately, saying he'd love to show them around. "Let's use my car," he said, "and I'll bring you back here after dinner." They piled in and began their journey around the Ring of Kerry. After that, Patrick promised even more dramatic sights when he turned off on a less-traveled route called the Ring of Skellig.

He drove slowly, stopping whenever an especially gorgeous ocean scene caught their attention. The rugged Skellig Islands were especially stark but breathtaking. He entertained them with stories about the largest island, Skellig Michael, pointing to its long, pointed rocks slanting upward. "Did you see the latest Star Wars movies? Luke Skywalker's scenes were filmed out there. What you may not know is that in the 7th century a dozen Christian monks actually lived in a monastery there. Too bad the surf is too rough to take a boat ride to visit the ruins."

Eve noticed how Patrick kept directing his eye contact to Lily as he talked, and only once turned toward her, except for playing the gentleman by opening the door for her when they got out of the car. It was to Lily he asked, "Are you warm enough with just a sweater? It's chilly today."

Still, he seemed so familiar, and Eve secretly thought Lily had nailed it when she said he reminded her of her brother, Colin. *It's true. He even looks like him.* But more than that, when Eve observed Lily and Patrick sitting in the front of the car or walking ahead to take in a stunning view, it was as if they moved in parallel universes and had known each other for a long time. What most annoyed her, though, was how all afternoon Patrick barely replied when she made a comment. Later, when they sampled different candies at the Skellig chocolate factory, Patrick talked only to Lily. Finally Eve's irritation blossomed into anger, but she tried to hide it.

Why did I even bother to come today? I guess I don't exist. Oh yeah, I forgot, I'm just a flirt, like Lily said.

Never one to give up, she tried a different tactic as they walked to their car. "So, Patrick, how do you know so much about all these famous sights? Did you go to travel school or were you in that business in your youth?"

Patrick finally returned her gaze, but the usual twinkle in his eyes was absent. His face had suddenly turned serious. "The sights of Ireland are a part of me soul. Ever since I left, I guess, many long years ago."

He'd reverted to a thicker brogue than she'd heard before too. Was it because he was talking about his past?

"You left?" asked Lily.

He turned toward Lily again. "Aye, I lived in Rome for a time but missed this Isle more than I ever expected. Since comin' home, I can't seem to get enough of travelin' to these ancient and gorgeous sights. I love to meet the people who make our land so faire."

Eve tried again. "How many years were you gone? I went to Rome on business last year. Stayed near the Roman Coliseum. I could walk to the Trevi Fountain in twenty minutes. Where did you stay?"

Patrick cleared his throat. "Umm, near the Vatican, I was. For eight years, then I moved to a place near to the Spanish Steps. The crowds mobbed those areas, though, and I missed the wide open spaces of our hills and valleys and the western ocean. I got used to them as a boy..." His voice trailed off. "...and especially the Cliffs of Moher, where I grew up. My heart is happy here now," he spread his arms out to the lush hills and waterways and valleys below the lovely vista where they stood, "not in faraway cities."

"Ah, the Cliffs of Moher—that's on our list of sights to see," Eve said. "After we leave here, we'll drive north. We've talked about going for a long time."

"The wild beauty of those cliffs is unforgettable, plungin' into the Atlantic Ocean," Patrick said. "They even surpass the Cliffs of Kerry we saw today."

Walking behind the couple now, Eve studied Patrick's broad back and muscular shoulders. He must be six foot three, he was so tall. Next to him, Lily looked petite. Eve wondered what it would be like to grow up in the lonely, western part of this island. What kind of man *was* Patrick? A guy who chose to live near the Vatican? Why? Was he a fan of Renaissance art? Was he a staunch Catholic? Maybe he wasn't like Colin after all.

Eve inched closer to overhear the twosome's conversation, even though the wind had begun to bluster in spite of the afternoon's sunshine. Patrick was talking to Lily about Wales.

Reaching the parking lot, Patrick took a travel book out of the car and pointed to a map. "Look here. It's only a three-hour ferry ride from Ireland to Wales, from Rosslare to Fishguard, then a short drive to some wonderful, original cottages and ancient sights. I wish I could take you with me next weekend. A spiritual energy reigns in Pembrokeshire, and pilgrimages are popular several times a year."

Eve noticed how fired up Patrick was as he talked. "Last year I hiked up in the Preseli hills with twenty others where we came upon a mysterious place called Bedd Arthur. I'll never forget the stillness that wrapped around us when we walked and hiked those hills together. And our nights by the fire with grog and song...it's etched in my memory, and fun too." His face was lit with a flushed excitement, yet Eve couldn't fathom from his description why he was enthused about a weekend retreat. "I plan to lead me own group next weekend," he continued. "I've called it a Vision Quest. Locals plus a few tourists have signed up."

Though Lily began to ask a question, Eve cut her off, "Not to change the subject, but what's your plan for the rest of the afternoon? We'll be nearing dinnertime in an hour or two."

"How 'bout I take you to see some famous horses? Everyone's heard how much the Irish love them," Patrick announced.

Back in the car, they eventually rounded a bend to view acres of fencing that surrounded a large, two-story stone house. An array of geldings and mares grazed quietly, their sleek coats shining in the afternoon light. One stood out among all the rest. He was much larger, with a shining coat as black as midnight.

Eve tried again from the back seat. "Has Lily told you how much we both love to ride? Goes back to our childhood. I started riding with my dad when I was only six and took lessons for years."

"Want to try it today?" Patrick asked. "I'm sure we can pick out just the right horse for both of you here." His face clouded over again. "You were lucky to have a dad like that. Me family had no money for frills. Me parents could barely make ends meet." He turned to Lily beside him. "Did you ride too, when you were small?"

"No lessons for me—we never had the money either. I got to ride at my Gram's cabin though, when I was little. Eve came with me on every vacation, and we rode through the southern California mountains together."

Patrick made his way to the entrance of the stone house, asking for his friend Tom Riley. After talking with him, Patrick turned and smiled. "We're just in time. His best horses are entertaining a few tourists, so we'll join them. You'll love it." Soon Lily and Eve were seated in the paddock watching the riders and their horses strut and manage difficult jumps, then parade in front of them, prancing in unison. Then Tom offered Eve and Lily the chance to ride around the ranch for a while.

Afterwards, Tom welcomed everyone into the ranch house for an evening meal. Lily heard him confide in Patrick during dinner. He took a long swallow of Guinness. "We lost some horses last night. It's the Travelers again, I think."

"What are Travelers?" Lily asked.

"They're bands of Irish gypsies," Patrick said. "Some call them Tinkers; they originally wandered our hills in horse-drawn wagons, earning money by mending tin pots and pans.

"Over the years they've branched out," Tom added, "breeding greyhound dogs, dealing in scrap metal or horse trading. That's where the horse stealing comes in. I've lost five mares this season. Local law enforcement hasn't been any help at all. It's costing me money," he rubbed his fingers together, "so I've decided to hire my own private investigator. I'm determined to drag those good-for-nothin's into jail."

"If I can help you, let me know," Patrick said. "Me brothers know a few law enforcement heavies in this county."

"Aye, I will!" Tom said and slapped Patrick on the back with a smile.

With dinner over and Tom and Patrick still engrossed in conversation, Lily and Eve wandered outside near the paddock. "I'm going in to see the horses. I stole a carrot and apple from inside," Eve said.

"I'll take a walk around the grounds," Lily said, looking up to admire the inky black sky. She hadn't gone far when she heard hoof-beats. Heavy ones. She tried to adjust her eyes to the darkness. A huge, shadowy figure of a horse emerged out of nowhere. An eerie, piercing whinny split the air. The mammoth black horse was coming right at her! His eyes were pools of golden light. She shivered. Fear rose from her belly. She darted through the gate. Her fingers trembled as she struggled to fasten the lock.

Secure behind the fence, she breathed a sigh, but only for a moment. The shadowy monster was still rushing toward her! He stopped suddenly, about to crash into the fence. Blaring out a blood-curdling scream, he lifted up his front legs. She froze, unable to move or take her eyes off his shimmering eyes. She turned and ran, huffing in short spurts. Her heart pounded louder than the strange hoofbeats behind her. It took forever to reach the car. Her hands shaking, she opened the door and sank into safety. Nausea made her gag. She peeked out of the window. No sign of the gigantic horse.

What was that? Maybe I'm totally losing it!

"You're awfully quiet, Lily," Patrick mused ten minutes later, as he backed the car out of the ranch parking lot and turned onto a main road.

"Yes, I thought you'd be really excited after our ride. We haven't done that in years," Eve said.

"Something...something strange happened to me out there. I'm embarrassed to even talk about it." Lily scrunched down in her seat.

Eve noticed her staring out the window, checking the paddock, but everything looked peaceful. Why was Lily so pensive?

"What happened?" Patrick's voice was full of concern. "C'mon, you can tell us."

She described the frightening incident as briefly as possible then folded back into silence.

"Any ideas about what that phantom was, Patrick?" Eve said. "That is, if it really was a phantom."

"I wouldn't make a story like that up," Lily retorted.

"Well, Irish legends might explain it, but—" he said.

"But what?" Lily asked.

"I happen to know some Irish lore about horses—or should I say pookas. But I don't want to scare you more."

Whenever Eve had shared one of her past "visions," her friend had never quite believed her. Maybe now Lily would finally open up to the spirit world. She needed to find out what this so-called phantom meant.

"Out with it, Patrick," Eve said. "Lily's not a child and I'm sure others can give us an explanation of pookas anyway, so you might as well tell us."

"Yes, it's okay," Lily said. "I know I saw a crazy black stallion, and it was ghostly. I want to hear what you have to say about pookas."

Patrick met Lily's gaze and she nodded. Then he finally looked at Eve, who thought she'd never seen such inscrutable eyes on a man. "Well, they say the pookas date back to the ancient little people who inhabited this island long before the Celts," he began. "They're called the Sid'e or a tribe of the Tuatha de' Dannon who were driven down to the underworld. But I'm sure you've heard them called faerie folk too: lordly spirit beings that resemble miniature humans. And other beings called leprechauns, banshees and pookas, creatures somewhere between gods and God. People out west here still believe that when the Celts invaded this Isle, those ancients went to live down in earthen mounds, faerie raths and cairns."

"Sounds intriguing, but do you believe it?" Eve said.

"Didn't used to, but the longer I live here, the more I wonder,"

Patrick retorted. He looked at Lily and she nodded again. "Well, I...I might as well tell you," he said. "In many places the Irish consider pookas to be quite dangerous. They're much larger than the other spirits. Some folk around here believe they're more mysterious too, issuing prophecies or warnings. They say they look a little like the black stallion we saw today, but more like the scary vision Lily described, with a coat the darkest ebony you've ever seen and those strange glowin' eyes. If you ever spy them, beware." Then he stopped abruptly.

"Really? Tell us more," Eve urged.

Lily scrunched lower in her seat, but whispered, "Yes, I can take it."

"Well...okay. They say seeing a pooka means...well, somethin' dastardly is about to occur...er, *might* appear in your future. It's not cast in stone, you understand." He paused for several minutes. Then he gestured toward Lily as his voice lifted, "But you'll also be happy to know that some Irish think all these legends are nothin' but superstitions and complete hogwash."

"I've seen dark horses at night plenty of times and nothing's ever happened to me," Eve countered.

"Ah, but the pookas are different from ordinary horses. They have bright yellow eyes and a long wild mane, much like...uh...like Lily said," he hesitated then went on as if he were reciting a story. "They say they roam at night, and can tear down fences, scatterin' livestock and tramplin' crops. Have you ever wandered the moors when the mists roll in? That's a time when they're supposed to...er they *might* appear."

"Maybe the Irish Travelers aren't Tom's enemies after all— maybe it's the pookas." Eve laughed, but Patrick didn't smile.

Lily's voice was low, "I know what I saw, but I can barely believe it myself. Eve has seen ghosts in the mists," she went on, "but I never completely believed her, and she was young then... Except the other night when she was walking on the moors—"

Eve cut in. "Patrick, see that truck weaving toward us? Better focus on the road! We'll have to squeeze by him. I swear, that driver in front of us hasn't even noticed him."

"Aye, don't worry, lass. I'm used to these byways. Been drivin' on them for years. You can always tell a tourist. First he crowds the entire road, drivin' as slow as a snail, then he'll move over when he finally wakes up. See? There you go, lad."

Eve took her compact, brush and lip gloss out of her purse in the back seat, primping, since she might stop for a drink in the hotel bar. *Whew! So glad he avoided that trucker. And glad I sidestepped that topic too. Why Lily would ever bring up my strange hike on the moors to Patrick, I'll never know.*

CHAPTER 40

*A*s Patrick drove to their hotel in Kinsale, Lily couldn't dispel images of the terrifying apparition she'd seen. She shuddered but kept quiet, unwilling to admit to either Patrick or Eve how troubled she felt. Patrick's pooka explanation made her feel worse. She tried to reason things out: even if this preternatural ghost had come to warn her, how could she possibly prepare for whatever disaster lay ahead? And why waste her energy worrying about something that might be a silly Irish fantasy? After all, she'd never really believed in spirits and she wasn't about to now. But it did disturb her to see how somber Patrick became when he explained the meaning of pookas.

She forced her worries away and focused her thoughts instead on the Vision Quest he would soon lead in Wales. That was more intriguing and she felt drawn to the idea. *I wonder if I can talk Eve into going with me.*

She yearned for the friend Eve used to be before this trip, and her heart warmed at the thought of sharing everything with her as they'd always done. She decided to plan a surprise. What if she arranged to hire Patrick to help finish Eve's ancestral search right here in Ireland? Maybe he would find some of Eve's lost relatives. It would mean the world to Eve, orphaned for so long. Then maybe she could talk Eve into going on the Vision Quest.

❧

Back in her hotel room, Lily had no sooner asked Patrick about her idea and completed her call, when she climbed into bed and her cell phone rang again.

"Want to share a nightcap together, like old times? You probably need a drink after the scare you had today," Eve said.

"Sure!" Lily scrambled out of bed to find her robe. She heard a knock at the door, and Eve greeted her with a bottle of sherry in one hand and Kahlua in the other.

"I couldn't decide which, so I brought them both," Eve said.

Soon they were sharing the alternate liqueurs and reviewing the day's activities. The pooka topic made Lily nervous, so she steered their talk to old times, laughing about softball games won and lost in high school, and the stories Gram used to tell them at her mountain cabin.

But Eve persisted, "I was surprised today...Patrick seemed dead serious about his pooka story. I knew the Irish were superstitious... well, I'm not really sure what to believe.

"Sort of reminds me of an article I read once about Icelandic superstitions. The Celts settled in that country too. Did you know about that?"

Lily sighed. "No."

"A town in Iceland was going to build a road, but neighbors began to fume about it. They warned that gnomes lived under the boulders that had stood for years in the middle of what was to become their highway. Everybody in the town was in such an uproar the project was finally put on permanent hold. But the leader of the project was so enraged that he built his house right near another mysterious boulder, despite everyone's warnings."

"What warnings?" Lily asked.

"He'd selected a plot on a hill, below some other ancient rocks where everyone believed the gnomes lived. They kept telling him bad things would happen, but he didn't listen. That's probably something I'd do," Eve said as Lily drained her second glass of sherry. "You'll never guess how things turned out."

"What?" Lily felt goose bumps forming on her arms and her stomach began to roil like it had that afternoon.

"One evening, during a horrible storm, the boulder situated above his new house got loose and rolled down the hill, crushing it. He and his whole family died that very night." Eve put her glass on the nightstand and slipped off her slippers to sit on Lily's bed.

"Really? I didn't think you believed in gnomes and faeries—" Lily held her drink up to the light, trying to divert Eve. These Celtic flights of fantasy were beginning to bother her. "Mm, look at the color of this sherry. It tastes fabulous." Seeing her hand trembling, she put the glass down, hoping Eve didn't notice.

Oblivious, Eve went on, "Well, maybe I don't believe in all the Irish little people, but you know I've believed in the living spirits of the dead ever since I was young...and my dreams of...of my dad too," her voice cracked. "In fact, I read somewhere in one of your books that the Celts believed that death is only a thin curtain between this world and the next. Their stories are full of people who moved easily between both worlds."

"I love that idea, and I have to admit," Lily said, "I felt something very peculiar when I went to Newgrange with Patrick. Spirits seemed to dwell inside the mound where the ancient bones of the dead were found. It was very eerie. I'll never forget it, but it was strangely comforting too."

Lily went on, "The only time I ever *really* believed in faeries was after that strange incident at our first Celtic Faire with Gram. I was never certain about how this," Lily fingered her gold Celtic Knot pendant around her neck, "got lost...and then, strangely, we found it hours later among those hazelnuts arranged in the shape of a heart. Remember? My pendant lay right in the middle." Lily emptied her glass of sherry and quickly poured herself another. She suddenly didn't want to talk about baffling fantasies anymore.

"Maybe you're finally coming around to my beliefs. I've always thought the supernatural was much closer to us than we think." Eve got up and changed her seat to a cozy lounge chair, "I think I'll curl up over here. You look ultra comfy in your bed. I won't stay much longer, but I need to change the subject and ask you something."

Relieved, Lily sat up, plumping the pillows behind her, then leaned back, scrunching her knees up and clasping her hands around them. "Ask away."

"Well, I haven't seen anything of Maeve since we came here or met her son, Seamus. I got a call from his friend minutes ago. Remember the wine merchant at the Dublin Theater you told me about? He might be a fabulous contact for me. I want to thank Seamus for the referral, but I haven't even met him face-to-face."

"Maybe we could all have lunch together soon," Lily said. "I don't know Seamus' travel schedule, but I could ask him. I'll call him tonight. Maeve will want to come too. Both of them keep asking about you."

"That's perfect. Let me know the date ahead of time so I can put it on my schedule. Oh, and one more question. What's your opinion of Seamus?"

Lily fidgeted a little, unclasping her hands from around her knees, inspecting her nails and then grasping her knees again. "Hmm, he's a nice guy. Has a magnetic personality."

"His photo in Maeve's little house got my attention. Is he that good-looking in person?"

"Uh...yes, he...uh sort of lights up a room, actually. And he makes friends easily."

"Did I say something wrong?" Eve pushed her hair behind one ear. "Your voice went down an octave and you're avoiding my eyes."

"No... It's just...well, I guess he's pretty special, at least I think so." Lily still diverted her eyes.

"Wow, sounds like you have a major crush on him. Am I right?"

"I don't know...I feel very attracted to him, if that's what you mean. I've never felt like this about someone...I mean it's *very* different...than Frank."

"So you're falling for him?"

Lily still diverted her eyes. "I...I'm not sure, maybe, I don't know... but I like him a lot and he seems to feel the same way..."

"You don't sound like yourself. Are you feeling guilty because you have strong feelings for Seamus? Because of Frank? But I thought Patrick was your new guy."

"Patrick's got a lot of great qualities and I feel really relaxed with him, but Seamus has something else..."

"You're trembling, Lily."

Lily nodded and emptied her glass. "I guess I'm pretty overwhelmed that both men are even showing interest in me. And you're right; Seamus is in my thoughts a lot, but Frank's only been gone four months... "

Eve got up and poured another shot of Kahlua into Lily's glass. "Don't forget why we came on this trip, Lily. We wanted to have the time of our lives, to be free of all those bars that were jailing us up at home. Lots of married women flirt and have fun doing it. You never did, and I guess I flirt too much sometimes. But you're a widow now —even though it's probably a strange feeling." She softened her tone, "Plus, you took care of Frank for a long time. Maybe you should let yourself go a little. With Seamus...or... Isn't that what trips are for?"

"Yeah, well...sometimes we differ... "

"I know, you think I've been out of control lately. Maybe I'm trying to feel free too. Getting away from Brad and the accident and...everything..." her voice broke for a moment, then she sat down and poured Kahlua into her glass. "Anyway, enough about that—I think getting back on the job has been really good for me. And if things go right, I might have another big order coming in due to Seamus. We'll see. I hope you'll set up a lunch date with him and Maeve soon, like you promised, so I can thank him."

With that, Eve left both bottles on the table and, taking her drink, sauntered over to Lily and kissed her on the forehead.

Lily was touched. They'd finally connected again. It almost seemed like old times.

Opening the hotel room door, Eve turned back to her friend with that famous smile Lily knew so well. "Don't waste time worrying about today's ghost. Sleep well, because we're in for an unusual sightseeing treat tomorrow. G'nite."

CHAPTER 41

*W*ith storm clouds gathering in the sky all around them, Eve caught sight of two somber, stone gray tablets pointing upward, capped by a large stone slab forming a crude roof. *Amazing, but definitely a gloomy scene,* Eve thought.

Though the site seemed far off, their tour guide, Molly, parked the car in a small, dirt lot. "Come on, you two, bring your umbrellas. We have a bit of a hike ahead of us," she was pointing ahead. "That dolmen or portal tomb, as they call it, is definitely worth seeing. And you must experience The Burren here in County Clare. It's like nothing you'll ever see in the States."

"What is The Burren?" asked Eve.

With a smile, Molly waved her hand at the weird landscape surrounding them. "This! Doesn't it look like pictures of the moon? People call it a place out of time. It's 100 square kilometers of gray Karst limestone, an amazingly unique habitat. One of the largest of its kind in Europe."

Lily and Eve followed Molly across an unusual, treeless expanse, where, for miles and miles, gray flat rocks were seemingly strewn everywhere. Molly pointed at several coral and mollusk fossils embedded in the weathered limestone. "They say these fossils date back three million years."

"So many mysterious stories and places are found in Ireland, but this one looks creepy, especially on a dark day like this," Lily said.

Molly nodded. "Yes, and you can get lost in the caves around here too, plus there are archeological sites galore but this is the best portal tomb you'll see in Ireland." She smiled again, but Lily couldn't imagine why. "Here's another scary story," Molly went on smiling, "a tourist once told me that he took a walk alone near an ancient tomb here and felt someone tap his shoulder. When he turned around no one was there."

Irritated at Molly, Lily shivered, remembering yesterday's scare and Eve's ghostly walk a couple of nights before. She tried to joke away her own trepidation. "I'd certainly call the Burren barren."

"Hah, too funny," Eve remarked, but Lily could tell she was glad for a little humor.

"After seeing nothing but bright green in Ireland," Lily continued, "these endless gray hills are even more desolate. Do flowers ever bloom here?"

"Come back in a couple of months," Molly said. "Blue gentian flowers and over twenty different orchids bloom everywhere, beginning in May."

Lily marveled up close at the two slender upright stones supporting a thin, horizontal capstone about twelve feet long, creating what looked like a crude shelter.

"This is an imposing megalithic monument," Molly said, "the famous Poulnabrone portal tomb believed to be constructed about 4200 B.C.E. After hundreds of years this tomb became a center for ceremony and ritual."

"Was this a burial site for the Celts?" Lily asked.

"No," Molly stopped to lean on one large, upright stone. "It was the pre-Celts who lived here at the time."

The Celts arrived much later, didn't they?" Eve said.

"Yes, around 500 B.C.E.," Molly said.

"People were buried here, right?" Lily asked.

"Not complete skeletons, but some remains. Obviously, the ancients weren't too different from us. They wanted to honor their dead." Molly's breezy comments had finally ceased. Her face was clouded over now—or was it the darkening sky that seemed to reach down and encompass all of them? Lily shivered from a breeze that seemed to chill her to the bone. She wrapped her arms around her chest as Molly's voice turned low and serious, "They also call this place The Hole of Sorrow because the remains of several adults and children were uncovered here, including a newborn baby buried over there at the entrance."

Eve pressed her hand to her abdomen and bright tears shimmered in her eyes. She swiped at them and suddenly turned away.

Lily's heart wrenched. For months Eve hadn't mentioned one word about her miscarriage. Why did today's sightseeing have to open up that tragic wound?

"Sorry, Molly, I've had enough of this." Eve murmured as she walked toward their parked car. "This whole Burren place is depressing me. Plus, I just felt some drops." She put up her umbrella. "I read that special Burren music plays at a pub nearby. Let's get out of here and do some partying."

.

CHAPTER 42

*T*he next afternoon was gorgeous. Lily couldn't take her eyes off the magnificent panorama in front of her. "I'm...I can't even...I'm just over-whelmed." She stood transfixed, admiring the immense grandeur of the Cliffs of Moher and the wild coastline of crashing waves below.

"Now are you glad you came?" Seamus asked.

"It wasn't that I didn't want to come," Lily said, "Eve and I had such fun at the pub last night, I was disappointed that she wasn't able to come today. We've planned this for so long."

"Tis a shame, i'tis. But I don't criticize her a bit for hustlin' off to Dublin this mornin'. I guess it's me you need to be blamin'. I didn't get around to talkin' to my friend at the Abbey Theater till two days ago. He was eager to see her today, and timin' is everything when it comes to wine orders. *Any* business, for that matter. And, low and behold, he's promised to introduce her to other Dublin contacts who own restaurants. Hope you don't mind too much if she ends up stayin' longer than tonight. I can keep you company if you want, lassie."

"It's tempting, but I need to get back to Kinsale. When Eve left this morning, I made an appointment with Rose at Blarney Castle. I'm really frustrated, though. Eve and I were just beginning to enjoy ourselves on our getaway. But I understand why she had to cut it short. I'm just glad you happened to be nearby."

"Believe me, lass, I am too. Quite a coincidence. Me mother Maeve tells me I've always been a lucky lad. Lucky too, because me work at Trinity College involves a good amount of travel. I'm studying Celtic artifacts in museums throughout the British Isles, you know, besides taking classes. It's a welcome change after drivin' the freeways rushin' to teach a class."

They talked as they walked along the cliff tops. "You taught college classes in California?" Lily suddenly stopped as close to the edge as she could. The fog was moving in from the sea surrounding the stark bluffs, which plunged down to the swirling surf. *What a wild and wonderful paradise*, Lily thought. For years, while perusing Irish travel books, she'd lingered over the pages of this scene. She could hardly believe she was here!

Seamus, sidling up to her, wrapped his jacket around her shoulders. She felt his warm breath on her neck sending delicious shivers through her.

"You're tremblin', lass," he said. "This late afternoon breeze isn't that cold, but I know you're used to the heat of the California sun."

"I'm shaking from excitement, not from the weather." The truth was his presence always seemed to catch her off balance. She took a moment to try to quiet the pounding of her heart. Better to focus on this amazing vista before her. The sun was spreading streaks of amber, ochre and scarlet across the sky. The scene caused a joyful stir in her, she rarely felt.

"I know what you mean," Seamus said. "Once you see these cliffs, especially at sunset, you never forget them. Did you know they are over seven hundred feet high? The way they jut out into the ocean repeating, one after another...well, this place can create a powerful feelin'.'" He pointed to his heart, "Touchin' us all here and connectin' us to the soul of this great land."

"Yes!" she said.

"You asked about me classes," he went on. "Yes, my girl, I'm known as the 'Itinerant Irishman' with a passion for arts and the ancients. Taught classes at three different colleges back home. They'll soon be interviewing doctoral students for permanent positions teaching Celtic studies, and that's what I'm after."

"When will you finish your degree?"

"Depends. I've been accumulatin' credits online for two years, but decided I'd better get over here and finish my courses and start my thesis."

Lily forced herself to make conversation, though she was really lost in a world of her own. As she studied the sky and the untamed cliffs, a shiver streaked down her spine to her toes. This stark beauty made words unnecessary. She remembered how Patrick had left her to her own thoughts at Newgrange. The stillness they'd shared had been so comfortable and had allowed them both to sense realities that weren't obvious to most.

"Now aren't you glad, lass, that I came here to study right at *this* time?" Seamus said. She noticed how his eyes were lit with merriment, and she had to admit his cheerful gift of gab delighted her.

They'd reached the parking lot now and headed toward his van. She turned toward him, enjoying his unfathomable smile and the dimple that winked at her. He had such a way with words, and his upbeat nature always lifted her out of her pensive moods. Suddenly she felt him moving closer, all the while his mischievous eyes were magnetizing her. She couldn't breathe and a passion she's never felt before was setting a fire throughout her body.

She was in his arms then, and his lips were pressing against hers, wonderful and warm, soft and insistent too. Gently she tried to pull away, but his mouth was unrelenting, caressing hers—then her neck, her ears, her eyes, one at a time, and oh, so softly. When he pressed his lips to hers again she gave in and let him have his way, his tongue forcing her mouth open, searching, exploring, and all the while his hands slowly massaging her shoulders and her back.

She returned his kiss then with a passion she'd never felt in all her life. Hot waves of new feelings crested inside her, heating her whole being. When he lifted her in his arms and carried her to the van, she shook her head as he opened the door. "I can't. It's way too soon."

So he shut the door on the large mattress inside and they stood next to the car, nestled inside each other's embrace, kissing and caressing for a long time. She'd never felt this urgency. Her body was tingling with desire. She wanted it to go on and on. How much time went by luxuriating in his arms Lily didn't know. By then Seamus had unbuttoned her blouse and began caressing her breasts. She wanted to stay here forever, but her body wanted more...much more. She suddenly stiffened and took a deep breath. *What am I doing? Frank's only been gone a few months and I'm ready to....*

"What's the matter, lass?" Seamus' fingers lightly massaged her back.

The sun had set by now, and the darkness of this lonely place penetrated her thoughts. *I don't even really know this man.*

"It's cold. I...I need to get back to the hotel," she said. "This isn't what I expected to..."

He put both arms around her shoulders. "Don't fret, lass, we can be in your warm and cozy hotel in no time, but not before we have a hearty Irish meal together. Yes?"

She looked up at him and returned his smile. She would let him take her to dinner but, as much as she wanted to, no way would he share her bed. At least, not yet.

CHAPTER 43

*M*esmerized by Kinsale's refurbished 18th century house, now called The Little Skillet, Lily admired the ambience. Quaint glass chandeliers, teal walls crowded with pictures and a warm, open hearth. Over in a cozy corner sat a beaming pixie lady waving to her.

"Hello, my lass, I'm pleased as punch to see you," Maeve said as she stood up. Her black slim boots and blue suede jacket and skirt accented her merry eyes and white hair. "But why're you all alone now, child? I thought you were fixin' to bring your friend along with you this time."

She handed Lily a menu and waved to a waitress, who came right over as Lily murmured, "Eve should be here soon." At least Lily hoped she would. Three days had passed since Lily had returned from the west of Ireland. Finally, late last night Eve had sent her a text to say she'd left Dublin and would soon arrive in Kinsale in time to meet for lunch today.

"What can I give you?" the matronly waitress asked, and, when she discovered Lily was a tourist, she began tempting her. "Our kitchen serves up a delicious Irish stew or shepherd's pie full to the brim with fresh steamed vegetables. My scones are just out of the oven too. And, of course, I have all kinds of teas to choose from."

Maeve checked her watch. "I wish me son would appear. Never saw a lad so late so often. But when he finally comes, mark my words, you'll forget it in no time." As soon as she'd spoken her son swept into the restaurant.

As Lily took Seamus' warm hand in hers she had to agree. That flashing smile of his always made her quiver with excitement.

He managed to set three mugs of ale on the table at once. "I've been across the street getting' your ale, my ladies. Where's your friend? I thought *I* got the prize for bein' tardy. I've heard all about Eve but, since I've never seen her, I'm wonderin', does she exist?"

"Oh, she's real, all right, I can vouch for that," said Maeve. "Where is she this time, child?"

Lily sipped her ale. "She landed some big orders in Dublin, thanks to you." She beamed at Seamus and he flashed his famous dimple. "One of the top California wineries she represents called her this morning unexpectedly, but she'll be here soon, I hope."

Time stretched on, so they ordered while Lily enjoyed Seamus' jokes, finding them almost as appealing as the steaming shepherd's pie the waitress placed in front of her. Or was she feeling tingly all over from the second pint of ale he'd bought for her?

She took another sip as Seamus talked, "Aye, I'm going to Wales one of these days to a university by the coast. They have quite a collection of ancient Celtic artifacts that were found not long ago. Maybe you could join me, lass," he said.

The thought of seeing long-lost Celtic jewelry with someone who was studying it—someone as brawny and handsome as Seamus—was almost too exciting to bear. "I'd love that," Lily said.

"And I'm lucky enough to have a stipend of money from the university to use, since I'm also working part time for Trinity as an anthropology instructor. I'll use me Irish blarney to allow you admission to see the other treasures stored there." He winked at her.

Lily was thrilled by his invitations, so much so she couldn't answer. Instead, she grasped her mug and took another sip.

Was he displaying that extra gleam in his eyes because of their intimate moments a few days ago? Or was he trying to tell her something else? Lily felt her breath quicken after she swallowed the Guinness; she tried to keep her hand steady when she put her glass down. She hadn't felt this way since high school, and back then any boy who thrilled her *always* treated her like she was invisible. She took a deep breath to calm herself. *He's just a friendly guy. My imagination's going a bit wild. Nothing seems real here in Ireland.*

Lily tuned in late to a story Maeve was beginning as Eve finally swung through the door, lighting up the room with her striking beauty as she always did. Her sleek gray dress, trimmed in silver, outlined the curves of her shape perfectly, and her dangle earrings, sparkling in the sun, matched the upbeat mood shining on her face.

After a flurry of hellos and an introduction to Seamus, Eve sat down next to Lily as he went off to get Eve some ale. Ordering her food quickly, Eve waited till he returned to thank him. "I'm so sorry. I was late getting here because the orders your friend and his colleagues gave me are so large that the winery has to schedule them in separate shipments. They're not used to that. I had to spend time talking to the production and shipping staff. They couldn't believe the hefty orders I submitted! I have you to thank for them, Seamus."

He beamed and, lifting Eve's hand to his lips, he kissed it, feigning bravado. "I'm your knight in shinin' armor, I am, m'lady," he said. "And you best not forget it."

"Oh, I'd never do that," Eve said, "and if you have any more friends who need wine, please let me know."

"I will, lass, I will," he kept her hand in his. "I've got some travelin' to do, so I may come across another lead for you. Shall I call you meself when I do or give it to your friend here?" At last he let go of Eve's hand and fixed his eyes on Lily.

"Well, I think you should call me because Lily's out and about a lot," Eve said.

Lily tried to keep her face neutral, but she knew her tension over Eve's answer showed.

Eve paused, "Um...actually what I meant was, our vacation isn't turning out quite... Lily and I are not together as much as we planned." She dug into her purse and gave Seamus her card.

Accepting it with a flourish of hand to forehead, he flashed his dimple, "My fair lady, I'm glad to help, and I'll put this in a very special place." He found his wallet and slipped it between a mass of Euros.

Maeve stood up then, her elfin height not much taller than the back of the large chair, and with an impish smile said, "Now, I was tellin' a story, I was, before you breezed in here, Eve, and I mean to finish it if you don't mind."

"Of course, of course," they all said.

She sat down and all eyes were upon her. "I was tellin' Lily that you should mind old tales, my lassies; they're full of whimsy, they are, but wisdom too. Especially you two, since your names call to mind one of the most ancient stories of all. Did you ever hear of *The Epic of Gilgamesh*? It's an ancient Sumerian tale both of you must read. And soon."

When Eve and Lily shook their heads, Maeve's face broke into a mystifying smile. *She looks like the Cheshire cat,* Lily mused. *I remember that smile when we came upon the Witch's Tree at Blarney Castle.* Maeve had promptly disappeared that day, leaving Lily fearful and confused by that sinuous, serpentine tree. Memories of that day still cast feelings in her she couldn't describe.

Maeve's pause fired up Seamus, "Stop your perennial teasin', Muther. Go on, will ya?"

With that, Maeve launched into a primeval tale about Adam and

Eve that Lily had listened to so many times in her Catholic school years that she began to yawn.

But Maeve flourished her index finger at all of them, just like a nun demanding attention, "Don't you close your ears to me now. Tisn't what you've heard before at all, though I know you're thinkin' it is. Cause before Adam met Eve in Paradise he was smitten with a dark beauty just like yourself, called Lilith, and that's your namesake, deary, now isn't it? I'm bettin' you've never heard about *that* particular favorite of Adam's, did you now?"

Lily sat up, riveted to the little old woman's words, gulping the last of her ale.

"Full of surprises, I am. And about your name, lass." Maeve flashed her puzzling grin again across the table and began a low keening, then said:

A serpent who could not be charmed made its nest in the roots of the tree,

Then the Anzu bird set his young in its branches

And the dark little maiden Lilith built her home in the trunk.

Hearing mention of the mysterious tree trunk and the bird, Lily felt a shiver run down her spine.

Maeve went on, "I'm tellin' ye the truth, lass, your name is one and the same as the She-devil, Lilith, who left Adam first, she did. These Sumerian tales go way back, they do, long before Christ. They say Lilith was Adam's first wife, but she wouldn't submit to him, you know, in the way he demanded. Under him was where he wanted her, so they say, on the bed where they lay. And she wanted none of that. So she left him, wearin' an angel's amulet, she did, to keep the devils away. Lilith went on to mate another and left Adam to a second wife whose name was Eve...yes, indeed. I'm sure you've heard of her, now haven't you?"

Lily followed Maeve's stare, which was fixed on her friend.

Eve's eyes were wide and her mouth slightly open. "I've heard part..."

Lily searched Seamus's face then but saw no twinkle in his eyes now. As she reached for a gulp of water, he put his hand over hers. "There now, lass, don't pay too much mind to me muther's tales. She goes on and on, she does, and we don't want her ancient tales scaring the likes of you and spoilin' your journey in our faire land."

But Maeve persisted, putting her own hand up to stop her son's talking, still flashing the enigmatic smile Lily had come to recognize. "Now what do you think of this tale, my lass? I've been thinkin' on it myself for quite some time, from the first moment I saw you two together on the New Year—you and Eve being friends for all your lives, you say. Because the story goes that Eve, the second wife, *did* submit to Adam's wishes in bed after all, but we all know, now don't we, lassie, that it was Eve who led poor Adam and all of us thereafter to sin. Or that's what the Mother Church has told us down through the ages."

Eve's voice was hard. "I left the Catholic Church long ago. Stories about Adam and Eve never enter my head."

"I don't know what to think," Lily said. "My mother named me Lilith in spite of my dad's arguments. My aunt claimed it caused a lifelong ruckus between them because Mother said she'd 'made a promise,' but no one ever knew why or to whom she'd promised. Dad wanted to name me Cara, after his mother, but Mom fumed and argued that it must be 'Lilith.' She finally got her way. Strange, because she never seemed to care much about *me*. Truth is, she cared more about my name." Lily suddenly felt an urge to leave.

"That's strange," Eve said. "You may not remember this, Lily, or maybe you never knew it, but Lilith was my grandmother's name. Only my father and I knew it, though, because everyone called her Lee."

"I never knew that. Why didn't you tell me?" Lily asked. She stood up then, using an excuse to find the *loo*, her erratic thoughts causing chaos in her mind as she wound her way to the back of the restaurant. Why was she spouting off about her childhood and revealing painful, personal stuff about her mother to Eve with all these strangers listening? And now, to find out after all these years, that she was the namesake of Eve's grandmother? How could that be? Was it a coincidence? Why had her mother insisted on naming her Lilith? *Very odd—because Mom never wanted anything to do with Eve's mother or her grandmother!*

CHAPTER 44

$\mathcal{E}$ ve looked outside the restaurant window at the leafless branches of trees where small buds had formed. Very soon it would be April. She and Patrick had been poring over Eve's ancestry papers for at least an hour in between nibbling on pub grub.

Suddenly he asked, "Do you want to give me a DNA sample today? It helps me narrow down relationships in a family. It'll give you a picture of your ancestors' ethnicities too."

Eve looked up from the family chart he had made for her when they'd started the project. He seemed deep in thought today, after delving into some data he'd received on the marriage and death records of her relatives. She found herself admiring the straight line of his nose and his high cheekbones under eyes the color of azure, framed by black lashes. She was struck by not only how attractive he was but how serious as well. *He needs to lighten up.*

"Of course," she said, brandishing her brightest smile and taking the small tool from him. She swabbed the inside of her mouth with it, trying to hold his gaze, then licked her bottom lip very slowly, on purpose, and handed it back to him. "Why don't we take a break? You're so intense about all this," she gestured toward the shaft of papers strewn on the table, "so much so that I wonder if you even enjoy it."

"I don't have to grin all the time like you do, lass, to enjoy something. I like the intensity of research. Most of my clients do too. Obviously, you don't. We've been at this an hour and you already need a distraction. I doubt another pint will satisfy you, but—" He got up from the table.

"My, such sarcasm," Eve retorted. "Why is it that whenever Lily's around you're all smiles?"

"My, such envy," he countered. "I thought you and Lily were lifelong friends." Heading for the bar, he didn't wait for her reply.

Me, envious of Lily? That's outrageous! What's with this guy? He manages to rile me even when I try my damndest to be friendly.

When he returned with a pint for them both and sat down again, she decided he looked less hostile and wondered if he regretted being so blunt.

"If I may, can I ask you an honest question?" he asked. When she nodded, he continued. "I'm wondering...why are you so interested in this project? Or am *I* the challenge?"

Hmm, he's more perceptive than I thought.

But she wasn't going to take his bait even though she knew he was dead right. While getting ready for their meeting today, she'd hoped to break down the barriers he constantly put up and take advantage of his talent and knowledge at the same time. Now she tried another approach. "I have no family. My dad died when I was nine, and when I turned eighteen, my mother died. All I've had is Lily's family since then, and even sometimes before that. For years I've dreamed of finding relatives somewhere, and since my dad's Swedish family seems to be nonexistent, I decided to try to search out my mom's ancestors over here."

"Aye, now I understand. I know a little about being an orphan," he said. "My own parents died before I was twenty, but I have three brothers and a sister quite a bit younger. In fact my sister has some of your sass." He tried to soften his words this time with a slight smile. "Sorry to say, she still causes trouble. They all needed me to take care of them for a few years after—"

She ignored his dig. "You're the oldest?"

"Yes, but me brother Sean insisted on taking over when I reached my late twenties so I could pursue me college education and travel too. I told you about that last time."

Eve understood him better now, but that only made her more curious. "So, did you start out wanting to find long-lost relatives like me? What do *you* get out of doing these genealogy projects? Besides money."

"When I took an anthropology class long ago, I was fascinated about ancient cultures, how they venerate their dead and how much they respect their ancestors. For example, I learned that ancient tribes in South America mummified their family and propped them up in their houses."

Eve tucked her silken hair behind one ear and gave him one of her dazzling smiles. "That sure would've crowded *your* house growing up. With all those siblings."

Patrick's smile was weak and his eyes stayed serious. "They didn't believe in heaven like some of us. Instead, they thought their loved ones' spirits still resided in their mummified bodies and were always with them. They set beer and food in front of them too. Theirs was a very different take on the afterlife than the Celts."

Eve sat up with interest. "What did the Celts think?"

"They believed the afterlife or Otherworld is very near to the living and the dead are not far away. That only a thin veil separates us from those we loved who have gone on to the next world, where their spirits move freely, even reentering our world at times."

His words hung in the air while images of her dad and mom invaded Eve's mind. How many times had she thought she'd seen them since they died? She couldn't speak, but noticed Patrick sipping his Guinness for several long minutes, lost in his own thoughts. She was relieved at his silence.

Finally, his eyes found hers and his words were gentle. "Does that surprise you, lass?"

"Well, I like the veil part and I like the beer part," was all she could manage, and she raised her mug to clink it with his.

CHAPTER 45

Flipping through garden brochures and magazines had become one of Lily's favorite things to do, even though she rarely had the time. Today she sat lingering over glossy garden images while eating breakfast in her hotel room. Taking Eve's advice, she'd decided to pamper herself today. She'd made a hair and nail appointment too, because tonight she and Eve were going to a special fundraising gala at Blarney Castle. The sapphire satin dress she planned to wear was hanging in her closet. She couldn't believe she'd bought a size eight. It fit perfectly!

Her cell phone rang and, unexpectedly, she heard a voice from home.

"Hi Mom, it's Tanya. How are you? We haven't heard from you much lately. Just wondering how you are."

Her daughter's voice didn't sound happy, and the old weight of maternal worry began to lodge in Lily's shoulders. "I'm surprised to hear from you—but it's wonderful! I'm fine, honey. Going to a big gala tonight at Blarney Castle with friends. I haven't gotten a call from you in eons." She bit her tongue then, not wanting to lay a guilt trip on her daughter. Nevertheless, she couldn't forget all the phone calls she'd made in these last weeks when no one answered. How many messages had she left with her daughters' roommates that were never passed on?

Gradually, as the weeks passed, Lily had forced herself to face the painful prospect that the girls wanted to be left alone. So she'd limited her phone calls and emails, resigning herself to the brief texts they sent, but replying immediately so they knew she still missed and loved them.

"How're you doing, honey?"

"Um...good, but... I have to change roommates. Now. My last one turned out to be a nightmare."

"Really? What happened?"

"Well, long story short, I caught her stealing my food and I think she stole my mini-iPad too, but I can't prove it. Anyway, we had it out so she moved."

"Oh no, I'm sorry. That's really disturbing. It can be so disappointing when a friend turns out to be a disappointment. Did you report her?"

"It doesn't do any good. It happens a lot around here, I guess. I asked Lisa to come and live here, but she's still mad at me about wanting to live separately, so that's out. Plus, she's...sort of changed, Mom, if you want to know the truth."

"Changed? How?" Lily began to pace around her room. Tanya's tone was worrisome.

"Can't talk about that now. I have to get to class. What I called about is Eve. Is she still traveling with you?"

"Yes, we're both going to a Blarney Castle dinner tonight. Do you want me to give her a message?"

"Yeah. You know that guy who caused Eve's accident? I think his name is Brad."

Lily's stomach suddenly felt like an elevator plunging to the bottom floor. "Yes?"

"He...he phoned Lisa the other day, out of the blue. Or that's who she thought it was."

"Really? I don't like that. Not at all. I hope she didn't tell him anything. Did she?"

"I don't know much more about it, because Lisa avoids me whenever she can. She sure knows how to hold a grudge. I didn't really do anything to her, Mom. I just wanted some space, you know, to spread my wings. She always comes on like a mother to me. I just wanted to be on my own, for once. Now, everything's gone bad."

Lily could hear Tanya's voice grind to a teary halt. She was sniffing now and blowing her nose.

"Oh, honey, I'm so sorry. I didn't realize you and your sister were barely talking. She's never mentioned anything. But I'm glad you told me. You must feel alone without her and your roommate too. Have you contacted the college to see about getting another roommate? What about your new friends?"

"Oh, yeah, I called Admin right away. They said they'll have someone moving in next week, someone who enrolled late, but it's a guy and I'm—"

"A guy?"

"Yeah, they don't have any girls available right now. It's pretty unusual—"

"Tanya, I'm not paying for your college room and board so you can live with a guy!"

"I knew you'd get upset about it, Mom. But it's not my fault. Hey, maybe *you* could call the Admin office and talk to them for me. All my friends already have roommates, but they've been sympathetic. I can live alone till the office finds me a female roommate. But it'd be easier if you complained. I don't want them getting mad at me."

"Of course, Tanya. I'm going to call Lisa too. We need to know more about this guy who phoned her. If it *was* Brad, I don't want her to have anything to do with him. Or you either. He's dangerous. Eve's totally done with him. You both know that, right?"

"Sure, but like I said, Lisa's in her own world right now. You need to call her—"

"What exactly is going on? You've got to tell me *some*thing."

"She's started to hang out with some low-lifes. At least that's what *I* call them. I don't think you or...or Dad," her voice cracked a little, "would approve."

"Thanks for letting me know. I'll definitely call her today. Please keep your phone calls coming too, honey. They're so much better than texts or emails. I want to hear your voice...to know how you are. I've tried leaving several messages but—"

"I know, Mom, I forget to call back sometimes, and with the time difference in Ireland..."

"So you did get all my messages?"

"Some, but like I said, I'm in class sometimes when it's a good time to call you."

"Well, I'm going to call the Admin office now and straighten out this roommate thing for you." Lily could feel the ache in her shoulders weighing her down. "Please do something for me, Tanya. Go over and see Lisa face-to-face, at her dorm. Today. You two have to make up. Tell her what I've said and ask her to call me. I'll be in this hotel most of the day. I need to talk to her now. It's important. Promise?"

CHAPTER 46

*D*usk was giving way to darkness in Blarney Castle's gardens as quaint lighted lanterns cast a glow on rows of decorated tables under a spacious white tent. Rose O'Sullivan had organized this fancy, fundraiser dinner, and had called to invite Maeve, Lily and Eve and their guests, Seamus and Patrick. They all sat together, Maeve and Rose at each end of their table.

Dinner over, Rose stood up to greet and thank the array of prominent professionals who had come from several Irish counties. Her husband, Sean, the head vintner from Kinsale, sat next to her, beaming with pride. Many wine merchants sat around them, enjoying special gourmet cuisine to match the wines they were trying for the first time.

Early on, during the cocktail hour, Lily had tried to shift her thoughts away from Tanya's phone call and the fact that she'd never gotten a call back from Lisa. But she had a penchant for worrying. When Frank was first diagnosed with cancer, she'd become an obsessive worrier, but realized that constant anxiety only made her more vulnerable to illness and depression. Her doctor confirmed it when he told her about her ulcers. So she'd sought out a counselor briefly to help her learn to substitute posi-tive thoughts for negative ones. Not an easy habit to form.

Now she sat among these friendly Irish people and decided she must not allow herself to dwell on events she could do nothing about. She vowed to get hold of Lisa tomorrow. *If it's the last thing I do!*

Fingering the napkin on the table, Lily watched Eve work the room, talking with Sean O'Sullivan, overhearing her make another sales appointment with him, and then, one by one, introducing herself to every other merchant, hotelier or restaurateur. For years, Lily had admired her friend's social skills. *She turns strangers into friends so easily!*

As Lily gazed around the candlelit table, she decided this evening was almost as special as her dates with Seamus at the Abbey Theater, the Cliffs of Moher, and their evenings together since. He treated her like a princess. But he'd also offered his affec-tions so suddenly, and so often, it had caught her off guard. No wonder thoughts of him had consumed her during these last weeks, despite other exciting news that had thrilled her too. Maeve had called last week and hinted that Rose O'Sullivan actually wanted her to become a part-time consultant and submit new faerie garden designs *for Blarney Castle!* And, sure enough, the next day Rose had done just that! Moreover, she'd offered Lily more money than she'd ever expected as a fledgling consultant, since, in her heart, Lily believed the job was more of an internship than a real position. Well, whatever her title was, she wanted to pinch herself to make sure tonight wasn't one of the faerie tales she'd always loved.

Though she'd purchased this special satin dress and sleek new sandals for this occasion, she was determined to wander the gardens again tonight. This time she had more than a tourist's purpose—to scope out an area where her faerie garden could take shape. Rose had given her free rein as far as its location on the grounds.

But she had to admit, she was more than a little nervous. This was the most important project she'd ever undertaken—far more challenging than submitting her garden designs to a contest and tons more important to her than any technical manual she'd ever tackled at Graylock. After Rose had phoned with her offer, Lily started sketching out a new plan, complete with a Celtic labyrinth that included whorled designs and favorite faerie gemstones, not to mention all the faerie flowers she'd learned about as a girl from the books Gram gave her.

Come to think of it, she thought she remembered a stream here on the Blarney grounds that might be a perfect setting for her garden. That way every tourist would learn about the Celts' belief in the magic of water, so much so that they often buried their treasures there. Mulling that over, she wondered about placing replicas of real Celtic medallions and goblets in the clear stream.

Up at the head of the table Rose O'Sullivan's speech to all her guests was coming to a close, "...and now I'd like to introduce you to someone you'll be seein' much more often here at Blarney Castle. Because I'm hirin' her as a special part-time consultant since she's won landscape awards in the States. I submitted one of her wee garden plans to our Board last week, and they had to agree with me that it's taken an American from California to appreciate our Irish faerie lore in such an endearin' way. As soon as I met her, I said to meself I must convince her to embellish our own Blarney Gardens. So please, Lily O'Malley, this is no time to be shy. I'm hopin' you'll stand up and take a bow."

All heads turned toward her, and Lily could feel a warm glow flushing her cheeks.

Eve nudged her and whispered, "For god's sake, stand up, girl. They're clapping for you!"

Lily wasn't going to let Eve chide her more. She rose up for a moment and managed to nod to everyone with a smile before she sank into her seat again.

Rose was still clapping lightly as she engaged the group again. "I think we surprised her with this public introduction." Her eyes sought Lily's and she smiled. "Didn't we, Lily?" Then she looked around at all those seated before her. "She's a modest lass, and I'm sure you're going to enjoy gettin' to know her. Be sure to go over and say hello to her tonight."

After most of Rose's guests had congratulated her, Lily found an obscure corner where she could relax, taking a few moments to breathe deeply. She sat quietly, basking in the joy of this evening and letting creative possibilities float through her mind again about her garden designs.

As she sipped the after-dinner sherry that Eve had donated for this occasion, she noticed how intent Eve and Patrick were at the table next to her, seemingly oblivious of anyone else. A unusual feeling came over her when she studied Patrick, but she couldn't name it.

Lily knew they'd met at least three times now to investigate Eve's ancestry, and she decided that searching out Eve's ethnic roots must be improving their relationship. She sighed with happiness to see her friend so animated, and for that matter, as gorgeous as ever. Not only was Eve's face gleaming, her blonde hair was swept up and wound in braided plaits accentuating a few wispy blonde curls. Her dress of icy blue silk matched the sea tones of her eyes which, right now, were fixed on Patrick.

At a far table she noticed Seamus surrounded by women and men alike; he was busy charming them all. *He couldn't be more different from Frank*, she thought. *Maybe that's why he intrigues me.*

Maeve approached Lily with a smile. "So, me darlin' girl," she gestured up to the new moon in the sky, "your dress is as beautiful as the cerulean sky tonight. But soon these shadows will give way to complete darkness and gloom. Shall we walk the garden now so you can plan your faerie playground?"

How did she know that's exactly what I wanted to do next?

Lily hoped to use this opportunity to find out more about Maeve. "I have you to thank for this amazing privilege and I'm really grateful."

The petite old lady walked a few steps ahead of Lily with a sort of gleeful gait, almost a dance. Lily realized that whenever she was with Maeve her spirits rose, and her doubts about herself and her future were suddenly cast aside. Sure enough, a thrill went through her again. "I have only one question, Maeve, if you don't mind. How did you know about my garden designs and the contests I won in the States? I don't remember telling you."

"Oh yes you did, child. You haven't forgotten the day we first met, now have you? You told me all about it. Though I remember I had to go about pryin' it out of you. Then, of course, I checked up on you with my friends who work at your college. I was so impressed I had to tell my friend Rose, so I wrote it in an email. She's been my closest friend for as long as I can remember, that is, since your..."

Her face suddenly turned downcast, as if a shade had been drawn. A second later though, her sunny visage was back and Maeve chatted on, "Rose takes my advice *seriously*, she does. Maybe like you and Eve? Uh, though I haven't talked to your friend lately as much as you, but I remember meetin' her at the Rose Parade after your Frank died. She seemed concerned about you then..." Maeve's eyes held a question and then she went on, "I always believe we meet certain people for a purpose, don't you, lass? Our true friends should be our special, kindred spirits who offer us just what we need. Here *and* hereafter too. Don't you think?" She gazed at Lily in a loving but mysterious way. She reached out her small, frail hand and clasped Lily's firmly in hers. Then she let go, dancing a few steps ahead.

They'd reached the Witch's Tree now, not intentionally, but suddenly they were upon it and Lily couldn't shake off the same ominous foreboding she'd felt the first time she'd visited here in broad daylight. Now the light was waning, leaving them in the gloom Maeve had predicted. Her words from the other day invaded Lily's thoughts:

A serpent who could not be charmed made its nest in the roots of the tree,

Then the Anzu bird set his young in its branches

And the dark little maiden Lilith built her home in the trunk.

Lily hugged herself then grasped her hands together to keep them from trembling. Maeve's words, describing her name, had been strangely menacing then. And her description of the tree sounded just like....

And Maeve was confusing her. Lily was *sure* she'd never mentioned her faerie garden designs to the little lady. And come to think of it, she didn't remember ever mentioning Frank to her either. Had Eve told Maeve about those missing pieces of her life?

Suddenly off in the distance she glimpsed a bird she knew she'd seen before, in the lowest branch of a tree nearby. She heard a weird, keening sound too, its volume violating the wooded glen. Lily shivered and her heart began to pound, but her curiosity won out. She rounded the huge serpentine trunk of the Witch's tree, inspecting it from every angle, and noticed the clear stream that ran near it. Despite the menacing sound that persisted, she was mesmerized by the tree's circuitous, sprawling shape; its numerous, tangled branches seemed alive, as if clawing at the sky. She gazed up at the branches' silhouettes, glittering in the remaining light like arms waving wildly. Lily blinked, not sure now of what she was seeing. How could this be? The branches were moving but no wind blew tonight and it was dark as pitch now. Evening shadows had closed in on her with only one lone star in the sky. All of a sudden the warm night evaporated as freezing air enveloped her. She shivered more than once and turned toward Maeve. The baffling little lady had disappeared—once again. But the bird remained on the same lone branch.

A keening started up, becoming an unbearable wail. Lily heard a mourning voice riding on top of it like a disturbing wave, "I must leave, though it's not what I desire! It tears my heart apart to leave you and be alone." A searing wail followed amidst a new wind that took hold. Soon it gave way again to a voice that was more like a woman's than something born of nature. Lily heard the same words repeated and she shuddered. She couldn't help thinking about Frank, and Lisa and Tanya too. Or was this an omen about her future?

Her skirt and hair, buffeted now by a stronger wind rising out of nowhere, Lily rushed off toward the white tent, where lanterns still blazed.

The scene had changed. Eve sat alone at the table, and Lily could see a tall, gangly man standing near her. It was Ian. Unsteady on his feet, he was wavering as he bent over Eve. Lily could make out a scowl on his face and eyes that flashed with rage. As she came closer, he bellowed at Eve and slapped her face hard, then slapped her again. Next he shoved her, and Eve fell out of her chair. She stood up to slap him back, but he grabbed her arm, and she teetered, trying to right herself, but fell again. Those still lingering at the tables turned to stare as Seamus left the bar and streaked across the lawn toward Eve. He landed more than one hefty wallop on Ian's chin and then pummeled his rib cage so that he finally fell backward onto the grass. Much taller, Ian quickly righted himself and slugged Seamus hard in the ribs. Their fight raged as Lily watched in horror. Eve was crumpled in a heap on the lawn, her face buried in her hands.

"You slimy bastard!" Seamus yelled, punching Ian in the ribs and groin over and over again. Security guards came running and finally pulled both men apart. As they huddled together Lily heard them questioning the two men and then call the police. Lily headed straight for Eve.

"Are you all right?" Lily asked.

"Of course," Eve looked up into her friend's eyes with embarrassment written all over her face. She swiped at tears welling up in her eyes. Her cheek burned with red welts.

In minutes Seamus was by Eve's side. "Who was that animal, lass? Where did he come from? Sure the likes of him wasn't invited here. But don't you worry your pretty head. They'll put him where he belongs now, in the local jail."

Patrick suddenly reappeared. "What happened?" he demanded. "I was only gone five minutes. What trouble did you cause, lass?" He stared down at Eve, who was holding her hand to her cheek and chin, massaging the red blotches from Ian's blows.

Eve moved away. "C'mon, Lily, I won't stay here." She glared at Patrick. "I don't need more abuse from you." She pulled her coat on as a wind blew around them. Lily held on to her, helping her stilted walk, noticing that all the flames igniting the lanterns and the candles on the tables were snuffed out.

The whole party was in disarray, everyone reaching for their wraps because of the cold wind, but rushing away because the beautiful evening was spoiled. Rose was trying to salvage the event by passing out the small, ribboned packages she'd saved as farewell gifts to each participant. It was obvious to Lily that she was horri- fied by the turn of events but was trying not to show it. She headed over to console Eve now, her husband, Sean, by her side.

"Let's make our thank you's as brief as we can and then get out of here quick," Eve whispered to Lily. "The last thing I need is to deal with their questions about what happened and who Ian is, especially in front of Sean O'Sullivan."

They forced some grateful but hurried good-byes as they rushed off, Lily waving to Rose and Sean. "Thank you again for everything," she called. "I hope you understand. We have to get Eve to the hotel. We'll call you first thing in the morning."

When they'd made it to the parking lot, Eve wouldn't allow Patrick to drive them, though he offered several times. Instead, she beckoned to Seamus. He took over then, putting his arm around

Eve. She clung to him as she walked, and he bent over her for several minutes, consoling her and helping her into the front seat of his car as cold raindrops began to fall. Lily sat in the back seat as they whizzed off, wondering why she felt so alone amidst the wind and sudden rain, hoping everyone would put the evening's dreadful finale behind them.

CHAPTER 47

*P*atrick couldn't sleep. It was just after dawn and he lay in bed looking up at the ceiling, going over last night's events. He wished he hadn't gone to the WC and missed the ruckus between Eve and Ian. What had started it? *Eve probably brought it on herself. She's a difficult lass. I know her kind—always bound to find trouble.*

She reminded him of his sister Nona and the friends she ran with. *Stubborn rebels, all of 'em.* Flirty too, but they didn't have a clue how dangerous it could be. He'd never been able to control Nora after Ma and Da died. When his brother took over, things got worse. Now he didn't know where she was and neither did anyone else in Doolin.

He rubbed his eyes as if to wipe away the old guilt he felt for leaving his brothers and sister alone. Back then he'd thought he had a calling from God. For ten long years he'd been a priest, his last years serving in the Curia at the Vatican, because the cardinal in Dublin had recommended him as "an unusual spiritual leader" to Rome. But the politics and hypocrisy there had filled him with concern then revulsion, and, though the Pope seemed faithful to God's teachings, when the scandals of pedophile priests broke again in the newspapers and were whispered all around him in Rome, he'd expected the hierarchy to act immediately, to console the victims and punish the priests.

But it didn't happen the way Patrick wanted. When letters and files were forced open, some Church leaders admitted their failures and resigned, but not all. Many just received forgiveness. Patrick felt the worst offenders were the cardinals and bishops who had simply moved the perpetrator priests to a new parish and hid the disgusting truth.

How could he look his Catholic congregation in the eye after that? Slowly, he even began to feel people looking at *him* as if he was a pedophile too. By then he'd begun to feel like a hypocrite when counseling divorced men and women. How could the hierarchy and the Pope justify their decrees to excommunicate them if they married again, but not banish a pedophile priest from the altar or the priesthood? It was ridiculous and the parishioners knew it! Patrick finally decided he no longer wanted any part of that nest of vipers.

Other problems had plagued him when living in Rome. He'd sorely missed his homeland and...and maybe he'd missed a woman's touch too. Even now it had been a very long time since he'd...

His cell phone rang and Patrick roused himself to answer it.

"That you, Patrick?" said Lily's sleepy voice.

Though drawn to her soft words, Patrick steadied his voice to make sure it sounded normal. She must've had a hard night with Eve. "Yes, how's everything with you this morning? And how is Eve?"

"She's pretty banged up, poor thing. I suggested she get a gentle massage later. She wants to stay in today and rest. We'll do room service for meals. Last night was...well, enough said. I was thinking, though, that when she takes her sleeping pill after lunch, I'll be sitting here doing nothing. Can I possibly hire you for a little genealogy time, if you can spare it? Or are you busy?"

"Not the whole day. I have an upcoming...well, it's sort of a retreat...you may remember. I have to prepare for it, since I'm the leader. But I'll be done with that by this afternoon. How about if I pick you up at two-thirty?"

"Great! Thanks."

Patrick reached into his briefcase, laying out his stack of programs for the weekend ahead and a copy of his presentations too. When, a year ago, he'd finally left the priesthood and come back to the wild western lands of this Isle, he'd become very excited to discover a way to lead people spiritually again, on what he called "Celtic Vision Quests." A getaway, coupled with pilgrimages to gorgeous, ancient holy places. After many months, he'd finally made a life for himself without the trappings of the Catholic Church. Now he just wanted to reach people simply and prayerfully with poetry and song, and connect them with the old Irish stories. His genealogy pursuits, his retreats in Ireland, Wales, Scotland and Britain, and frequent freelance articles for travel and anthropology magazines paid his bills. That was enough for now.

Patrick and Lily squeezed into the hotel's pub, which was crowded with weekend tourists. Patrick knew many of the locals, and several would be part of his retreat in a few days.

After he and Lily had sipped their first Guinness pints, she began to ply him with questions.

"I need to talk to you about something more urgent than genealogy. Last night started out to be a dream come true for me, but it quickly turned into something else. Because of Ian." She paused trying to select her question carefully. "I remember what you said to us that night in Dublin when he charged into that pub. That he was dangerous. Why exactly?"

"I knew him long ago. We were boys together, but Ian was always in trouble. He had a hard time of it. He came down alone, without his family, from the North several years after his father was murdered by the British police. Back then his whole family got involved with the IRA, determined to avenge that murder. He was the youngest of the brood, a lad of only thirteen when I met him. He had more brothers than me. Older ones and a sister too. Some of his older relatives died in the terrorist raids in the late 80s and 90s. Finally the police ordered what was left of his family to get out of the North. They were trying to negotiate peace treaties then, but weren't very successful. Firebomb attacks still happened often. So, he came to Doolin to live with an aunt and uncle. When I met him he wouldn't talk to anyone in school. He was bitter, full of hate. Always in a fight, and the nuns punished him good. Finally, he was kicked out of my school. He got into real trouble then. A few years passed and I heard he was released from juvi jail at eighteen and went back to fight, this time in the New IRA with his cousins. After the peace finally happened, I didn't hear much about him, until one night he got into another brawl and pummeled a good friend of mine, outside a pub close to Galway. It was near midnight. The two of them had it out. Who knows why. It was brutal. My friend ended up in a hospital. It would've been Ian's word against his if it ever went to court, but my childhood friend never woke up. That's why Ian didn't want anything to do with me that night in the pub. Ian went free. My friend's mother is still trying to get the case to go to trial.

"Now do you see why I didn't want Eve hanging around him?"

Lily was stunned. She bit into her lower lip and clasped her hands, looking down at her whitened knuckles. "That's quite a story."

Now it was Patrick who began to ask questions. "Why did Ian

show up last night? I thought he lived in Dublin now."

"I don't know. I can't get Eve to even talk about it. She's been seeing him lately, though. What I do know for sure is that all of a sudden he was standing next to her last night, weaving back and forth like crazy. He was stone drunk. Then he laid into her, slapped her across the face more than once and shoved her down. Seamus was at the bar, but he saw it and went for him. They had it out, and it was a raging fight. That's when you showed up. He's still in jail, based on Seamus' story as well as everyone else's testimony at the party. I called the police just now to make sure."

Patrick moved forward in his chair. "I was only gone from the table for a few minutes. When I was walking to the WC, I saw him arrive. Several minutes before that Eve had been arguing with someone on her cell phone."

"It was probably him."

"Why she lowers herself to be with scum like him is beyond me." Patrick reached for his Guinness again.

Lily stared into his eyes. She knew he felt guilty for not rescuing Eve. *Like her brother, Colin, a protector.* She looked down at her clenched hands. "Eve does that. Always has. Off and on since her mother died. Men are her weakness, and sometimes the drink too. It's gotten worse since we came here. I don't know why and I don't know what to do."

"Don't worry, lass, we'll get her help." He leaned back to finish his ale, then put a short stack of files on the table. "But we can't solve it all today, now can we? Let's focus on you for a change." The smile he gave her didn't waver. She could feel herself blush and she couldn't utter a word. "So, my lass, what is it you want me to do about your genealogy search? I brought some family tree forms and a swab to test your DNA."

She took them, and as she accidentally brushed his fingers, she felt herself tremble. *What is this?*

"Shall we get started?" he said.

CHAPTER 48

*T*hey were nearing the Rosslare ferry dock in a caravan of cars, Patrick in the lead. Eve and Lily followed close behind in their rental car. Lily looked out the passenger window, admiring the indigo sky and yellow and gold wildflowers covering the emerald hills on every side. Soon they both glimpsed the sparkling Irish Sea ahead.

It had taken some doing, but finally Lily had persuaded Eve to join Patrick's pilgrimage retreat this weekend. After several no's, Eve relented when she heard he was holding it in a treasured nature spot in Pembrokeshire National Park, not far from the Welsh ferry landing in Fishguard. Lily had suggested that after two nights at the "Vision Quest," they could drive through Wales, giving Eve "opportunities to call on several Welsh wine merchants." That clinched Eve's decision.

Lily's real desire to go on the retreat was to give Eve a chance to forget the ugly night that had embarrassed her in front of her wine colleagues and offer her an opportunity for some soul searching. Lily and Patrick had come up with the idea, hoping to help Eve. Neither of them expected Seamus to invite himself along. And Lily had to admit, she was thrilled that he had! He'd called her as they were getting ready to leave, saying he'd checked with Eve first, found out she was mending okay, and after hearing about their plans, asked if he could tag along. "It's the best opportunity I've heard yet to be with two gorgeous women and see the famous blue-stone circle," he'd said. "Remember, lass, I'm the one who told you about the ancient sites in Wales in the first place. You're in for more unforgettable experiences if you agree to go to other mysterious stone circles with me. I've been studyin' about them at Trinity College."

§

After a week, the bruises on Eve's arm and neck had deepened into sizeable puffs of blue and purple on her ivory skin. So, for this evening, she chose to wear a wispy white eyelet blouse with long sleeves and a high neckline. Pearl earrings would go with it perfectly, and she finished off her outfit with black slacks and black wedge sandals. She decided she looked regal but breezy as she brushed her shiny, golden hair.

She reached out to close the casement window. *Ooh, that green patchwork...what a lovely sight. Maybe this was a good idea after all.*

She and Lily plus Patrick, Seamus and several others had checked into this charming 300- year-old farmhouse a few hours before. It was nestled near the moor, with sheep grazing in fields below the sloping Preseli Hills. Tempting dinner smells wafted up the stairs. Eve checked her image in the mirror. She wanted to look as attractive as possible this evening. Seamus had seemed so concerned and caring on the phone yesterday. *He's quite the flirt, and Lily doesn't seem to mind at all. Thank god he's here. He'll amuse me when Patrick gets boring.* She applied a rosy gloss to her lips.

Hearing a knock, she opened the door to find Lily beaming. Eve could feel her shoulder and neck muscles tighten as she surveyed her friend in a new deep teal top that hugged her figure, accentuating her generous bust. Lily looked so slender in the black skirt and skimpy sandals that Eve had helped her buy in the States. *Lily actually has a sexy figure now...* "Wow, you're really dressed up," was all she could muster.

Lily's face fell. "Too much?"

"No." Eve left more doubt than reassurance in her voice. *Why do I do this to her?*

"Should I wear something more casual?"

"Lily, for god's sake, stop second-guessing yourself. You look fine."

They made their way down the wooden stairs to a room Anna, the proprietor, called a "farmhouse diner," complete with rustic pine furniture and a corner woodstove. Blue and white homemade rugs were scattered across the worn hardwood floors. Candles on the long rectangular table and a lone lamp in a corner cast a cozy glow all around. In spite of her travels, Eve had to admit she'd rarely seen such an inviting, authentic room.

Everyone was all smiles as Eve and Lily seated themselves at opposite ends of the long table in the only empty chairs left. Lily sat near Seamus and Eve next to Patrick. Nevertheless, Eve sought out Seamus' eyes, and he winked at her. She twisted her hair behind her ear and smiled back. That was all that was needed for now, in spite of the fact that Lily had managed to grab the seat next to him.

A wave of annoyance distracted Patrick when Eve took the seat next to him. *Great, the consummate attention hound, back for more,* he thought. Secretly chiding himself for being unkind, he stood up, told a favorite joke, causing chuckles all around the table and led the group in a prayer of thanks. Then he gave them all a brief idea of what was in store in the days ahead.

During dinner, he launched into a lengthy conversation with a Canadian lady at his right, but eventually feeling guilty, he turned to chat with Eve. But he got nowhere. Was it his imagination or was she deliberately ignoring him? Was she really that mesmerized by the Frenchman next to her describing the history of French wines in heavy-duty detail?

With the group's meal over, though the evening breezes were a bit chilly, Patrick led them all out to sit on the patio. He didn't want them to miss the sunset beyond the moor. The black hills silhouetted in the distance formed a perfect backdrop and compelled him to snap a photo of them all. He wanted to make this weekend a memorable experience for everyone. He sat down beside Lily this time, but when Seamus made room for Eve on a garden couch that barely accommodated them, he noticed Lily gazing down into her lap. In fact, Eve and Seamus were so crowded together that Eve was sitting half on the arm of the couch, and Seamus jokingly offered his lap to her but Eve coyly refused, emitting a giggle.

A hot irritation flowed through Patrick. *They're not here for a spiritual experience, that's clear.* Looking at Lily, he sensed she felt the same way. Determined not to show his feelings, he tried to get everyone's attention. "Look at the new moon rising, a good omen for all of us," he said, relieved to notice Lily's rapt gaze was now fixed on the sky. "For it is my hope that we will not only receive the inner light from God on this retreat, but we'll reflect the light we receive, like Sister Moon, on and for others. What we learn here will come principally from within our own hearts, but I will do my best to elicit peace and joy in this tidy group, as well as a good measure of laughter too." Then he took up his guitar and began to sing while the fire blazed, warming them all.

CHAPTER 49

*A*wake before dawn the next morning, Lily called Lisa not once, but three times. Finally, her daughter picked up. "Hello?"

"Perhaps I shouldn't care so much, but I thought you might call me back after receiving half a dozen calls from me."

"Oh, hi, Mom." Her daughter's voice was lackluster and faraway.

"Can you speak up? I can barely hear you."

"How's *this*?"

"You don't have to yell. I hear you now." Lily knew Lisa was blasting into the phone on purpose. She also knew her daughter couldn't bear the slightest criticism and always made sure anyone who dished it out got a generous dose right back. "Tanya promised she'd tell you that I wanted to talk to you *right away*. It's been two days."

"Oh, Mom, why am I always the one who screws up? I haven't seen Tanya in ages."

Who was Lily supposed to believe now? Her oldest daughter or her youngest? Tanya had promised to contact Lisa, but now Lisa swore she hadn't heard from her sister. Lily took a deep breath to squelch her annoyance.

"Well, I give up. You girls are telling me different things. One thing I do know for sure, Lisa. I never seem to reach you. You know I care a lot about you, and based on what Tanya told me, I'm concerned about Eve too. I heard you got a strange phone call. A guy asking about Eve."

"Yeah, it was weird, and I meant to let you or Eve know about it, but I never hear from you...Uh, I mean, my roommate never tells me you called. And I didn't really know where you were, so..."

Lily couldn't help it, her temper began to rise. "So, what happened to the detailed itinerary with phone numbers that I emailed you? Tanya has it. Why don't you?"

"Oh, I forgot. Yeah, I have it. It's right here pinned to my bulletin board."

"Okay, you have it. What did the guy say? And when did he call?"

"He wouldn't give his name, even though I asked him three times. He basically wanted Eve's phone number or address. Said he wanted to tell her about a surprise, something she'd be really excited about." Lisa laughed. "Made me wonder if she'd won the lottery or something."

"Did his voice sound familiar? You met Brad a couple of times. Do you think it was him?"

"I'm not sure. He didn't sound like a college guy. He was older. Had a friendly voice. Very persuasive. Said he knew Eve was traveling in Europe and he needed to get a hold of her right away. He asked me to try to find her info and he'd call back in a few days. I said I would. Oh, and he said to keep his phone call just between us. That's weird, isn't it?"

"This is serious, Lisa." Lily could feel her body tense up. "Brad's very dangerous. Even if it wasn't Brad, you shouldn't give out information to strangers. But I don't want Brad contacting you or your sister. Or Eve!

"Calm down, Mom."

"I am calm." But Lily felt anything but calm. Secretly, she knew the call was from Brad. He was on the prowl again. "Eve doesn't want anything to do with him. You remember that, don't you? She has good reason."

"'Course, Mom, why do you think I kept everything under wraps? I figured if he called back I might be able to squeeze more out of him. You know, to help Eve out."

"I know you meant well, Lisa, but I don't want this guy contacting you again. If he calls, just ask for his name and phone number. Say you'll give it to Eve. And tell him not to call again. Then please call me back. Immediately."

"Even if it's three in the morning?"

"Ha, ha. No, of course not, but as soon as possible. Promise me?"

"Sure, Mom."

"Now what about you? How are your classes and your grades? The semester's half over, isn't it?"

"Yeah, midterms are coming up. Didn't Tanya tell you? That's why I haven't been in the dorm much and didn't get your messages. I'm in several study groups; one is full of nerds. But they help. I'm not the greatest when it comes to tests. You know that."

"Well, one of these days I'm going to fly home to see you."

"You are? Why, Mom? I thought you were having fun."

"I am, but I miss you and I'd like to see you in person. Meet your new friends too."

"Uh, well...I think you better wait a few weeks. I've got lots of projects due right after midterms."

"Okay, but please promise you'll contact me in a few days? I want to know either way if this guy calls you back. And, Lisa, please ease up on Tanya. She just wanted some space of her own during her first year at the college. You understand, don't you? But now her roommate—"

"Okay, okay, Mom. Yeah, she's hurting. That roommate did a number on her. I'll try to cheer her up."

"Okay honey, I have to go now. I've got things to do today."

"Wow, that was quick. Aren't you even going to nag me about who I'm dating? You know, like you and...Dad..." her voice cracked, "like you always did when I was home?"

Lily smiled to herself. "No, not now. You're off the hook for the time being."

Instead, she gave Lisa the details about her job offer at Blarney Castle and then hung up, proud she'd finally been forceful with her daughter but still puzzling about which of her two girls to believe. Lisa sounded like she was on-task and focused on her studies, in spite of what Tanya had said. Tanya, on the other hand, was emotionally strung out and lonely. Lily vowed that she'd keep in better touch with them both.

This was a breakthrough, finally. I haven't had straight talk with either of them in a long time. She paused. *Hmm, maybe never...*

CHAPTER 50

*A*t the sound of the proprietor's bell, everyone in Patrick's group rose before sunrise to begin the weekend Vision Quest. Boxed meals waited in the kitchen for them. Dressed and ready, they all sauntered into the dining room, picked them up and assembled quietly outside, gray light still shrouding the farmhouse and beyond. The sun was peeking over the horizon and the air was chilly. Wild rabbits hopped across the grassy expanse of land, and fat little brown birds flew from tree to tree. Soon they'd begin their trek up and through the Preseli hills.

Barely awake, Eve stood off to the side. She noticed an unusual bird with gray and black feathers, its head a flash of red. Tap, tap, tap. It pecked a branch as if trying to get her attention. She blinked and it was gone. She wasn't used to rising this early. But Lily had been so adamant about coming she hadn't dared turn her down. *Well, I'm here in body if not in spirit,* she mused as she watched all twelve participants forming a circle around Patrick. "Hmm, the twelve apostles," she murmured.

Apparently only Lily heard her because she shot her a scowl from across the patio. Eve offered her a wicked smile. Lily happened to be standing next to Seamus, with none other than Patrick flanking her other side. *She's certainly not hurting for male attention,* Eve mused.

Patrick stepped forward, opening the circle. "I'm grateful you're all up at this ungodly hour. But I guess I shouldn't be startin' this sacred trek with the word 'ungodly,' now should I? Let's just say I know the sacrifice you made this mornin' because I'm anythin' but an early riser. It'll be worth it, I promise ya, but I bet I'll be hearin' all your different opinions about that, later on."

Everyone laughed.

"Well, we've all come together here from different homes and even from far off lands," he began, "each of us with a wish for our future. A Vision Quest is a time apart from regular life. So, for these two days, we'll give ourselves a new name, which is a symbol of the changes we'll experience. I'll be calling you 'pilgrims' now, meself included. All of us are searchin' for more meanin' in our lives. We'll be venturin' off on a trek, but an internal journey too, explorin' our own insights and if we feel inclined, we can write them down. I hope you brought a notebook. If not, I have some here. Help yourselves." He distributed pencils and small tablets to anyone who stepped forward.

"While you walk this mornin', ask yourself questions," he continued, "the big questions you don't have time for during the hustle and bustle of your everyday life." He passed out sheets of paper.

Eve scanned through the questions on the page as Patrick's voice droned on.

What is the real reason I find myself here in this particular spot? What is God or the universe inviting me to explore? What do I need to cast off? What do I want to embrace? What steps should I take to find and grow the passions inside me? How have I changed from last year or years ago?

Finished reading, Patrick picked up his box lunch from the

picnic table and turned toward the hills. The group did the same, and Eve followed behind.

"Some say these are sacred hills, a sacred center of energy," he said, "where we'll find mysteries no one quite understands. It's my hope that you'll not only appreciate what you sense here but awaken to a multi-dimensional spiritual experience most people rarely acknowledge.

"I see you've all taken me suggestion and worn comfortable clothes. We'll eat this simple food today too. Some Vision Quests require fasting, but I've chosen not to. However, it's best to plan a mixture of silence and alone time for yourself along with socializin'. You're free to interact, but I'd encourage you to try hikin' off to the side by yourselves too. Not too far away, though. I don't want to lose you in those hills. Above all, breathe in the cool breezes and absorb the beauty of nature all 'round us."

Patrick set off then, leading the group. Eve still followed at the end of the line and noticed Lily veer off by herself too, though she didn't walk far from her two male friends.

The terrain was alternately rocky and full of brambles and moss. As far as the eye could see, different shades of low green bushes and plants covered the expanse of semi-flat farmland. Gazing up at the hills beyond, Eve thought of the much higher mountains where she'd wandered as a child. Different from here, but wild too. Roaming in the pine tree forests back then, usually with her dad or Lily, had always offered unforgettable delight. She felt the beginnings of that same exuberance now. To be under a brightening sky, a gentle wind playing with her hair, savoring the country's stillness minus the noise of traffic with its low, inhibiting roar--*maybe the weekend will be good for me after all.*

She thought a little about what Patrick had written. When he talked about "spirituality and God" she couldn't identify. But, she could mull over where she was going with her life. What were her passions and what changes did she need to make? After walking for a while, she had to admit she didn't have a clue. *I'm trying to get back on my feet again. Trying to resurrect the old Eve—the pre-Brad Eve. But who was I back then?*

She'd dated Brad for four years, and the time before that had been a shaky few months of adjustment too, following her divorce. *I was trying to "find myself" after that eight-year fiasco called a marriage.*

Still lagging behind, she absorbed the expanse of blue sky and green hills, pondering over the questions. Despite Ian's recent hint about marriage (*was that what he'd meant?*), she decided her passion now must be her career at the wineries. *It has to be. I'm not going to let any man disappoint me again, and I've never really been good at anything else but selling wine.* Well, school... She'd always excelled in school. Riding too. *And I guess I do a pretty good job at decorating, but it's not a passion.* She climbed up on a boulder in the middle of the vast fields and turned around on the top, her arms spread out, as if twirling in a very slow dance. She smiled at a good-looking guy in the group below. *I guess Lily would say my main passion is men.* She started to jump down as he reached out to her with a helping hand. She locked him in her gaze. *Maybe she's right.*

The distant hills beckoned to Lily too. She saw Eve flirting again with a strange guy in their group, but she left her behind and hiked ahead of Patrick and Seamus as well, wanting to find some quiet time to think. *His questions are deeper than I expected. Such an intriguing guy...Patrick.*

"Why am I here? What *are* my passions now? How have I changed from last year and years ago?" Answers eluded her but she could answer the third question. ...So many monumental changes— grieving Frank's passing, discovering she had an inheritance, quitting her job and finally, following her dream to come to the British

Isles, where her ancestors resided long ago—all in the space of only a few months. This land had already changed her.

The pre-Celtic sights Lily had seen and the mythical Celtic stories she'd heard here were exactly what she'd yearned for since she was a girl. From Gram's stories years ago had sprung an avid curiosity about her roots that this trip was beginning to quench. She knew now that these ancient places and this wild beauty of nature were somehow part of her soul. And after hearing about the courageous Celtic women, Grace O'Malley and Boudica, who were her ancestors, she felt a new grounding and a strong identity growing inside her that she'd never felt before. And her new job! Who would've thought that could ever happen! Plus the people she'd met, who had freely given her their friendship—Seamus, Maeve, Patrick and even Rose O'Sullivan—were changing her as well.

Lily smiled to herself, thinking about the male attention she'd received here and the flirtatious smiles even Irish strangers kept sending her way. Finally, at 40 plus, she was actually feeling...attractive. *Probably like Eve has felt all her life.* But, more important, *I feel a new power inside me.* She wondered if Eve had any idea what that felt like.

But what are my true passions? What will my next step be? Thoughts of Tanya and Lisa flitted through her mind. Other than the recent phone calls, she suddenly realized she hadn't thought of them much at all. Or her need to care for them and everyone else... *Maybe that's why my heart feels a bit heavy at the thought of planning a trip home.* She wondered if she really *needed* to find out what was going on with Lisa's friends and her grades. And shouldn't Tanya solve her own roommate problem?

Maybe I should leave them be. She reached up to massage her shoulder and neck, her old uncertainties turning into a familiar ache.

Her mind pressed on. What about Brad and his phone calls?

Shouldn't she spend her energy finding out more, to shield Eve from danger? Or...would it be better to tell Eve and let her handle it? *But Eve's still bruised from Ian. It's not the right time...* Or was it? Lily was full of indecision and she knew it. That hadn't changed.

Just then Seamus came up beside her, touched her hand and waved her forward as he hiked a bit ahead of her. The unmistakable quiver of his touch thrilled her, tempting her to pick up her pace and walk by his side. Instead, something told her to hold back; she shook her head at him but smiled with her eyes. She needed some alone time to sort out her thoughts.

More than twenty minutes had passed before the group reached the circle of stone monoliths at the top of the hill. Soft breezes blew the grass in waves all around them below a deep indigo sky.

"This is an ancient outdoor sanctuary, dating to the Neolithic Age, which stretches back to over 6,000 years ago. We're told the indigenous people carried out spiritual rituals here, likely worshiping the sun and stars," Patrick told them. "It's not important to figure out what they thought or felt, but rather use the beauty of nature and the mystery we feel here to revisit our *own* deeply held convictions. Why did *we* come here...now? And why are we here on this planet at all? We have the right, you know, to live our lives our way, and not base our path on everyone else. Go ahead. Feel your own destiny, your own beckoning and intuition. Let me share a piece of a famous poem with you, *The Road Not Taken* by Robert Frost:

Two roads diverged in a yellow wood, And sorry I could not travel both. And be one traveler, long I stood, And looked down one as far as I could, To where it bent in the undergrowth,

...I shall be telling this with a sigh, Somewhere ages and ages hence,

Two roads diverged in a wood, and I— I took the one less traveled by, And that has made all the difference.

He sat down on the soft grass and the others followed. "Remember, you have only one life in this place called earth. Your choices create your life. And your life is yours, no one else's.

"If you're willing, let's all write down our thoughts about our own journey and a couple of answers to the questions I raised."

A petite lady with an English accent and furrowed brows leaned toward him. "Those are difficult questions."

"Well now, take it easy about it." Patrick's voice was calm. "I don't want you gettin' uptight. But just so you know, I've hired a masseuse back at the farmhouse after you've done all this hard work I'm demandin' of you." His face lit up with a grin. "Just in case you'll be needin' one."

The group tittered.

"Now don't be thinkin' on this *too* hard. All we need to do is crack open our hearts and minds a little, put pencils in our hands and trust the universe to do the rest. Now take a few deep breaths, relax and let your words start flowin'."

Silence settled among them, except for the breeze swaying the tall grass.

Several moments passed. Patrick's voice was just above a whisper, "That's right. Get comfortable and enjoy the silence. You'll be surprised at what emerges on paper."

After what seemed like forever, Eve lay down in the grass, closing her eyes, listening to the sounds of nature. She couldn't remember ever doing anything like this, but multiple images began crowding her mind: Exploring with Lily outside her grandmother's cabin during school breaks. Riding at home long ago. It had been years since she'd ridden a horse, except for the other night. *Why?* She'd forgotten how wonderful it felt and decided she'd find a way to ride again here in Ireland. Patrick could set it up with his friend Tom.

Just then his smooth tone interrupted her thoughts. "I hope some of us might be willing to share our written insights now. Most of us don't know each other, but sometimes that offers a special freedom. Be willing to risk. It's an adventure you shouldn't miss."

"Are you willing to share with us too, Patrick?" Eve asked.

She could tell he was taken aback by her question, but he mustered a smile. "Of course. I wouldn't ask you to do anythin' I won't do meself."

The breeze became stronger. Her notebook pages began fluttering, so Eve sat up again. She thought for a moment but knew she didn't have answers about why she was in Wales, or on this earth, for that matter. Yet she noticed all the others were dutifully bent in thought or writing away. *I guess the only reason I'm here today is to calm Lily's worries.* In these last weeks, Lily and Patrick and even her dad in that mysterious vision, had been relentless, pestering her about the dangers of men and her harmless trysts.

She sighed and decided she couldn't write one word, only to look up from her notebook to see Patrick staring at her empty pages.

He walked on, encouraging others to share, one at a time, as the sun moved up into the sky and almost everyone peeled off their jackets and hoodies. After a bit, Eve's stomach began to growl. She decided not to open her lunch pack, though. Patrick had a steely way about him that reminded her of a stern professor she'd known in the old days. *He was outrageously handsome, but I never dared mess with his "rules."* She knew enough not to mess with Patrick's either.

When she heard Lily talking, Eve reigned in her distracted thoughts. Her friend was sitting right in the middle of the group.

"I feel as if most of my life has changed in the space of a few months," Lily mustered in a soft voice.

Her dark hair shone and its ginger streaks were lit by the sun. Her eyes were sparkling too, glowing green against her emerald sweater, and her cheeks were rosy from the sun. *She looks...amazing! So different now.* Eve shifted her gaze then, noticing Seamus, who was lying on the grass near one of the standing stones, one hand propping his head up.

Lily continued, "Sometimes it's overwhelming and I'm not sure what parts of me I need to shed...or grow," and her eyes began to tear up. After a few moments, she smiled. "But in spite of my uncertainties I don't think I've ever been happier!

"As for my next step, I feel a brand-new awareness when it comes to...to my inner strength...my heart," she paused as her eyes demurred from connecting with anyone. "Other people have always been my focus, but now I think I need to follow my own path a bit. I have a new job too, very different than in the past, allowing me to be creative. I've always loved gardens, but now perhaps I need to plant seeds for *myself*." She paused and heaved a sigh. "What else the universe has planned for me, I'm not sure."

"Thank you for sharing," Patrick said, as he led her out of the center of the circle. "Those were simple but profound insights, lass. Dante himself wrote of the uncertainty you've shared, '*In the middle of the road of our lives/ I awoke in a dark wood/ where the true way was wholly lost.*' Yes, it can be dark sometimes because we don't know exactly where our path leads, but we need to start, nonetheless. And that's exactly what you've done." He put his hand on Lily's shoulder and she heaved a sigh at his touch.

Lily's face was shining with a glow Eve had never seen. As she sat down on the grass Seamus moved closer to her, taking her hand in his.

Eve closed her eyes then, unable to watch them.

Twilight shadows surrounded the patio's fire pit as Lily and the rest of the group listened to Patrick. "The next phase of our journey is to try meditating on a friend of mine's ideas about a pilgrimage."

Everyone was gathered together in the low light of the waning day, after enjoying a late lunch and then spending several hours of silence time in their rooms at Patrick's suggestion. But Eve had decided to take a long nap after lunch, saying she wasn't interested in more reflection.

Lily had knocked on Eve's door before this session and tried to chat, but soon gave up. *She sure sounded antsy and cross,* Lily mused, as she watched the orange and yellow flames lick through the kindling in the pit, *but I guess she's still willing to participate.* Eve had found a seat across from her, between Seamus and the guy she'd been flirting with earlier.

Patrick went on, "My friend talks about a *finisterre* moment, which means 'end of the earth.' I like to think of it as the end of a pathway in our lives, when we step into the unknown. If you've studied the ancient tradition of a pilgrimage, you know it always involved some sacrifices. But we won't engage in those old, painful rituals now. However, periodically casting off some parts of ourselves can bring new energy to our lives, like a new butterfly breaking out of its chrysalis." Patrick motioned toward the fire. "So, it can be very cleansing to burn something you've brought with you or leave an item of clothing behind. It's a way to cast off an irrelevant part of ourselves, like a snake shedding its skin.

"We go 'round with many labels, don't we? A way of bein' that we've clung to even though we know in our hearts it's time to tone it down or leave it behind. We all have phases of our lives where we collect these labels, such as 'cancer survivor' 'intern,' 'unemployed,' 'widow,' 'alcoholic,' 'married,' 'philanderer,' 'divorced,' 'girlfriend,' even 'mother' or 'father,' or... 'flirt.'"

As he said the last word, Lily noticed Eve look up and stare at Patrick, but he didn't turn his gaze toward her.

"These become our identities. Think about it. What name or label do you want to get rid of now? Who would you like to give up being?"

The word "fat" flashed like a neon sign in Lily's mind. Even now, when she looked in the mirror she couldn't believe she was shapely and attractive, even though she'd received more compliments in the last few months than in her entire life. For years she'd hated for anyone to take her photo. She thought of the clothes in her suitcase upstairs. Most were too big for her now, but she'd been unable to part with them. Why? Because secretly she thought she might need them in the future...yes, when she was fat again. *Wow, I really am unwilling to part with my old self.*

As if he heard her thoughts, Patrick asked everyone, "Do you have something with you you'd like to burn or leave behind? Our proprietor will be happy to give any unwanted articles of clothing, books, symbolic jewelry, etc. to the poor. She has a box next to the door. Don't hesitate. You can do it now. We'll take a long break before dinner—an hour should be enough—while you think about this. I hope you'll act on it too. Anyone for another glass of wine?"

Pushing her long blonde hair behind her ear, Eve noted how Seamus was gazing at her with his irresistible dimpled grin. When he took off upstairs she decided to follow him. "So, you're getting into this after all?" she asked.

He reached his room. "Why not?" he said. "I can afford to lighten up my suitcase. Maybe my life too. What about you?"

"Yeah, I guess so. What are you going to discard, if I'm not being too nosy?"

"I have some tin trinkets," he said. "They don't mean much to anyone but me, but it's time to offload them along with that part of my past."

"Tin trinkets? How fascinating."

"Yes, my family used to sell tin. For generations. That's definitely over now. I don't want anything to remind me of those years as a Tinker."

More concerned about herself, Eve missed the meaning of Seamus' comment. "That gives me an idea. Maybe some trinkets from my past can go into the box for the poor or even into the fire," she said.

"Sounds like you're on the right track, lass."

Eve went down the hall and disappeared into her room. Most of what she'd brought was costume jewelry, but she had a few more valuable pieces she always kept with her. One was a present Brad had given her when they'd first met, a tiny silver rose charm, but she'd never bought a bracelet to go with it. She couldn't fathom why she'd brought it in the small velvet jewelry purse she took on all her trips. Except, if she was honest, she had to admit that whenever she glimpsed it she thought about Brad in those early days, when a bright future stretched ahead.

She took the shiny charm and stroked it between her two fingers, suddenly realizing she'd been hanging on to it, hoping that he'd change, that they'd somehow be able to revive that early promise in spite of the trauma that had ruined their relationship. She dumped the tiny charm into a plastic bag, put it into her pocket and went downstairs to join the others.

She met Seamus standing near the box. "Ah, my pretty lass, so you found something to contribute to the poor after all?"

"Yes, jewelry someone else will love much more than I."

"Hmm, I bet it's wrapped around a lost love, isn't it?" he said.

Eve's words popped open. "Yes, and all the dark and unhappy memories that go with it." She dropped the pouch among the hats and clothes already piled there, noticing Lily nearby. She was putting some familiar blouses and a black skirt into the large box.

"Casting off the 'big' clothes?" Eve said. "Maybe you should burn the girls' email addresses and phone numbers too."

All Lily could do was stare at her, and then walk away.

Seamus edged next to Eve and placed his own heavy bag of tin trinkets, along with a cup and an old pot, on top of her offering. "Should make us feel lighter now, eh lass?" He walked away.

"Yes," was all Eve said, noticing where Lily sat. *Why am I being so mean to her?*

The whole group was milling around the patio now. The sun had begun to drop behind the hills, its ribbons of light painting the sky and matching the orange flames crackling in the fire pit. Gradually, the rest of the participants took their seats around their leader, armed with glasses of wine.

A middle-aged British lady held up an envelope to Patrick. "I've decided to burn this letter." She looked around at them all as she began to explain, "If you must know, it's from my daughter, who's been nothing but trouble for me since she turned eighteen. I've been letting her ruin my life for...yes, it's been ten long years. I don't quite know what my next step will be, but burning this is a very good start..." her voice faltered at the end, but she placed the letter carefully in the fire pit while, in a hushed silence, they watched it curl into blackened fragments. Then someone began clapping and they all joined in, as Patrick held the lady's hand for a moment, and Lily stepped forward, away from Seamus, to hug her. Eve stared. *Of all people. She used to be shy. Why is Lily so friendly to strangers all of a sudden?*

They settled down again, but Patrick remained standing. "I must be true to me word as well. I've written here some Bible verses that I've carried in me wallet for these long years." He took out a worn piece of paper and unfolded it. "It's been holdin' me back from livin' my life in the present. So I must destroy it." He lit a taper with a flame and the note began to burn, then he dropped it into the fire.

Eve couldn't control her curiosity. "But won't you share what it said, as the others have?"

"Aye, I will if you'll agree to do the same."

"I don't have any scripture quotes in *my* wallet."

"Don't you have something you'd like to leave behind like the rest of us? A name, a label, a habit?"

"Well, I guess we all do," Eve stammered.

Patrick looked at the group. "Well now, I think Eve's made a good point about me sharing. The quote I burned said, 'Come, follow me, and I will make you fishers of men.' From the Gospel of Matthew, Chapter 4, Verse 19."

Everyone murmured, wondering why that particular quote would hold Patrick back. Lily had an inkling what the quote meant and decided to ask him later. They all hushed as Eve stood up.

"I've decided to write something down. Something I need to leave behind, and I'll burn it here. It's a bad habit of mine, or so I've been told." She took a pencil and wrote on her notepad, then ripped the page out and lit it with a taper. "Flirting. Flirting with strange Irish men," she said, and dropped it triumphantly into the fire with a wide smile.

Everyone laughed except Patrick and Lily, who exchanged glances. Lily folded her arms to her chest, trying to contain her frustration.

After a few more admissions, the group broke up, heading for the wine bar before dinner.

It was late, after eleven o'clock. Most of the group had retired upstairs. The fire pit was out, and Seamus and Lily sat inside on a comfy couch, with Eve facing them in a creaking rocking chair. Announcing she'd had enough for one day, Lily got up and made for the stairs.

Eve began to follow her then veered toward the restroom first. Expecting everyone to be gone when she returned, she was surprised to see Seamus filling up her wine glass once more. "Oh, I can't. I've got to be a good girl here," she said.

"A good girl? Why?"

"Oh, Lily's bound to scold me if I act out again. And, of course, our noble leader too."

"You mean drinking might bring on the flirting again?" His dimple winked.

"Oh that. No, I told you...and everyone...I've given it up." Her voice was firm, "No. More. Flirting." But as she lifted her glass to the light, she flashed a mischievous smile as she clinked her drink against his. "One more of these won't hurt, now will it?"

"I guess not, lass. Wine tastin's part of your job, isn't it?"

She drained her glass, watching Seamus' eyes widen, and then took the half-full bottle from him.

"Sure is."

Seamus sunk back into the couch. "Come here, my beauty," he said. "Keep me warm."

"Oh, I thought only Lily do could do that," Eve said, feeling a bit tipsy but pouring more wine into her glass anyway.

"Aw, don't you know? I'm not a one-woman man. Never could abide it." He put his arm around her as she leaned back beside him. "*You* can understand that. Right, lass?"

"I didn't know that," she said, sipping more and meeting his eyes.

"Your friend Lily and I are friends, nothing more."

"You sure?" She drained her glass again and Seamus obliged by refilling it. "I think she likes you a lot."

"No, she's a shy one, she is. So, I never touched her. Or rather, 'knew' her in a Biblical way, and I'd swear on a Bible about that, but I have none here. I 'spose Patrick has one." He chuckled and Eve joined in.

"Yes, I guessed that's why he spent so many years living near the Vatican," Eve said, sure she'd guessed right. They exchanged a knowing glance.

"Oh, he did, did he? That fits with the Bible quote he burned.

Well, I think priestly ways still cling to our flawless leader. Don't you?" Seamus said.

She smiled and drank the golden liquid, adding to the delicious buzz she already had. "Hmm," she said, "this wine is delicious." She knew her words were beginning to slur, but she didn't care.

"Aw, c'mon," he said, taking her empty glass and putting it on a nearby table. Then he moved closer and began stroking her cheek with his finger. "You're a bit like me, aren't you? Despite your resolution, lass, you're a flirt who enjoys affection. And maybe even rockin' in the hay. You love it, so you'll never quit, lass. I saw it in your eyes when first I met you." He stroked her hair, then his fingers found her breast and he pressed her nipples as his mouth found hers and he took sudden hold of her whole body. "You know I've been waiting to steal a kiss from you since the first day we met." His voice was husky with passion.

She stayed in his arms, returning his kisses, softly rubbing his neck and hair, knowing she should move away, go upstairs. He was persuasive, though, and his clean scent was unmistakable, his body welcoming...stirring her own. She heard his breath accelerate as he massaged her back and arms and a delicious heat moved up her thighs, her own breath rising. He kissed her again, his tongue enveloping her mouth, languid and moist, too tempting to resist. Then she stumbled upstairs with him, giggling in the dark, trying to keep quiet, and the next thing she knew she was at the door of his room. He took her in arms again, and she couldn't help it, the urge to wrap her body around his was too much to resist. Soon he was reaching his hand down to pleasure her under her skirt as he kissed her, this time with an urgent passion. His fingers lingered, stroking her, and all she wanted was to unzip his fly and— Thoughts of today's retreat filtered through her mind. *What am I doing? Is this what I want? Lily would never forgive me if...*

When he opened the door of his room she pressed her body to him one more time but whispered, "I can't. Not tonight."

His voice was raspy, "'Course you can, my lass, I can keep a secret."

"No!"

But when he pulled her inside and took her in his arms, though she tried to resist, he enveloped her completely, the muscles of his arms strong and solid. So she relented, lifting her arms up, clasping her hands around his neck while she kissed the dimple on his cheek, then his warm neck several times, and finally, she found his mouth, kissing him deeply. When she heaved a delicious sigh she felt him hardening on her thigh, and she leaned in to stroke him, while his tongue and lips caressed her over and over.

He shoved the door closed then and picked her up and laid her gently on the bed. His voice was low. "Aye, lass, no more flirting now. We have other business now."

CHAPTER 51

*D*izzy from so much wine at the Vision Quest dinner, Lily had no sooner put on her nightgown and climbed into bed than sleep overcame her. Instead of a peaceful oblivion she began wrestling with a mysterious dream.

She was a child again and the woods were dark. She was climbing an immense tree, and kept scrambling higher and faster, up near the sky. She found a large cavity in the trunk, big enough to hide in, and squeezed inside, trying to cover herself with her jacket, a shield from the cold, blowing rain. When the storm finally stopped, she looked out. A full moon shone through the forest with a crystalline, streaming light. On a branch far down below she spied small, pudgy birds chirping in a nest. A strange rattling sound started, silencing their chirps. She looked further down at the ground. *Snakes! Must be half a dozen! Slithering up the trunk.*

Shaking, she pulled her head and body inside the tree's cavity and took off her jacket to create a barrier where the opening was. She kept a tiny slit open, watching...watching helplessly as the snakes began to attack the baby birds. Someone was talking over the wind's howl, a horrible keening sound. She'd heard it before:

A serpent who could not be charmed made its nest in the roots of the tree,
    Then the Anzu bird set his young in its branches
    And the dark little maiden Lilith built her home in the trunk.

"I must save the birds!" she screamed. "They can't save themselves!"

Her eyes popped open then to discover her shadowed bedroom, perspiration wetting her face and forehead and her chest heaving with sobs.

She sat up, trying to calm herself, dried her eyes and put on her robe; she needed to use the restroom they all shared down the hall. Closing her door, she turned toward the bathroom and saw Eve in the hall, in the shadows many doors down, still in the outfit she'd worn at dinner. Wasn't that Seamus? Yes! Eve was turning toward him, wrapping her body around his. Seamus began kissing her...

Lily froze. Their kiss seemed to go on and on. She saw Eve disappear into Seamus' room and the door closed. She couldn't breathe. She knew they hadn't seen her. She turned back but couldn't reach her room. Her breath wouldn't come. A wild nausea she'd felt once long ago took hold. The room began to spin. Was she going to be sick right here in the hall? She felt herself falling. An unyielding blackness had begun behind her eyes...it spread out before her and her queasiness mingled with it, like a dark shroud suffocating her.

Muffled voices. Someone was walking near her. Lily squinted her eyes open. Everything was fuzzy. She looked up and managed to make out the brown beams and white ceiling of the farmhouse living room. She put her hands up to her ears to stop the buzzing. One lone lamp beamed next to her. Where was she? Was that an EMT lifting her arm to take her blood pressure? Then he took her pulse. He had kind eyes. Another EMT was asking her questions:

"How do you feel now? Does anything hurt? Any more nausea? What's your name? Can you give me your address? Tell me exactly what you remember." Lily tried to answer him as best she could. Then she noticed Patrick sitting silently in the easy chair close beside her.

The EMT was checking her pulse again. "Well, Ma'am, all your vitals are normal." He turned toward Patrick and shrugged. "I think she just fainted. No serious bumps on her head. That's good. I don't think she needs to go to hospital. But don't let her go to sleep for a while, and if she has any unusual symptoms, bring her in to the local clinic right away." He handed Patrick some paperwork.

"Thanks for coming so fast and for being quiet so as not to wake anyone else." Patrick nodded good-bye to the two men as they detached Lily's oxygen mask, packed their paraphernalia and set off, closing the farmhouse door.

Moving his chair closer, Patrick offered her another pillow, propping it behind her head. "You gave me quite a scare, my lass." She noticed worry lines around his eyes and between his eyebrows.

The windows were still dark. No light yet. "I'm sorry to cause you trouble. What time is it?"

"Close to three o'clock," he said. "Do you feel better now?"

She nodded. "I've only fainted once...a long time ago. Were those EMTs? Is that what they call them here too?"

"Yes."

"What happened?"

"Couldn't sleep, so I went for a walk then stopped down here to make myself a hot toddy. Must've dozed off briefly by the fire. When I woke and climbed the stairs, you were lying on the floor in the hall. So I carried you down here to this couch. No one else was around. What were you doing out in the hall so early in the mornin'?"

Images of Eve and Seamus floated through Lily's mind. Why hadn't they come to her aid? *They probably didn't see me.* Bile began to burn her throat. Nausea sickened her again. She couldn't squelch the images tumbling through her mind... Eve wrapping herself around Seamus...kissing him passionately... Numbness wound its way around her heart, taking her breath away. She began to cry. Her hands shielded her eyes as she sat up and bent over. Tears she couldn't hold back dripped from her cheeks, wetting her hands, trailing down her neck.

Patrick knelt down by the couch, his face close to her. "Oh no, my lass, don't cry. You're okay. They said you're healthy. All you need is a little rest." He put his hands on her shoulders, and for a moment his touch warmed her. But Lily moved away from him, curling up on the couch, turning her face away. "It's not my health I'm worried about!" *How could...how could Eve do this? I trusted her. I told her...I told her how I felt about Seamus. She knew I was falling in love...maybe for the first time in my life.*

And Seamus...I meant nothing to him. He never cared at all. She let herself weep.

Patrick stood up, putting his weight first on one foot then the other, not knowing what to do. Women's tears had always frightened him. He'd never been able to solve his sister's problems when she cried. He waited. Lily's wrenching sobs were the only sound except for the moan of the wind outside. He put his hand on her shoulder, but she kept turning away. He paced some more, then finally went to the wine bar and poured them both a glass of chardonnay. *Maybe this will calm her.*

He sat down again, placing his hand on Lily's arm."There, child, don't worry more. Whatever is troublin' you so much, or whoever it is who hurt you, they aren't worth it. They don't deserve your love nor your time. And you don't deserve this anguish—from anyone.

Please believe me when I say you're a very beautiful, smart lass with many, many talents."

She turned toward him, her cheeks red, her eyes swollen. "I am?" she whispered.

Her response shocked him. He reached out and pushed back her hair, then cupped her chin his hand. She looked up at him, "Of course," he said. Her wet eyes sparkled. Then he slowly traced her lips with his finger. She was the dearest soul he'd ever met. "You don't know your own value, do you, lass?" Should he do what he'd dreamed of since the first day he met her? Her eyes seemed to invite him. Taking her in his arms, he kissed her with a depth of feeling he rarely allowed himself.

She didn't respond at first, then he felt her lips seeking his, soft and welcoming. She placed her hands around his neck and he lay down with her, cradling her as she hugged him with a warmth so sweet he almost couldn't bear it. Soon she'd fallen asleep in his arms.

CHAPTER 52

*T*he Vision Quest group began to assemble again, as planned, in the shadowy kitchen. It was six o'clock, and only a few of the sun's first rays shone through the window as Eve made her way down the stairs to join the others. Seamus came toward her and, strangely, his mother Maeve was by his side. Eve already knew Maeve's quirky, unexpected ways, so she was more amused than surprised at her sudden appearance.

"Well now, if it isn't Lily's friend," Maeve said quietly, offering her hand to Eve, her pixie grin beaming. "I decided to join you today. You know, to offer everyone some faerie lore amidst Patrick's solemn speeches." She winked, and Eve felt an unusual strength in her hand.

Patrick began, "Good mornin', everyone. I'm afraid our original group is one less this morning. Lily isn't feelin' herself today, so I told her to sleep in. She'll be joinin' us later. But we do have a new visitor, Seamus' mum." He nodded toward Maeve, and when she offered her merry smile and an exaggerated curtsy, they laughed.

"We each have a special Sunday brunch meal today," he went on, "so take one for yourself and we'll start right away on our mornin' trek through the Presili hills, this time in a different direction. It's important to reach a new stone circle by noon."

Patrick was soon five yards in the lead as the group all began trudging up the hill.

Eve moved ahead to ask him about Lily, but his answer was brief. When she pressed him, he shook his head and turned his back, leading the group forward. "Well, if you won't answer me, I'm going back, to see for myself how she is."

He whirled around. "Don't bother her, Eve. It won't do any good. She's taken a sleeping pill and is sound asleep. Give her a few hours."

"What's wrong with her? She seemed okay last night."

Why was Patrick staring at her with a question in his eyes? Eve shrugged at him. *Bastard!* If Lily was sound asleep, no way could she find out what was wrong with her. She flounced away toward Seamus. When he held out his hand to her, she accepted it, deciding for the time being to enjoy him, along with the gorgeous waving grass and pastel sky all around.

They'd traversed the first slopes of the hills, when Patrick turned to say, "I've changed our itinerary a bit and the topic of our excursion too. Today will be more of a sacred journey, different than yesterday. Each of us needs to experience and savor the gift of being alone. Some of you may be afraid of it. I once was. As you hike in silence, ask yourself these questions: What do I have to give to this universe? What are my unique gifts? What is most important to me? How do I spend most of my days? Connecting with others? Being alone? What has brought new life to me? How will I change when I leave here?

"I give you some advice too: Believe me when I say that being alone, while keeping silent here and at home, can open you to special insights and awareness. Don't forget the spirit that dwells within you and the voices within this mysterious universe. They all can speak to you." He opened his arms up toward a pink sky that deepened as he spoke. "You might be surprised what you'll learn while listenin' to your heart. Dwell on your thoughts and answers as you go your own way today. Refrain from talkin' with your companions. Use the silent, natural beauty of this place to give you all you need. They'll be plenty of time for chattin' this afternoon before we all say good-bye."

Eve squeezed Seamus' hand and moved forward by his side. "C'mon" she said to him loudly, "let's hike together."

Patrick winced as he watched them.

After a couple of hours of hiking Patrick reached the sacred stones first. They weren't huge, but they were striking and mysterious nonetheless. He decided he'd bring Lily here later if she was feeling better, perhaps at sunset. *She'll love it! Maybe it will wipe away her strange sadness.*

The others seemed to be inching up the hill today. He watched them all, straggling individually, picking their way between the rocks in the unusual heat. Except Eve and Seamus, who hiked only inches apart, holding hands, their heads together as they laughed and talked. *They didn't listen to a word I said—why am I not surprised?* He felt his teeth clench and knew his temper might flare if he didn't control it. Negative vibes had welled up inside him before around Eve, and he wondered now why she was sticking so close to Seamus. The guy had dated Lily more than once. *So why is he so friendly with Eve now? Could that be why...?*

Maeve reached the top of the hill first, hiking by herself, looking more sprightly and energetic than all the rest. Her face seemed to shine as she winked at him. *She must be eighty,* he mused. He didn't know her well, but wondered why she looked familiar. He'd felt the same way about Seamus when he'd first laid eyes on him. And why had he thrown away tin items last night? A strange choice. The

Travelers had sold tin for decades, but he didn't look like one of them. Maybe he'd changed his ways. And why had his mother, Maeve, suddenly appeared at the Vision Quest? He didn't know when she'd arrived. After he'd put Lily to bed this morning? Maybe five or six o'clock? He wouldn't ask the little woman anything now, determined to keep the silence he'd advised for everyone. Maeve sat down far away, nestling herself near the tallest standing stone, closing her eyes as if to take a nap.

Patrick opened his backpack and took out the surprise he'd planned, his flute. He loved Celtic and Irish ballads and began to play one as the others gradually joined him, sitting down next to one or another stone in the ancient circle. The wind came up, blowing all around him as the tender strains of the old Irish song rang out. The music calmed the inner unrest he'd felt earlier. He thought of Lily as he played. After he'd kissed her last night, they'd napped for a short while on the couch and then, she'd seemed so unsteady, he'd almost carried her upstairs. Now he pictured her lying in her bed where he'd left her. As his flute reached the highest note of the gentle tune, he remembered kissing her once more on her forehead before he'd closed her door, wishing he could stay longer, but knowing she wasn't ready for... He paused a beat, then pressed the flute's keys once more, creating the final longing notes of the soothing melody, repeating them softly till he played the last one. Only the sound of the wind blew around him now. *A mysterious sadness is clinging to Lily's heart,* he thought, as he looked out at the lovely horizon. He knew he was helpless to transform her into the vibrant, eager lass he'd met weeks before.

Then he began playing several Celtic ditties, and mournful tunes too, and after what seemed like an hour, he laid his instrument down to get a bite to eat. After they'd all finished their boxed meals, Maeve approached him with an impish grin. "Hello, Patrick, I know you said we must be keepin' silent up here. But I've started wonderin' if an old Celtic story might entertain us all a bit—we must listen to the voices of the universe, you said. Perhaps mine could be one of them. What do you think, lad?"

Those wide blue eyes holding his for what seemed like several minutes were so endearing...and strangely mysterious too...that he suddenly changed his mind and nodded yes to her.

She stepped forward and lifted her arms up, using a louder voice because of the wind, "Come closer, everyone, and gather 'round me, will you now?" She motioned for them to sit in a circle. "Patrick has said yes to my request just now, so I'll be telling you a story that you've probably never heard. It's about the hags and banshees of Ireland that often wreak havoc in people's hearts, instigatin' all kinds of trouble with others. Even evil, if things go too far... But a brave maiden and an ancient Faerie Queen pit themselves against this unrelentin' evil.

"Want to hear more?"

Everyone nodded and settled down around her.

"Even if you don't believe these tales at first, soon you'll come to know they're present in our lives even now. The Faerie Queen too, as sure as this wind's blowin' near us. We don't see the wind either, now do we? But we see what it does. Do you see what I mean?

"So I'll begin my story: There was once a mortal called Finnegan who grew to manhood but nonetheless seemed lost to himself, his desire for riches and women a constant urge in him, but alas, he had no way to gain his every wish. Unknown to him, he was soon to lose whatever conscience and caring he'd been taught as a youth. About to be a soldier and enamored by fair maidens, one day he looked into a crystal pool and saw his impressive reflection. His physique was somethin' to behold, his muscled arms and legs as impressive as Neit's, the Irish god of war. Very soon after, both in battle and in a woman's bed, he became aware of his remarkable prowess, far excellin' other men. The only desire he had besides was to plunder after his battles to gain the riches of the world.

"It was then that the evil hags' and banshees' voices completely overcame his soul. He kept killin' by day and makin' love to a different maiden every night, so many that the wicked banshees came to him at night further influencin' his revoltin' pursuits. As the months and years went by, he'd murdered thousands of men and bedded hundreds of maidens. So many that the cryin' and wailin' in the world from their souls became a shriekin' wind that would not quit. Everyone who was left living there clasped their hands to their heads, it was such a mournful, grievin' sound violatin' their ears and hearts. No one could sleep at'tall, and finally the only faire virgin left in the land, Fiona, gathered every wee child around her from far and wide to help her stop Finnegan, and thus, stop the horrid, shriekin' sound.

"She was so frantic about the sadness and tears of them all that she took off with them on a journey to find the Faerie Queen and ask her assistance. Surely Her Highness would not reject the children's pleas even if she would not listen to Fiona's. But as much as she petitioned on her knees and the children cried out to her, the Queen seemed deaf to their pleas. 'It must be the loud shriekin' and weepin' sounds,' Fiona said to the little ones. 'That terrible noise overwhelms our voices so the Faerie Queen cannot hear us."

"Finnegan himself heard the constant shriekin' far worse than anyone and thought he'd surely go crazy from the constant shrieking. Soon he became haggard from years of lackin' sleep and no longer feelin' any inclination to eat. When Fiona returned from her trip, he came upon her, where she was sobbin' in vain at her failure, sittin' in a meadow among hazelnut trees near a crystal pool. As exhausted as Finnegan was, he reverted to his old antics and set about trying to capture her attention, as only he knew how, but she would not look at him no matter how much he tried. Instead, she spied shinin' gold coins lying in the pool under the water.

"'Why don't you come closer,' she said to Finnegan. 'I promise you'll find a treasure you'll love. A way for you to find the inner solace you've searched for all your life.'

"He ventured toward the maiden and glimpsed with amazement at the golden coins shimmerin' in the pool. Then he looked into Fiona's eyes with the usual flirtatious way he'd used to lure hundreds of maidens to his bed. This time his eyes became fastened to hers, locked in a strange magnetic vise, and he could not take them away no matter how much he tried. Then deep inside her orbs he saw the Faerie Queen, her wrinkled faerie face, her white hair gleamin' and a sparkling crown upon her head.

"'From this day forward, Finnegan,' said the Faerie Queen, 'you are banished from this land. You'll be escorted to the underworld as punishment for your selfish, horrid deeds, for a time so long it's useless to count the days. Take only one golden coin this day from the pool. A token to buy your freedom once the specters and seers decide you've suffered enough for all your wickedness in this land. Long before that happens, only excruciating screams and whimpering sounds, even worse than here, will torment your ears and your soul in the underworld.'

"Then before their very eyes, Fiona and the children watched Finnegan disappear, and gradually the horrible shriekin' and cryin' sounds dissipated into a comforting silence, a silence they had not heard in years. They each bent over the crystal pool to discover a gold coin for themselves, and all went back to share them with everyone who lived in their land."

With that, Maeve smiled at them all, but saved a mysterious knowing look for Patrick.

Patrick sat stunned. What kind of story was this? He'd never heard anything quite like it in all his years living in this Celtic land. He watched Maeve rise to take a bow as the others clapped, then she walked away to the farthest stone in the ancient circle where Seamus sat with Eve.

This time taking a tin whistle out of his backpack, Patrick decided a cheerful ditty would lift the mood of everyone now. As he played the most upbeat melody he knew, he watched Maeve carefully--surprised by what he saw. Motioning to Eve, first Maeve gestured with what looked like angry words, then pointed both hands toward the land below the hills from where they'd all come, as if she wanted Eve to leave. When the tall blonde got up and began the trek downhill, Maeve began talking to her son, her hands even more animated now with sharp, staccato motions. This went on for several minutes until the old woman put her hand in her pocket and gave Seamus what looked like a bundle of Euro bills. At that he stood up, without a smile or good-bye motion, and turned away, following after Eve.

CHAPTER 53

The sun's rays blistered through the farmhouse windows. "Unusual scorching heat for early April," Anna, the proprietor, said as she prepared Lily's lunch. A few minutes later, her apron discarded, she told Lily she was off to visit the open air market nearby "to fetch the freshest vegetables and fruits 'round here," and, with basket in hand, she breezed out the door. Lily was relieved. After she'd come downstairs at noon, she'd found it almost impossible to fake polite chit-chat, so she'd told Anna she was still sick from the night before. Sitting alone at the table now, Lily wiped perspiration from her forehead. Once she finished eating, she'd go upstairs and change into cooler clothes.

Quiet pervaded the spacious room now except for the larks' trills outside. *They're twittering up a storm, enjoying their lunch,* Lily thought. But their chirping made her heart ache more. She slowly bit into the sandwich on her plate, indifferent to its taste. The last thing she wanted to do was eat. She put down the bread and sipped her tea instead; its tepid warmth was usually a comfort, but not today.

Comfort. Her thoughts turned to Patrick. It was the best way to describe him. She pulled his note out of her pocket. She'd found it next to her cell phone when she'd awakened late this morning:

Dear Lily,

I'm hoping you slept plenty late. When you get up, don't worry about joining the rest of our group. Take the morning off. Take care of yourself. I'll come to look in on you this afternoon. I hope you're feeling better by then.

Sincerely,

Patrick

The screen door behind Lily slammed. She turned to see Eve come rushing in, a preoccupied frown on her face. Once she gazed across the room and spotted Lily, she smiled. "Well, Sleeping Beauty, how are you doing? I heard from our esteemed leader you were under the weather."

Lily turned her back to Eve. She couldn't look at her. Under the table she dug her fingernails into her thighs. Nausea began to overwhelm her again. *I will not talk to her.* She tried to breathe deeply. *I will not faint again either.*

Eve came over to the table and pulled out a chair. Her voice softened, "I was only joking. What's the matter? Are you sick?"

With slow precision, Lily moved her plate and cup aside, folded both arms on the table and put her head down. She'd do what she'd done as a child when her mom and dad yelled at her and each other for hours. Pretend they didn't exist. Now, as she listened to the larks continue their songs, she willed herself to block out everything else. *I won't say a word!*

When Eve put her hand out and touched Lily's arm, she flinched as if she'd been burned. "Don't touch me!" She raised her head, holding it high.

"What's with you?" Eve said.

"What's with *me*? What's with *you*? Or maybe I should phrase it more carefully—*who's* with you? Which one this time? That's right, it's Seamus *this* weekend, isn't it? So where is he? Why isn't he tagging after you?"

Eve pulled her hand away and stared at her. "What?"

Lily glared back as seconds turned into minutes. "I saw you. I saw both of you last night. You were going to his room. You wrapped yourself around him, like you do with all the men. You were giving him your come-on kiss before you and he—."

Eve sucked in breath. Guilt gleamed from her eyes. Lily knew she'd caught her.

"It wasn't what you think," Eve protested. "Don't make a big deal out of a kiss. I didn't go to bed with him. I swear it."

"Don't lie to me."

"I'm not lying. I've *never* lied to you. You have to believe me." She pushed back her hair. "Okay, I admit it; we were messing around in the hall. We'd both had too much to drink, and I kissed him a few times but I cut it short and went to my room. I never went to *his* room, even though he asked me. Lily, I couldn't do...I wouldn't do that to you. After you told me how you felt about him...."

Lily waved her hands as if swatting flies. "No more lies. Just leave."

"But—"

Lily took a deep breath. "I mean it." Her words were granite stones. "Leave. Me. Alone." Then she lowered her head and rested it on her arms, retreating to her childhood refuge.

"Lily, I—"

"Why won't you listen?" Lily yelled. "I said leave!" Her arms were still hugging her head.

Silence suffocated the room. She knew Eve hadn't moved.

A minute later, the screen door beside her slammed again. Lily pretended she was asleep, forcing herself to listen to the birds. Their songs were beautiful trills, as if inviting each other to play. She couldn't bear it.

Footsteps came close. "What's this?" It was Seamus' voice. "My two beautiful lasses in the same room? Wish I could enjoy your company. Wish I didn't have to leave, but me muther Maeve has laid down the law. Says there's a danger to my stayin'. So I have to disappear and quickly."

Lily lifted her head up to find Eve and Seamus' eyes on her. "You *both* should leave. Now."

Seamus' face turned pale. He held Eve's eyes in a question.

"She saw us last night outside your room," Eve said. "But we were just kissing, weren't we? Tell her, Seamus. She won't believe me."

"That's right, lass. It was just a little good night kiss. You wouldn't begrudge me that, now would you?"

Lily wanted to scream but she tried to rein in her voice but it came out low and loud. "Do you expect me to believe that? I saw you both go into his room, Eve. You were doing what you always do. I've always been your loyal friend, but I'm not stupid. Get out of here, both of you. I can't stand the sight of you." She stared at them, though it sickened her.

In silence, the couple slowly climbed the stairs together, and Lily breathed a sigh of miserable relief.

Several minutes later in her room, Lily lay on her bed, wishing for sleep. A numb, cold ache pervaded her whole body, even as she felt a gaping hole in her chest. She willed herself to visualize something beautiful instead...anything to take her mind off this betrayal. She began painting it in her mind, a dreamlike memory, the green velvety hills of Ireland against the setting sun—the scene she'd glimpsed from the plane months ago. *Everything was ahead of me then, freedom to explore, excitement. Eager to discover my homeland, my roots, myself.*

Two hours passed. Restless and unable to sleep, Lily called a cab and then changed into a cooler cotton blouse and beige slacks, choosing comfortable sandals for her trip home. Yes, it was time to fly back to California. After all, she'd promised to visit her daughters.

No makeup today. No time, no need. She noticed her body in the mirror. She almost looked thin, though she could hardly focus because she felt so sick at heart. Her suitcase was almost packed when she heard a gentle knock at her door. Patrick asked to come in, and soon he settled into the only comfortable chair in the room. Lily sat down on the bed to face him.

"How do you feel now, lass?" he asked. "Your cheeks look far rosier than last night, but you still don't look well. What're you doin' packin' already? None of us plan to take off today until after dinner."

"I've called a cab. I must go now. My cheeks might be pink but I don't feel myself. Not at all." She clenched her teeth to dam the tears behind her eyes. "Maybe not ever." Though she tried, she couldn't turn her gaze away from him. His eyes were kind, his voice so gentle.

"I know enough to realize this is not a physical problem now," he said. "It's your heart that's heavy, isn't it, lass?"

She saw only those dark blue eyes, full of caring and concern.

He stood, and taking her hands tenderly, he pulled her up and took her in his arms, hugging her. His warmth was so comforting. "There, child, I don't know the details, but I know you've had a terrible shock," he whispered. "You're not yourself. I can see the hurt in your eyes and in the way your body sags. If you need to cry then do it now, not when you're all alone in that cab out there. Please."

Safe within his arms, she finally let her tears seep out at first, vowing she wouldn't lose control. But all at once a torrent followed until she leaned in on him and let herself sob. She couldn't remember when she'd ever felt so hurt, so lost. *After so many years, my only friend betrayed me....* His warm arms around her gave her a consoling shelter she'd never imagined. *What a gift.* She wished she could stay like this forever.

When she'd quieted down, he whispered in her ear, "I'd like to help you. But I know your pain goes deep. Please believe me, though; eventually it will heal. I know it will, just not soon, lass. Remember, I'll be here for you. I'll do anythin' I can."

She let him hold her a long time, until her tears dried and she'd wiped the rest away. "I must go now," she said and motioned toward the window. "The taxi's waiting." With that, she looked up into his kind face and kissed him full on the mouth, surprised at the shivers that ran through her. She picked her suitcase up off the bed. "Thank you so very much. You'll hear from me. I...I guess you're my best friend now, Patrick."

Then she was gone.

CHAPTER 54

*T*aking the stairs together, Eve parted ways with Seamus, telling him she needed to be alone. Later she hiked in the hills for a couple of hours, but it didn't do any good. Even sitting quietly under the trees and sipping the wine she'd brought didn't relax her or raise her spirits. The muggy heat and overcast sky only added to her angst. Giving up, she headed toward the farmhouse. In the distance she saw a taxi drive up and watched as Lily put her suitcase inside and, without a look back, climbed in and closed the door. The cab made its way back up the long driveway and disappeared in the distance.

Reaching the house, Eve ran upstairs, opened the door to her room then slammed it shut. Or she thought she did. When it swung wide again, she shoved it closed with all the force of her shoulders and hips. "That hurt!" She rubbed her body, wondering if she'd see bruises tomorrow. It didn't matter. The pain actually felt good. *How sick,* she thought.

She punched her fist hard at the wall. "I've had it!" She was yelling now and suddenly realized they might hear her because the others were all packing. But she didn't care. "Patrick's probably still up on that friggin' hill where all the Druids did their chanting eons ago." She toned her yelling down to a growl. "He loves that stuff, but I'm sick of listening to him. Who cares what happened up near those old monoliths? I'm done with this place."

She took out her suitcase and plopped it on her bed. She might as well pack too. Her eyes burned as she pictured Lily leaving without her and never looking back. But she was determined not to feel...anything.

Poor Lily...she's been trying so hard to get me to talk about all the stuff I've been avoiding. I actually thought I was making some progress here until Patrick kept muscling in. But now I've done it. I've messed up everything. Eve knew with a revolting certainty that Lily wouldn't speak to her for a very long time.

Dumping her clothes into the suitcase, she finished packing in less than five minutes. She'd done such a dreadful job, though, she couldn't close it. "Hmph," she said aloud, and began refolding each piece of clothing and fitting them more carefully into her suitcase. In the midst of it all she was aware she was rushing, caught in an awful frenzy. But why? She didn't have any deadlines. Everyone else was about to leave to catch the ferry to Ireland. Well, she knew where Seamus was. Down the hall, packing too. With the door to his room ajar just now, she'd seen him and waved. But Patrick? She didn't know and she didn't care!

Seamus planned to leave promptly after a brief dinner here, stay somewhere local and sightsee all afternoon tomorrow in Wales. He'd tried to talk her into going with him, saying he had some business in the morning at the nearby university. Now that Lily was gone, she decided she didn't have many options, so why not go with him? She could keep her sales appointments with the Welsh wine merchants tomorrow morning as planned.

Finally clamping the suitcase shut, she sat down on the bed. The room was quiet. She had nothing more to do, except think. ... No, not now. She got up and paced the room. But, no matter how much she tried, she couldn't sweep her thoughts and feelings away. She'd had lunch with Lily only a couple of days ago, and they'd had such fun planning their itinerary through Wales. Now, because of one night of sex, everything had changed. Lily had even detected she was lying.

Why did she take it so personally? She and Seamus weren't really a couple. She made a big deal about his attention. No, Seamus was never taken with her. So he was fair game, wasn't he?

Eve shoved the suitcase aside and began rubbing the temples of her forehead, trying to wipe away a headache that threatened to send her to bed. Maybe it had something to do with all the wine she'd drunk last night, and all the stress.

Still with her back to the door, Eve studied the encroaching darkness outside. A soft knock distracted her. "Come in. It's open."

No sound penetrated the stillness. When Eve turned around she saw Maeve. The petite old lady never looked so serious. The little woman's eyes pierced hers, so much so that a grim streak ran through her.

"All packed, eh?" she said. "I'll be goin' myself soon." She sat down in a chair across the room, "Before I leave, child, I must warn you. Only because I think of you and Lily as me friends, though I've seen much more of her since you both came to this faire isle."

"Sorry. I've been pretty busy the last few days."

"Yes, busy with your job and busy with your men," Maeve said. Her eyes were like bright blue weapons aimed at Eve.

Still massaging her temples, Eve stood up and walked back to the window, noting how the trees' shadows outside were casting dark patterns on the lawn now. Clouds had been hiding the sun all afternoon, and now that it was nearing dinnertime, the rest of the landscape had changed to a palette of charcoal and gray. It was exactly how she felt. Dull. Colorless. Sad. Regretful, too? Maybe. Yes, she'd kissed Lily's...yes, Lily's *boyfriend*. And then he took over her whole body. A strong guy. What could she do?

A minute stretched into many, but the two women didn't move or say a word. Finally Maeve spoke, "So you're done with your friend then, are you? I hugged her good-bye earlier, before she got into the taxi. She was the saddest I've ever seen her, and it's no one's fault but your own and me Seamus." She slapped her hand so hard on the table that Eve jumped. "And it's no surprise to me about me son."

Eve gave no response. She kept staring out the window. She had nothing to say to this little woman. What did *she* know?

"And you're goin' off with me son now, instead of your friend?" Maeve continued, "I'll warn you once about him, but not a second time, mind ya. The truth is, he's me son and I love him like the good muther that I am. But I know all his faults, every one of them, and I know them well.

"I wished and wished when he first met you two that he would change. But though I have some mysterious and sometimes magical ways, I've learned that I cannot alter a person's choices, not even me son's. I'm sorry to be admittin' it and telling you too, he's a lot of things, but he's not a loyal chap when it comes to women. And that's not all, lass. In spite of what he says, he doesn't have one gold coin or any money to his name. If it weren't for the college scholarship he won, he'd never be in these faire isles. And if it weren't for the money I earned in my gardening shop back home, I wouldn't be here either. I never thought I'd have to be tellin' you this.

"I'm sad to be sayin' it, but he reminds me of the Celtic hero Finnegan, who couldn't get enough of women or gold. Do ya know what happened to him? Banished, he was, to the underworld for punishment, for many a long year. You should read his story, me lady, and not forget it, because many a faerie story has come true for mortals over these years. Even though I'm sure you, above all, won't believe this now, a day will soon dawn when you will." Her eyes pierced Eve's again. "Mind my words."

Eve didn't know what to say. All she could do was turn away and stare at the growing darkness outside.

Then Maeve raised her voice so loud that Eve turned around to see her blue eyes still blazing. She pointed her index finger at Eve like a fierce schoolmarm. "If you're after a faithful man, he's not the one. Me Seamus is bound to disappoint you, sure as this hair is white." She pointed to her head and lowered her voice. "The same way he disappoints everyone, includin' me, over and over again. I advise ye to watch your wallet too, my fair lass." She glared at Eve again for a full minute before turning toward the door. Then she disappeared. But, strangely enough, Eve noticed the door of her room remained closed the whole time.

"Sit," Patrick stared at Eve and pointed across the room. He'd come into the farmhouse kitchen after spending some last moments up on the hill in the gathering shadows. He'd prayed for guidance, communing with the ancient spirits that seemed to surround him among the circle of standing stones.

Eve stood staring at him, her golden hair pulled back in a sleek bun, her makeup perfect, her suitcase by her side. Her eyes flared. "Wow, the holy ex-priest, and not to mention Vision Quest leader, shouting profanities? I'm shocked."

Patrick stalked across the room and pulled out the chair. He was so rough it almost keeled over. "I said sit, not shit." His voice was so deep she could hardly hear him.

"Yes, sir!" she saluted, then stomped over to stand next to the chair but refused to sit down. She wouldn't grant him that. Nor would she give him a glance. She turned away and gazed through the window again. No stars tonight.

"I won't bother to tell you," Patrick began, "the details—"

"What details?"

"—of how much you hurt your friend."

"I know all about it."

"I don't care. You'll hear me out. Because of you, Lily is hurt and alone now, Eve. She's like an injured fawn, and it's your fault. If I were you I'd wait a long while before you talk to her—if she'll allow it."

Eve turned around to face him. "I didn't do anything,... except maybe that *grave* sin you're always accusing me of—a little flirting." She wouldn't look at him.

He knew for sure now. It *had* been Eve's antics with Seamus that had caused all the trouble. Lily must've...she must've had a thing for....

He wrung his hands, a habit he'd tried to break, but whenever he was hurting he resorted to it. So, Lily *had* been involved with Seamus. But for how long? And Eve had...yes, she'd probably seduced him. Or...he remembered Seamus taking Eve to a car after the Blarney Castle debacle and their antics together last night around the fire pit. Today on the hill too. So last night the two of them had...

Now he strode over to Eve, wanting to slap her. But something inside him reared up, making him stop. He'd vowed his whole life that he would never hit a woman, and he wasn't going to start now.

Footsteps on the stairs distracted him. Seamus was loaded down with his own suitcase and a basket of wine bottles he'd apparently brought with him. "Aye, so you're down here, are you?" he said to Eve. "I was wonderin' where you'd gone. I knocked on your door but no answer." Then he spotted Patrick. "Aye, and you too? Oh, so what's *this* little powwow about? You're both lookin' a little green. Have the ancient ghosts up yonder been following you about?" He gestured toward the hill outside.

Then he swept down into the kitchen and showed his basket of wines to Eve. "I thought this would liven up our travels today and tomorrow. What do you think, lass?"

"Sure. Good idea." She buttoned up her jacket, gathered up her suitcase and her purse and starting walking with him to the door.

"Well, Patrick, I guess we're goin' now," Seamus said. "That...what did you call it? Oh yes, Vision Quest--that was quite a time, wasn't it, Eve?" He winked at her. "Quite a time, indeed. So long, then." He tipped his hand to his head in a jaunty salute and whisked Eve out the door to a waiting taxi.

Patrick couldn't have been more relieved to see them go. But inside him raged a fire he'd never felt before. He knew for certain that if they'd stayed one more minute he might have broken his vow. He would have slugged Seamus more than once and, at the very least, shoved Eve out the door as well.

CHAPTER 55

Stretching after a fitful night's sleep, Lily eased herself out of Tanya's bed, opened the dorm room window and made her way out to the tiny balcony. Ominous clouds hovered across the horizon, much like Ireland's skies just yesterday. Today's predicted storm would dump two inches of rain on Berkeley, an unusual amount for late April in northern California. *It's a good day to stay in and sleep,* Lily thought. *That's all I want to do.*

She'd taken the first flight from Ireland she could find yesterday, and when the plane finally began its descent in San Francisco, she'd glimpsed the twinkling lights of the Golden Gate Bridge. So much sadness had weighed her down that she barely even looked out the window at this, her favorite sight.

It was close to midnight when she'd finally arrived at the dorm last night. Tanya's new roommate had welcomed her, "Hey, Ms. O'Malley. Come on in. You must be tired from your flight." She'd led Lily over to her daughter's bed. "Let me help you with your baggage. You can sleep here tonight since Tanya won't be back. In fact, I was just leaving too." She began gathering her books together as she talked. "It's finals week, so a bunch of us planned an all-nighter in the library. I'm meeting Tanya now. She asked me to let you know what's going on. We have two exams tomorrow. Can't wait till they're over." She'd no sooner loaded all the books and notebooks into her book bag, than she waved good-bye and left.

Well, that's that, Lily had decided. *All I can do now is try to reach Lisa by text or phone.* Though it was crazy late, she'd called Lisa three times, but again, no response. Disappointed but exhausted, Lily had peeled off her travel clothes, dug out a nightgown from her overnight bag and settled into bed, falling asleep immediately.

Now, seven hours later, she walked back into the cramped two-bed dorm room and spotted a note pinned to the wall above Tanya's bed. She'd obviously been too tired last night to notice it.

Hi Mom,

I'm off to Chem Lab and then to the library to study all day and all night. I'm sorry I won't be able to be there when you arrive tonight. I wish I'd known sooner that you were coming, but I probably couldn't have changed my schedule anyway because of exams. Thank god, it'll all be over soon. Then we can have a good visit, okay? Who knows, maybe with Lisa too. In the meantime make yourself at home. And wish me luck!

Love,

Tanya

Lily wadded up the note. She was glad one daughter was studying hard and wondered what the other one was up to. She could see they were both busy, but she couldn't help feeling let down. A craving to see nature suddenly took hold of her, and she headed for the balcony again. Sometimes immersing herself in the beauty of mountains, hills and wildlife worked like a balm when depression assailed her.

Though the weather was cool, it felt good. Like the weather in Ireland, she thought again, then quickly banished the comparison from her mind. She studied the clouds, billowing up like dark blue and gray bruises, in the eastern sky. A sizable lawn spread out below, surrounding side-walk paths as well as aging oak trees, their leaves bright green. Though it was early, she watched a few students heading toward their classrooms or the library. She wondered what it would be like to attend college on a *real* campus. She'd never had that privilege.

As much as she tried to immerse herself in this idyllic scene, a melancholy she couldn't shake plagued her. She thought of Eve then Seamus and reached out to grasp the balcony rail, realizing she was clenching her teeth as well. The emptiness she felt overwhelmed her. She wished she could find an elixir to heal the wounds inside. Maybe then she'd feel more herself. The dry numbness that had taken hold ever since she'd seen Eve wrapped in Seamus' arms still gripped her. Even Patrick's gentle words before she left for the airport hadn't triggered any emotion. She knew she needed some sort of relief. She felt locked up inside with no way to escape.

Why had she come here? Had she simply trumped up reasons to leave everyone in Ireland behind, even those who had befriended her and offered her that goldmine job? *No,* she convinced herself. *Last week I told the girls I was going to visit them. I need to find out why Tanya is making innuendos about Lisa's friends. And...and see if they're really keeping their grades up.*

Besides, Rose O'Sullivan had told her this would be the best time for her to visit her daughters at UC Berkeley. "Then you can fly back to Blarney Castle in a week or so and start your consulting job here with your mind at peace." *If she only knew...that seemed impossible now.* But yes, this *was* an opportune time and she'd grabbed it for all those reasons. Yet underneath it all, she had to admit, this trip was a convenient escape. One she desperately needed.

Large raindrops began to fall all around her, and she rushed inside, closing the balcony door. She tried to enjoy the tap, tap, tapping sounds plus the swish of cars in the distance. She'd always loved the sounds of rain, but her usual delight was missing. She climbed back into Tanya's bed, pulled up the covers and hid under them, wishing she could stay there for days. *No, I'll only sleep for an hour or two,* she promised herself, *and then I'll go find Lisa.*

&.

Lily spied her daughter sprawled in a large leather chair near several other students seated at a nearby table in the library. Lisa was reading a thick chemistry book while the others were studying from textbooks and notes spread out on the table. The library was quiet, so Lily whispered hello before Lisa got up to hug her.

"Can you take a break?" Lily asked. "I don't need to be entertained while you study for your finals, but I'd like to talk to you for a few minutes. Can we go to the coffee shop?"

Lisa nodded yes and they made their way across the quad to the campus bookstore café.

"So, how are you, honey?" Lily asked as she bit into a bran muffin.

Stirring creamer into her coffee, Lisa met Lily's gaze. "Just tired from studying all night. I didn't know you were coming, Mom, until yesterday. Tanya texted me. It's great to see you, but what made you come?"

"I'll be starting a new job in Ireland at Blarney Castle soon, so I thought I'd better make this trip now. Let's talk about you, hon. How're you doing with your classes and your roommate?"

"I'm doing well. I got lucky—my roommate situation is good. I've got a B average in most classes too, and I want to keep it that way. Chemistry is really difficult, though. I'm struggling—that's why I'm studying so hard."

Lily was relieved. Because of Tanya's negative comments about Lisa's friends, Lily decided to broach that subject later.

After her daughter finished giving details about each of her classes, Lily tackled the subject of strange phone calls. "Tanya said she thought you'd heard from Eve's old boyfriend Brad about a week ago. He hasn't contacted you again, has he?"

"I texted Tanya about that," Lisa said, "but we don't exactly spend much time together. It's funny you asked though, because I got a weird phone call again the other day. This time the guy actually wanted to talk to you and he sounded really familiar and friendly but avoided giving me his name. Unlike before, he said he'd been in touch with you, but couldn't remember where you were staying. He asked if I could help him out 'cuz he couldn't reach you. Before I realized it, the words were out of my mouth."

"Oh, no! What did you tell him?"

"Not much the first time he called." Lily watched her daughter's face cringe as if she were going to scold her. "But the second time... I'm sorry, Mom. I...didn't want to give him your cell phone number. So I told him you were staying in Kinsale, but I couldn't remember the name of the hotel. Did you...did you ever hear from him?"

"You didn't! Thank God I went to Wales for a few days right before I flew here. Wait a minute, I can't believe Tanya didn't warn you! We spoke on the phone just a few days ago," Lily heard her voice rising and knew it would make Lisa clam up, so she took a deep breath and lowered her tone. "I told Tanya to tell you not to take any more calls from him. Now he knows Eve is in Ireland with me, and he even knows we've been staying in Kinsale."

Lisa leaned forward. "I said I was sorry, Mom. I didn't mean to. Who is he, anyway? You think it was Brad? Like always, I'm out of the loop."

"Yes, I'm sure it was Brad. He caused Eve's accident, remember? He's abusive and dangerous. Now, he's decided he wants to find Eve. So he's calling you to find out where I am, and then he'll track me down, then Eve and who knows what else?"

Head lowered, Lisa began stirring more creamer into her coffee. "Great, I guess I fucked up good. I'm *really* sorry. I've put you in danger, haven't I? Eve too." She laid the spoon down and began

355

rubbing her forehead. "If he finds you and hurts either of you, it's gonna be my fault." She squeezed her eyes shut and scowled.

"First, Lisa, watch your words. I don't appreciate hearing you use the f-word. I hate it and you know it. Don't worry about the Kinsale thing. I'll figure something out. Whatever you do, if he calls you again, refuse to speak to him. I'll say it again. He's dangerous. Do you understand?"

"'Course," she said, but from then on, no matter what small talk Lily offered, Lisa would hardly look at her mother, let alone converse.

Lily decided to cut their time short. She'd try again later to find out how her daughter really was, and who her college friends were. After telling her a little about her new job, Lily set a time when she could talk to both girls together.

Walking through the college campus back to Tanya's dorm, Lily tried to digest what Lisa's revelations meant. Should she contact someone in Ireland right away? But who? Call Eve direct? No! She couldn't do that. Not now. *I feel sick just thinking about her.* Pains jabbed inside her stomach, and she reached into her purse for her meds. She really didn't owe Eve anything. But by the time she reached Tanya's dorm, she'd mulled it over some more. She realized she couldn't keep this news to herself. She had to tell someone. If Eve returned to Kinsale, her life could be in danger.

CHAPTER 56

"That's a bonny outfit you're wearing this mornin'," Seamus said as he got up from the table and leaned over to kiss Eve's cheek. She turned away, wondering how anyone could be so cheerful on this dreary day. The sky was dark pewter gray. Tree branches were tapping wildly at the window. The cold wind outside sent chilly drafts through the breakfast room. This gloomy weather was getting to her. Obviously, Seamus had risen early and eaten his breakfast long before her. They'd stayed the night in Pembroke.

No matter how jovial Seamus had been yesterday, as they drove through the town, sightseeing, Eve found herself longing to be alone. As soon as they checked in at this quaint B&B, she'd feigned a migraine, declined his invitation for dinner and retired to her room. But it hadn't helped. Images of Lily's stricken face kept invading Eve's mind along with the echo of Patrick's and Maeve's warnings. After picking at the sandwich and dessert the proprietor had insisted on sending up to her room, she drank some wine, then took a sleeping pill and turned in early, unusual for her.

Perhaps she'd taken too strong of a dose. When the alarm

sounded this morning, she could barely stand up and walk, and even now, after a hot shower and a cup of Joe in her room, she was feeling drowsy and lightheaded.

"What's the matter, my girl?" Seamus asked. "You're lookin' a bit weary and you were late gettin' up. " He stared at the scowl she offered him, then softened his tone, "Or a little later than I thought you'd be."

"I'll be fine. It's not that late," Eve insisted, ordering only a roll with jam. "I'm going to spend an hour here before I make my sales calls today. We can meet somewhere for a late lunch."

He took a final swig of coffee from his mug, wiped his mouth with a napkin and stood up. "That'll be fine, me love. I hope you don't mind, but I need to be gettin' along now or I'll be late for my appointments at the college. I'll call you when I'm finished."

She nodded and watched him leave, wondering why she felt so uninterested in this handsome Irishman when two nights ago he'd seemed so hot. She even wondered what Lily had seen in him. *He's just an Irish skirt-chaser—I've met hundreds like him.*

A half-hour later, she was in the middle of checking out, when the B&B proprietor handed her the bill and she noticed that the total included the price of Seamus' room as well as her own. When she questioned it, the lady said, "I haven't seen your friend this morning, but last night he told me that both rooms would be covered by your company's expense account."

"Hmph." Eve scowled as she handed the woman her credit card, remembering Maeve's warning.

Several hours were enough for Eve to call on three Welsh restaurant owners, who weren't as enthusiastic about her wines as the proprietors in Ireland. She sighed as she sat down on the stone garden bench in front of the B&B. After texting and calling Seamus but receiving no replies, she'd driven back here for lack of anywhere else to go. Finally her cell phone rang, and Seamus asked her to drive over to the college so they could go out to lunch. His rental car had caused trouble and he was stuck there.

Despite his predicament, he was beaming a broad, dimpled smile when she arrived and began introducing Eve to two young women. "Molly and Shannon, meet Eve Olson, my gorgeous and successful friend from the States," he said. "She's an award winner, she is, sellin' California wines in the U.S. and throughout these Celtic isles too." He directed his gaze to Eve, "And I've been investigatin' Celtic artifacts here, thanks to these other two beauties." With that he waved one arm in the air with a flourish, and bowed to all of them.

"Nice to meet you. You're not twins, are you?" Eve asked, noting that both young women were dressed in jeans and matching thigh-length boots.

They smiled and shook their heads. Their pastel sweaters accentuated their fair skin and long, silken hair, one a brunette, the other a redhead. *They can't be much older than Lisa and Tanya*, Eve mused.

"I was thinkin', Eve," Seamus continued, "Molly and Shannon here should join us on this bright day. They know their way around the college much better than I, as well as a few good pubs we could visit, bye and bye. I was thinkin' maybe you can sell your wines this afternoon."

Eve decided she might as well be agreeable, plus this might be the opportunity she needed after her disappointing morning, so they all piled into her rental car. Seamus and the girls showed her a few Celtic artifacts displayed at the college, but soon they parted ways. Eve chose to visit three different restaurants in the area on her own. By the time dinner rolled around, she joined the threesome at another pub across the road from Pembroke College.

She could tell they were all tipsy when she met them laughing together in a corner booth. She noted too that Seamus hadn't bothered to order her a drink even though she'd asked him to have one ready for her. Her temper flared but she bit her tongue and walked to the bar. When she glanced back she realized Seamus was so preoccupied he didn't even notice she'd left. *Well, I've dumped men before...*

The pub was much larger and more crowded than the ones Eve had called on earlier. The floor space and booths were thick with college students, so Eve couldn't even see Molly, Shannon and Seamus sitting across the room as she waited for her drink. She tried to spot them, but no luck. It didn't really matter. Earlier she'd grown tired of the girls' banter anyway—they were at least a dozen years younger than she was—and Seamus' jokes had become tedious too. So she struck up conversations with the men around her, who were close to her age. She was about to order dinner from the menu the bartender gave her when she spotted the threesome getting up and crossing the room. She waved to them but they didn't notice. Instead, they made their way up the stairs adjacent to the front door. "Where does that lead?" she asked the bartender.

"Oh, the second floor is part of the inn," he answered. "Why, lass? Do you want a tour? I'd be happy to show you one of our gorgeous bedrooms. We could spend some time...uh, studying the décor or, better yet, we could do whatever we like..." He winked.

"Well, now that you mention it, I might need to stay overnight here," she said. "I'd like to talk to your manager if he's here. But I can do without a tour, thank you very much." She winked back.

"So, I'm not good enough for your tour, am I? Well, my manager's off travelin' in Spain right now so you'll have to put up with me, if you don't mind. I'd be happy to put you up," he said, "with or without a tour." He smiled.

As the evening wore on, Eve didn't see Seamus and his "twins" again, so she arranged to stay at the inn rather than drive the unfamiliar roads at night. After a while, her head cloudy with liquor—maybe because she never ate dinner—she'd had enough chitchat for one evening. When her efforts to reach Ian failed, she made her way upstairs to turn in.

Tomorrow was another day, sure to bring another surprise too, at least for Seamus. Her plan was to leave just after dawn tomorrow. And this time *he'd* pay the bill for *her* room!

CHAPTER 57

*I*an's gruff voice at the end of the phone sounded so sexy. *Finally he's calling me back, and his apologetic tone seems sincere.* Even though Eve couldn't completely erase the trouble he'd caused her at Blarney Castle, an urgent longing engulfed her as she listened to him.

"Where are you?" Ian asked. "I have a few days off and I thought you could help me with a job I'm doing. It involves a large order of wine, and with it, quite a hefty amount of money...for both of us."

"I'm in northern Wales," she said. "Hmm, sounds tempting. Depends on what you want me to do, though." But underneath her offhand reply all she wanted to do was wrap herself around his strong, muscular body as soon as possible. Their lovemaking, though a little edgy, turned her on more than any man she'd ever taken to bed. She hoped he wasn't too far away. "Are you near the coast?"

"Not far from the Irish Sea. I can get to the station where the ferry comes in within an hour. If you leave Wales soon, I'll even foot the bill for your crossing."

Eve's breathing quickened as her body began to tremble. He

must want her more than she thought. She hadn't been with him in over a week. The last time she'd seen him he'd brought her flowers and lavished her with a very expensive evening "to make up for the trouble I caused," he'd said. After their extravagant dinner they'd indulged in one of the most memorable sexual escapades she'd ever experienced. But each time she saw him, he frightened her a bit more when their lovemaking became unusually fierce. Sometimes it hurt a little and she felt she was wrestling with a fighter, Ian's muscles were so hard and strong. "Please stop," she'd whined more than once, and finally he did. In fact, he wouldn't even touch her, but she knew he was playing with her. So she'd begged him in the sexiest tone she could muster to lift her onto the bed and lick her nipples and then her thighs, "oh so slowly." When he refused, she'd caressed his body for a long time, so slowly and long that he grew crazy with desire, finally giving her exactly what she wanted. From then on in between their incessant wrestling and deep kisses, his tongue found all the places she'd pleaded for... And when she moaned and begged again for more, he mounted her and rode her hard until she squealed with pleasure.

Imagining it all now, her nipples hardened, as she grasped her phone. Even so, warnings echoed in her thoughts, along with images of Patrick's scowling face, then her dad's ghost, smoking his pipe on the dark moor, as he delivered his stern advice. She pictured Lily's soft green eyes too, pleading with her to be careful.

But she dismissed it all.

"You've got a deal, Ian. I'll take the next ferry to Ireland, and I'll text you as soon as it leaves, okay?"

When she walked off the ferry boat and saw him coming toward her, it was all she could do to stop herself from rushing toward him. Instead, she held herself back, measuring her steps as he came near, offering him her best smile. His gray, steely eyes and his opened arms told her he was holding back too. Then he crushed her to him. When he began to pull away she resisted, pressing her breasts to his chest again, kissing his neck, listening to the pounding of his heart.

When he finally moved away, she pouted. "Did you miss me?"

He nodded, granting her a rare smile. "I see you're hungry, girl, and it's not food you're wantin'. But we've got work to do now." He took her hand in his as they walked to the parking lot.

Once they'd settled themselves in his truck, he drove toward Dublin. On the way, when he braked at intersections, he kissed her more than once. Long, sensuous kisses, his tongue exploring her mouth gently, then with sudden passion, his breath still rising and falling when he began driving again.

She'd figured out a while ago that he was a master at hiding his feelings, someone who probably hadn't been loved much. That's why he almost never smiled or admitted how much he cared. But it was plain he couldn't control his feelings around her. And that thought gave her a sensuous triumph, coupled with a thrilling heat that moved throughout her body.

She couldn't wait for tonight.

Ian pulled the car to the curb and parked in front of an old warehouse. Eyes closed, Eve leaned back, picturing the evening ahead as he fumbled through the glove compartment.

"What the fuck? Damn it, where is it?"

Her reverie was cut short and she sat up. "What's wrong?"

"Oh shit, here it is!"

A cold chill gripped her at the sight of the revolver in his hand. "What's that for?"

"Let's just call it insurance, eh?" He stared at her with a gleam of triumph in his eyes that she didn't understand.

"Ian, you could...you could end up in jail if you—"

"Quiet, lass. I don't even have ammo, so calm down. I'm only going to use it to get my point across, if you know what I mean." He shoved it into his jacket pocket. "This deal could land us a cool million each, and these punks need to know who they're dealing with."

Anxiety must have shown on her face. He gave her a long look. "Hey, I said don't worry. I probably won't even need to flash it at them." He gently traced his finger down her cheek.

She breathed deeply, aroused by his touch, and now, strangely enough, by the danger he exuded. "Really? A cool million each?" She made good money at the winery, but not that kind. Money like that would guarantee she'd never have to work again. But she was stunned. Stunned that he planned to carry a gun and stunned that he was involved in such a lucrative deal. "What do we have to do?"

"Nothing much, at least where you're concerned. Ah, I know underneath your sass you're pretty straight. Aren't you now? So, I made sure you don't have to do much. I only need one big wine shipment, only one, to come from your winery's warehouse in Kinsale to this warehouse here in Dublin. And, after a few days, I need it shipped to London. You have plenty of inventory in Kinsale, don't you? All you have to do is place the order today and make sure it gets shipped out as soon as possible." He fixed steely eyes on her.

She shrugged with a nonchalance she didn't feel. "As long as you give me a legit order I can ship it wherever, although I'll have to check with headquarters in California, depending on how large it is. And shipping to two locations is a bit unusual. You'll have to pay for that."

"No problem with the double shipping costs," he said. "I think you'll be able to persuade them to sell a hunk of their inventory when they see the money they'll make." He motioned toward the warehouse. "My contact here has the order all ready for you. It'll be the easiest sale you'll ever make. As far as a million each, maybe I was exaggerating, but it'll mean a load of money."

She noticed how animated his voice was now, new electricity lifting it. "The money'll be more than enough to buy one of those slick, gentry houses in the middle of this lovely city," he continued. "You know, over in that rich section of Dublin where folks flaunt their money at cocktail parties, ride their sleek horses. Those upper-class snobs are respected around here."

What had he just described? Was he asking her to marry him?

Unusual for him, he was still talking, "Their names are in the paper every other week. Wouldn't you like to be one of them? Own racehorses, shop wherever you want, travel the world." He paused. "Do. Anything. You. Want?" This new urgency in his voice struck her as genuine. Ian was usually careful not to show his feelings except when it came to sex, but now he persisted in a low voice while his eyes burned with determination. "It's not too late, Eve. Not too late for us to have it all."

He smiled that crooked smile again, and she realized it was only the second time she'd seen his face light up like that. He kept smiling, leaning down so close she could feel his breath on her face. It was minty and fresh. "Eve, then we can do anything we want," he whispered. "You get that, don't you?" His fingers began caressing her lips and she felt an uncontrolled passion taking hold of him again. She heard his heavy breathing between long kisses, and felt his ravenous tongue exploring her mouth with sudden pressure. Soon he was licking her ear and nibbling her neck too. She felt his fingers reaching up her dress, massaging her thighs, then finally reaching down to her wet spaces and stroking her slowly, his hardness pressing up against her. Delicious thrills ran through her body.

Slowly he moved away from her, his voice husky, "But if we want all that, we have to do a little work. Yeah. Seal the deal today," his tone rose again to that same emotional pitch, "and then we can go see the neighborhood where we're going to live. I've got a place all picked out. You'll like it, I know. Fancy houses all around it, full of nice families and...and kids too. What you've wanted, right?"

She couldn't stifle her feelings now. They ran deep. Something inside her wanted to cry out. She reached up with both arms to hug him, stroke his chin and his face. She found his lips and explored his mouth with her tongue, just the way he liked it. Quickly undoing her blouse and her bra, she lifted her breast to his mouth as she held him, massaging his back and neck. She would pleasure him now and much more later. A foreign excitement welling up inside about their future was more than she could bear. This man wanted her not for one night or a week or a year, but *forever*. She unzipped his pants, stroking his hardness slowly at first, then leaning down, she gave him all the pleasure she knew he wanted.

As she caressed him, she pushed the danger he'd hinted at earlier into a dark place far away, wanting nothing to do with it. Instead, her mind and her body were alive with the desperate wanting he'd described—as if he'd discovered all the secret long-ings she'd hidden for years, even to herself.

Minutes later when they rested in each others' arms, she whis-pered in his ear, "Did you mean all those things you said?"

He nodded. "Yeah, we're not that different. I've wanted those things too. And I want you." He turned and looked at her full-on, a timid, half-scared look in his eyes, and she knew he was divulging something he'd never told anyone before. He was in love with her. She was sure. She hadn't felt hope like this in a long time. Maybe she *could* have everything she wanted. A husband and a filthy rich house in a posh Dublin neighborhood. No, she couldn't have a child... But...but she could adopt one. She felt sure she could talk him into it. She'd only allowed herself to think about it once, then thrown the idea away, along with all her other broken dreams. But he'd been so emphatic when he said earlier, "Do. Anything. You. Want." Was the idea so completely outlandish? He'd said it wasn't too late, and she wouldn't be alone. He'd take the lead and she could finally let her feelings out, break down the dam of her lifelong resistance and indulge in the dreams she'd never let herself desire: a husband who actually loved her, a mansion in a neighborhood she could be proud of and at least one child she could mother...it was everything she'd ever wanted. Family. Everything her friend Lily used to have, but never seemed to appreciate.

They'd finally reached their hotel room after Ian's meeting, which had lasted over an hour in the warehouse while Eve tried to doze outside in the car, though her nerves made her fidgety.

Now she rolled over on the bed, away from Ian, gasping for breath, perspiration wetting her face, neck and behind her knees. But he wasn't done with her. He picked her up and turned her into the doggy position and she knew what was coming. Yes, she knew, and she wasn't sure she wanted it. They'd been at it for at least two hours and, for the first time, most of her body ached. He'd gone too far. Why was she putting up with this new treatment? She groaned like a person drowning, as he grasped her thighs. His fingers hurt, his nails cut into her skin, and even though she cried out, he pressed them deeper, hanging on to her as he penetrated her body. Hard. Then, over and over he plunged into her, and she stifled a scream. It was too much! Something was wrong. No matter how many times she'd told him no, he wouldn't listen. It was all happening again— what Brad had done to her.

She had to be *sick*. Sick in the head. And now, sick of the pain. She screamed louder, "No!" and disentangling herself, found the bathroom and locked herself in. This had all happened before. How many times? Could she change it with Ian?

By the time she finally showered and returned to bed, she was determined to have things her way. Even though he wanted more of the same, she talked him out of it, whispering in his ear with all the sexy talk she knew. She stroked his arms and legs, felt his muscles calm and his breathing slow as she leaned down to play with his sex, caressing him all over, then asking him to massage her crotch. "Gently this time. *Only* gently. *Please*," she whispered, as he felt her up and licked her nipples at the same time. He was doing what she wanted now, finally, and his sensuous teasing was pure ecstasy. Yes, she knew how to tame him and have it her way!

Slowly, gradually, his touch evoked a passionate fury inside her. Shivering with pleasure, she took a deep breath, mounting him quickly, and now it was she riding him back and forth her own way, until a crescendo of pleasure lifted her up high. Then a pause and a sudden, hard push, and she rode him again until they moaned their final release together.

"Ah!" She heaved another sigh as she rolled over, and lifted the sheet to cover them both before they fell into a deep sleep.

When she woke, Eve heard Ian on the phone in the bathroom and wondered what time it was. She tiptoed over to the door and listened. He was talking loud—something about "false bottoms" and "adding the stuff after midnight" and then, "It can't take too long. We won't have much time."

She was tired from their strenuous lovemaking, even woozy. They'd finished off two bottles of wine before having sex last night. So why had she taken a sleeping pill at two a.m. on top of all that? She lifted the blinds in the hotel room and glimpsed the lines of cars building up out on the highway under a cloudy sky. Then she dropped the blind and fell back into bed hoping for more sleep.

It seemed like an hour later when he came out of the bathroom and sat on the bed. "Well, love, it's all set."

Groggy, she tried to open her eyes. "What?" He sounded so completely awake it annoyed her, plus he was all dressed, though the shadow of his beard still covered his jaw. But that was his scruffy look, the look she'd liked from the beginning. "Why are you up and ready to go? It can't be that late."

"I told you yesterday, we've got a deal to close, so I need you to get up now, my girl. C'mon, get ready. It's after nine. You need to check on those wine shipments. I need to settle more details with my contacts here in Dublin. Then we'll drive to Kinsale to make sure it's done right. We have some more drivin' to do today too. When we get it all done, I promise you more than the money, lass." He looked into her eyes as he fondled her breast and squeezed her nipple. "You'll want more of this later." He placed his hand on her bare thigh.

She placed her hand over his. "Please, can't the job wait a little?" She moved closer to kiss him. "I want to spend more time here now."

His face turned serious, but his kiss was brief. "You're insatiable, girl. Or maybe you're a nympho." He moved away. "Not now. We have business to attend to. Get up, and when we're all done we can play all day and night in that Kinsale hotel you like so much." He smacked her ass as she made her way to the bathroom.

CHAPTER 58

"Why did you lie to me?" Lily couldn't hold back her anger. She was sitting across from Lisa and Tanya, having coffee in the college bookstore the day after their final exams.

Tanya hung her head and focused on her chipped, purple nails. Lily got up and paced around the table. Luckily, the store was empty of students. Most had left the Berkeley campus for a three-day weekend. Well, it was now or never. She had to lay it on the line. She sat down again and faced her daughters. "Tanya, why would you tell me those things about your sister? Her friends seemed polite, friendly and plenty concerned about their grades. Yesterday we all went out to lunch. They're the kind of friends Lisa needs. And her grades are great too." Then her voice rose, "But when I first got here, I didn't believe her because of your lies. I even made her traipse over to the Student Services office yesterday and *show* me her transcripts. Now I've hurt your sister because of you. I believed you, so I didn't trust her!"

Lisa fidgeted with her cell phone, "Mom, can I go now? Don't get me wrong, I'm still mad at both of you, especially her. But I'm trying, Mom, to at least understand why you didn't believe me. I need a break from this drama."

"Put yourself in my place for a minute, Lisa. I care about you both and I've always trusted you. But in this case, who was I suppose to believe? I *had* to check that you were telling me the truth. In my place you would've done the same thing. It's not like either of you have been in communication with me. Yes, I've been traveling, but I've called regularly and neither of you *ever* bother to call me back."

Tanya finally looked up. "I did, Mom."

Lily shook her head. "Pretty rare, though. You have to admit that."

Each girl was silent, avoiding eye contact.

Tanya swiped at her hair, pulling it out of her eyes. "Gees, Mom, you've changed. You're awfully strict now and well...much more assertive than before. But yeah, I guess you're right, we haven't been in contact. The time difference from Ireland makes it—"

"Don't give me that excuse again. *I* manage to call you in *spite* of the time difference." When she heard the sarcasm in her voice, Lily knew she'd exposed her raw irritation. But maybe she needed to let them know how *she* felt for once. "Anyway, I've been in the dark about both of you, and maybe that's what you want—for me *not* to know every detail of your lives. I get that. But it also means I'm not in the loop at all, and so I have no clue if you're hanging out with the wrong crowd or what kind of grades you're pulling. All I have to go on is what you tell me about yourself and each other."

Silence fell like a curtain over all of them. Lily gulped down the last of her coffee. Lisa fidgeted with her cell phone, and Tanya, hands in her lap, continued inspecting her nails.

"I guess I was lonely." Tanya's words were barely audible.

"Lonely? What do you mean?" Lily stared at the top of her daughter's head. "C'mon, look at me, please."

"I don't get it," Lisa said. "You were lonely, so you lied about me to Mom?"

Tanya lifted her head and looked at her sister. "Well, not exactly. I guess...well I guess I was feeling left out. I had a bomb of a room-mate, but you got a perfect one and a whole crowd of new friends. That's what usually happens to me; everything always falls into place, but this time...this time it didn't," Tanya managed. Her words were muffled and her head began to droop again.

Lisa squinted at her sister. "No, you got it wrong. It wasn't easy for me, Tanya. It never is." Her lips tightened as if she wanted to say more.

"Yeah, I guess I know that now, but you sure didn't seem to miss me." Tanya raised her head and dug deep into her satchel for a Kleenex. Two fat tears rolled down her cheeks.

"Miss you? You were the one who didn't want to room with me, and you made it clear you didn't want me hanging around you," Lisa said.

"Tanya, are you telling me that lying about Lisa's friends was your way of telling me you were hurting? So I'd be concerned and fly back here?" Lily asked.

"It wasn't that, Mom, we...I know I have to solve things on my own. You don't need to take on all our problems now and fly back here whenever. We both need to grow up and find our way. I guess I was just mad at Lisa, at how she made friends so easily and...she... she seemed to fit in so well. I wanted that too. So I...did what I did... because I was mad. I was jealous, so I wanted to get back at her." She began studying her purple nail polish again. "It was pretty stupid—but it's just like me to do something like this, isn't it?"

"You're not stupid," Lisa said.

"No, you're anything but," Lily countered as she pulled out both of their transcripts. "In fact, it says here that your grades are higher than your sister's."

"And you've made a couple of good friends," Lisa said. "I don't really have as many as you think."

Tanya looked from one to the other. "Mom. Lisa. I apologize...for lying. Neither of you deserved this. And I'm sorry I interrupted your stay in Ireland, Mom. Maybe I've been a spoiled brat sometimes in the past too. I admit it." She stared at Lily. "Looks like you're not going to allow it any longer. That's good, really. You deserve some happiness now that...now that dad's gone. I promise not to mess things up again." With that she began to cry in earnest, and both her mother and sister got up and enveloped her in a warm group hug.

CHAPTER 59

*T*wo more days in Berkeley with the girls and Lily knew it was time for her to go. After heartfelt good-byes, Lily flew to southern California, looking forward to a few days of solitude. She knew her house would be crowded with memories from a life that now seemed vastly far away, but she felt a responsibility to check with Kinza's caretaker and ask her about her future schedule, plus check her property.

She'd no sooner arrived and unloaded her luggage, than she dressed in casual clothes and made her way out to the backyard. This had always been her favorite place—for thinking, meditating. Frank never enjoyed the yard like she did. So now it provided some distance from Frank's memories inside the house.

The neighbor who had taken care of Kinza for months promptly brought him over, and then left on an errand. Overjoyed to see Lily, the dog nuzzled her nonstop as she sat under her favorite trees in the welcome sunshine of southern California. From habit she scratched Kinza's head, then began weeding her garden. That and the comfort from her faerie village of tiny houses, the wishing well and the thriving faerie flowers she'd planted was all she needed. For

KATHLEEN O'DONOVAN

a while she felt almost carefree as she cleaned up the garden. Then random thoughts began to bombard her.

Memories of Ireland drifted through her mind along with a choking feeling in her chest, a resistance rising up inside her, plunging her into a sadness she hadn't let herself feel since leaving the farmhouse in Wales. Remembering Eve's betrayal, a dark disappointment enveloped her like a suffocating fog. But she also recalled Gram's words long ago, "Don't summon up all your energy to chase your feelings away, Lily. You need to *be* with your feelings, even if it's really scary or sad. That way you'll meet the fierce dragon inside of you head-on, and guess what, child? You'll find he isn't as powerful after all. If you stop being frantic to hide your feelings, they'll show themselves. Then they'll eventually disappear and you'll become yourself again—wounded yes, but strong and more resilient." Back then Lily had been so young she hadn't known what "resilient" meant, but after looking it up, she never forgot it: "flexible but tough, the opposite of rigid and weak." That's what she wanted now, to be pliant and feisty like Gram always was.

She breathed deeply to relax and tried to open the invisible door inside of her that had slammed shut in Wales. Finally, she let herself think about all the horrid details: Eve's mean remarks, her constant need for attention and finally, her complete dismissal of Lily's budding attraction to Seamus *which she'd shared with Eve*, and then... then she let herself picture Eve with her body wrapped around Seamus. The hurt was like knives piercing her insides.

Lily held her hand to her breast, absently petting Kinza, who put his head in her lap as she mulled over the past. Why had Eve changed so drastically during their trip? Never in a million years would Lily have expected their friendship to end. Yet it had.

Pain overcame Lily now as she let herself feel this monumental loss. Like a brimming river, dammed after a storm, all the mixed-up feelings she'd been harboring inside forced their way out. Letting herself weep for several minutes, she became exhausted, then dried her eyes. She stared at the bright colors around her. This familiar beauty gave her comfort. Kinza, sensing her sorrow, began to lick her leg with his rough, warm tongue, then laid his head in her lap again. He'd always done this when she was sad or upset. She patted him now and whispered, "Thank you, my dear friend."

She suddenly got up and set to work clipping branches, raking up old leaves, trimming dead flowers, thinking all the while about her future prospects. Slowly, the realization came over her that she would miss too many amazing opportunities, let alone friends, if she didn't go back to Ireland and dive into the job that she'd never, in a million years, thought would be hers. She pictured Blarney Castle, Rose O'Sullivan and Patrick. She paused at the thought of him, remembering his caring words and his kiss. Her breath quickened.

A stray image of Seamus came to mind, and she realized he had rarely intruded into her mind in all the days that had passed since the Vision Quest, whereas hundreds of memories of Eve haunted her day and night. Now the thought of him made her slightly nauseous.

"Enough of this pity party," she said, taking off her gardening gloves and straightening up. Kinza's ears perked up and he gazed at her with soft, adoring eyes. "I have to find a way to bring you to Ireland too, don't I? And today I'm not going to hibernate here, my friend. I'll go and buy a few things to spruce this place up." He gave her his usual squeaky reply. "Okay, boy, I won't make you stay here alone today." She found his leash. "C'mon. We'll be back here in no time."

Was it just a random whim that made her drive by The Garden Getaway shop a half hour later? As she glanced through the shop's windows, she admitted to herself that she missed Maeve with all her whimsical ways. Lily also felt unmistakable sparks of rage flare up inside. After all, Maeve was Seamus' mother! But, she reasoned, just because he was her son didn't mean Maeve had betrayed her too. Nonetheless, she couldn't dismiss the disappointment she felt in the old woman, even though she knew her anger was irrational. So why was she hoping to find Maeve here in this shop today? Was it simply her nature to try to recapture the warm memories she'd felt toward this magical lady?

Noting the "Open" sign in the shop window, she parked her car and walked in with Kinza on a leash. She admired the front fountain surrounded by pink impatiens. She'd loved it the first time she'd visited. It seemed so long ago. *But, really, it's only about three months. And yet so much has happened...*

An insistent trill interrupted her thoughts. Looking up, she saw a white and black bird with a red spotted head. It was sitting in a tree behind the glass door that led outside to where the shop's plants were laid out for sale. Strangely enough, she recognized it as identical to the one she'd seen at Trinity College. And hadn't she seen one like this near the Witch's Tree at Blarney Castle? Kinza's ears perked up, but he didn't strain at his leash, as he usually did, to go after it. The bird flew into the shop then, but just as quickly Lily lost sight of it, wondering where it had gone.

She ventured over to her favorite corner in the shop, the shelves full of faerie items. At first Lily didn't see the little old lady, bent over way back in the shop, digging in the soil and planting pansies in a circular planter that looked like it used to be a bird bath. She tiptoed forward hoping... Yes, it *was* Maeve! How absolutely amazing!

Lily stared into those crinkly blue eyes that twinkled with merriment as the petite lady came forward with both arms outstretched. She folded Lily into an inviting hug. "Well, and it took you some time to find me here, now didn't it, girl," she whispered in Lily's ear, "but here you are again in my wee shop, like so many months ago."

She released Lily and gazed up at her. "Let me look at you, my sweet lass, and your special friend here too." She patted Kinza.

"Come, let's sit back here so we can talk, child. I'm needin' to tell you some things that you need to be hearin', my Lily."

Settled near a window full of sunlight, Maeve began setting the table with the white cloth trimmed in lace and small china dishes and cups Lily remembered from New Year's Day. Maeve produced warm scones too, full of cranberries and bits of orange peels.

"When did you arrive back in California? And how did you know these are my favorites?" Lily asked, as she bit into the soft, sweet dough.

"Haven't you noticed yet, me friend, that I have a way of keepin' secrets as well as knowin' them, even sometimes before they happen?" Maeve smiled mysteriously and sat down across from Lily, pouring a tawny liquid into their cups and spooned a few silvery grains of what looked like sugar. "Here's some magic that will soothe you, my dear," she said. Her eyes had suddenly turned serious; her gaze was fixed on the table, away from Lily's face. "I only wish I could discern the hearts of those I love before they mete out pain to soft and caring souls like you. It's my Seamus I'm talkin' about now."

She put her hand out and covered Lily's and finally gazed at her full-on. Disappointment was etched in the lines around her eyes. "I wish my son would stop hurtin' those I meet and love. I have some special powers, you know, but I lack many too. I cannot keep others from their failin's, though I sorely wish I could. I was hopin' Seamus would come to his senses when he met you. It's about time he did."

Her hand became a fist on the table, as she paused for a moment, wrinkles forming between her eyebrows. "But now I...I finally know for sure that he won't, and nothin' I can do will change him, child...except...except banish him from my life. And, if you want to know the truth, that is what I did."

"Really?" Lily said in a whisper.

Maeve breathed out a sigh. "I've had enough of his philanderin', child, and his lyin' ways, and I'm sure you have too. I, for one, after many a year of pleadin' with him, am not hopin' for anythin' more from him anymore."

Lily squeezed Maeve's hand as tears formed in her eyes. "It's okay, Maeve, it was really only a schoolgirl crush on my part, and it didn't go on very long. I never experienced that much sudden attention from such a handsome, friendly man, but believe me when I say that I've nearly forgotten him completely. So...so it must've only been my vanity that was hurt when he turned to..."

Now it was Maeve who squeezed Lily's fingers. "Yes, my dear, I already know. It was Eve who wounded you most. I know that...yes, it must've broken your heart, my dear." She leaned over and put her arms around Lily for several minutes and whispered, "I am so sorry." Sitting back, she cleared her throat and quickly sipped more tea. "Drink some more of my brew, child, it's sure to soothe you and bring you cheerful thoughts. It's an ancient, magical recipe of mine and a secret that I rarely share—but you, my lass, are different. Here, take some back with you to Ireland." She got up and opened a nearby cupboard. "When are you leavin'? You're goin' to take that special job at Blarney Castle my friend Rose offered you, I hope?"

Lily nodded yes as she sipped the tea. Yes, she'd decided. Already she felt a strange, pleasant glow soothing her throat and chest and tummy.

"Good, that's the girl! Rose would never forgive me if you didn't." Maeve produced a large box of tea decorated with clovers and shamrocks. "I promise this will help, and I've put some of my secret formula of sweet packets inside here too."

"Thank you, Maeve, you've helped me so much. I'm grateful. I know a little about how children can disappoint us, being a mother myself, and I feel for you," Lily said.

They sipped her brew for several moments, the quiet in the shop surrounding them, except for Kinza's snoring as he lay near Lily's feet.

Maeve went on, "Believe me when I say, child, that I gave Eve a piece of my mind too and I will again. Mark my words. She may have been a loyal friend of yours for many decades, but now she's turned into far worse than an empty-headed flirt. She doesn't know her own heart or her own soul."

Maeve paused while Kinza woke up and began to nuzzle Lily's feet. Then Maeve took several moments to study the inside of Lily's empty teacup where stray tea leaves lay. Closing her eyes, she pressed her finger down inside and spoke in a hushed tone, "But mark my words, soon Eve will have to face the true stirrings of her heart and soul. Finally. I know that for sure, but I'm sad to say it will cost her loneliness and pain. Lots of pain." Her voice sounded so ominous that Lily glanced outside, straining to recapture the sun's light, knowing the future would assure the same in her own heart. As far as she was concerned, she and Eve were finished.

CHAPTER 60

*I*t was terribly early, only 5 a.m., but Patrick was determined to reach Lily, so he got out of bed and called her. The time since he'd seen her seemed like forever and her replies to his texts had seemed unusually brief, weakening his hope that she would return to Ireland anytime soon. His grip tightened on the phone as the ringing went on and on.

Finally she answered. "Hello?"

"Oh finally, Lily, where are you?"

"Oh, it's wonderful to hear from you, Patrick. I'm at LAX. I leave for Ireland in a few minutes. My flight arrives in Dublin this afternoon. I don't think I'll reach Kinsale till late. I'm sorry I haven't been in touch with you. I guess...I guess I needed some time to myself. I hope you understand."

"Of course, it's okay. I was just worried about you. It's a relief to hear your voice. How are you?"

"I'm okay. My time in Berkeley with my daughters, plus a week alone in southern California, was just enough. It's hard for me to admit, but I think..." her voice faltered, "...I think four days of visiting with their mom was plenty for Tanya and Lisa. Then I flew to southern California and I finished my To-Do list yesterday."

"I'm so glad you're coming back. I've...I've missed you," he said.

"You did?" Her voice trailed off and a long pause followed. "I'm still not myself, Patrick, after...after the whole mess with Eve. I'm plagued with memories. But keeping busy helps. I'm so glad I have my new job to look forward to. It's what I need."

"Yes, that'll be a plum position for you, workin' for Rose O'Sullivan. Blarney Castle is a special place. Not an opportunity you should pass up." He tried to sound upbeat, but inwardly he felt disappointed. Was her new position designing gardens the only reason she was returning?

He'd missed her more than he'd ever expected and realized he hadn't been able to put her out of his thoughts during all the days she'd been away. This was new for him. He'd never let himself feel like this about any woman. Lily not only excited him whenever he touched her, she was a good and loyal friend like none he'd ever known. Hoping she would return soon, he'd even made a list of all the places he wanted to take her in Ireland. He kept picturing how she'd lit up with joy when she'd learned about Celtic customs, castles and wells. Images of the day they'd explored the ancient mound at Newgrange crowded his thoughts. He had so much more to share with her.

As if she'd read his mind, she said, "And I still have to discover all those mysterious ruins and sights that you promised me, plus how's my genealogy project coming? Have you discovered my ancestors yet? You know, the famous Irish queens and Celtic goddesses?"

His spirits lifted and he laughed. "Yes, we have lots of explorin' to do, my lass. I'm finishin' up an article now about sightseein' in Kinsale. I can take you to Desmond Castle if you like. And, since you're from the States, I'll take you to Ringfinnan Garden too. It's a gorgeous memorial for the 343 NYC firefighters who lost their lives on 9/11. As you probably know, many of their ancestors were Irish. It's located on a hill overlookin' the town. Each firefighter's name is inscribed on a tree...a peaceful place if there ever was one.

"And your family tree? Well, let's just say we have lots to talk about, for sure. But I'm not finished yet." Inwardly though, he'd already decided Lily wasn't ready for those discoveries.

"Patrick, I know you're going to find this request very strange, but have you...?" her voice lowered to almost a whisper.

"Speak up, lass," he said.

"I need to ask if...if you know where..." she paused, "where Eve is. Have you seen or talked to her at all?"

"Of course not. After what she did?"

"Yes, I agree. But...but something's come up and I just can't contact her. Patrick, I'm asking if you will. I know this is a special favor. Please, would you do it for me?"

He noticed Lily had trouble even mentioning Eve's name. She went on in a painful, halting way, "A man, his name is Brad, Brad Philips, who... Well, let's just say he can be very irrational and very dangerous too. He used to be Eve's fiancé, and he hurt her badly in a car accident last year. Up to now we've kept her whereabouts a secret from him, but not anymore. He's found out where Eve and I have been traveling in Ireland and he's looking for her. Patrick, when he's in a rage there's no telling what he'll do, and apparently he's dead set on finding Eve. A few days ago I found out he knows we were staying in Kinsale, but not the name of the hotel, thank God!"

"Why does she date such low-lifes?" Patrick said. "Well, don't worry, I'm bettin' she's still in Wales, so she's safe for a while. But if you want me to try to find her, I will."

"Maybe it's not too late then. Please find her before Brad does. Even after everything that's happened, I can't *not* warn her. I've thought and thought about it, lost sleep over it too. Patrick, I can't contact her myself. I doubt...I don't think...I can't imagine ever talking to her again."

"Okay, Lily, much as I dislike her too, I'll do it for you, but before you hang up, give me a description of the guy. It's possible I might see him in Kinsale. Don't worry. I'll find Eve somehow. After you left, I know she went to Rhos-on-Sea, where the college is, with that demon, Seamus."

"Don't even mention him."

"I know. I'm so sorry he hurt you. What Eve did... Well, you didn't deserve it, lass.

But I get why you want to warn her, and I know what to do."

They talked a few minutes more, and when he finally hung up, he couldn't push thoughts of this loving, gorgeous woman out of his mind. Her last words to him before she said good-bye made him wonder, but also told him what a special person Lily was. With a pitiful sadness in her voice she'd said, "Patrick, I need to ask you something. I can't stop thinking about what Eve said. Do you think, do you possibly think that Eve wasn't lying to me after all? That she only kissed him that night? She's never lied to me in all the years I've known her. Do you...do you think she would lie to me now?"

Had he found the right words when he answered her? All he could say was, "I don't know, Lily. I don't know what kind of a friend she was to you before. All I've seen is a selfish woman who doesn't deserve a friend with a carin', sensitive soul like yours. She's consumed with jealousy and insecurity, and whether she lied to you or not I can't say. But even if she didn't, why was she even kissin' Seamus if she knew he was datin' you? One thing I'm sure of, lass, if she ever comes back into your life, she owes you the highest level of loyalty and trust, because that's what you've given to her. She'd better work long and hard to earn your friendship back. Because you're precious, my love, even if you don't know it now."

Though Patrick longed to meet Lily at the Dublin airport, he kept his promise to meet her later at the Blue Haven Hotel in Kinsale, where she'd stayed before. He also made some calls to people he knew in Wales, but no one had seen Eve. After his meeting with a magazine editor, he left Connemara and headed to Kinsale to look for Eve and this thug named Brad. He'd tried to reach Eve by phone several times too, but so far she hadn't texted or called him back. He wasn't surprised, based on their past interactions, especially the last heated one at the farmhouse.

While driving, he phoned Seamus, but all he got was a quick brush-off and some damning words about Eve. *So she turned Seamus off too,* he mused, as he steered his car around winding roads. Or better yet, Seamus had probably rejected Eve and found another easy woman. "They were made for each other," he shouted out loud.

Imagining Seamus with Lily as he drove, Patrick couldn't help pounding one fist on the steering wheel. But the last thing he needed was a car accident, so he tried to calm down. His promises to Lily pestered him as he drove through the countryside. No need to travel to Wales tomorrow or the next day, he thought. No one he'd called had seen the couple. And Eve wouldn't stay long after splitting with Seamus. So he was right to go to Kinsale first and see if Eve had checked into the Blue Haven. It was a longshot, but a start. He doubted she would stay anywhere else after she arrived back in Ireland. It was just a matter of time before she appeared. As for this Brad guy, Patrick didn't have much to go on except the sketchy description Lily had given him. "Blonde, tall and muscular. With a tan." Well, anyone with a tan this time of year would stand out.

A new idea emerged. Maybe, just maybe, Eve was back with Ian again. *She can't do without a man, and Ian is the only person left she can cling to, except for the good-for- nothin' loafers who hang out at pubs lookin' for a good lay.* He decided to call his friend Tom at the horse farm, who had plenty of law enforcement contacts. They'd know Ian's comings and goings. In fact, Ian might be involved in the wave of horse stealing Tom had mentioned weeks ago.

"Yes, I've seen that rascal Ian, all right," Tom replied when Patrick phoned him, "but we haven't been able to catch him in the act, though I've heard lots of rumors of his horse dealings and I'm helping my friends follow leads. One thing I do know—lately rumors say he's involved in a much bigger deal. A shipment of some kind, and they just got a tip that it's going to go down right where you're heading, in Kinsale of all places. Have no idea when. Has something to do with the Wine Geese organization. Don't they have a big wine warehouse in that town? Some of my *Garda* friends are heading down there. You'd better be careful, friend. You don't have a badge, you know."

Patrick's hunch about finding Eve with Ian seemed a sure thing now. Wine was her business. When he drove into town, instead of going to the hotel first, as he'd planned, he decided to check out some of the pubs where Ian usually hung out, and then he'd have a quick dinner and go around to the warehouse Tom mentioned and case the joint. Even if it was empty, maybe he'd pick up some clues.

By the time the sun had set, his stomach was growling, but Patrick was still scouring Kinsale, looking for Eve and Ian or her boyfriend Brad. No luck. At the last pub, he set aside the search in favor of some food. He surveyed the room the best he could, but it was so crowded with wall-to-wall workers and drinking buddies that he barely managed to find a seat at the bar. Waiting for his meal, he plugged the address of the Blue Haven Hotel into his cell phone. He'd go there next, since Lily should arrive soon.

Finally digging into a meal of bangers and mash, he spotted a lone guy who didn't seem to fit in. He was sitting across the room, gulping down a pint. His poker face and crouched position in a shadowed booth, despite his athletic build and blonde hair, almost made him invisible, as if he was trying to disappear. Patrick was keen on getting to the wine warehouse, but this guy looked like he might be Brad.

"Hey," he asked a middle-aged barmaid, "do you happen to know that dude?"

"No, and I'm glad I don't. He's a surly sort. I'm sure he doesn't know anyone here—he's wearing a Rolex and designer clothes and he's got an American accent. He's no tourist, though. Don't ask me how, but I know."

As Patrick got up to talk to him, the guy glared straight at him and made for the back door of the pub. Patrick managed to push through the crowd, aiming to follow and at least have a few words with the guy. He'd almost caught up to him in the alley outside when he called, "Brad!" and the guy turned around.

"How do ya know my name?" the stranger growled.

"A good guess," Patrick said. "Been in town long?" By now he'd caught up to him and realized what a big thug he was. Maybe 6'4" and calling him brawny was putting it mildly.

"Who are ya and why're ya asking me questions?" His stance was so aggressive Patrick glanced down at the guy's hands to make sure he didn't have a weapon.

"I heard from a friend of yours that you might be lookin' for someone here—thought I might be able to help." Patrick wanted to calm the guy down and steer him out of town with a few lies.

"I can carry on my own business, thanks!" Brad snarled, his mouth twisting into a scowl.

Patrick tried again. "Is her name Eve?"

Brad's eyes widened with a crazy glint. "What'dya know about her?"

"So her name *is* Eve then? Well, I know she isn't in this town," Patrick said. "She's in northern Ireland with another guy. I wouldn't try to find her if I were you. The guy she's with is known to be a killer."

His smirk smoldered with rage.

Why did I have to add that last part? Patrick thought. It was clear the guy was a jealous cuss.

"Oh he is, is he? How do you know so much? You been with my Eve too?" His massive body moved toward Patrick like a tank, and he punched him hard in the jaw.

Patrick staggered, then righted himself, knowing full well he couldn't run but was no match for this guy either. "No way," he said, "I'd never go for *that* woman." But his anger rose up in spite of himself, and he dove into Brad, both hands pummeling his ribs.

"Ya don't call her 'that woman.' Ya don't call her anything!" Brad yelled.

The last thing Patrick saw was the hulk going for him and felt a terrible crunch in his ribs as he fell headlong into a brick wall.

Brad stood over the stranger, kicking at the stupid dude a few times more. "You won't wake up for quite a while, dick." He spotted the man's cell phone where it had fallen by a trash barrel and grabbed it. It wasn't set for password protection, and he clicked to Patrick's last entry. There it was, the name of a local hotel called The Blue Haven. "Humph, so she's in northern Ireland, eh? You lying bastard."

CHAPTER 61

*E*ve shivered. This dirty, isolated street full of sagging, colorless buildings, gave her the willies. She hadn't intended to come to this seedy side of town with Ian. He'd never ordered her to do anything before, but when he got a phone call telling him two of the four guys who were supposed to show up had flaked, his demeanor changed. It frightened her, enough not to resist when he told her in no uncertain terms, "You're going with me tonight."

Well, at least he wasn't angry with *her*.

According to Ian, "this project," as he called it, needed to be completed, and soon. She didn't want to know any more than that. She just wanted the whole thing to be over.

When they reached the warehouse, two weird-looking dudes met them inside. They'd already dragged most of the winery cartons next to the door. Eve noticed all the labels—sure enough, these were the cartons she'd ordered from her winery a few days ago. One guy was taping up an open box.

"What are you—?" she said.

"Keep quiet!" Ian shoved her aside and began stacking cartons the dude handed him.

"We'll go get the truck. It's parked on another street near here," one guy said, and they both left.

While Ian inspected all the cartons, Eve kept quiet, but her mind was whirling. *What's going on?* She'd assumed Ian was marking up her prices to make an unbelievable profit on the wine by shipping to some outfit in Dublin that would then deliver the wine further east. Certain countries paid big bucks for California wines. When she was hired, her employers had told her never to get involved in shipments to places like Indonesia and the Far East, but she figured they'd never catch her this one time. And she'd never questioned Ian further because she didn't want to know what he was up to. So why had these weaselly guys tampered with her wine cartons? She noticed that all the cartons stacked near the warehouse door had been re-taped too. Why? It wouldn't be obvious to other people, but Eve knew exactly how her winery prepared their cartons for shipping.

Finally the guys were almost done transferring the cartons to the warehouse door and then to their large truck. They began carrying empty bags out of the warehouse with the cartons too. They were almost ready to go and, as Ian began doing a final count, he barked, "Hurry, I want to lock up!" But one guy suddenly went back in the warehouse for something, and Ian yelled at Eve, "Go get him." Eve hated to go back in, but the last thing she wanted was to aggravate him more, especially when they were all rushing to leave.

She stole through the warehouse, but she couldn't find the guy. The clock was ticking and she was nervous. Finally, she spotted him by a window, enough to make out he was snorting cocaine then trying to hide it in one of the bags. "Hey!" she said.

He rushed toward her, "What're you starin' at? Don't you dare blab about this, cunt! C'mon!" When she didn't move, he smacked her. She lost her balance, her body banging backwards against the wall, and she hit her head against a lead pipe. "That'll make ya forget. C'mon!" he growled.

Ian came out of nowhere then. *He must've got tired of waiting.* As the weaselly guy made for the entrance, Ian shoved him hard out the door. Then he was upon her, dragging her out too.

"Ooh, you're hurting me! Don't," she tried to pull away from his grasp. Her head was throbbing. She noticed small clumps of fine white powder on the warehouse floor. She pointed to it. "Ian, what are you doing?"

"Shut up, woman. C'mon!"

Swiftly he exchanged paperwork with the two guys in the truck, then grabbed Eve's arm again and heaved her across the street to their car. "Quick, we can't be seen here."

"What—?"

"I said shut the fuck up! Get in!"

CHAPTER 62

*L*ily sat on the bed in her hotel room, propped against soft pillows. Her body ached with exhaustion, as if weights were strapped to her arms and ankles. She rubbed the back of her neck and tried to knead each shoulder. She remembered when she was a teen coming home from slumber parties after a few measly hours of sleep. That's how she felt now. The vague headache that had plagued her on the plane from California to Dublin had blossomed into a mini migraine. At least her nagging stomach pains were gone; thank God the meds she carried with her now always worked.

She felt at home here at the Blue Haven Hotel. Well, almost. The gold décor of her room was familiar as was the lovely crème satin pillows and brocade drapes surrounding her bed. The soft sheets she remembered had been turned down just right and the maid had put a shiny little package of chocolate on her pillow. She didn't lose any time putting on her nightgown.

Then she remembered Patrick. He'd promised to meet her here. As exhausted as she was, she got up again and put on her velour robe. She sat in the velvet wingback chair by her bed and phoned him. No answer. She tried a second time, but after no response, she left a message. She was surprised how disappointed she felt that he wasn't here yet. He'd told her he would arrive in Kinsale several hours earlier, and he was always so dependable. Should she worry? A longing she didn't recognize overwhelmed her, an unmistakable eagerness to see him again, talk to him... She sent him a text and popped a couple Advil, leaning back in her chair to wait.

A few minutes passed and a knock on the door startled her. Lily got up to discover the bellboy holding the tray of tea and food she'd ordered when she'd checked in. He put it down on a nearby desk as she fumbled through her purse for a tip. As the young man turned to leave, another much taller, blonde man appeared at the door, a face she hadn't seen in months. *My God! Brad? Yes!* He barged in as the bellboy backed out of the room, nodding to her, meeting her eyes and leaving the door ajar.

Brad's cold smirk reminded her of a cobra she'd seen once, rising up to pounce on its next meal. "Ah, if it isn't Lily, Eve's precious friend. I finally tracked you down. Ready for bed, I see. Waiting for Eve?" As he moved toward her she backed away.

"I have no idea where Eve is," Lily answered as boldly as she could. "We had a major falling out. I haven't seen her in weeks. I just flew in from California."

"Ah, my dear, you're not very good at lying. Eve could never lie either. She tried it once, but I saw through her. She never tried it again, at least with me." He flashed a wicked smile. "I made sure."

He planted his feet on one side of the desk as if ready for a chat. She wished the bellboy hadn't left her alone. She knew her hands were shaking, so she hid them behind her and tried to slouch in a casual pose as she composed her voice in what she hoped was a normal tone.

"Well, whether you believe me or not, Eve isn't here, and she won't be coming here anytime soon. I'm telling the truth when I say I have no idea where she is. She might still be in Wales. That's where I saw her last. But I have some hot food here. I'd be happy to share." She pointed to the food on the desk.

"How sweet of you. I remember how *sweet* you were to her too." Like frosting on a cake, he was laying sarcasm on every word. "I doubt she noticed, though. Eve was never big on sweetness. Can't forget her other talents, though." His leer turned Lily's stomach. "Not the same as your talents, I bet.

"Inviting me to eat? Yeah, that fits. You're the little lady who takes care of everybody, right? That's what Eve always said."

Lily's stomach turned over at his mention of Eve. Brad seemed to enjoy taunting her. Should she take a chance? Slowly she stepped to the side, away from the desk and nearer to the half-open door.

"Ah, not so fast, my little pigeon, I know what you're up to. I'm not hungry either. I just finished eating some pub grub tonight, but a brawny Irish guy tried to ruin my meal. Said he knew Eve too. I *bet* he did! He got what he deserved."

Lily sucked in a breath, fearing for Patrick. "A brawny guy?"

"Yeah, you know him? He wasn't near my size, but he's solid all right. Got nerve. Tried to hammer me." His eyes glittered with an ugly light. "No one gets away with that."

He stepped toward her. "Fess up, chicklet. I'm tired of waiting and I'm sick of your excuses. Where's Eve?" He came very near her now, and she smelled beer on his breath and his clothes too. Then he raised both his hands and grabbed at her neck.

Lily backed away but, still squeezing her neck, he moved with her. His smell sickened her.

"You little cunt. You won't get away."

She stumbled into the desk. The large teapot turned over and hot water spilled over, scalding her bare leg. She tried to scream, but it sounded more like gurgling—his big hands were choking her.

"Where is she? Tell me, you bitch!"

She tried to squirm out of his grasp, but his hands held tight. She could barely breathe. She tried to push him away. He didn't budge. Instinct told her to make a loud sound. She croaked out what she hoped was a scream. Dizziness gripped her. She began falling.

With the whole messy business at the warehouse completed and the loaded truck on its way to Dublin, per Ian's orders to his crew, Eve sighed as he swung the car around a familiar corner in Kinsale and she saw the Blue Haven Hotel in the distance.

Ian seemed calmer now, more like his old self. He'd put his hand on her thigh when they left the warehouse, and slowly he began stroking it as he drove. When they stopped at intersections, he brushed his fingers on her breasts, as if by mistake. She knew what he was doing. He could turn her on in a second. Hot from his constant touching, she leaned into him, pressing against him, excitement sending shivers through her body. Soon they'd be alone together. She longed to feel his hands stroking her everywhere, arousing her like only he could.

When they checked in at the hotel, she asked, for reasons she wouldn't think about, for a room on the second floor, where she'd stayed with Lily. Soon she and Ian were whisked up in an elevator and were carrying their luggage down the hall. But why was the door to the room next to theirs half open? A strange, hoarse howling invaded the hall. She heard a man's voice coming from the same room.

"Someone's in trouble!" She pushed the door wide and saw, of all people, Lily falling out of the grasp of a man whose back was turned. Had she fainted or...? The guy swirled around to face them and she gasped. "Brad! What are you doing?"

She rushed to revive Lily, but she seemed lifeless. Eve sucked in air, feeling light headed herself. She couldn't bear it if... Eve looked behind her. "Ian, c'mon, help us. Call the ambulance and the police." She knelt down and lifted Lily's head up a little. She was breathing, but barely. Large red welts stood out on her neck.

"No way, Eve!" Brad yelled, "No one's going to call anyone. That dude either." He pointed to Ian, who was standing there staring at him. "I knew you'd show up. This little pigeon said she hadn't seen you in weeks. She's a good-for-nothing, lying bitch."

Eve gave Ian a long look. Why wasn't he stepping in to help her? *I'll have to try to distract Brad myself.* She got up from Lily's side and slowly moved forward, crooning, "Wow, you look just the same, Brad—you always were so hot. I've missed you. You don't know how many times I've thought of calling you since I left the States, but I didn't think you wanted to hear from me."

That adoring looked she'd forgotten flickered on his face just for a moment. She hoped it would stretch into two or three as she moved closer to him in the sexy way he used to like.

"Bother me?" Brad said. "Really? I wish I'd known. You could've at least texted me. You know I'd never forget you." For another long moment he stared straight at her, and then he glanced over at Ian who was talking on his phone.

"You sonna of a bitch! Didn't you hear what I said?" Brad yelled. He lunged at Ian, tried to grab his phone, but it fell on the floor next to Lily. When Ian slammed him in the ribs, Brad careened backwards, but pulled something out of his jacket. Was it a knife? Yes. It glittered in the lamplight. Staggering, Brad came forward, waving it in front of Ian's face. Eve shuddered.

"You dickhead!" Brad yelled. "Do you think I don't know what you've been doing with *my* girlfriend? She's *mine.* Always has been. I'm outa here *now,* and she's coming with me." He grabbed Eve's arm and turned toward the door, trying to pull her with him. "C'mon, baby, you want to be with me!"

Eve's throat closed and she couldn't breathe. Brad's grip was gouging her arm. Frozen with fear, her body was slowly losing strength to resist. Her eyes fixated on the shining blade in Brad's other hand. *Ian, do something!*

Ian began to close in on Brad. Something black was in his hand. She blinked. It was the gun he'd shown her the other night. *No!* Was it loaded after all? *Did he lie to me!* She tried to stand her ground, but she knew she had to follow Brad. If she went with him, she'd save everybody's lives. Still staring back at Ian, she saw him point the gun at Brad. Brad raised his hand to pierce Ian, and in that split second, Eve looked down on the floor at Lily's face. Her eyes were now open, watching everything. The gun exploded and Brad fell toward her, the knife he'd meant for Ian heading straight for Lily. Eve moved toward Lily to block it and felt a searing pain in her back. She toppled over onto Lily. Closing her eyes, she gave in to darkness.

Was it minutes later when she opened her eyes? Or hours? Why was Patrick bending over her? He stared at her from above, deep lines indented around his mouth and between his eyebrows too. She'd never seen him look so worried. "Where's...where's Lily?" Eve asked. "She isn't...she isn't hurt, is she? I tried to..." He didn't answer. Then she heard sirens and her heavy eyelids closed.

Sometime later she pried her eyes open again. People in face-masks and white smocks hovered over her. The lights above blinded her; she had to close her eyes. Then nothing... darkness enveloped her.

CHAPTER 63

*P*atrick put his arm around Lily. They sat in the waiting room of the ER, each comforted by the other's presence. She sighed as she nestled her head in the crook of his arm. The doctor had finished examining her a few hours ago, saying, "You're okay now. You're cleared to go home, and when you do, please don't do anything but rest." Instead, Lily insisted on waiting to talk with the doctors following Eve's surgery.

"Doin' okay now, love?" Patrick asked, noticing the dark pink band around her neck. She nodded and, still very pale, tried to smile. "Why don't you try to rest now," he said.

Rest was what he needed too after the events of this horrendous day. It had all been so unreal. The fight in the alley with the man who had to be Brad, then cleaning himself up and hurrying to the hotel to meet Lily. The moment the elevator doors had closed he'd heard a deafening bang—a gunshot! Fear gripped him...Lily? In danger? His heart felt like it would explode. He could hear moaning and ran toward a half-opened door and looked in. He saw Eve—the last person he expected— crumpled on top of...was that Lily? All he could see of Lily's face were those beautiful wide green eyes pleading with him to help her. Eve's white dress was smeared with blood. She lay still and Lily was trying to move out from under her.

On the floor, face down, lay a man. His straw-colored hair and deep tanned arms were unmistakable. It was the guy who'd beat him up earlier. Was he dead? Patrick looked across the room. Ian was standing still as a statue, eyes glazed over, looking down at a gun in his hand.

"What the...?" Patrick moved fast. He carefully lifted Eve's limp, bloody body off Lily and laid her on the bed. Not a sound came from her, but he could tell she was still faintly breathing. He bent down on the floor to cup Lily's head in his hands. "Are you all right, love? What happened?"

Lily nodded her head yes, but began to cough uncontrollably. After a moment, she began to choke. She managed a deep breath, but started coughing again. He held her head, gently stroking her shoulders and arms to try to calm her. When the coughing stopped, he lifted her up to sit. Her neck was streaked with new red welts. She kept rubbing them. He went to the bathroom to get her some water. When he came back, her breathing was a bit easier.

Ian was still standing in the middle of the room, staring vacantly at Patrick, who tried to shake him out of his catatonic state. "For god's sake, Ian, what happened here?" No answer. "I said what happened? Do you even hear me?"

Patrick shook his head and lifted the glass again to Lily's lips. She took another sip of water.

Sirens began screaming outside and the *Garda* converged on the hotel, EMTs following close behind. The sound of the sirens had filled Patrick with relief. Thank God Ian hadn't had time to escape because, just in case, Patrick had moved toward the door to barricade it with his body. He learned later that the bellboy, who had lingered in the hallway suspecting something was wrong, had phoned for help immediately after he heard the gunshot. *Thank God for that,* Patrick thought now, as he went over everything in his head.

He still didn't know why his friend Tom had come with the *Garda*. He'd heard sketchy details about horse-stealing—and something about Ian being in trouble with drugs too. All Patrick knew for sure was that after the police lugged Brad's dead body away to the morgue, they'd hauled Ian away to the police station. Within minutes the EMTs had rushed Eve to the hospital, but the *Garda* were adamant that she'd have to answer their questions as soon as she was conscious.

Feeling a cramp in his leg and aches in his ribs and shoulders, where he'd been pummeled earlier, Patrick got up and stretched. The dark patches of the windows told him it was still night-time. With Lily beside him, they'd sat here for hours in this dull white room, surrounded by other tense strangers.

Sitting down again, Patrick pulled Lily closer to him. She snuggled against his chest. The huge relief he felt amazed him a little-- she was safe. He wanted nothing more than to be near her. After all these years, how had this sweet California garden designer captured his heart so completely?

As if reading his thoughts, Lily looked up at him and managed a sleepy smile. "Thank you. You're so protective, just like my brother, Colin." As tender as a gentle breeze, she kissed his cheek.

"I'll protect you, lass, you can count on that, but you must realize one thing. I'm not your brother." He wrapped both arms around her then and kissed her full on the mouth. She was rigid for a moment, then returned his kiss with a passion he'd not felt from her. Ever.

CHAPTER 64

A few hours passed. Then a tiny sprite of a lady opened the waiting room door. "Yoohoo!"

Maeve sashayed toward Lily and Patrick. "So sorry to see you two holed up in this depressin', antiseptic place. But knowin' what problems your friend, Eve, has laid on you, I can only say I'm not surprised." She held her hand out to shake Patrick's. "And, my fine friend, I see you're keepin' Lily company. I'll be thankin' you a bunch for that."

"Thanks so much for coming, Maeve." Lily rubbed her sore neck again. Her head hurt now, and her fingers still trembled, though she'd been hiding them from Patrick so he wouldn't worry. In spite of how she felt, glimpsing her friend Maeve was exactly the magic elixir she needed. In fact, she hoped Maeve had brought some of her mysterious brews.

The little lady sat down across from them and began rummaging through her handbag. "Yes, of course, Lily, I brought just the goodies you're thinkin' of. They're somewhere in here."

Lily stared at her in wonder.

Out came a little box decorated with bright green shamrocks,

407

the one Lily had glimpsed on her recent trip to California and many months ago in Maeve's rundown cottage. She jumped up and went over to a small alcove to find a tall thermos-like container of hot water. She then produced her own tea bags and poured water into paper cups. When she stirred in some sparkling grains and tiny seeds, Lily heard her whisper some words that sounded like a chant as she waved her right hand over the steam in a solemn motion, then brought the cups to them. "There now, lass and laddie, this will fix up the both of you, for sure. Mark my words, you'll be feelin' like sunshine after you drink this!"

Into her bag Maeve's hands went again, and she brought out scones like the ones Lily had eaten months ago at the Rose Parade. The warm buns just as Lily remembered, fresh from the oven. Lily didn't question this, though. She knew Maeve didn't have an oven in her hotel room here, but no oven had graced her Pasadena cottage either. And when had she flown back here to Ireland? Lily had seen her just a few days ago at the Garden Getaway in California. Lily shook her head. All she knew for sure was that this little woman had strange, mysterious ways that Lily never failed to cherish.

Once they'd eaten Maeve's delicious gifts, both she and Patrick were feeling as Maeve had promised, revived and even exhilarated. Lily wasn't surprised at all. She would never completely understand it, but that was okay. Her new friend had come to help her in a serious hour of need, and Lily couldn't be more grateful. Watching Patrick gobble down one scone and ask for another, she knew he was grateful too.

Maybe Maeve should visit Eve with her healing spirits, Lily thought. Then she quickly corrected herself. *That is, if she...if she makes it.* The doctors hadn't made any promises when Eve was wheeled into surgery.

Yes, she thought to herself, Eve had caused her a horrendous degree of sorrow and anger, more than she'd ever experienced. Yet,

Lily wouldn't allow herself to even consider the possibility that Eve's stab wounds might take her life. The sober-faced medical staff she and Patrick had talked with hadn't promised a complete recovery, far from it. And they'd warned that predicting Eve's future right now wasn't possible. "The knife wound hit several core organs," was all the surgeon revealed, and Lily hadn't been able summon up the courage to question him further.

They'd been waiting here now for over six hours and still no news about Eve. Patrick nudged Lily, then put his arm around her again. "Hey, where'd you go off to, my love? You turned so quiet all of a sudden."

With that, Maeve took both of their empty cups and went to the corner of the room to find hot water and begin her mysterious wizardry again.

"Say, what's in that special tea? Do you know?" Patrick asked. "I feel like a new man."

Lily smiled and shrugged. "I don't have the faintest, but it works for me. I feel much better. Let's just enjoy it, okay?" She leaned into him and closed her eyes.

Soon Maeve was pouring more cups full of her magic potion and waving her hands over them as before. "This will banish your fears, heal your aches and open up a new, bright world for you," she promised. But when she pulled two larger scones for Patrick and herself out of her small satchel, Lily couldn't help sitting up with surprise. How had all those scones fit in that miniscule bag? A purse like that could only hold spare change, lipstick, a Kleenex pouch and *maybe* a very small hairbrush. Another crazy mystery... But Maeve's refreshments were more than wonderful, weren't they? So Lily absolutely didn't care how Maeve managed it. Right now, she just wanted to bask in her euphoric gifts.

CHAPTER 65

$\mathcal{N}$ ow the dawn light was filtering through the hospital. Another hour had passed and by then Maeve had met everyone in the waiting room, serving up her goodies to each one. Patrick watched them sipping her mysterious tea, one by one, but he couldn't figure out how each one got a scone to munch on. Devour them they did, and soon the waiting room was lit with everyone else's smiles too, Maeve's the brightest of them all. Lily had finally dozed off and was sleeping soundly while Patrick napped off and on, but when he heard loud talking, he sat up on high alert. Two policemen were conferring with Eve's surgeon in the hallway.

Carefully, Patrick disengaged himself from Lily, who was sound asleep, and wandered over to the open door of the room to listen, pretending that he was gazing at a large framed photo on the wall of some celebrated hospital personnel.

"When will she be awake?" asked the taller policeman.

"Not for a few hours. And she may not be completely lucid for a few days."

"Well, we know that she's definitely implicated in a drug case we're following. Timing is critical. So is the information she can give us. The heist is massive. And it's still going on. We've got to prevent those shipments from leaving the country. We'll need to interview her, and soon," said the shorter, stocky policeman.

"I don't advise it," insisted the surgeon. "She'll be groggy to say the least. So, whatever she tells you today will be sketchy. You must understand, she's just been through a life-saving operation."

"I can't care about that right now," said the first officer. "Once she's recovered, she'll have to pay for what she's done. It'll mean a trial for sure. Possibly jail time. Her accomplice gave us enough info already to make sure of that. No love lost between those two."

So Ian had blamed Eve. *Just like that bully to lay the rap on a woman.*

Patrick wasn't surprised Ian had become involved with an unbelievable money-making scheme involving drug deliveries. Ian had always been his own worst enemy, and during the battles of the Irish Resistance, he'd made many mistakes. He was a disloyal cuss to his friends too, Patrick was sure of that. Hearing he'd blamed Eve for this heist wasn't a surprise either. But why would a smart woman like Eve get suckered into a low-life drug deal? He shook his head in dismay. She was a lot of things, but he'd never thought Eve was a fool.

As if the stocky officer had read Patrick's thoughts, he went on, "Doctor, let me shed some light on how serious this is. This woman, Eve Olson, must've been lured by her boyfriend's promise of lots of money in this heist. Cuz it's not just domestic, it's international. These losers and their hired crew stuffed cocaine into the false bottoms of hundreds of wine bottles last night at a local warehouse and then boxed them back up. From there, we know they trucked them off to who knows where, based on an eyewitness who was near the warehouse area. We also know that an enormous shipment of wine is heading out of Dublin harbor as we speak, bound for Indonesia, of all places. And other shipments are going out too, in cities all over Ireland, but not necessarily wine. I'm telling you, this is a giant drug ring. So to say this poor woman's input is critical is an understatement. We *must* have your permission to question her as soon as she wakes up, even if her information might be hazy."

My God, Eve is in real trouble. What will this do to Lily? Should he tell her? No, it could wait till tomorrow. She'd been through too much trauma in the last twelve hours. One thing he was very sure of —whatever happened next, he and Maeve must stay by Lily's side.

The police disappeared, and after a few hours passed, Patrick, Maeve and Lily went down to the hospital's lunchroom. All during their meal Patrick vacillated again between telling Lily about Eve's alleged criminal activities and keeping silent, but decided his earlier decision was best. Returning to the waiting room, they saw Eve's surgeon beckoning to them. "She's very groggy, but you can visit her now. Only very briefly, though, and I *mean* briefly."

Patrick searched Lily's stricken face. "Are you sure you want to do this now? You've been through so much."

She gazed up at him, "Yes, I'm sure. I...I admit I feel like I don't know her anymore, after everything that's happened, but I owe this much to her. She did save me from the knife, Patrick. *I'd* be in that hospital bed now if she hadn't blocked it."

"Well, if you're set on going in to see her, I want to go with you," he said, putting his arm around her shoulders.

"Me too," Maeve whispered, and she took Lily's hand.

Lily said nothing, but ventured forward with them through the swinging doors to the hospital's recovery area.When they reached Eve's bed, Patrick saw Lily's face turn ashen. "Oh, no," she whispered. He held onto her and was relieved to see Maeve still grasping her hand too.

Eve's once lustrous blonde hair was pulled back from her face. Her skin was tinged a greenish white. An IV and other medical contraptions blinking and pinging data packed the room.

Irish hospitals aren't that different from the States, Patrick mused to himself, remembering that Lily must've spent many days sitting by her husband's bed.

Eve's eyes fluttered and she reached out, but she stopped short of touching her old friend's hand. Lily stood rigid. Patrick put his arm around her and saw Maeve's fingers pressing hers. They all heard Eve's labored breathing. Patrick sensed that every muscle in Lily's body felt strained with knots as she tried to hold herself together.

Eve's eyelids fluttered again and then opened. She gazed into Lily's eyes and then her own glistened with moisture.

"Hi," Lily said. Gently she dabbed at Eve's pale cheeks with a Kleenex.

"You came." Eve's voice was just above a whisper. "Thank you." Then she was unconscious again, and the nurse motioned for them all to leave the room.

Later when they were alone, Lily confided in Patrick... her words and feelings spill out... "Always before I followed my natural impulse to help Eve, to care for her, or at the very least empathize. But not now. My feelings are so chaotic and confused. Yet I feel relief, gratefulness too, and even sympathy toward Eve, but all the wrenching hurt is still there. Worst of all, anger is burning through all my emotions. I can't remember ever feeling like this, Patrick. It's scary. Seeing Eve in that bed, an overwhelming certainty came over me: Things will never be the same between us. All I feel is sadness."

CHAPTER 66

*L*ooking through the steel barbed fence that surrounded the county jail, Eve noticed how the Irish golden hills were fading under an iron gray sky. The hours of twilight were dipping into night. She noted the nearby apple orchard, feeling a strange, involuntary chill at the sight of the round fruit, but she brushed it off as superstitious nonsense. The inmates had reminded her that tonight was the eve of Samhain, a fall festival ending summer and a night believed to be full of portents for the future. They'd told her that the dark side of Halloween originated here.

Even her cellmate, Shirley, usually a quiet woman, had added her two cents about this Irish lore. "It's believed that on the night of Samhain, the Irish evil faeries will spit on any unharvested apples to make them inedible. In the old days people often got sick, and even now police report that poisonous apples are given out on this night. Huge bonfires are lit too, to ward off the evil that's let loose everywhere. So most people wear ugly disguises to confuse the spirits. It's supposed to stop the dead from identifying people they disliked during their lifetime."

As Eve limped across the yard toward the prison's cafeteria with the others, she scowled from the pain in her leg as she pulled her jacket around her against the October chill. Mulling over Shirley's words, Eve couldn't help thinking of her mother. She had never heard the woman say, "I love you," nor seen her hug anyone. Ever. *Too bad I don't have a mask to protect myself from her tonight,* she thought.

But she didn't dare say this aloud to her cellmate, who wouldn't appreciate Eve's sarcasm. When Shirley had waxed on this morning about this Celtic tradition, her face had shone with an unusual conviction. "For our ancestors, Samhain was a spiritual transition time. Many Irish still believe that the mysterious curtain between the Otherworld and the human world becomes less secure tonight. And, Eve, I definitely believe them. Banshees, bad faeries and other good spirits come and go freely. Friends of mine even tell tales of seeing 'shape shifters'."

Eve hadn't bothered to reply. She'd learned one thing in the last five and half months. It didn't do any good to upset these people. They believed what they believed. And they could turn volatile. She'd already seen certain inmates get irate over nothing and cause a violent ruckus, then pay for it dearly.

Walking faster, they all reached the mess hall, Eve among them. The scent of beef stew permeated the air as the sour-faced warden opened the door, and they promptly filed in and stood around the long gray tables. Eve surveyed the barren faces of the women around her. This was the life she'd been given since last May, and as far as she knew, it might go on for a very long time. Her preliminary trial was set for January, and her lawyer thought she might have to do at least another year in prison for aiding and abetting criminals, maybe more. She'd finally accepted that the life she'd known was over.

Tonight was movie night, an event she looked forward to. It took the edge off a little, from the horrible monotony and routine of the leaden days that stretched on and on, colorless and uneventful.

This place was goddamned boring, and even though she sometimes tried, she couldn't force herself to listen to the others with whom she shared her work, her meals, her cell. It wasn't that they were mean or sadistic—well a few were. But for the most part, these were all just sad, forgotten women. Most had been poor and uneducated all their lives. It didn't take her long to realize she had nothing in common with them. That was the difficulty. If she even tried to compare her life with theirs she kept coming back to the same conclusion: They had valid reasons why they were in jail. They'd all committed crimes, and she'd heard their personal stories in counseling sessions: These women all had very cruel and abusive parents or husbands, and had battled poverty, alcoholism, drug addiction, rape, even incest.

How had *she* ended up in a place like this? Surrounded by women who could never dream of the advantages she'd taken for granted? That reality had pulled her into an even worse depression than the stark alienation she'd chosen here. She'd built thick walls of not caring, not listening, not paying attention to any of them. Eve felt her only alternative was to keep herself apart. And that was hell too, a special kind of hell. She'd avoided, even run from loneliness all her life. Ironic how she'd ended up all by herself here, in this dark hole. Being alone had been her greatest fear. Always. She knew that now. She'd finally faced it, and she was trying to accept it. She'd even told the prison counselor she *wanted* it. She couldn't exist any other way in here.

She sat down next to the other women now, their comments only gray noise, as she scraped her plate clean, finishing up "the gruel," as she called it. She looked up to see Ole' Ms. Crawbuck at the door, beckoning to her in her predictable, mean way, always demanding absolute obedience. A familiar heat grabbed at Eve's throat and constricted her neck and shoulders as she picked up her plate, dumped it into the kitchen to be washed, and made her way toward the dumpy kitchen warden. She hated Crawbuck.

"You've got an unexpected visitor." The old woman's voice was crusty.

"Now?" Eve mustered. Why would anyone come in the evening?

"Don't complain, bitch. It's your lawyer, and it's urgent. Or so he claims, otherwise there's no way I'd let you speak to him."

❧

Eve's meeting with the lawyer was over, and she figured the prison movie was almost over now too, as she made her way back to her cell. The guard took his time locking her in. She noticed how he stared at her; she knew what he wanted. If she gave him even a crumb of encouragement, they'd be rolling on her bunk in a minute and who knew what favors he could arrange for her? Now, with everyone in the auditorium, would be a perfect time for a brief tryst. But she'd decided weeks ago she'd have none of it, and she'd made it known to him over and over. Lucky for her he wasn't hostile or violent like some. He seemed to actually have a soft spot for her, kind of a crush.

Once she entered her cell, she turned her back to him and finally heard the key click in place in the cell lock. He slowly walked down the corridor. He'd given up. Good. She'd had it with men. Every man she'd ever known had disappointed her, used her over and over, or at worst, betrayed her. Yet she couldn't quiet a small voice inside her that kept reminding her that her troubles were her own fault.

The jail was quiet. The rest of the women wouldn't be back for a few minutes. She was alone, and glad of it too. She had no desire to explain to anyone yet why her lawyer had come. In this place no one ever missed a thing. She was sure the other women would question her, up one side and down the other tomorrow, when they all went out for exercise in the yard. At least her cellmate, Shirley, didn't pry. Thank god, she kept to herself most of the time.

Eve sat on her bunk in the shadows, considering what her

lawyer had just told her. It was hard to grasp. Should she finally believe him? He'd rushed over here, in the evening no less, to tell her the good news: If she identified some of the local men involved in the cocaine heist and gave information on anything else at that warehouse where she'd gone with Ian, there was a good chance she could obtain an easier verdict and sentence at her trial. Apparently, many of the criminals involved in the heist had finally been captured, some in Dublin and others in Cork, Galway and Kinsale. But law enforcement needed witnesses like her who would speak out. She'd kept totally quiet about any details so far, based on her lawyer's directives, much as she'd hated to follow his advice. Because of her silence Ian had been able to lay a lot of blame on her. That's why she was in this hole now. But as of tonight, it looked like her lawyer might have been right all along. He'd hoped this would happen and had promised her she could take advantage of it when it did.

A lighter sentence for her after these criminals were tried and put in prison meant she might eventually be able to return to the States, but they'd stressed she shouldn't return to California or to the winery business. Instead, her lawyer advised her to protect herself from anyone who might want to harm her after she testified.

Suddenly Eve felt weak, even dizzy from this news. She bent over now, putting her face in her hands. The impact of this possibility overwhelmed her. She'd held back tears for a long time, but now they began to fall on her cheeks, on her blouse and in her lap. She let her emotions go, wave after wave of regret and suffering flowing over her in a torrent. Even as she cried, she began to slowly allow herself to visualize a return to the United States, a reality she had believed would be out of reach for many years.

The news didn't seem real—but it was. Her lawyer had promised this, but she hadn't believed him, remained skeptical and depressed. Now his promises might finally come true. He'd gotten the agreement in writing from the higher-ups in Irish law enforcement—he'd even shown the contract agreement to her. She'd signed it promptly at his urging, and now her future could take a dramatic turn.

This news was wonderful, but heartbreaking at the same time —since she had no one to share it with.

Hours had passed. The darkness was deep now and the air colder than usual. It had to be past midnight, Eve thought groggily, as she turned over on her bunk, half asleep. She lifted her head, looking through the barred window next to her top bunk, watching the bonfires on the hill in the distance. Yes, the Samhain festival was still going strong. She could hear the screaming her inmates had warned her about. *I guess the townspeople really do turn into banshees at midnight. Ha, maybe their horses and coaches turn into mice and pumpkins too.*

She pulled at the thin blankets that usually warmed her, plumped the flat prison pillow and tried to go back to sleep. Her teeth chattered and chills moved through her body like the rivulets of a stream. She put on her jacket and covered herself up again but the cold closed in on her with a strange force. Determined, she closed her eyes and tried to visualize a peaceful scene, a strategy that sometimes relaxed her and helped her fall asleep. But the night screams went on and on, and the peaceful scenes she pictured refused to stay put. Instead, she kept seeing a shadowy figure. Each time she tried to banish the image, it forced its way back into her mind. She realized it was a man and he began to speak, " Don't condemn yourself, my Evie. I made grave mistakes too. Soon you will find out, my girl."

She saw the pipe then and smelled its signature aroma. *Daddy!*

The scene expanded and she saw herself out on the shadowed moors again, where she'd wandered months before. She was trying to reach him again, but he turned away and made his way up the dark hill. "Daddy, don't you dare...don't you dare leave me! Do you hear me? If you do it again, I'll...I'll banish you for good. Out of my life." She started to follow him, but then she stopped and stood her ground. She watched him slowly move off, climbing up the hill into the mists. "Daddy, I said I won't allow it. If you leave me like this, I'll put you out of my memory...and my heart. Forever."

His voice was getting fainter. "I know, Evie, and you should. But do me one last favor. Find Lily. Do that much. Go to her, Evie. Promise me you will."

Then he disappeared and the dark scene slowly turned pitch black. He was gone. The keening screams and the fires outside had vanished too.

Strangely relieved, Eve laid her head down and finally slept.

CHAPTER 67

*T*he rain of November's last days cast a gloom on the prison yard. The women who gathered outside wore gray hooded slickers. Eve was feeling poorly—a bronchial virus had kept her in most of the week. But today she was determined to go out and breathe fresh air. Unusually, her cellmate Shirley sought her out in the yard. "I hear your lawyer has come to visit again," she said in low tones, which Eve appreciated. "Someone saw him get out of his car just now."

Her eyes told Eve she was happy for her. Though Shirley had never spoken a word about her early release, Eve knew that somehow all the inmates knew. Rumors had a way of feeding the women who craved them.

Eve's dug her nails into her hands as she focused on the yard's entrance, her heart beating fast. Would he bring her good news?

Minutes later, she saw him standing next to the prison warden, a faint smile on his face as he raised his hand to wave.

Shirley saw him too and reached out to high-five Eve. Her eyes were kind. "Go on now, girl. He's waitin' on you."

Her lawyer led her into an empty waiting room and greeted her with, "You won't believe this, Eve. Sit down so I can tell you." He paced in front of her, buttoning and unbuttoning his blazer, a habit he had when he was excited or nervous. Eve felt a tingle down her spine and her stomach was turning over. Should she let herself hope? Did he have more good news?

He was still pacing, but his eyes sought hers. "They've finally found big holes in Ian's story. Two of his drug hooligans talked, and talked plenty. They went back a long way with Ian, back to IRA times. No love there. Anyway, these guys separately got a plea deal in exchange for naming Ian as the sole leader of the heist in Kinsale. Yeah, even though he tried to pin you down as more than his equal partner."

Eve's stomach was reeling now and she felt nauseated. She couldn't stand even thinking about Ian or hearing his name.

Her lawyer sensed this and paused as he sat down across from her. "I don't know why they ever believed him anyway, Eve. But now you can be sure he'll be doing time, and for many long years indeed."

"Good," was all Eve said. It was so quiet in the room they both could hear a stray bird twittering and tapping outside. It kept on tapping and Eve found the sound strangely comforting.

"What does this mean?"

"The district attorney doesn't need your testimony as much and the case against you is a lot weaker now. My big news is, a meeting will be held tomorrow to decide whether you can be tried before a judge *very soon*. With no jury! And the winery in California has dropped their lawsuit too, turning over your punishment to the Irish authorities. There's even talk you could get out of here sooner by doing community service here in Ireland. And, if they grant you that miracle, after your service is done, I strongly suggest you go back to the States for good...not leave a trail. You can't ever go back into the wine business anyway. The judge might even lay out directives on this. These drug cartels are dangerous. You need to cover your tracks for a few years, stay away from old, familiar places. After a chunk of time they'll forget about you—after all, you were only a small cog in a massive, global operation."

With no curtains on her cell window, an unusually bright December sunrise woke Eve. She gazed at the hills through the window's bars. Was she really going to leave this place today? It all seemed so unreal.

The warden had handed her the judge's orders yesterday morning after she'd left his courtroom: She was to dye her hair black before she left and wear only plain clothes from now on, like the ones they'd given her. She would live at a halfway house in a small village near Kerry, and during the day she was to work at a rehab center for young adults who had previously committed a crime and were under court orders. Her community service work would last six months, and if approved upon her completion, she could then fly home to the U.S. Even the winery's lawsuit had weakened considerably, requiring she pay a fine, but she would never work there again.

As she dressed, memories of her plane trip to Ireland less than a year ago crowded her mind. Everything had changed. Everything. Back then, she and Lily had shared such excitement about their future. Would she dare contact her friend now? She wasn't even sure Lily was still working at Blarney Castle. But how could she face her or even begin to mend what had happened between them? Lily had visited her only once, right after her surgery. Eve barely remembered that day, but what she faintly recalled was Lily thanking her for blocking the knife meant for her. Since then Eve hadn't heard a word.

Pushing those thoughts away, Eve buttoned up her dark brown blazer, slinging a navy wool scarf around her neck, then put on a long black coat and matching gloves. She was almost ready. She gave Shirley a final, silent hug and walked out of her cell for good. Even the guard was smiling. Maybe he was a good guy after all. He seemed happy for her.

Walking down the hall to the entrance of the prison, she wondered what she would do in her spare time during the weeks that stretched ahead? Or would she have any? She had no clue. Everything and everyone she'd known before was gone. She shivered.

CHAPTER 68

*H*er stomach doing flip-flops, Eve stepped through the prison door. The path stretching to the steel fences that surrounded the prison seemed incredibly long. Slowly Eve put one foot in front of the other, anxiety and elation gripping her like the prison smell that had clung to her for seven long months. No houses graced the street across from the jail; only bare winter slopes surrounded the prison, and masses of trees covered the hills behind them. Once she reached the guard, he solemnly said good-bye and opened the massive gate. She walked through, turned right and began walking up the hill. Someone had told her this was the way to town, where a rented room was waiting for her. "Bet it's a doozy," Eve said to herself.

She heard the creaking of gears mixed with tires shifting on gravel, and turned to see an old Ford Focus creeping up behind her. It stopped next to her as suddenly as it had appeared. A petite driver jumped out of the old dusty heap, waving one hand and smiling from ear to ear.

Was it...? No, it couldn't be.

"So, how're you doin' on this fine winter's day, my lass?" Maeve clasped Eve in a warm hug, though she was so tiny, she barely reached Eve's shoulders. She looked up, surveying Eve for several moments. "You're thin as a rail, you are, and pale. So I'd be guessin' that ugly place doesn't have much of a cook. And what happened to your lovely hair? It used to remind me of spun gold when the sun shone. Now it's black as a raven."

Eve was speechless. Maeve was the last person she'd expected to meet today. In fact, she'd never expected to see her again. But Maeve always turned up without warning.

Her hand smoothed her dark tresses, "I had to follow orders and dye it."

"Oh, no. Well, I'm hopin' that won't last long. Now c'mon, young'un, stop your staring. I'm as real as an old lady can be, even though some may call me a faerie godmother." She motioned to Eve, "Get into my loaner heap here. Time's a wastin'." Maeve opened the passenger door and scurried around to the driver's seat. "It's not an expensive carriage, but it'll do for today, child, won't it? My real car is in the shop and this is all they had to loan me." With Eve settled inside, she stuck a key in the ignition and started up the engine. The car snailed up the rest of the hill with plenty of sputters and groans.

An hour later Eve had checked into the halfway house, Maeve at her side. The two women then explored the village, stopping for a simple lunch outside the social services office, where Eve signed up for her nine to five community work. She learned that each of the young adults registered had committed a serious crime and were doing charity work for several months. Throughout the morning Eve marveled at Maeve as she circulated among the social services personnel and the villagers, introducing herself as if she were Eve's friendly aunt. She always added that Eve was "as happy as could be to be movin' to this new town to do good works for the communi-ty." Some raised their eyebrows and others managed smiles.

When the setting sun began to sink behind the hills, Maeve

announced that Eve better return to the halfway house "to get to know her roommates." Her cheerful chatter started all over again at the dinner table where four other women sat with them for a simple meal of potato pie. The woman in charge of the "rooming house," finally invited Maeve to eat with them since her lively prattle engaged everyone so much that no one wanted her to leave. As soon as the matron brought a simple Irish bread pudding to the table for dessert, Maeve stood up, putting on her jacket and moving toward the door, waving her hands and promising she would "return in no time." Eve guessed she wouldn't. She was used to Maeve's strange exits and her abrupt disappearances too.

Lying that night in the cramped bedroom, noting the rise and fall of her new roommate's breathing, Eve wondered about her future. She didn't harbor hope that Maeve's happy aura would permeate this town again. No, she was stuck here for six long months. She might as well accept it. At least she wasn't behind bars anymore. As she watched Molly sleep in the bed beside her, she decided, for the first time in her life, to make the best of *all* the experiences ahead of her—embrace the good ones along with the difficult.

CHAPTER 69

*P*atrick skimmed through the reports on his desk for the second time, then slipped them into a folder and laid it aside. He intended to hide this folder in the bottom drawer, but his phone rang, interrupting his train of thought. It was Lily. She would arrive in a few minutes. She'd insisted on meeting him this time at his office after she finished her workday at Blarney Castle. He knew why and he had mixed feelings about it.

He gazed out the window at the bright green leaves rustling in the robust breezes. Under the trees and all around, spring was in full swing with May blooms filling the garden beds. Lily loved this time of year. Every garden she saw energized her. He counted the months since he'd met her—well over a year. All he wanted was to make her happy and banish the disappointment that still cropped up in her eyes and turned her lips downward when she thought he wasn't looking.

Her daughters weren't causing her moodiness anymore. He was sure of that. He and Lily had flown to California to visit them last February, meeting all the girls' friends and their new boyfriends too. They'd been aloof and quiet around him at first, but he'd managed to melt their resistance by the end of the visit.

Patrick could still picture Lily's face when she'd boarded the plane to Ireland and settled into her seat next to him, her eyes shining with what she called happy tears. "Patrick, you're the best thing that's ever happened to me," she whispered as she cuddled next to him, "I'm so grateful to you for this trip. It's given me so much happiness. How can I ever thank you?"

He answered her with a question, "What about this?" Folding her into his arms, he kissed her with a depth he'd never known and she welcomed it with a warmth he would not forget.

He smiled now, reliving that intimate memory and many since. He wished she would ask that same question again; he'd prepared the perfect answer. Up to now he'd hesitated, wondering if she was ready. Nevertheless, he'd planned a surprise when the time was right. He pulled a small velvet box out of his jacket pocket, but at the phone's persistent ringing he put it back.

"How're doin' today, my friend?" Maeve's voice was like no other's, crackling with her well-known blend of magical exuberance. He talked to her for a while, trying to persuade her to change her mind, but it was no use. She was hell bent on coming over too.

Patrick turned toward the window again. Why spoil such a gorgeous day? How could he avoid telling Lily the truth this time? He'd unearthed an amazing find in her genealogy and DNA reports that would *not* make her happy. For weeks she'd been prodding him to complete the ancestry study she'd hired him to finish. She'd used every female wile to persuade him to meet tonight to learn his discoveries, and he'd come up with so many empty excuses already. Maybe it was a good idea that Maeve was coming over after all. She'd be the perfect distraction. And that she was.

"I'm plannin' a little celebration, I am," Maeve said to both of them as she circled Patrick's desk with what looked like new dance steps. Her eyes wide, she waved both of her hands in the air. "I want to invite all the people who came to Blarney Castle many months ago when Rose announced your new role as her landscape consultant, Lily."

Lily's mouth opened in surprise, but her eyes turned dark with anguish. Patrick knew why. The stark images of the banquet's end last summer were still vivid. How could Maeve forget? That evening had started with such promise for Lily but had ended in a chaotic mess. Because of Ian. Because of Eve. And Seamus too, playing the ridiculous charade of a savior. Not many days later, he and Eve had betrayed Lily. Bloody bastards!

Maeve noticed Lily's face and stopped dancing around the office. She reached out to her as she cleared her throat. "Oh, my lass, I didn't mean we'd want *everyone* who attended back then to come this time. That's the last thing we'd be wantin', my love. Please put those horrid people out of your mind this minute, now will you, child?

" But I've already invited many of the *chosen ones* around here that you've learned to love and cherish durin' these many days and months since you started buildin' your faerie garden. And I'm wonderin', Lily, if we might include your two daughters? They'll not be studyin' this summer. Will you give me permission to book their flights?"

Lily's eyes still held that unmistakable sadness Patrick still glimpsed off and on. Her response sounded hollow, "Oh that sounds great and to be able to show my daughters what we've accomplished here would only add to my excitement, Maeve. But why now?"

"Yes, why now?" Patrick was less than thrilled.

"Why not? You've been working at Blarney Castle a year now, Lily, and your amazin' faerie gardens are almost complete. Besides,

Rose is so excited that she wants to have a grand openin' to show all our friends before she opens up the garden again to the public." Maeve picked up one of the large rolls of paper she'd brought with her, unwrapped it and waved the colorful poster around, stopping to show them the announcement of the opening of the new faerie gardens. It held an invitation to all the towns and villages in the counties within easy driving distance of Blarney Castle.

Patrick and Lily examined the poster while Maeve explained, "It'll be a sort of private celebration in the evening and maybe... maybe even the faeries will attend. Or their magic might be with us..." Her brows lifted as her eyes sparkled. Patrick breathed a sigh of relief as he saw the light in Lily's eyes returning, along with her beautiful smile.

Watching her, he was overcome with pride at what Lily had achieved. "Maeve's right! It's a great idea. You deserve this celebration." He held his arms out to her. "Come here." And she let him enfold her for several long minutes, as if she belonged there.

Patrick couldn't contain the joy that suddenly flowed through him, knowing how much he loved this sensitive, talented woman. The gardens Lily had created had become the talk of all the surrounding villages and towns. Rose had even welcomed lookie-loos as long as they stayed behind the carefully constructed barriers on the pathways that exhibited Lily's gardens. Neighbors from the nearby towns had often visited Blarney Castle in the last five months to watch Lily's imaginative plantings of faerie flowers, the laying out of miniature pebbled pathways, bridges, tiny stone cottages and little stick houses. It had become a local pastime for the villagers. And beside it all ran the creek that now contained miniature golden coins.

Patrick hugged Lily tightly as she clung to him. She looked up and nuzzled, then kissed his ear. He couldn't contain his passion any longer. He kissed her long and lovingly, then kissed her again, and when she returned his kiss with equal feeling, it was if no one else but Lily was in the room.

When Lily reluctantly pulled away from him, they both realized they really were alone. Maeve had suddenly vanished. They exchanged a smile and shrugged, enjoying another long kiss.

Only later, after they'd finished dinner, Lily began plying Patrick with question after question. So much so that he agreed to return to his office to retrieve the genealogy file. She seemed determined this time to hear about the results of his study. As they drove back to his office, Patrick remembered he hadn't hidden the folder after all. How would he avoid telling her what it contained if the file was laying out in the open on his desk? But, strangely, when they arrived, it had disappeared!

Keeping their conversation going on another topic, he carefully searched for the file inside the desk drawers, not once but three times, without letting on to Lily that he was frantic to find it. In the end he had to fib to her that he must've left the folder at home. She wasn't happy with him at all after that.

How had he lost all the information on Lily's Irish ancestors that he'd so carefully compiled? He didn't remember putting the file away in a secret place...or had he?

CHAPTER 70

Surprise and anticipation lifted Eve's mood when she heard Maeve would visit the halfway house this evening. Many months had gone by since she'd seen her. All day Eve wondered what the enigmatic old lady had in store.

"You must drink. You must," Maeve said, her eyes part twinkling, part serious. The housemother had allowed her to prepare a special brew of tea for all the women. But Eve couldn't wait to drink it, knowing how it would make her feel.

"You must come to my party, too. You must, child," Maeve said quietly. Eve shook her head, then savored the amber liquid that tasted like cherries, cinnamon and lemon wrapped up in one amazing flavor.

Later, when the other women had retired to their rooms, Maeve made a different brew of golden liquid, a special ancient mead she'd raved about all day to Eve and saved as a special nightcap for the two of them. Its honey julep taste was odd at first, like nothing Eve had ever tasted; soon she felt more upbeat and relaxed than she'd felt in months. When she mentioned this, Maeve told her how special her recipe was, and suddenly launched into a story about her Celtic ancestor.

"I was her namesake, I was, and all around Ireland they still call her the Goddess Queen Maeve, even today, in a place called Tara. Have you heard of it, me lass?"

"Yes, I've always wanted to go. Lily and I had planned—"

"Yes, 'tis a special place in Ireland," Maeve went on, "where many a king was crowned in olden times. Another place is near Tara's famous hill, called Rath Maeve. It's an ancient *'henge'*—a sacred circle of flat land enclosed by an empty ditch. The story me muther told me, while I sat on her knee many a long year ago, is that Maeve was well-known there as an ancient warrior and fertility queen. That's not all! She was the wife and lover of, not just one, but *nine* Celtic kings."

"Nine?" Eve wanted to smile, but thought better of it.

"Yes, me love, she was quite a woman, you see. Ambitious, strong-willed, cunning too," Maeve's eyes looked demurely downward for a second, but then flicked up to meet Eve's and she went on, "...and I'm afraid, worst of all, she was promiscuous too." Maeve looked long and hard at Eve then, so much so that Eve wondered what she was thinking. In a soft whisper, the little woman added, "Perhaps a bit like you...uh, hum," she cleared her throat, "like you *were*, I meant." Maeve's hopeful eyes washed over Eve right then, like an unexpected wave of forgiveness.

Eve took a deep breath and let a smile break through her doubt, "Yes, *were*."

"Why, the Goddess Maeve's name even means 'she who intoxicates,'" the little woman continued. "So I'm guessin' she used her many brews to her advantage when she dealt with men and others at Tara, wouldn't you say?"

"Yes, definitely." Eve was beginning to see another dimension to Maeve. She had always seemed so harmless, actually just a cute old lady. Now she seemed to personify something different. She was a woman with an old soul, whose words were layered with deeper meanings. Eve leaned in to hear more.

"Me muther carried her name too, and her muther before that, many times over, and so me own legacy in this land was set long ago by that famous Goddess Queen whose secret recipes of food and drink were handed down to me."

A brief silence fell between them like a cuddly blanket as they sipped Maeve's new gift of mead.

Finally, Maeve whispered, "I've been meanin' to explain me ancient legacy not just to you, but to Lily and Patrick too. They need to know about me ancestor, the Goddess Queen, don't you think? She believed in parties too and, I was told, made sure her special brews were served up at all the king's gatherings, so that everyone mellowed out and avoided disagreements. They say she fostered peace and forgiveness, and even prevented wars that way."

Eve wasn't quite sure what to say. Even forming Lily's and Patrick's names felt off-limits to her now. "Yes, they should hear your story."

And though Eve knew what Maeve had been driving at all evening, she'd told the little lady many times she couldn't possibly attend the Blarney Castle party. No matter how many times Maeve asked her or filled her cup with magical liquid, Eve knew it would take much more than an ancient drink or two to mend the deep rift she'd carved in the last year with Lily, and Patrick too.

She couldn't resist one question. "So, does your son Seamus know about this ancient story, Maeve?"

The old lady's eyes widened with a look as sharp knives. "Yes, my lass, he does indeed. Unfortunately, he's followed in the footsteps of his own philanderin' namesake, and the shameful Finnegan we all know from ancient stories as well. I tried, with all me recipes and magical powers handed down, to change him. But his father's legacy killed every faithful bone in his body. I've finally disowned him, I have, since that day in Wales when he took off with you. I knew what he would do, and I warned you too. He's always been a brawny lad and a handsome piece of manhood. Many a woman thought she could use her wiles to capture his love. He knows it well, he does, and he uses it. But I know now that no one will change his flirtatious ways. Make no mistake, he will go to his grave payin' for his shallow and heartless philanderin'."

"Yes," Eve said. "Your predictions came true, at least for me."

"What, may I ask, did you learn from it, lass?"

"I learned what betrayal is," Eve said, "and I finally faced...I faced my own demons and failings too. I...I am...was a lot like Seamus."

"Then you're already much wiser than me son, you are. And you've already taken the most difficult step toward a special knowin' that many will never admit."

Eve could barely eke out the courage to ask, "What is the special knowing you're referring to, Maeve?"

"'Tis the first step in real love, my child—knowin' the realty of every true friendship—and that it must contain the seeds of mutual forgiveness. Without tolerance and mercy, friendship eventually dies. But before we can learn that lesson, we must let the soft light of awareness and love fall upon not only another's darkest side, but most of all, upon our own. Once we start admittin' our own flaws, and make reparation to those we've hurt, then we can truly love ourselves and others too."

She leaned over and touched Eve's cheek very softly, "You must now begin to forgive yourself, me lass. When you focus on that, and do it with a deep awareness you've not known before, you'll soon know what steps to take next."

CHAPTER 71

*L*ily watched the lights twinkling in hundreds of trees in the Blarney Castle Gardens. Her spirits lifted, dispelling for a moment the trepidation she'd felt all day. Why had Maeve asked her to come here at eight o'clock, the night *before* the celebration of the garden's reopening?

She looked up to discover a white halo moon shining down on her surroundings, casting friendly shadows on the Witch's Tree up ahead. The tree had once foretold only tragedy, as the black pooka did, and Lily shuddered at those memories. But she'd weathered all kinds of storms now...months of caretaking Frank and then his passing, quitting her horrible job and turning her disappointing ties with her daughters into healthy, adult friendships. Most important, she'd finally managed to move on from the profound disappointments Seamus and Eve had meted out to her. Instead of dwelling on their betrayal and the deep loneliness that tore at her heart for months, she'd immersed herself in creative efforts to enhance these castle grounds. And she'd *so* appreciated Patrick's constant caring too.

Glancing again at the mysterious moon above, she stepped

more lightly down the paths she'd helped to create on either side of the new faerie gardens. In these last months the marvelous possibilities of a new life's work she'd never imagined had actually overwhelmed her with joy—and now it was all complete! Tomorrow the whole town of Blarney and people from the nearby villages would come out to view it and then party all night. Maeve was right; a celebration was just what she needed!

She stopped suddenly, noticing the snake-like branches of the Witch's Tree hovering near her. They were lit by the bright moon that had begun to move behind the clouds. She felt a pang of fear and strained to make out who was waiting up ahead. Was it...? Oh, my God!! Yes! Standing stone-still about ten yards away was...Eve! Maeve stood next to her, and Patrick too.

Lily couldn't move. Her heart pounded so loudly she could hear nothing else. Her nails dug deep into the palms of her hands. Dizziness threatened and she longed to sit down.

As if Maeve had read her thoughts, she called, "Come here, child, we've set up a special table and chairs for us all." The little lady skipped forward as if she were floating. "Please." She held out her hand to Lily.

When Lily managed to reach the table, she saw that it was covered by a white tablecloth that looked familiar. She couldn't raise her eyes to meet Patrick's or Eve's. She struggled to breathe; her throat was dry. She held her head down and studied the familiar items on the table. Shamrocks adorned Maeve's lace napkins. The same quaint flowered teapot, the same dainty china cups. Maeve had used them all on that long-ago New Year's day. Her special scones were also piled on a flowered china plate, their delicious aroma tempting Lily. The tawny golden liquid Maeve was pouring into each cup was the elixir Lily sorely needed now, but not yet.

Instead Lily reached up to rub both of her eyes, hoping to somehow subdue the confusion and anguish she felt. Why were

Patrick and Maeve here with Eve, of all people! What was Maeve thinking? The shock of it withered Lily's heart and took her breath away. Why had they planned this horrible surprise just when she was beginning to trust and love them?

§&

Weak with anger he knew he must hold in check, Patrick sat down at the table. What else could he do? Eve's sudden appearance just now had shocked him, and he saw shock mirrored on Lily's face as well. This was Maeve's doing and his head ached with regret that he'd trusted her when she'd asked him to meet her here with Lily. She'd been so persuasive with her twinkling eyes, as only Maeve could be, and he'd fallen for her promise of a "lovely surprise and unforgettable night here with Lily."

When Eve had arrived minutes ago, without a word to either him or Maeve, he'd gasped, staring at Maeve as she nodded back at him, a strangely determined look on her face. What a disaster! But there'd been no time to straighten the situation out, or to prevent it. Only seconds after Eve appeared, Patrick saw Lily walking toward them in the fading moonlight.

Now it was done and he had no idea how to mend this terrible situation. He reached out to touch Lily's bent head, but she flinched and moved away, shuttering herself from him. Maybe all he could do now was be a mediator between the two women who had once shared a long friendship. As for Maeve, he wished she would disappear for good!

§&

Wrapping her cardigan around herself, Eve sat up straight, though she felt sick to her stomach as she exchanged a knowing glance with Maeve. The little old woman nodded, encouraging her to start.

443

Well, here goes...I have nothing to lose. I've already lost everything and everyone.

She noticed the utterly silent wood, then cleared her throat and dove in, "Lily...Lily, I...um...as usual, I'm the offender. I asked Maeve to arrange this meeting with you, and Patrick too. I wanted to meet here because I won't be a part of your creative celebration tomorrow night, but I wanted to share it with you now and congratulate you. You've done an amazing job! Everything looks enchanting.

"Please don't blame Maeve for setting this up. She was only trying to help us both, mostly me. And believe me when I say that I don't blame you if you never want to look at me or talk to me again."

Eve knew she was babbling and noted that Lily's head was still bent down; she hadn't moved an inch. "Please, after all these months of separation, Lily, just this once, do me the favor of listening while I explain.

"I've tried to face my demons while I was in prison, and when I was working out my sentence at that halfway house, helping others. We all rolled up our sleeves and helped poor teenagers from broken homes every day, trying to prevent them from committing crimes again or ever doing what we'd done. But in spite of living with others, I've been more alone than I've ever been...and...and that's the one thing I was always afraid of." Her voice broke, but after a pause she went on.

"After so many months living with myself in isolation, I figured out that I've always craved and demanded attention because I was petrified of being ignored and alone. That's why I drank too...to forget my fears. I became obsessed with sex because it was the best way I knew to get a man's attention. I thought it gave me power. What a twisted view, huh? It's why I put up with those men and their abuse. Weird, isn't it? I allowed men to treat me like chattel because I was petrified of being left alone. Doesn't make sense, does it? You always said you looked up to me, Lily, because I was supposed to be the smart one. You told me many times I was accomplished and successful. But underneath I was only a wounded little girl inside a stubborn, headstrong facade of a woman who wouldn't face the truth. Until I had to. Until now."

Patrick leaned forward, a scowl on his face. "Even with all your remorse, you're still doing it, Eve. So far every word out of your mouth is about you. What about Lily?"

Maeve lifted her hand up. "Stop! For just a moment. Let me share this brew before you continue."

"I don't want any," Lily said, her head still bent.

"Please, child, this meeting is for you too, not just Eve. We've got secrets to tell and hearts to mend. Even if you never see Eve again, I know you've wanted this meetin' in your heart, haven't you, lass?"

Maeve gently lifted Lily's chin up with her gnarled hand, enough for Lily to meet her eyes and give her a slight nod, then she held out her cup to Lily. After she'd sipped some brew she sighed, giving Patrick an accusing gaze for the first time.

Eve held out her cup too and Maeve poured it to the top. "We're going to need this special brew," Maeve said. "Truths need to be told. Then what will be will be." Eve took a sip.

The silent wood closed in on them all, then Eve went on, "Yes, Patrick, you're right. I started this by talking about myself because I want Lily to know that all the meanness and jealousy I inflicted on her during these last months had nothing to do with her. And, Patrick, you didn't think I listened to your words at the Vision Quest, but I did. Later, much later, in prison, I faced up to my deep flaws...the ones I wouldn't confront before. They'd gotten completely out of control, and it was no one's fault but my own. I'm deeply sorry." She stared again at Lily who still had not raised her head.

Eve's voice softened, "Your goodness, Lily, your generosity, your eagerness to give me a family all these years were your constant gifts. You wanted nothing but to give me love and friendship, but you gave me way too much. I gladly took it all and I took you for granted too, not just for years, but for decades.

"Then, on this trip, you started to change, and it was...yes, it was truly the best thing for you. You lost weight. You became attractive and men wanted you. You began to truly shine in a new job. You became more confident than you've ever been. But I couldn't stand it. I've finally admitted that to myself. Suddenly you no longer needed me as much. Maybe not at all.

"Me? Share the limelight? I couldn't. Or the real truth is, I wouldn't. I wouldn't listen to your warnings either or Patrick's. So I ran headlong into the arms of yet another philanderer, Seamus. Someone like me. But Lily, and this is the god's honest truth, I couldn't regret that night more. I hope you'll believe me. Yes, he kissed me and I didn't make him stop. And I enjoyed our tryst, I admit that too. But I'm very, very sorry. I truly am."

Eve kept staring at Lily, who finally lifted her gaze to meet hers. She *must be trying to decide whether to believe me at all*, thought Eve.

Then Eve lifted her cup and drank all her tea down. "Then I got what I deserved when he dumped me a few days later. So I turned and ran to another abuser, Ian. Who led me into a worse disaster. A disaster you both tried to prevent, not once, but several times. But, as usual, I wouldn't listen.

"I'm sorry...so *very* sorry. And I know it's too late. I don't deserve your trust or your friendship anymore, Lily. I wanted to at least tell you...tell you both... how sorry I am." She put both hands up to her face, as her shoulders quivered with emotion.

Lily didn't know what to say.

All of them sat in silence, under an ebony sky amidst twinkling trees. The moon was still hiding behind the clouds. Darkness enveloped them. Finally Maeve leaned over and pulled a large white candle out of her bag. Placing it in the center of the table, she lit it. The flame emanated a soft and gentle light all the way to the edges of their table, casting a peculiar radiance on each one of their faces.

"This special taper belonged to an old friend of mine. I've been keepin' it for many a long year," Maeve said, as she gazed at Lily and then at Eve.

Maeve turned her glance to Patrick for a moment and pulled a folder out of her bag. She looked straight at Lily and Eve again. "As difficult as this may be, you both must know the truth now. You must take the next step, me girls. What you do with this revelation is up to you, and the decisions you make thereafter are yours to choose in future days, months or years." She opened the folder, pulled out a paper and began to read:

"A genealogy study based on DNA evidence, prepared for Lilith O'Malley Doyle, daughter of Hans Olson and Colleen O'Keefe O'Malley, born in Pasadena, California, at Huntington Hospital on July 15, 1973. Half brother, Colin O'Malley. Half sister, Eve Walsh Olson. Grandmother on mother's side: Kathleen J. O'Keefe"

She looked up briefly at the two women. Then read on:

"A second genealogy study based on DNA evidence, prepared for Eve Walsh Olson, daughter of Hans Olson and Deirdre Walsh Olson, born in Pasadena, California, at Huntington Hospital on Feb 11, 1972. Half sister, Lilith O'Malley Doyle. Grandmother on father's side: Lilith Norland Olson.

Both Eve and Lily sat up, stark as stone tombs.

Lily faced Eve. "*You* are my half sister?"

Eve nodded, too stunned to speak.

Patrick sat stiff and quiet as Maeve poured her mysterious tea for everyone at the table. They all sipped it in silence while soft breezes moved through the garden. The moon came out of the clouds, lighting up the faerie garden path again where they sat.

"No wonder my mother didn't ever want you around," Eve whispered, staring at Lily. "That's probably why she hated my father, constantly battering him and driving him out of the house. She hated it when my father showed so much love to me, and you... because he'd betrayed her."

Lily held Eve's gaze. "My mom didn't want me around either. Neither did my dad. Remember? Colin was always their 'golden boy,' and when he went into the military they treated him like a saint."

Eve nodded. "Yes, I remember. And I saw how it hurt you."

Lily went on, "The only thing my mom ever cared about was my name. She even embroidered it on my things...remember my little laced handkerchiefs? And those pillowcases and towels she was so excited about? She kept giving me gifts monogrammed with Lilith, my formal name. No one ever called me that except her. I always thought it was strange.

"But I remember hearing over and over from Gram O'Keefe that my dad tried to talk her out of naming me Lilith. He wanted to name me Cara. But no, Gram told me Mom insisted... and now I get it. Because she wanted me to have *your* grandmother's name, Eve, even though she'd already passed away. Because your dad must've asked Mom. *He* wanted it. Eve, your dad...your dad was my dad too. That's why he was so ultra kind to me. I'll always remember his warm bear hugs, though I saw him seldom."

"I know," Eve said. "He was gone all the time. Mom drove him out. And that's why *your* mom was never really welcoming to me when you invited me over on holidays. In fact, she was incredibly cold—she must've been biting her tongue the whole time. By that time my dad had passed away, but she must've hated seeing me because I reminded her of him and their secret past. Maybe she hated him too, for coming onto her, for being a philanderer."

"We'll never know what their relationship was," Lily said, pausing for a long moment. "Maybe he wasn't a philanderer, Eve.

Maybe he truly loved my mom. Maybe she loved him as well. Though we both were pretty young, I remember how she cried at his funeral and I wondered why, because I rarely saw her shed any tears. Most of the time she seemed so unhappy...so bitter. Now I know why."

"This is shocking. I wish one of them were still alive so you and I could talk to them," Eve whispered.

Then they looked at each other and said in unison, "What about Gram O'Keefe?"

"Yes, what did she know?" Lily said.

"I bet she knew everything," Eve said.

"It all makes sense now," Lily went on. "How she brought us to her mountain cabin whenever she could, took us to the Celtic faires to teach us our Irish heritage. She wanted to make us feel so special. Not just me—she always asked me to invite you along too. She was not your biological grandmother, Eve, but she knew how you felt. She knew how we both felt. Cast out. Ignored. She saw that both of us reminded our parents of their transgression, and even though we didn't understand it, we could *feel* their rejection. She tried to make up for that. Gave us the love we'd never had."

"She knew the secret, that we were...really...we are half-sisters." Eve hesitated, "...Gram brought us together, and she wanted us to become lasting friends. She made sure..." Eve's voice trailed off.

"...we had each other," Lily finished.

Suddenly Maeve stood up and lifted the large taper up high. The candle's beam cast a circle of golden light on their gathering, and as Lily looked up she noticed the moon had grown much larger. It was a great spotlight enveloping all four of them, diminishing the huge, sinuous branches of the Witch's Tree nearby.

"Yes, your Gram was a very special person, she was," Maeve began, "and after she died she asked me to watch over you both from afar, because I was mostly livin' here in Ireland by then, though once in a while I'd travel to California to see her. The Garden

Getaway shop was her idea, my lasses. She paid for it, to stop me from havin' to sell the Travelers' tin here, and givin' me a way to earn my way. She knew my son would never help me. Your Gram and I were friends for many a long year, we were, and we shared many ancient myths and stories. After she journeyed to the 'other side,' I kept my promise to her. I watched over you two in spite of the distance, I did. But in secret. That was her wish.

"You were grown then, and you both leaned heavy on each other. Your Gram thought it was way too much. Many a time she wished you'd each unfasten your hold and discover your own worth. Now her desire can finally be granted. Each of you must find and settle your own path before friendship can intervene. I know you both will."

Maeve set the candle on the table again, and it seemed to glow with an unusual, shimmering light. "I remember only once meetin' you girls in person. At a Celtic faire in the California mountains, when you were only ten and eleven. Your Gram never introduced me, but I was there, all right. I'd traveled across the sea special, at her request. Remember a little lady with dark wavy hair dressed in a white robe? That was me, it was, before me hair turned white. I showed you all those faerie things and ancient books in a white tent, right before Lily ran off in a dither lookin' for her lost pendant. I was the one who led you, Evie, though you didn't know it, through the fog to meet your father behind the curtain of life. Yes, it was me, it was. That was the first time your dad visited you, one among several visits, aye, lass?"

Eve nodded, her eyes bright with amazement.

"And, Lily, I helped you too that day. You were fussin' about losin' your special Celtic Knot necklace, the one your Gram gave you as an infant. It truly was the faeries who stole it, they did, on the faire's first day, but I persuaded them to give it back. So they laid it under the hazelnut tree. Remember?"

Lily was speechless. Eve met Lily's eyes, as she nodded her head up and down.

Maeve blew out the candle's flame and began gathering her things together in a large basket. "My friends, it's time to be goin' on our way." She turned toward Patrick, "I hope you're not too angered by my meddlin' in your genealogy. The faeries stole the file off your desk, they did, a night not long ago, and soon they came and told me what was in it. Once I read those long-held secrets, I knew you'd hidden this file these many weeks from Lily. And I knew why—because you love her so. It's no secret, now is it, son?"

Patrick turned his gaze from Maeve to Lily, and she saw emotion filling his face, his eyes too, as she moved toward him, reaching out to clasp his hand. He'd kept this secret to himself all these months for fear of resurrecting her pain from the scars of Eve and Seamus' betrayal. But as the months passed, she had learned a lot about the difference between infatuation and real caring. Patrick was truly the man she loved, she knew that now. He'd been a pillar of support and concern all these months, encouraging her at every turn, propping up her spirits over and over after disappointment and betrayal. He'd been waiting... waiting for her all this time, to finally realize what she knew in her heart now: She wanted nothing more than to be near him...make love to him, yes, forever. She couldn't do without him--she *must* tell him and soon.

"Nonetheless," Maeve went on, still gazing at Patrick, "I knew it was finally time for these two to learn the truth about the family ties that bind them, ties that will remain, though jealousy, disillusionment and many a day of pain have scarred their friendship.

"Well, I've finished with my truth tellin' now, except to say that if you think you know and understand me, think again. I come from an ancient legacy of faerie goddesses here in Ireland, armed with a few faerie powers and potions, but I'm still very much a human, with flaws galore. I'm sure you know that now.

"I'll be sayin' good-bye to you tonight, but I'll be sure to attend the celebration tomorrow, Lily. In the future when you least expect it, I'll appear, my lasses. But it's you alone who must each choose your way. Your paths have gone awry here in Ireland for the first time in your lives, and it's up to you what choices you make, whether alone or together. Whatever you choose I will be by your side. You may not see or hear the breezes of affection I blow your way or the whispered bits of advice I give, but for sure they'll be with you as they've always been, and your Gram O'Keefe's love mingled with mine as well."

With that she meandered down the path into the hovering darkness, disappearing into the mist beyond.

CHAPTER 72

"*I* didn't know whether you'd come tonight," Lily said to Maeve, who sat down next to her at the banquet table. "What you said when you left last night sounded like a good-bye to all of us."

"Oh no, child, I wouldn't have missed this celebration for the world! My words last night were mainly for your friend." She nodded at the empty chair across from them and paused. "I was talking about...about the connection you two have had these many years. I'm wonderin' now if you expected Eve to come, but I felt sure she wouldn't."

"No, Maeve," Lily said. "I knew she meant it when she said good-bye to me last night. Neither of us is sure whether we'll see each other again. I...I had to tell her...I'm not ready yet for that...or to even think about being her friend. If and when we do connect, we'll have to create a very different friendship. And that will take a lot of time. And," Lily's voice broke, "... she agreed with me."

Maeve took her hand under the table and squeezed it. "There, child, don't spend too much time now mournin' this loss. The road that mends loyalty is long. Feelin's often must foment and age like fine wine before we can forgive, let alone reconnect. And that's as it should be, lass. Your sister Eve still has much growin' to do, and her own inner journey to make. But I see a bright future ahead for you... and for Eve too, dependin' on her choices."

At that moment the garden lanterns were lit, casting a glow on all the banquet tables arrayed with fresh flowers and sparkling candles. Patrick arrived in their midst just in time, his eyes bright with excitement, and gave both of Lily's daughters a hug. He selected the chair next to Lily, and when he leaned over to kiss her on the cheek, she kissed him full on the lips instead, prolonging it, then enjoyed the surprise shining in his eyes.

Rose O'Sullivan, manager of Blarney Castle, went to the podium as the crowd quieted, and acknowledged the hundreds of towns-people, villagers and Irish dignitaries who had flowed through Blarney Castle's gates. Her welcome speech was short but full of Irish flare as she described the new gardens the audience was about to see. White satin ribbons partitioned off the new terrain, she explained, but she would cut them very soon, so everyone could explore the new designs—but not before she lifted a glass of cham-pagne in a toast.

"I want to express my deep gratitude to all who made this happen over these many months, but I must especially thank one special person. Her name is Lily O'Malley, and though we hired her as a part-time consultant from the States, her creative ideas and diligent study of our Celtic tales have made all the difference, as you'll see in a moment. Lily, please come up here." She motioned with her hand. "Join me at the podium to receive a special award, which you well deserve!"

Stunned, Lily sat speechless. She reached up to touch the Celtic Knot pendant around her neck, fingering the chain, remembering Gram. *If only she were here tonight....* When both Maeve and Patrick urged her on, she finally stood up amidst an explosion of applause and made her way to where Rose stood.

Rose held up a silver statuette of a winged faerie holding a bundle of flowers in her arms, and the crowd clapped and roared "Bravo! Bravo!" as Rose handed it over to Lily.

When the audience quieted, Lily spoke, "Thank you, thank you all so much. I have only joy in my heart for all you've given me since I came to your Emerald Isle. This fabulous project has turned out to be everything that my Grandmother O'Keefe taught me long ago, but much, much more." Her voice wavered, but she took a deep breath and lifted up the faerie statuette, saying, "It is I who am grateful to you." As the crowd stood up and clapped again, Lily handed the mike back to Rose and made her way to the table, where Tanya, Lisa, Maeve and Patrick waited.

"I'm so glad you stayed, Maeve. I thought you might disappear again," Lily said.

"Oh, no, lass, tonight I'm stayin' for the entire celebration!" she said, as they watched Rose cut the satin ribbons.

Patrick stood up and placed his arms around her, kissing her long and sweet. He took a small velvet box from his pocket, and Lily opened it to discover a gorgeous diamond ring. "Will you marry me?" he whispered. Her face shone with joy as she nodded, and he slowly put it on her finger. In response, she lifted her arms up to embrace him for another very slow, precious kiss, as the crowd clapped and roared again, this time even louder, "Bravo! Bravo! Bravo!"

The End

455

FROM THE AUTHOR

Dear Readers,

After taking an unforgettable trip to Ireland, I couldn't wait to trace
my ethnic roots. Soon after, I discovered my Great Grandmother
Annie O'Donovan, who left Cork County and came to the U.S. in
1871. Because she was only 14, her journey astonished me, and she
wouldn't let go of my imagination. Finally, I decided to write a story
about her homeland, and learn everything I could about Ireland in
the process. After all, one of the reasons I read books is to learn, as
well as get to know characters inside and out, characters who are

grappling with problems and searching for love. So it occurred to me: Why not write a story that gives readers exactly what *I* like?

But what *kind* of a story? Female friendships have always intrigued me, but also the rocky road created by female jealousy. Also, from the time I was six years old, I've always loved fairy stories. With those ideas simmering in my imagination, I began the saga of the *Celtic Knots*. Yes, I changed the story once or twice, after listening carefully to the thoughts and reactions of my writing critique groups. Sometimes I used their ideas, sometimes not. So, the *process* of writing this book has become a very fun adventure! And discovering pre-Celtic and Celtic beliefs, their rituals, folklore, and mysticism also warmed my Irish-American heart and soul.

I hope when you read this book you'll feel the magic I felt when I was writing about my Lily and Eve's journey. They searched out their Irish heritage and did some soul-searching too. And as with any journey, they forged an unexpected path in their lives as well. I wish you an exciting reading journey too!

Irish Blessings to You,

Kathleen O'Donovan

P. S. I'd love to hear from you! KathleenODonovanAuthor@ gmail.com Don't hesitate to send me an email. Or sign up for my contests via my website, www.kathleenodonovan.com, and learn more about the Irish places mentioned in this novel, Irish fantasies and stories, along with some genuine Irish recipes too! Will the recipes produce magical tea and scones like Maeve's? I'll let *you* decide!

P. S. S. And while you're navigating through my website, social media sites, or sending me an email, don't hold back about sharing your story ideas. I'd love to hear one or two. And in the future you might find a story similar to yours in my next novel! But only with your permission, of course!

facebook.com/KathleenODonovanAuthor

twitter.com/KathODonovan